Praise for

THE LOCALS

Named a Notable Book of 2017 by *The Washington Post*
and a Best Book of 2017 by *Publishers Weekly*

"Thoughtful . . . [Jonathan Dee's] prescient sensitivity has never been more unnerving. . . . Amid the heat of today's vicious political climate, *The Locals* is a smoke alarm. Listen up."

—RON CHARLES, *The Washington Post*

"This novel is a big machine, and Dee drives it calmly. . . . He's a warm, earnest, sympathetic writer whose sentences [are] wired . . . with a low, almost subliminal, sarcastic hum."

—*The New York Times*

"Addictive reading . . . [Jonathan Dee] captures the deeply ingrained resentment and disillusion that seem to define the present moment. . . . *The Locals* confidently sutures broad social travails with individual destinies."

—*The Wall Street Journal*

"[A] magnificent new novel . . . a transcendent look at the battered state of the American psyche in the interim between two key years in our recent history: 2001 and 2008 . . . With rueful sympathy and acuity, *The Locals* conjures all the cares and quandaries of flawed characters coping in a faith-corrosive world."

—*The Boston Globe*

"Engrossing . . . Clearly, Dee has been paying attention."

—*The New York Times Book Review*

"After 9/11, New York hedge fund billionaire Philip Hadi retreats to his summer home in the Berkshires. In thrall to his new town, he runs for office to keep it sleepy, sweet and free from tax hikes. Is he benevolent, arrogant or both? No one gets off the moral hook in this propulsive, brilliantly observed study."

—*People* (Book of the Week)

"Captivating . . . [Dee's] knowing gaze and elegant writing work well throughout *The Locals*, which is infused with a sense of desperation and dread. His characters are vivid, and the emotions raw."

—*USA Today*

"*The Locals* is a steady, intelligent probing of family ties and sibling rivalry and themes that illuminate how we live now—inequality and status envy, individualism and community, the high life and the good life."

—*Newsday*

"Stunning . . . In Jonathan Dee's thoughtful and witty new novel *The Locals*, set in the years between 9/11 and Occupy Wall Street, dozens of the trends and ideologies that make up our current American moment come to insistent, demanding life. Dee hits both the fun pop culture ones and the scary political ones, because he can see how closely connected they are."

—*Vox*

"Brilliant . . . *The Locals* has an air of satire, but there's nothing in here that's implausible. It's more like a tragedy about people who allow themselves to be made ridiculous. At times, we might be reading a magazine article about the rural death spiral that birthed

"After 9/11, New York hedge fund billionaire Philip Hadi retreats to his summer home in the Berkshires. In thrall to his new town, he runs for office to keep it sleepy, sweet and free from tax hikes. Is he benevolent, arrogant or both? No one gets off the moral hook in this propulsive, brilliantly observed study."

—*People* (Book of the Week)

"Captivating . . . [Dee's] knowing gaze and elegant writing work well throughout *The Locals*, which is infused with a sense of desperation and dread. His characters are vivid, and the emotions raw."

—*USA Today*

"*The Locals* is a steady, intelligent probing of family ties and sibling rivalry and themes that illuminate how we live now—inequality and status envy, individualism and community, the high life and the good life."

—*Newsday*

"Stunning . . . In Jonathan Dee's thoughtful and witty new novel *The Locals*, set in the years between 9/11 and Occupy Wall Street, dozens of the trends and ideologies that make up our current American moment come to insistent, demanding life. Dee hits both the fun pop culture ones and the scary political ones, because he can see how closely connected they are."

—*Vox*

"Brilliant . . . *The Locals* has an air of satire, but there's nothing in here that's implausible. It's more like a tragedy about people who allow themselves to be made ridiculous. At times, we might be reading a magazine article about the rural death spiral that birthed

the Trump voter. They're deplorable, these locals, but are they culpable?"

—*Bookforum*

"Keenly insightful [and] gently humorous."

—*BookPage*

"Admirable . . . [Jonathan Dee] appears to have outdone himself."
—*The Guardian*

"Dee does a fine job of evoking the texture of small-town New England life in the twenty-first century. . . . Well written [and] engaging."

—*Financial Times*

"*The Locals* provides an incisive fictional map of post-9/11 America, where fear and paranoia have pushed citizens to compromise
their faith in democracy. . . . The author draws his small-town cast
with loving care."

—*The Sunday Times* (U.K.)

"The residents of a small town in the Berkshires have their world
overturned by a billionaire in their midst. This is a novel with political motives, so much so that it recalls *The Fountainhead*, except
[Jonathan] Dee is a better writer than Ayn Rand by several orders
of magnitude, and his point seems to be virtually the opposite of
hers. . . . [*The Locals*] plays both as political allegory and kaleidoscopic character study. An absorbing panorama of small-town life
and a study of democracy in miniature."

—*Kirkus Reviews* (starred review)

"Engrossing . . . His blue-collar characters, each of them pursuing the American Dream, are vividly developed, and his insights into how they think about the government (ineffective and corrupt) and their rights as citizens (ignored, trampled) are timely. . . . [Dee] handles the plot with admirable skill, finding empathy for his bewildered characters. He creates tension as a reckoning day arrives, and strikes the perfect ending note."

—*Publishers Weekly* (starred review)

"Good old social novels are hard to come by these days, great ones harder still. Leave it to Dee to fill the void with a book that's not only great but so frighteningly timely that the reader will be forced to wonder how he managed to compose it before the last election cycle."

—*Booklist* (starred review)

"*The Locals* is a bold, vital, and view-expanding novel that thrills technically and emotionally. Jonathan Dee, big-hearted and masterly, summons up a small American town at precisely the right moment in our history, using his signature gifts (fairness, poetic precision in the language, affection for all) to cast light over a dark time—to suggest the root cause of our political problems, but also a way forward."

—GEORGE SAUNDERS, *New York Times* bestselling author of *Lincoln in the Bardo*

"Blackly comic, effortlessly authoritative, *The Locals* is almost criminal in its perceptiveness about the screwed state of the American union. Jonathan Dee is a modern American master."

—JOSEPH O'NEILL, author of *Netherland* and *The Dog*

"In this moving study of how the housing bubble's burst sets a small town's citizens against one another, Jonathan Dee tells a must-read story for our age. Class struggle, tyranny, America's disillusion-ment after 9/11—*The Locals* creates a delicately drawn world im-possible to forget."

—MARY KARR, *New York Times* bestselling
author of *The Liar's Club* and *Lit*

" 'A palpable contract between the very rich and the people who distrust them the least,' Joan Didion once said of the Getty Villa. Jonathan Dee understands this impossible, enduring contract, sometimes called populism—other times, theft—as well as Did-ion does. *The Locals* might be the first great Occupy novel of the twenty-first century."

—RACHEL KUSHNER, *New York Times* bestselling
author of *The Flamethrowers*

"There could not be a more timely novel than *The Locals*. It exam-ines the American self and American selfishness from 9/11 until today. Jonathan Dee has given us a master class in empathy and compassion, a vital book."

—NATHAN HILL, author of *The Nix*

"Jonathan Dee's manner is so forthright, his approach so quietly intelligent and direct, his small-town America with its dreams and ambitions and sense of order and rectitude so familiar, we realize we have acknowledged nothing particularly alarming about our weakening grasp on a functioning democracy. Hiding in plain sight is the blueprint of our decline—our easy corruptibility and willed ignorance, our ethical wobbliness and eagerness to sanitize history. *The Locals* is an absolutely riveting novel that dares to prod us awake. Whoever has ears let them hear—Indeed."

—JOY WILLIAMS

BY JONATHAN DEE

The Locals
A Thousand Pardons
The Privileges
Palladio
St. Famous
The Liberty Campaign
The Lover of History

the Trump voter. They're deplorable, these locals, but are they culpable?"

—*Bookforum*

"Keenly insightful [and] gently humorous."

—*BookPage*

"Admirable . . . [Jonathan Dee] appears to have outdone himself."

—*The Guardian*

"Dee does a fine job of evoking the texture of small-town New England life in the twenty-first century. . . . Well written [and] engaging."

—*Financial Times*

"*The Locals* provides an incisive fictional map of post-9/11 America, where fear and paranoia have pushed citizens to compromise their faith in democracy. . . . The author draws his small-town cast with loving care."

—*The Sunday Times* (U.K.)

"The residents of a small town in the Berkshires have their world overturned by a billionaire in their midst. This is a novel with political motives, so much so that it recalls *The Fountainhead*, except [Jonathan] Dee is a better writer than Ayn Rand by several orders of magnitude, and his point seems to be virtually the opposite of hers. . . . [*The Locals*] plays both as political allegory and kaleidoscopic character study. An absorbing panorama of small-town life and a study of democracy in miniature."

—*Kirkus Reviews* (starred review)

"Engrossing . . . His blue-collar characters, each of them pursuing the American Dream, are vividly developed, and his insights into how they think about the government (ineffective and corrupt) and their rights as citizens (ignored, trampled) are timely. . . . [Dee] handles the plot with admirable skill, finding empathy for his bewildered characters. He creates tension as a reckoning day arrives, and strikes the perfect ending note."

—*Publishers Weekly* (starred review)

"Good old social novels are hard to come by these days, great ones harder still. Leave it to Dee to fill the void with a book that's not only great but so frighteningly timely that the reader will be forced to wonder how he managed to compose it before the last election cycle."

—*Booklist* (starred review)

"*The Locals* is a bold, vital, and view-expanding novel that thrills technically and emotionally. Jonathan Dee, big-hearted and masterly, summons up a small American town at precisely the right moment in our history, using his signature gifts (fairness, poetic precision in the language, affection for all) to cast light over a dark time—to suggest the root cause of our political problems, but also a way forward."

—GEORGE SAUNDERS, *New York Times* bestselling author of *Lincoln in the Bardo*

"Blackly comic, effortlessly authoritative, *The Locals* is almost criminal in its perceptiveness about the screwed state of the American union. Jonathan Dee is a modern American master."

—JOSEPH O'NEILL, author of *Netherland* and *The Dog*

"In this moving study of how the housing bubble's burst sets a small town's citizens against one another, Jonathan Dee tells a must-read story for our age. Class struggle, tyranny, America's disillusionment after 9/11—*The Locals* creates a delicately drawn world impossible to forget."

—MARY KARR, *New York Times* bestselling
author of *The Liar's Club* and *Lit*

"'A palpable contract between the very rich and the people who distrust them the least,' Joan Didion once said of the Getty Villa. Jonathan Dee understands this impossible, enduring contract, sometimes called populism—other times, theft—as well as Didion does. *The Locals* might be the first great Occupy novel of the twenty-first century."

—RACHEL KUSHNER, *New York Times* bestselling
author of *The Flamethrowers*

"There could not be a more timely novel than *The Locals*. It examines the American self and American selfishness from 9/11 until today. Jonathan Dee has given us a master class in empathy and compassion, a vital book."

—NATHAN HILL, author of *The Nix*

"Jonathan Dee's manner is so forthright, his approach so quietly intelligent and direct, his small-town America with its dreams and ambitions and sense of order and rectitude so familiar, we realize we have acknowledged nothing particularly alarming about our weakening grasp on a functioning democracy. Hiding in plain sight is the blueprint of our decline—our easy corruptibility and willed ignorance, our ethical wobbliness and eagerness to sanitize history. *The Locals* is an absolutely riveting novel that dares to prod us awake. Whoever has ears let them hear—Indeed."

—JOY WILLIAMS

BY JONATHAN DEE

The Locals
A Thousand Pardons
The Privileges
Palladio
St. Famous
The Liberty Campaign
The Lover of History

THE LØCALS

THE LØCALS

A Novel

Jonathan Dee

RANDOM HOUSE

NEW YORK

2018 Random House Trade Paperback Edition

Published in the United States by Random House, an imprint and division of Penguin Random House LLC, New York.

RANDOM HOUSE and the HOUSE colophon are registered trademarks of Penguin Random House LLC.
RANDOM HOUSE READER'S CIRCLE & Design is a registered trademark of Penguin Random House LLC.

Originally published in hardcover in the United States by Random House, an imprint and division of Penguin Random House LLC, in 2017.

LIBRARY OF CONGRESS CATALOGING-IN-PUBLICATION DATA
Names: Dee, Jonathan, author.
Title: The locals : a novel / by Jonathan Dee.
Description: First edition. | New York : Random House, [2018]
Identifiers: LCCN 2016055310 | ISBN 9780812983395 |
ISBN 9780679645016 (ebook)
Classification: LCC PS3554.E355 L63 2018 | DDC 813/.54—dc23
LC record available at lccn.loc.gov/2016055310

Printed in the United States of America on acid-free paper

randomhousebooks.com
randomhousereaderscircle.com

2 4 6 8 9 7 5 3 1

Title-page and part-title image: © iStockphoto.com

Book design by Dana Leigh Blanchette

For Claire

"What I struggle with is, how bad do I want to blow it up?"

The New York Times,
October 10, 2015

Ø

They were saying that all appointments were canceled, indefinitely, that it was the end of everything, but why would they assume that? The subway was running again, for example, parts of it. So people must have been going places, meeting other people. So there were still meetings. So maybe my meeting was still on. I found the lawyer's card and tried to call his office, but cell service was fucked, still, after like a day. I didn't know what to do. I couldn't even ask Yuri for advice, because the phones. What if this meeting was still happening and I wasn't there? What if everybody showed but me? The lawyer had stressed over and over how important it was that I not miss it. Nobody'd told me it was canceled, technically, according to the letter of the law or whatever. So I put on my shoes. It didn't start for a few hours yet, but I had nothing to do, and there was fuck-all on TV that day, that's for sure.

Broadway was frozen, like a screenshot. Nobody on the street. It was cool at first, actually, having it all to yourself like that, like one of those end-of-the-world movies. But then I saw an empty bus with its doors open just sitting in the middle of an intersection, and I started to feel a little creeped out, so I cut west into the park. Saw people there, at least, a few people out with their dogs, just standing there like drugged lunatics while the dogs chased each other around the grass. Then further on I could hear voices, loud voices.

There's this playground in that part of Riverside, at the bottom of a steep hill, all fenced in. And that's where everybody was, it looked like the whole West Side in this little enclosed playground. It was packed, people were up against the fences, it was like a detention center for kids or something. Parents were in there too, on the fringes, talking to each other, while the kids just ran around screaming like usual. Well, not quite like usual: it was a Wednesday at eleven in the morning, but nobody had school. That's probably why they were having so much fun. Technically I am still not supposed to be in playgrounds, I think, but it was so packed I figured who'd even notice, and I squeezed my way in.

I had the day off too. It didn't make a ton of sense to me, but I wasn't complaining. To make my meeting with the lawyer, I'd been deliberating between taking an unpaid personal day and calling in sick; the paid sick day was obviously the smart way to go, but one thing about me, I am actually a pretty bad liar. Even on the phone, Yuri tells me, my poker face sucks. I took up a position near some parents who were talking with their arms folded and with the look on their faces that everybody on TV had, which I would describe as sort of gray. "Someone in my building," this one dad was saying, "used to go out with someone who was a broker at Marsh and McClennan."

It was so loud in there, like mayhem. The kids were going nuts. I think they were really into having all the adults lined up, watching them.

"I was in the kitchen," this other mom says. She was super hot, actually, with a ponytail through the hole in the back of her baseball cap, and tights like for running, and this really toned milfy thing going on. Black hair. "Josh was home sick from school. He's watching Sesame Street, and I'm in the kitchen, and they break into Sesame Street with a live news feed, for God's sake. He starts yelling."

"Jesus," I said, just to get her to look at me.

"Right?" Her ponytail swung away from me in the sunlight. "It's just like, no sensitivity at all. I'm Julie, by the way. I feel like I've seen you here before. Are you Teresa's dad?"

My mouth opened and kind of stayed open, and she started to frown a little bit, and so I turned and squeezed myself through the crowd until I was outside the gate again. I went back up the path toward West End and on to Broadway and kept going downtown. It was probably about noon, and I was hungry, but nothing was open. Why?

Even though the day off helped me out I was actually somewhat torn about it. I knew we were all getting paid, and would get paid until the lab reopened. There's no way they'd use a national tragedy or state of emergency or whatever to dock our pay, I mean granted they're Columbia University, so they're assholes, but they're not insane. They care how things look. So fine, whatever, a paid holiday. "Safety concerns," they said, which made me laugh. You really think somebody somewhere wants to cross the world to blow up some random research lab? To bring down, what, the evil cosmetics empire? We get the PETA people, for sure, but that's a whole different order of magnitude. They mostly just carry signs, and they yell their little gay rhyming chants that are actually the funniest shit. If they were ever going to shut us down, that would have happened years ago, those clueless douchebags. Holding up their pictures of rabbits with no eyes or whatever.

But now the whole city had lost its mind and that was that. Everyone thought someone they'd never met was suddenly coming for them, had been planning it for years. Pretty arrogant, if you think about it. Who gives a shit about you, really? Not that many people.

What made me pissed about missing work was that work was where I saw Yuri. He'd started as a lab tech about a year after I did, but that wasn't how he made his real money. He always had clean credit card numbers for me. I don't know how he got them. All those fucking Russians know each other. Sometimes he charged me, if he felt like being a dick about it, and sometimes he just threw one my way for nothing, because he said I was funny. I needed at least one, the last one he gave me was getting flagged now when I tried to use it. I thought what with the whole patriotic air or whatever, this would be a good time to catch him in a non-mercenary mood where he would lay one on me for free, but as long as the lab was closed I wouldn't see him, and the guy changed his cell number like every two weeks.

The lawyer's address was all the way down on West Forty-eighth Street. His name was Greg Towles. I was saying that second bit like "towels," which I wasn't sure was right, but every time he called me now he'd just say, "It's Greg." A few months ago he'd met me for lunch at a diner near the lab; he explained what a class action was, and asked me if I wanted to be a part of it. I said would I get my money back or did that mean I would have to split it with a bunch of other people. He said I'd get my money back and probably more besides. I said what's your fee, and he said zero, my fee comes out of the money you win, so I thought what's to lose, other than a day of work to go downtown and get, what do you call, deposed, and now thanks to this Tragic Time I wasn't even going to get docked for the day.

All of a sudden the little voicemail chime goes off on my phone in my pants pocket—I must have walked into some zone that had service restored—and I stopped on the Broadway median to see if maybe it was Yuri, or Mr. Towles, but no, it was from my mother, hysterical as usual. Freaking out right along with everybody else. She should have known better—she's lived in Bayside her whole life, for God's sake, you'd think she could remember on her own that Manhattan is a big place. I'd sent her an email to let her know I was fine but she never checks her fucking email, it's too complicated, you might as well ask her to tune up her car. She couldn't put it together herself that I lived all the way up on 131st Street, miles from everything, and so obviously nothing had fallen on me and I

4

wasn't dead. It was true that when the wind was right, like it had been last night, even up on 131st you actually got that burning smell, to the point where I'd had to get up and close my window. It was almost worth telling my mother that story just so she'd maybe have a stroke from it and be paralyzed and not able to dial her fucking phone anymore.

I was deleting the message, looking down, and walked smack into some huge dude on the sidewalk outside La Caridad. Completely my fault, I just bounced right off him. And those were the weirdest moments to me, actually, the scary moments, because no one was acting fucking normal anymore, everyone was all like, are you okay? All the time. Over nothing. Are you all right? So where normally this guy—who was wearing a tank top, who had a neck tattoo, who looked like he would maybe welcome the opportunity to get into a little beef with a rude stranger—might have at least made an aggressive remark to test me out, instead he just puts his hand on my shoulder, really gently, and he says, like he was the one who'd been looking at his phone while crossing the street, "Sorry, bro, you okay?" I did not like it, man. I did not like the way people were acting. This was New York. People were always looking for an excuse to go off on you. They were hoping for it. Now it was like being in this cult. It creeped the shit out of me. But I didn't dare do anything but smile back at this guy, because he was pretty ripped, and it's like they say, be careful what you wish for.

Beautiful out, one of the ten best days of the year, like the weathermen say. But it was a ghost town. In the windows of the locked stores, and especially on the upper floors where the apartments were, you were just starting to see that thing of where people put up flags, or else just taped pictures of flags to the inside of their window, some of them just cut out of the newspaper, some of them just black and white.

The lobby of the building on West Forty-eighth was humongous. Ceilings like four stories high. Completely empty, except for a few security guards, and two of them were right on me. They actually ran, or at least the young one did. The fat one tried. To be fair I didn't look like someone who was in that building on legit business. Especially after walking eighty-some blocks. I understood their reaction, is what I'm saying. They positioned themselves right in front of me.

"What's your name, sir?" the first one said. The younger and faster and more dickish one.

What's my name? What the hell kind of useless question was that? Did he think maybe he'd recognize it?

"Who," said the older guy, "are you here to see?" They both wore these matching maroon jackets, like suit jackets. It looked pretty gay. I told them I was here to see Greg Towles. He's a lawyer, I said.

"What firm?"

How the fuck should I know? I just thought it was a big building and this guy Towles had an office in it. It was probably on the guy's card, but if I reached into my pocket right now one of these jumpy no-necks would just shoot me dead. The older guy had sweat on his face. Everybody was on edge. The other guards were looking at us. Maybe the old guy was the young guy's father, and he'd gotten him the job, I thought for a moment, but no way, if it weren't for the Team Gay jackets they didn't even look like they were from the same country.

"Rice and Powers?" the dad asked me.

That sort of rang a bell. I nodded.

"They're closed today," he said. "In fact everybody's closed. There's not an office open for business in the whole building."

Then why did you bother asking me where I was going, I felt like saying, but instead I just asked if I could call upstairs to make sure.

"No," he said. "What, do you have a package for him or something?"

I held out my empty hands. I was getting irritated now.

"Try again tomorrow," he said, and gestured with his fat hand toward the door.

So then the same long fucking walk back home.

I went through Central Park this time, just for something different. In at the south end, out at the north. Fucking empty. On a day like that. Everybody was all frightened, but really that was just a way of trying to make the whole thing more about themselves, which it wasn't. Either you were actually there when it happened or it was something you watched on TV, period. But whenever something major happens it's like everybody wants to insist on their little piece of the suffering. People had no idea what was coming next, that's true I guess—when something as fucked up as that happens, something you weren't even imagining, it wakes up your imagination pretty good—but still, they were just overdoing it, I'm sorry. Get over yourselves. You weren't there, it didn't happen to you. Plus you know anything built that high is going to come down sooner or later, one way or another.

But it was that other weird thing going on, that whole kumbaya, brotherhood-of-man thing, that made me way more jittery than anything else. Like when I exited the park at the top, just near the foot of that hill behind the cathedral, there was a line outside this one restaurant with its lights on, and when I got up there and heard people talking, it turned out that the owner, who had just reopened, was letting everybody eat for free. He was standing there on the sidewalk, and people were fucking hugging him, and he was crying. Little skinny bearded dark-skinned guy. He looked kind of Arab, so maybe he was just thinking this was a good way to discourage people from killing him. "Come in, my friend," this guy says to me when he catches me staring through the window at the people sitting at the tables. "Fourteen years I have been in this location. These are my neighbors. I would do anything for them. You, you are my brother, you look hungry, no place to sit right now but I bring you, wait right here." I was starving, it's true. But the whole

7

scene creeped me out something fierce, so when he went through the door to the kitchen I started walking again and kept going until I was back in my apartment.

Not a whole lot to eat at my place. But there was no way I was going out again. I'd walked enough. In the freezer I found a Swanson's chicken TV dinner and stuck it in the oven. I buy four or five of those things at a time, telling myself they're for emergencies, but then I eat them all in like two weeks. Still no message about work tomorrow. I called the lab and got through but no one answered. Nothing but news on TV. I wasn't hungry anymore but I still felt restless. I guess "restless" would be like a polite word for it. I definitely, definitely needed to unwind somehow.

Here's the problem with porn: if you get too into it, like I probably was, then quality starts to become an issue. I mean, when you're a kid you watch it and it truly doesn't matter what it is—it's all basically the same, you're seeing stuff you've never seen before, the fucking Victoria's Secret catalogue does the job just fine for you. But then you get a little older and more sophisticated. And you start noticing things. If you're me, you can get a little caught up in the question of how real it seems: I mean none of it's actually real, but you can still suspend your disbelief or whatever. They can at least make the effort. And that's good enough for me. I mean it sort of has to be. Let's just say that pursuit of the real is what's gotten me into hot water before.

I won't say I was an addict or anything, but you do get kind of used to ending your day a certain way, and this had been a bitch of a day. But, as with everything in this life, if you want the good stuff, you have to pay. This is why I needed the credit card numbers. The last card I got from Yuri had been declined last time I tried it. I tried it again now, stupidly, and no go. Behind me the TV kept showing people crying. Great. Even though I knew better, I went to one of those free sites that promises Spy Cam Videos or whatever. This guy is sleeping in a bed and some chick comes in, and it's okay for like the first thirty seconds, and then I realize I can see the shadow of the boom mike on the girl's ass. Are you fucking kidding me? I'm supposed to not notice that? I felt like throwing the monitor out the window, but instead I turned it off and went to bed and did not sleep very peacefully at all.

In the morning there was an email from the lab. Closed for the rest of the week now. I was able to get through to Towles's cell phone, but it went straight to voicemail. Voicemail at his office number too. So I sat and thought. I figured if your work got canceled for one day, circumstances beyond your control, logically everything on your schedule would just get pushed forward a day. Everything at the same time, just twenty-four hours later. So I didn't see what other option I had except to go back down to Forty-eighth Street again, at two, in case the meeting was on.

How all this got started is that I got hit by a bus, a city bus thank God, one night like six years ago, not too long after I moved to Manhattan. I stepped off the curb, I had the light, I was in the crosswalk, and the M104 just makes the turn on Broadway and cold flattens me. I was drunk, for sure, so drunk I actually don't remember most of it, but in the eyes of the law or whatever that didn't matter, because the bus driver, some fat black chick, was at fault. So there's this fucking lawyer beside my bed at Metropolitan Hospital practically the moment I wake up. Not Towles—this was way before that, and this guy was like something Towles would flick off his shoe. He has a camera with him, right, and he's taking pictures of me while I'm asleep. If I could have got up, I'd have decked him. But then he says who he is and he shows me the pictures, and Jesus, I looked like shit. Most of the skin was off my face, my arms, my hands. I had a broken pelvis too, but that wasn't quite as visual, I guess, and this bottom-feeding motherfucker just wanted to get some photos while my wounds were still fresh, before there was any healing going on. He said his name was Bond, which I thought was hilarious, and he would take thirty-three percent of whatever he got for me.

I felt stupid for not having thought of it myself already, even though to be fair I'd been unconscious most of the day: Run down by a city bus? Lawsuit! As long as you don't die it's like hitting the Lotto. The whole thing was such a slam dunk they never even finished picking a jury. Three hundred and sixty thousand dollars, though of course a third of that came off the top for old Mr. Bond. He earned it, don't get me wrong: he got the business about me being drunk excluded, and man, you should have heard him, it was like he was arguing for his own life. He asked me, right before we signed, if I wanted the driver fired as a condition of the settlement. I said nah, why bother, let her run over some other lucky asshole and make him rich too. She's like accidental Robin Hood, this mama.

So I don't know if you've ever had a lot of money, but it fucking weighs on you. I mean you can have a thousand bucks and feel pretty smart, but when you've got $240K just sitting there doing nothing, it can make you feel pretty stupid. I was at the lab then, but it was before Yuri was working there. The only guys I had to talk to were basically morons, and they started getting in my ear, you know? You've got to invest it. You've got to put it to work for you, otherwise it just sits there and gets the shit taxed out of it until it's gone, either you grow it or it dies, it's the American way.

So fine. I'm on the internet a lot anyway—that's one thing I'd done with all the money, I bought a decent computer for once, with a DSL connection, and a new TV too—and I go on Ask Jeeves and I ask for advice on how to invest money in the stock market. It sounds incredibly naïve, I know, and it was, but at that point my two choices were pretty much Ask Jeeves or Ask Those Ignorant Dicks You Work With. I go to a few of these top sites, and before long I start getting these emails, addressed to me personally, from someone who clearly knows I've got some money to my name. His name is Garrett Spalding, and he wants me to go in on a fund, a private fund—that's all he kept calling it, a fund—where I had a guaranteed return on my money each year of nine percent. Probably more—he sent these annual reports I couldn't read, but the upshot was that he was some kind of stock-picking genius, he just needed enough of a stake from a handful of select clients so that when he called the big banks to make a trade, they'd take his call. Nine percent minimum was his guarantee, good times or bad, bull market or bear.

So you are smarter than me and can see where this is going, probably. I sure couldn't. I kept ten grand and gave him the rest, and that was pretty much that, I never heard from the fucker again. A total con man. A good one too. Not that I made it very hard for him. I never even met him face to face, if you can believe how stupid I was. I did have one meeting, in an actual office, with some underling of his, because of course a legit stock-picking genius like him was way too much of a big shot to meet with every single new client. I swallowed it all. Now I wonder if the underling wasn't just him all along. Secretly laughing his ass off. I mean he was a pro. Those fake-ass annual reports couldn't have been cheap.

I won't say I felt relieved—I was pissed as hell about getting clowned like that and for months I kept trying to pick fights when I was out, just so maybe while getting my ass kicked I could land one punch on some face and pretend it was Garrett Spalding's— but I will admit that, in a weird way, just going back to living paycheck to paycheck made me feel less stressed, because I was okay at that, it's what I know. Four years go by. And then out of nowhere, I get a phone call from Towles the lawyer. Young guy, not too much older than me. I don't know how these fucking guys keep finding me, but what the hell, the last lawyer worked out pretty good for me, right?

"We found your contact info in his records. You aren't the only one he's done this to," Towles says. "He's defrauded a lot of people out of a lot of money over the years. Millions."

"You're suing him?" I said. "So you've found him? You know where he is?"

"Not exactly. He's fled the country, we think. But we're starting to learn where some of his assets are. And legally that's all we need."

"This fund thing. Does it even exist?"

"Well," Towles said, "yes and no."

Whatever. I just heard the part where it didn't cost me anything. And who knows, maybe I get my money again.

Towles said he didn't know how many people would be joining me, because he was still in the process of uncovering how many people this Spalding guy had ripped off over the years. The more the better, he said, though it also seemed to me like the more of us there were, the less money I'd get back. But a suit like this had to have what he called name plaintiffs. He had five of us so far, and he wanted to go ahead and file the suit, it wouldn't prevent other names from being added later, but he thought it was very important to be first out of the gate and so he wanted to go ahead with the five of us, five ordinary, non-institutional investors, five idiots retarded enough to hand their life savings to a con man. He set up a meeting at his office where we would all get together and agree on strategy and be deposed. That was the meeting that was supposed to have taken place that Wednesday afternoon, except I was the only one committed enough or dumb enough to still show up for it.

So now it was Thursday and I walked again, because the walking helped level me out. It always does. I had a stop to make first, at the post office. It's a condition of my probation that I have to send pay stubs to my officer every month, and I have to send them registered mail. Whatever, I'm used to it, and it's almost over anyway. The only drag is that the Morningside Heights post office is the worst post office in the world, and of course I can't base that on having visited every PO in the world or even in New York. I am basing it on the fact that it is impossible to even imagine any place more aggravating. The people who work there are the stupidest, laziest, slowest, fattest, most sadistic people you have ever encountered in your life. They must recruit from all over the city to find these people. I hate them. Everybody hates them. But not half as much as they hate you back.

I get there that day and it's crowded, like always, but it's as quiet as a church. People are just standing in line. And eight of the ten customer windows are open. That has literally never happened. The day before Christmas you might see like five of them open at the same time. Then there are these little conversations. Usually the only time two strangers start talking in a post office line is just before some kind of shouting match starts, maybe with some mild shoving or, once in a thousand times, an honest-to-God fight, between two women if you're really lucky. I've seen one or two. But now people are kind of whispering to each other, and I realize these are people who don't even know each other, and the little bell keeps going off nice and regular—62, 63, 64—and suddenly this one whisperer a few people in front of me starts crying, and the woman she's talking to puts down the tube mailer she's holding and puts her arms around her.

"What's eating her?" I say, out loud apparently. This old guy in front of me turns and gives me a funny look. Then he sees I'm just holding a regular envelope.

"You look like you'll be quick to finish," he says. "No reason to spend all day in line. Why don't you go ahead of me?"

What the fuck was wrong with everybody? I mean I knew. I'm not a complete idiot. I'm not saying I didn't know what the cause and effect were. I'm just saying something about it seemed put on to me, performed. The cause was real, but the effect was fake. Or maybe the other way around. I don't know how to say it so it makes sense.

The lobby of the building down on West Forty-eighth seemed a little more normal than yesterday, less haunted-looking, more going on. I saw the same two security guys, but not before they saw me: their eyes were right on me. They stayed where they were, though. The younger guy said something into his walkie-talkie. I went up to reception and told the girl I had an appointment with Mr. Towles at Rice and Powers. Then I sort of held my breath while she called upstairs, because I wasn't sure what I'd just said was strictly true anymore. I didn't feel like getting thrown out of any-place, especially with everybody so tense. The phone call went on for a while, way past what would've been needed for somebody to just say "Send him up." I tried not to look at the security guys to see if they'd started moving in my direction. Then all of a sudden, hal-lelujah, the chick at reception hands me a Visitor pass and points toward one of the elevator banks.

It was still pretty empty, not like usual, you could tell, and I rode up to the twenty-seventh floor all by myself. This Rice and Powers joint was a palace. Lots of leather chairs. Lots of phones blinking but you couldn't hear anything. There was one other guy waiting in reception, rugged-looking dude, wearing a tie but otherwise dressed like he was there to fix something. He nodded at me. I went to the girl and said I was there to see Mr. Towles, I had an appoint-ment. She said what time, and I said what time is it now? She was fucking hot, by the way, like model hot, so hot it probably made me a little irritable, especially when she spoke to me in that way hot women speak to invisible guys and said would I mind just having a seat. She pointed to the chairs, like I wouldn't have worked that out myself, like a creature like me might just sit on the floor unless someone explained things to him. I took one of the leather chairs that faced the picture window, looking downtown. And that was the first time, other than on TV, that I could see the actual smoke. That's how high up we were. It was wild. And when you looked up from it, you were looking pretty much straight into the blue sky, which was pretty unnerving too, like, empty as it was, something might suddenly appear out of it.

"Excuse me," I hear, and it's the other guy in reception, the one who nodded. I raise my eyebrows. "You're here to see Mr. Towles? Sorry, I couldn't help overhearing. It's pretty quiet in here."

He was only a few years older than me, probably, though he looked like a dad, like somebody's dad. Very fit and tan, but not like someone who goes to the gym all the time. Like someone who's outside a lot. But I was psyched when I realized what he was doing there.

"I have a meeting," I said.

He stood, walked two steps forward—still kind of half-crouching, like he didn't want to get all the way up—to shake my hand, then backed into his leather chair again. "Mark Firth," he said, then he left a kind of pause, like I was supposed to tell him my name, which I didn't. "I have a meeting too. Or I'm not sure if I still do. I had one scheduled for two days ago, but then, well."

"Where are you from?" I said. "I'm surprised they let anybody into the city at all."

You live in New York for a while, you develop a sense for when people are from someplace else. "I got here Monday night, if you can believe it," he said. "I'm down from Massachusetts. I left my car up in Wassaic and took the train in from there. Mr. Towles had the firm put me up in a hotel. It was only supposed to be for one night, but now I don't know."

"Sweet," I said.

He gave me kind of a look, like he was worried maybe I was making fun of him. But I wasn't. "It's possible to make the drive here and back in one day," he said, "but it's about four hours each way. I would have done it if I had to. But Greg was very generous about it."

"I should have said I was from somewhere else," I said, just trying to be friendly. "Free hotel room. That's the shit."

"So you're from the city?" Mark Firth said, in a strange, kind of careful tone, like it was a big deal. "You live here in Manhattan?"

I nodded.

"So, um, is everyone—did you know anybody? Do you know anybody, I mean, who's missing? Everyone close to you is okay?"

Everyone *close* to me? I actually misunderstood him for a second, because I said, "No, man, I was nowhere near it. I live miles away."

He nodded, his head down, still looking all somber.

"It's all so unbelievable," he said.

I guess. He seemed pretty shaken up. I was waiting for him to start in on his own personal story of where he was when it happened, but he didn't.

"So you don't know anyone," he said. "Anyone who worked down there."

"Man," I said, "do I look like someone with a lot of friends in high finance?"

He choked out a little laugh. "And you—I mean I guess I shouldn't assume we're here for the same reason, Mr. Towles has more than one case to work on at the same time I'm sure—"

"Garrett Spalding?" I said.

His shoulders sagged.

"Yeah," I said, "me too. How much did he fuck you out of?"

"Oh," Mark Firth said, "I'm not really sure if—maybe we're not supposed to talk about that?"

I didn't really care, I was just hoping that there'd been someone out there even stupider than me. If he didn't want to say how much, I figured it must have been a lot. "Whatever," I said, "we're all on the same team, right? Team Gullible." He smiled, kind of sickly. "Let me ask you this, though: did you ever meet him? Because I'm not sure I ever even met the guy, and I kind of regret it. Not to mention that it makes me feel like an even bigger idiot."

Mark dropped his head. "Believe me," he said, "it's worse hav-ing met him."

"No shit?" I sat forward, and he kind of sat back. "You met him?"

"I had him in my home."

"You had him in your *home*?" I said, too loud for sure, and so when the hot receptionist pointed at us and some other little pale guy in a suit started toward us silently on the carpet, I figured it was to tell me to behave myself.

"What did he look like?" I said. "Did he have like a, like a—"

"You're here to see Mr. Towles?" the suit said. He was balding and he had no chin.

"Yes, sir, that's right," Mark Firth said, polite as hell. He stood up again and said his name. "Do you happen to know if any of the others are here?"

"I don't believe so," the guy said. "Of course the depositions would all have been scheduled for different days and times." I couldn't tell yet if he was another lawyer, or just an assistant with a really positive opinion of himself. His head reminded me of a lightbulb.

"Well then, can we go in the back and see him now, if we're not waiting for anybody else?" I said. "I came a long way to be here, and my fellow plaintiff Mark here came a lot further than I did."

"I'm afraid not," the little guy said. "He isn't in."

Great. "When do you expect him in?" Mark said.

"I'm not sure," the guy said. He looked more and more rattled, the more he talked.

"What are you talking about, you're not sure?" I said. "Where is he? We didn't just wander in off the street, we're here because he told us to be here. I had to take a day off work."

Something in the little lackey dude seemed to crack, and he sat down in the seat that was more or less between us, so that we were like three sides of a square. Mark and I gave each other a look and sat down too. "These are frightening times," Lightbulb Head said. "A lot of our staff isn't in today. A lot of the lawyers too. Even though we're officially open for business again. Some of them have friends or relatives who aren't yet accounted for."

"Oh my lord," Mark said.

"And no one really knows what's going to happen next," he said. For some weird reason he had taken out his phone and was just kind of fondling it. "No one knows if whatever is going on in the world right now is over or not. So my point is that it's not that unusual, not that hard to understand, that Mr. Towles and his wife have apparently left the city for a while. He has family somewhere on Long Island, and he's gone to be with them."

"So you don't know when he'll be back," Mark said. "Or where he is, exactly."

"A lot of people are panicking," the guy said.

"Long Island," I said. "And so us working folks are supposed to what, stay here and take our chances?"

The guy stared at me. The more impatient I got, the more he looked like he was about to cry. We sat there in our little open-ended square, on the fancy furniture that was just waiting-room furniture but that was ten times nicer than anything I'd ever owned. Just for the waiting room. I'd never really seen the inside of an operation like that before. Some people live in a world made of money. You think you know it, but you don't know it.

"I don't blame him," Mark says, his voice as soft as the other guy's. "It's hard to be away from your family at a time like this. You want them close to you."

Chinless reached out and put his hand on Mark's arm, which was so inappropriate. Everybody was putting on an act, but not for each other, it was more like they were their own audience, if that even makes any sense.

"So can we still go inside then, since we're here?" I said, and stood up. "Get deposed or whatever?"

The lackey looked miserable. "I'm sorry—"

Mark's cell phone rang.

"Sorry," he said. He pulled it out and muted it.

"I was just saying how sorry I was that only the two of you, out of six? I think it was six. That the two of you were scheduled when you were scheduled. I know it was hard to make it all the way down here. I know we all want life to go on just like before." And the motherfucker is flat-out crying now. I just felt furious, for some reason. "But there's no way we can take depositions without Mr. Towles here. And he isn't here. And he's left no word when he'll be back. So I don't know what to tell you except go home and be with your families and we'll be in touch just as soon as there's further word."

"Or we could try again tomorrow?" I said.

"Or you could try again tomorrow, though I would definitely call first. I'll be here, that much I can promise you."

He walked us to the elevator. He was acting like a funeral director. I was just like, buddy, do you know what kind of horrible shit happens to people you don't know every day? But then he gets even weirder. "Do you," he says, "have a dog?"

"Hell no," I said, but he was looking more at Mark, who was nodding.

"I just get overcome," the guy says, "thinking of all those thousands of pets, dogs especially, waiting by the door. Just waiting. I know it's crazy, what happened to those people is so awful, but I get fixated."

The elevator came, thank God. Mark and the guy did that thing where you shake hands but then you put your other hand on top of the pile of hands. Then we were in the elevator, going down in silence.

"Dogs!" I said finally. "What a fruitcake."

We walked side by side through the giant lobby. I saw my security-guard pals and waved, but they were looking at something else. We stopped on the sidewalk and looked up, and just then some kind of military fighter jet went over, the only planes that were flying then, those first few days. It happened a lot, but you never quite got used to it. Every time one went over, you'd see people on the sidewalk freeze.

"It just feels like nothing will ever be the same," Mark said.

And for some reason I felt it all come spilling out of me right there: all this hate, like it had been building for days. Why at this guy, at fucking small-town Mr. Clean? I don't know. I could mention that he looked an awful lot like the guys who used to kick my ass all the time for no reason in high school. Stick my head in the toilet and what have you. And now he's pretending we're brothers. Not pretending—he believed it. He believed that that was what he thought. He was just so clueless about himself that it fucking pissed me off. Or maybe what I was really mad about was thinking that I did have something in common with him. Look at him. He's a rube, a sap, a greedy fucking imbecile, and I'm just as bad as he is. And he's just as bad as I am. There's your fucking brotherhood of man, am I right? Anyway, I suddenly had had it with this Mark guy. I wanted to restore the distance between us.

"We're all New Yorkers today," I said.

He nodded, like I had said something very wise. He put his hand over his eyes to look down at me, like a visor, like a salute.

"Are you hungry?" he says to me.

Yeah, I'm hungry, you condescending douche, but I do know how to feed myself. Some people look at me like I'm some kind of unfortunate. Because maybe I don't look a certain way. I have a job, I have my own place, I live a life, fuck you, you know? That well-meaning sympathy is the worst. It makes me crazy. You be you, and I'll be me. You know damn well it's just about making yourself feel superior anyway. Like in case the building you're in falls down and it turns out there really is a God or something, you want your ass covered, you want to be able to make your case. Good luck with that.

"You know, this is silly," I said, "but everything just seems like—it could be our last day on this earth, you know?"

He put his hand on my shoulder and squeezed. He was fucking strong, this Mark.

"And we're sort of thrown together by fate, you and me, and this is such a bizarre time, it feels like the world might be ending—"

"I know."

"What hotel do they have you in?"

"What hotel?" He jerked his chin in the general direction of downtown. "The Marriott. Right on Times Square. Just a few blocks from here. Do you know it?"

"I've seen it," I said, "from outside."

"It's quite something." He paused. "They evacuated the whole hotel. They made us all go stand in the street. Just stood there for a couple of hours, watching the news on that giant video billboard, and then at some point they just said we could go back in."

"This is going to sound kind of gay," I said, "but I don't really feel like being alone right now."

He invited me over. I knew he would. What everyone in New York was suddenly trying to act like—neighborly—this hick was actually like that 24/7. Probably he was a churchgoer. He had a lot of wrong ideas about himself, you could see that. Anyway, it was only like a five-minute walk and we were there. The Marriott has this rooftop restaurant that spins around while you eat, which sounded awesome to me, but of course that had been closed since Tuesday and was unlikely to be up and running any time soon. "Room service?" I suggested. He seemed reluctant but I asked at the desk and room service was technically back in operation but not fully staffed, so it might take a while, is what we were told. So many of the kitchen and hotel workers were illegals, and there was no easy way to get ahold of them to tell them to come back to work. They'd come back when they felt it was safe, I guess. Mark's room was all the way up on the nineteenth floor. The lobby elevators are made of glass, so it's like watching yourself go up in a rocket or something. Revolving restaurant, glass elevators—the whole place is designed to make you piss yourself.

I could tell he was uncomfortable. He handed me the room service menu and then called down to the front desk to ask if all the trains upstate were running on their normal schedule, and I guess the answer was yes. Maybe he wanted to pack up and go home right then, but he was Mr. Polite, and brother, I wasn't budging. This place was sweet.

The second he hung up the room phone, his cell phone rang again. "Hi, honey," he said. "I was just about to call you back." He looked at me for a second, without meaning to, and I understood he wanted some privacy, but I didn't really feel like giving it to him and anyway where was I going to go?

I smiled at him and mouthed, "It's okay," which seemed to puzzle him.

"Just came back from there," he said. Little pause. "Well, sort of. Towles wasn't there." Littler pause. "Nobody seems exactly sure."

I looked at the art on the wall, which was abstract, like a picture of nothing, like they were afraid of getting sued for accidentally reminding you of something.

"No, for God's sake, no, he wasn't killed or anything. He was nowhere near all that. He's just taken off for the suburbs somewhere. His family's there. Just to be safe, I guess."

"I'll just go into the bathroom," I said, like it was to be nice to him, but I didn't close the door all the way, so I could still hear him.

"I am safe," he said. "I'm perfectly safe, as safe as you, that's not what I meant."

Sometimes you can learn a lot from snooping out a person's bathroom. But he'd only been living there two days. He had this grungy leather toiletry kit like a kid would have, a kid at camp. The only interesting thing in there was a prescription bottle of Vicodin, which I was like, what? I had it halfway into my pocket—not for me, but stuff like that might be valuable to Yuri or to someone he knows—but when it shook I could hear that there was only one pill left in it. So I just put it back.

"They did?" he said. "Well that's—I mean that's sweet, but—"

The bathroom itself was nice. So clean. I don't want to say why I was so struck by that. Huge mirror. Huge tub. People live lives where they stay in different rooms like this all the time. That's got to be the best. Anonymous and cleaned up after.

"I know, but who would organize a thing like that? What did you tell them about why I was here?"

I wondered why he didn't tell her I was right there with him, especially if he wanted to get off the call, which it kind of sounded like he did. I walked back out and lay down on his bed. I just smiled. I don't know, there was something about the guy, you just wanted to provoke him. He looked like some reformed bully. It was like drinking in front of somebody who's in AA. Part of you is curious to see what he's like drunk, right? How bad it would get.

"I should go," he said. "Room service is here." A lie! I hadn't called them yet! "No, if she's outside, just let her play. Tell her I love her and I'll see her tomorrow." Little frown. "I'll just have to come back here another time. No, I know. Me too. I love you. Me too. See you tomorrow."

He looked at me sheepishly, that's the word. I think he probably wanted to lie down too, but he wasn't about to stretch out next to me. I make people nervous, I don't know why, so I just try to enjoy that quality about myself when I can. He stood by the window. All day long I'd been way higher up than I'm used to being. It didn't feel that different.

"My wife," he said. I nodded. "She was telling me that they had a candlelight vigil at the Town Hall last night. For me. For my safe return. I don't know whether to laugh or cry."

He stared out the window at all the neon and the blue, and he dropped his head.

"Everybody was totally shocked to hear I was in New York City, because I hadn't even told anybody I was coming here. I mean Karen knew, of course. But we agreed not to mention it to anyone else. Because I actually haven't told anyone, not even the rest of my family, about the whole Garrett Spalding disaster. Because I was ashamed of what they might think of me. And now they're all out there holding candles and praying for me. I feel like kind of a low person right now."

"What's she look like, your wife?" I said.

He was really making an effort to roll with it, with this whole particular interaction, you could see. And then he does exactly what I'm hoping he'll do, he pulls out a picture of his wife and their daughter from his wallet. The wife is just like you'd figure a good-looking yokel like this would wind up with. Country girl. Great body, not fat but nice and curvy, lots of long, naturally shaggy hair. Great, full mouth. Outstanding tits. The kid just looked like a kid.

"You have a lovely family," is what I said.

He smiled, a little sadly. He didn't ask me if I had a family. He could probably tell. "I've been very lucky," he said.

So I did it up with that room service, man. The prices were ridiculous. I know Mark disapproved, but it was all free, right? I mean it was all on Towles the lawyer, and even then it's not like it was coming straight out of his pocket, and did I mention that fucking office? You think a few extra apps or a bottle of cognac is going to break that place? Come on.

We ate like kings. Once the food was there, and it was too late to do anything about it, he gave in and enjoyed himself a little. He even had a beer, while I had three and figured I could carry the other two home with me. I could tell he was worried about getting in trouble with Towles. But who knew if we'd ever see that paranoid asswipe again, unless we wanted to go out to the Island buddy-movie style and track him down. I started flipping around on the TV, still all just news, but then it hit me: pay-per-view! I'd heard about it but I'd never seen it. He was just sitting in the chair not saying anything. I looked through all the sad-ass vanilla porn trailers just for fun, but I wasn't really tempted: porn is meant to be watched alone, not with another guy in the room, regardless of whether you're beating off to it or not. That's why porn was invented, to give everybody something to be alone with.

"So where do you live exactly?" he says. "The subways and buses are running now, right?"

"So was your wife pretty mad at you?" I said. "About the money. She looks like the fiery type."

"Well, yeah. I mean, it's—not that I mind your asking, you know, but it's kind of personal."

"Sure. You're right. I mean, it's just I don't have a family myself. So I get curious. Especially now, right, when we're still in danger, maybe, for all we know. So yours might be like the last new story I ever hear."

He went right for it. He told me the whole thing. He's a contractor up in Massachusetts someplace. He restores old houses. It's some kind of a summer town, where rich assholes from New York or Boston buy vacation homes. All that money in his face all the time, so he gets kind of envious and he starts to put his money in the stock market. And he's actually pretty good at it for a while, or else just lucky, and his wife is all proud of him, just dropping to her knees and blowing him all the time (okay, I added that last part, but it's his fault for showing me the picture). Then he decides he's got to move up to the big leagues, and he starts shopping around for an investment manager—because he figures that's safer!—and he's looking around online and in some fucking chat room he comes across somebody raving about this guy Garrett Spalding. He gave the man everything. Didn't even tell his wife he was doing it. Now they've got debts up the ass and they had to call off having a second kid.

And get this: "Can I confess something to you? After everything happened on Tuesday, part of me was a little relieved, because Karen's whole attitude changed, she was just like, forget about all that, forget about our problems, it's just money, none of that seems important anymore, all that matters is that you're safe. But I know that feeling might not last forever. I don't know, maybe that's why I don't feel as scared about being away from home as I probably should. I actually feel kind of safe here. In a weird way. But it's disrespectful to say so."

There might have been more than that. But the cognac was open and I was pretty drunk at that point.

"Your daughter, though," I said.

He smiled. "Yeah, fortunately I think she's too young even to be scared. No idea what everybody's so worried about. I know they gave her the day off from school, and she was mad about that."

"What? They canceled school all the way up there? Why?"

He shrugged. "School's closed all over the country, I think. The country is under attack."

"But that's so fucked up!" I said. "I mean you live in the middle of nowhere, right, you said? Out in the woods basically?"

He looked a little startled, like he didn't get what was upsetting me.

"Why would anybody want to attack you?" I said.

He just sort of made a neutral face. "Who knows what they want," he said. "Or even who they are. They just hate us. They hate what we stand for."

"What we *stand* for? Jesus. Why does everybody suddenly think it's like Judgment Day or something? You know what most people's judgment of you is? Their judgment is that they couldn't give less of a shit about you. You don't exist to them. But people would rather think that they're hated. It makes them feel important. Anyway, to me it's conceited as fuck."

I don't think I was making myself too clear. "It's getting late," he said.

He wanted me to go. It's not like I didn't see that. But I loved it that he couldn't just say it. Who was this guy? Why didn't he just throw me out? You know he wanted to. And you know he could have, even if I'd been sober. But he was being such a fucking pushover. Big handsome guy with his hot wife. I couldn't let things go his way.

"It's crazy," I said, "all the different things that had to happen to bring you and me together. All the coincidences, I mean. Because we don't seem like guys who would normally be hanging out."

"Absolutely," he said. "It just goes to show you."

"I mean, the whole tragedy. But also what brought you here in the first place. The fact that the same guy ripped us both off. Different as we are. The fact that we still went out and showed up for that appointment, we still cared that much about our own money even while thousands of people were dying."

"Well, I guess," he said.

"Even the fucking lawyer pussied out of it. Not us, though. We want that fucking money back. You got to want it. You can't let a terrorist attack stop you. That's what we got in common, man. We're selfish."

"I guess at a time like this, our differences don't seem so—"

"Selfish and greedy and naïve," I said. "That's not a winning combination."

"Listen, I'm getting pretty tired," Mark said. I think I'd maybe fallen asleep myself. I opened my eyes. At the foot of the bed the huge TV played silently. Same old shit, on a loop. Nobody wanted to let go of it, of what had happened. It made everybody feel important.

"Yeah, me too," I said. "But, Mark, I'm scared. I don't think I can go out there. Not at night. Nighttime is the worst. It's like ninety blocks back to my apartment. Do you know I walked to Towles's office and back, the whole way? Both days. I just can't deal with crowds right now, enclosed spaces. I can't deal with not being able to see what's coming out of the sky. The buses seem like prime targets. Like in Israel. And the subways? Forget it. I can't even think about it."

I tell you, I got so into it I started crying a little. It was hilarious!

"I'm so scared right now. I don't know why I'm telling you. They're talking about bombing, about world war. It's just, you never know: is this my last night alive? We've been through something together, man. I don't know why people hate us. Why there's this kind of evil in the world. But I just have this feeling, like you said, like nothing will ever be the same. On my way downtown yesterday, I passed this playground, and it was full of kids, and I just can't stop thinking about them. It's like, they're so innocent, and they're going to have that ripped away from them. I want to find some way to stop it, you know? To stop them from ever knowing about what happened. But you can't stop it. It'd be like turning back time. They're not afraid of anything yet, of anything real anyway, but man, I'm so afraid for them right now—"

And that is how I spent my first-ever night in a king-size bed on the nineteenth floor of a luxury hotel. For free.

Best bed I ever slept in, but still, I tend to wake up early. It was dark. He was sleeping in the chair, his face propped up by his fist. The TV was still on, with the sound down. Very carefully I rolled to the edge of the bed and stood up and listened. Fucking quiet up that high. Can't hear the street at all. That must be why people like it. His phone and his wallet were on the table beside his chair. I took his MasterCard and the photo of his wife and kid, pocketed them, and put everything back the way I found it. I knew he wouldn't come after me. He could have gotten my address from the lawyer, maybe, but then he would have had to explain why he wanted it. Instead he'd just convince himself the whole thing was his fault anyway. Which it kind of was.

I rode the subway home. Even under the usual roar you could hear a quiet. Just a bunch of numbed-out people, on a train in a tunnel under the street, letting themselves be rocketed around to wherever they remembered somebody expected them to go.

I got straight online and guess what, fucking Mark Firth's card was declined, everywhere I tried it. Two possibilities. One, he'd already reported it stolen. Two, it was useless because he'd maxed it out anyway. I wanted to laugh but it didn't seem that fucking funny.

I took off my shoes and lay on my bed with my hands folded and what I wound up fantasizing about, bizarrely, was the money. All of a sudden I really wanted that shit back, and then some. I wanted punitive damages, I wanted pain and suffering. I wanted the fact that my pain and suffering were obviously fake to be the punitive part.

And then before I knew it the day was gone, and it started to get dark. I guess I was so bored and frustrated that I was in a kind of trance that made the time jump by without my even knowing. I'm sure I slept some too. But mostly I was just in a bad state of mind. I know I meant to call Towles's office again, just for the hell of it, but somehow I forgot even to do that.

Nothing to do, nowhere to go, no one to talk to. What a fucked-up world, I thought, that had put me in this spot. I don't like idleness. It works on me. I think too much. Everything starts to connect. This is what's gotten me into trouble in the past.

I made another one of those chicken TV dinners. I dicked around online for a while but that just made everything worse, everything I was locked out of. Those sites I like, you knew they hadn't stopped posting or changed their routine in any way just because some building full of stockbrokers and other assholes fell down somewhere. They were still uploading fresh, new, authentic-as-shit clips every day. And there's so much of it that things generally only stay up a few days before they're taken down again, sometimes for legal reasons, most times just to make room for the new. So I was missing things, things I wouldn't have the opportunity to see ever again. It drove me fucking crazy.

So in the end, I took the big risk, I made the big mistake, I did the one thing that night that's really fucking self-destructive for me to do. I admit it. I went back out on the roof. Basically I'm the same guy now as I always was: I get worked up and I need to get off somehow in order to settle down again. But I've learned to channel it. Thank God for the fucking internet. Because this is how I got into trouble in the first place. You know how long it took me, after last time, to get that job at the lab? Getting caught out on the roof again would put all of that at risk. I'd have nowhere to go but back to Bayside to listen to my mother cry like I'm not sitting right there. Which made it incredibly stupid of me.

But on the other hand, who did I hurt? I mean ever? You think I don't know how to avoid being seen? It's like my middle fucking name. And if you don't see me watching you, if you don't even know I'm doing it, then what fucking difference does it make to you?

Anyway, if I got caught I figured I could claim post-traumatic stress or whatever. Why should I miss out?

I walked up to the fifth floor—on the outside edge of every step, to cut down on squeaking—and when I tried the roof door it was open, just like it always was back when, just like the old super hadn't been fired for not locking it. In the middle of the roof there's an exhaust vent, and I walked across the tarpaper as quickly as I could and flattened myself against it. If you make a sort of tight circle around it, you can see through windows in a total of five other buildings. One is some Columbia housing, like fifteen stories.

The lower-floor windows especially are so close you could almost reach out and open them, but people leave their lights on, their blinds up, they don't have a clue. I used to see people every night. There was a high school girl in the high-rise, she was the best, my downfall in fact, though she was probably long gone by now. Couples fucking, mostly in a really boring way but still, when it is on the real it is always oh so stimulating no matter what they look like. Other guys beating off too, sometimes, which doesn't exactly do it for me—but then also, this one woman who used to sit on the couch in front of her TV and just rub one out with a dildo or a vibrator or something, damned if I could see. That was the absolute best. I would have given anything to be able to hear her, but there's always a lot of noise rising up from the street and she was too far away.

I made a circle around the vent, looking in every lit window, feeling my heart pound even worse than I remembered. Then another circle, and another one. Then I just stepped away and stood in the middle of the roof, on top of my building, under the stars. I couldn't believe it. There was nothing out there. Everyone— everyone—was just watching their fucking TVs, and on every TV was the same thing, like the whole city was the window of an appliance store or something. Shadows of people's heads in front of the TV news. I just stood there and stared. I saw a new light go on and some nice-looking chick in a t-shirt and shorts, but then she just sat at her kitchen table not moving, and I realized she just couldn't sleep, that was all it was. How long was this shit going to go on? When were people going to drop it and go back to acting like nobody was watching them? They were all still alive. They were all still their own nasty selves. They'd forget, because that's what people do, they forget what they feel. They go back to being animals. They go back to being savages.

Monday I went back to the lab, and I've never been so happy to go to work in my life. I was twenty minutes early. "You okay?" everybody kept asking me, and I got paranoid I looked sick or something, until I saw they were asking everybody that, first thing. "You okay?" Jesus, yes, I'm fine. Enough.

Then Yuri saw me, and I tried to act cool, but he just smirked. That shit never works with Yuri. "Somebody looks a little tired," he said with his dumbass accent. "I tell you what. Meet me in the break room at ten forty-five. Uncle Yuri is feeling generous, in this time of national mourning."

"Not you too," I said.

He clapped me on the shoulder, then he leaned over and I thought for a second he was going to kiss me on the cheek. He puts his lips almost against my ear. "Fuck these people," he whispers very softly to me. "Fuck this whole country in its big fat ass."

The end of that same week, I'm on my break at work and I see I've missed a call from Towles. "You're back," I say when I finally get through to him. "You know, I came looking for you. I'm not the one who missed our meeting."

"So I heard."

"So now I have to get another day off, but when do you want to do this?"

"We have a problem," he says. "Not with the suit, which will go forward. With you as one of the name plaintiffs. You're in the registry. I don't know why you didn't tell me that, though I also can't fathom why my staff didn't turn it up before now. Anyway, you can understand that this is not what we want, public-image-wise."

I was seething, for a minute. But he explained to me that I'm still part of the whole class action, I'll still get my money back if he wins. This just keeps my name out of it. Cool with me. Just as soon keep my name to myself anyway.

Maybe two weeks later, maybe less, I'm in the Morningside Heights post office again. I've got my envelope and my registered-mail form all filled out. It's quiet in there. And crowded, twenty people at least waiting in line, in spite of which only two of the ten windows are open. You can see other employees walking around back there, of course, doing fuck-all, talking to each other, scratching their asses. But God forbid any of them should speed things up for us by opening a third window. Probably against union rules, right? We're all staring at that light with the green arrow on it, waiting for the little bell. It's like hell on earth in there. But nobody says anything. Then a woman leaves the second window, the guy at the head of the line—some older guy wearing a suit and sneakers, bald on top but with this scraggly white Bozo hair around the sides—starts forward with his package, but instead of the light going on, the woman behind the counter puts up her NEXT WINDOW PLEASE sign and gets up and walks away.

You can kind of feel the air go out of everybody in line. But then the guy in the suit, halfway between the front of the line he's just left and the shuttered window, says out loud, "Are you kidding me?" Maybe it wasn't that loud, but it sounded loud.

Nobody made eye contact with him.

"Are you kidding me right now?" he says.

And then he just goes off! He drops his package on the counter and he starts banging on the window, pounding on it. "Hey!" he says. "Hey! I see you back there! I can see all of you! Can't you see us? What is wrong with you people?"

The woman behind the one remaining open window all of a sudden shuts hers too, and disappears. Now it's ten closed windows. Like war.

"Is this any way to run a goddamn business?" the guy yells. His face is dark red. He turns to look at us, but no one will meet his eye. "You disrespectful government vermin! I demand that you open up these windows right now! I've lived in this neighborhood for twenty-eight years! I will not be treated this way! None of us will! Come out of there, you coward, you lazy fucking bitch!"

They had to call security. Two of them, it took. He was still yelling when they dragged him out to the street. Jesus, it was beautiful. Some woman in line accused me of laughing, but I wasn't, I swear. I just felt this huge sense of relief. There we go, I thought. Thank God. Finally!

THE LØCALS

1

The lazy, nearly empty train ride north to the end of the line, the long, featureless ditches and bright foliage, the towns diminishing in size and vitality—White Plains, Valhalla, Katonah—all of which looked like ghost towns now, though maybe they'd looked the same a few days ago, before the air of loss had attached itself to everything. Mark was one of just three passengers in his train car. At Brewster came the transfer onto a much smaller train—a Budd car, it was called: the term popped back into his head from boyhood, when he was obsessed with such things—and there he found himself the only passenger at all. He leaned his forehead against the scratched plastic window and watched the trees flow by, lifting his gaze only when the conductor came to ask softly, almost apologetically, for his ticket.

"Thought there might be more people getting out of the city," Mark said.

The conductor, a man about Mark's age who wore a short-sleeved white shirt and a tie with a clip, expelled air through his nose. "Need to bomb those people flat, is what we need to do," he said.

They seemed to be talking about different people, but the misunderstanding wasn't worth pursuing. Mark passed him the return portion of the round-trip ticket, purchased Monday, and saw him linger over the date on it.

"Get home safe," the conductor said. Mark mouthed, "You too."

Old towns, colonial towns, towns too far north to posit themselves as suburbs. Rusted swing sets and above-ground pools in backyards perpendicular to the tracks. He felt like one of those nineteenth-century robber barons with his own private rail car, except for a lot of things, principally the absence of food and the faint mildew smell and the deep cracks in the vinyl upholstery of his and most every seat and the faint, permanent stains on the murky industrial linoleum of the floor. Mark couldn't think offhand where you might go to replace that grade of linoleum anymore. It had to be as old as the car itself.

Why was there no one else on the train? Maybe because you were now supposed to think of mass transit as a target. It was pretty hard to consider this particular train, which ran in a straight line away from New York City for two and a half hours and then just stopped in the middle of nowhere as if due to an expiration of interest, an asset worth the resentful or strategic notice of anyone anywhere. But danger and ill will were loose in the world, anarchic and unreasonable. He could see the back of the neck of his conductor, sitting in the front seat of the car with his hat on, gazing straight ahead, at attention, Mark imagined.

In the parking lot in Wassaic he found his truck—Karen wasn't comfortable driving it, so he hadn't wanted to leave her without the Escort for a few days—and continued north up 22, through the valleys of stony farmland, cows standing dumbly on the slopes. In Hillsdale he turned east on 23 and crossed the state line. He'd told Karen what train he was taking just before he left the hotel. He was low on gas but he didn't want to stop, and anyway his credit card was missing; he thought maybe he'd left it with the front desk, for incidentals, when he checked in to the hotel. He didn't specifically remember doing that, but then he barely remembered Monday at all. In Howland, just a mile from home, he was suddenly nervous at the two stop signs he had to observe; he didn't want anyone to see him, or even the telltale truck with his name on the side. They'd make a fuss. He'd been touched but mostly embarrassed by Karen's report of friends and neighbors and even people he'd never liked very much standing on the Town Hall steps holding candles and praying for him. "Well, technically, you are a survivor," she'd said. "It can be looked at that way. Anyway, you just put a face on the whole thing for everybody, that's all. Otherwise it's so massive people don't even know how to pray about it, what to ask for."

"But it's just so random that I'm here at all," Mark had said.

"It was random for everybody. Right? It was just as random for the people who were killed. It's not like a bunch of soldiers dying. Just a bunch of people going to work. But those people are heroes now."

Were they heroes? He guessed they were. You could become a hero without doing anything, if your end turned out to mean something to others. Anyway, he could certainly admit now, to himself at least, how frightened he'd been. He took the last bend before his turnoff and another car, one he didn't recognize, honked as it passed him going the other way. Mark flinched and waved at his own rearview mirror, and then swung left onto the dirt road that led to his driveway.

The house was a perfect old New England saltbox that had been added onto once, in a less than sensitive fashion, long before they ever saw it. His initial plan was to restore it properly himself, maybe even tear the addition down, but in those early days of the marriage Karen had encouraged him to save his time and skills for paying work. Every winter they closed off part of it to save on heat and still had rooms to spare. They'd taken on so much more space than they needed, mostly because the house was an unmissable bargain; he'd been tipped off to its foreclosure by his brother Gerry, a real estate agent in Stockbridge, who'd had a girlfriend of sorts who worked at Citizens Bank. Mark bought it at auction, on a Wednesday morning in midwinter, for what he had to keep reminding himself was practically nothing. Gerry's advice was to fix it up a bit and flip it, and that too was the plan for a while, but then Haley was born, and Mark's business picked up, and he started to feel the sentimental pull of the idea of a house that his children and their own families would want to return to on holidays, on summer weekends, that they could eventually inherit from him. Interested as he was in making money generally, he wanted his home to be a home, not an investment, not an asset to convert at the top of the market. Of course, they could have used the cash right now. But in his heart it was still out of the question, and Karen hadn't brought it up in a while.

Where the driveway turned into lawn, Mark stopped and switched off the truck. His heart was pounding. Even though there was no sign of the Escort, he hit the horn twice. No one came through the door. He checked his watch: Karen must have gone to pick up Haley at school, which had resumed today. Fair enough, he thought: she couldn't very well make Haley wait, just in order to stay there for him. Still, the silence of the house, the fact that his wife and daughter were gone, put an irrational lump in his throat that made him think the trauma of the last few days had worked on him more than he realized. He stood in front of his truck and listened. Nothing but a breeze moving the ryegrass at the point where the mowing line ended. When they'd bought the place, it was utterly private—two point seven acres, and you couldn't see another house in any direction, on either side of the road, which was just the way Mark liked it. Unfortunately, that had changed. About four years later, when Haley was two, a gap had appeared almost overnight in the stand of trees to the east of them, across the ryegrass meadow, maybe five hundred yards away; the gap turned into a square clearing, then a hole, into which a foundation was poured, by which time Mark had the whole story. The house was going up at the behest of somebody from New York City named Philip Hadi, a Wall Street guy, like so many of them up here. He'd rented in Howland with his family for two weeks the previous July and, based solely on that, had decided to build a home here. That kind of financial spontaneity seemed to Mark both reckless and enviable. He had expected the worst, of course—some ostentatious zillionaire, building on a whim—but in the end the design fit in decently, and the house, while plenty big, was not monstrous. Karen was angry that their view was marred. But this was how towns like theirs survived, like it or not—people who grew up here usually tried their damnedest to get out, and outsiders and their money had to be attracted and accommodated. And anyway, the Hadi house was only occupied two or three months out of the year. From September to June, it was unlit, and on a moonless night you couldn't see it out there any more than you could make out anything else.

Haley's elementary school was ten minutes away, so Mark could easily have waited. But the need to see them, to hold them, was now overwhelming him. Without even dropping his suitcase on the porch he got back in the truck and drove to school; he didn't make it halfway across the parking lot before people started shouting to Karen that he was here, and then, in front of many of their friends and neighbors, he was treated to the homecoming, his daughter followed by his wife reaching him on the dead run across the concrete like he was a POW on an airport tarmac. A few people cheered. He and Karen kissed several times in a loving way that respected the presence of their audience, which now included ten or twelve second graders. For Haley everything was back to normal in an instant, so much so that she chose to ride home in the Escort with her mother, while Mark followed. She never liked riding in the truck; she said it was too noisy.

· · ·

His little sister Candace called, and then Gerry called because Candace had called him, and so Karen just wound up inviting them all over for a drink or dinner or whatever—really just to lay eyes on their brother. Candace swung up to Pittsfield to collect their parents, so they were there too. All the Firths except the oldest of the four siblings, Renee, who lived in Colorado Springs—but she called as well, sobbing, and Mark told her the whole story over again while standing on his porch in the twilight, half-drunk, grateful, missing her in a way he usually neglected to do. Before everybody got there he'd asked Karen, a little ashamedly, what she'd been telling people when they asked what he'd been doing in the city in the first place. She said she'd told them he was showing plans to a client. So that was the story he went with.

His mother cried, and though Gerry was the youngest of the four, Mark could already see how he was turning into their dad: the way they held it in, the stoic, hyper-masculine, one-emotion-fits-all look on both their faces. Candace, with her prim adult hairstyle that Mark could never get used to, kept wrapping her arms around him—Candace, whom he could reduce to tears when they were kids just by repeatedly touching her with an index finger. Only six years separated the four of them, and maybe the intensity that had generated was what made their adult selves seem less real to Mark than their childhood ones, when they fronted with each other less adeptly, when everything within them was closer to the surface, like it was tonight. Only Renee had managed to move more than thirty minutes away from the house in which they had all grown up. Their love was more important to him—more unconditional, more reflexive—than he remembered; he regretted not having let himself feel closer to them, safer with them, not being honest about everything that had happened, though now was certainly not the time.

Haley got to stay up late because the family was over, and when inevitably she started to melt down, the others took that as their cue to leave. Mark and Karen put her to bed together and then went downstairs and had another beer in the living room, side by side on the couch, carefully silent, just as on most nights, not talking until they were confident Haley had gone to sleep. He smiled at her, whereupon she put her face on his chest and started to cry. She too, like his siblings and even his parents, seemed to be responding to something new or different about him, something he didn't get and thus felt slightly guilty about projecting. In Karen's case maybe it was just the thought of how close she had been brought to the idea, at least, of having to go forward in life without him. But even that didn't seem to account fully for it. They hadn't had sex at night for he didn't know how long—Haley had a stubborn habit of waking up in the small hours and stumbling wordlessly down the hall and into their bed—but somewhere in the middle of this night Karen woke him up and they did everything, in total darkness, in charged silence. At some point she took him by the shoulders and pushed him forcibly down beneath the comforter, leaving her fingers in his hair. When that was done, and he could feel her whole body trembling in his hands, she pulled him back up to her. He felt her tears on his face, but whatever she was thinking, she couldn't say it.

Monday everybody went back to work. Mark's knee ached below its surgical scar, but he was still superstitious about taking the last Vicodin; he'd held on to the one pill for a month now, worried that the day he didn't have it would be the day he'd stumble or fall on the job and the pain would become unbearable. He stopped, as he did whenever feasible, for a coffee and an egg sandwich at Daisy's, on the county road just inside the Howland line, where he saw another half-dozen people he knew. He accepted their hugs, and the tears of Chase (Daisy's daughter, middle-aged herself now), who worked behind the counter, and he told his story again— Times Square, the evacuations, the video billboards, the angry, weeping crowds. The repetition made the temptation to embellish very strong, but he resisted it, even when he could see he was disappointing people. Then he drove out to New Marlborough, where he was putting in a bid on the restoration of a Dutch colonial for new owners fanatic about period details, a job that was as much research as it was construction. The owners were currently asking for bids only on the kitchen—they said they didn't want to start any work that would open up the walls of the house during the winter months—but having met them once, he felt good about the larger prospect, because they were just the kind of city people he did well with, good-looking entitled perfectionists who prided themselves on not appearing demanding or unreasonable even though you could tell they would turn out to be both. He was good at instilling confidence in clients like that, the wives especially.

In the end he got the kitchen job, which occupied him and a crew of two until mid-October; but then, the night after the custom-salvaged gamekeeper's sink went in, the wife called Mark at home to tell him sheepishly that, even though they were thrilled with what he'd done, the rest of the renovation was going to have to be put on hold indefinitely. Her husband was an executive at American Airlines, as bad luck would have it: all the airlines were suffering and this guy was basically waiting for the ax to fall on him and his whole department. This, for Mark, was not good news. Karen suggested they ask for an increase in their credit limit, or else just apply for another card, as they'd done before to help them through lean months; but when Mark tried both those things, he was told that he'd been placed on something called a security freeze. That was a whole day of phone calls right there. The card he'd previously reported lost had been used, they said. He asked where, and they said Russia. Russia? It had occurred to Mark, in trying to recall what he could of those jumpy days and nights in New York, that maybe he hadn't lost the card at all, maybe that twitchy little co-plaintiff who came up to his hotel room had stolen it. But the Russia business seemed to rule out that suspicion, farfetched as it was in the first place. Probably he had dropped it somewhere and some eagle-eyed criminal, some guy who did this for a living, had scooped it up. Guys like that never took a holiday. Disaster and panic were like good growing weather for them. Anyway, the credit agencies assured him it would all be straightened out, though it might take a while, because the Russia thing was a real red flag.

He was owed another eleven thousand for a job in Lenox he'd completed in August, but past that there was nothing definite on the horizon. And that's if he could even collect on the eleven grand. It was all over the TV that the economy was hurting, and there was a sense that everyone else's hardship in the wake of catastrophe was your hardship too, which made it awkward to go after people to settle their debts. Not that Mark had ever excelled at that aspect of the job anyway. Karen had volunteered, a few times, to become a kind of office manager for him, but he didn't want to set that precedent. He felt like some distinction ought to be preserved there, between business and family, days and nights. Anyway, there were always lean times like this in the life of someone who did what Mark did. It was the nature of the work, not to mention the nature of having only yourself for a boss. You socked some money away for winters like this one was shaping up to be. But thanks to Garrett Spalding, they would enter this winter with their savings gone.

He spent mornings in his office—really just one of the empty bedrooms at home—doing random but still valuable professional research online, mostly just thinking. The day after Halloween Karen asked him to do the school pickup that afternoon, without explaining why; and then when she came home at four thirty, she announced that she had gotten a job.

"At the school," she said. "It's kind of informal. Teacher's aide, some admissions-office help. Eighteen, twenty hours a week. It doesn't pay, but they will knock fifty percent off you-know-who's tuition. You hear that, Haley? You're going to see Mommy at school!"

"Yay!" Haley said.

"You didn't want to talk this over with me first," Mark said, resenting her for starting this conversation in front of Haley, which meant he would have to keep his tone light.

"What's to talk over?" she said brightly. "That tuition bill is due at the end of December, in case you forgot. So the alternative is for me to home-school her, and I know you're not suggesting that."

The more reasonable alternative was actually the public school in Howland—where Mark's sister Candace was vice principal—but he knew better than to bring that up.

"Daddy, you can come to school too," Haley suggested.

"Sure," Karen said while searching through the fridge, her back to them. "You can restore some of its period details."

Some of his regular hires—Hartley, his cabinetry guy, and Kurt, who was a master plumber—were already wandering, committing to other jobs with other contractors in the Berkshires and elsewhere, which of course was understandable. They had to work. But it meant that even if he got the opportunity to bid on something now, he might not be telling the truth if he said he could get started right away.

He mowed the grass for what would probably be the last time this year, and he went up on a ladder outside the house to rehang one of the shutters before it got too dark. Karen was picking up Haley from a birthday party. Mark opened a beer and stood with his shoulder against the newel post atop the three back porch steps, and as the sun went down over the ryegrass field, he saw something he had previously seen before only in the summertime—and never so clearly as now, when the trees were beginning to lose their leaves: all the lights blazing in the Hadi house, just on the far edge of his property.

. . .

The locals spotted Hadi's wife—at the Price Chopper south of Great Barrington, tipping some teenager in a smock to put what looked like eight or ten grocery bags in the back of her black Mercedes SUV—before they ever saw him. Which was odd only because the wife seemed all but invisible whenever the Hadis were in town for the summer; it was Philip who was the gregarious type, one of those guys who just assumed he fit in everywhere, with anybody. They all had a Phil Hadi story. The wife—they couldn't even all agree on her name; Karen was pretty sure it was Rachel—would materialize once in a while, at the drugstore or the post office; she was polite, semi-friendly, answered questions, said goodbye. But none of them, not the year-rounders at least, had ever had more than a four-line conversation with her, so none of them was about to approach her now in the Price Chopper parking lot, or in the Rexall the next day, to ask what she and, presumably, her family were doing in Howland on a weekday in November, why they were opening up their summer house again. Planning to stay awhile too, judging by the eight bags of food.

After several days of happily reckless group conjecture, Karen found herself in a debate after morning dropoff as to whether Hadi himself was in town at all. A couple of women were confidently putting forth the idea, based on nothing, that Rachel had left her rich husband and fled to Massachusetts with the kids. Not that anyone had seen the kids either. But it was unthinkable that she'd be up here without them, even though it seemed likely that a woman who led the kind of life she must have led would have full-time live-in childcare to see to the kids' needs wherever they went. And there was still the initial evidence of all the groceries. She had to be feeding somebody.

It was Rachel herself who broke the ice. A friend of Karen's named Sue Scoville was in Grindhouse, getting a coffee for herself and smoothies for her two sons, one of whom had wet-combed hair and a red face and smelled like chlorine and had clearly just gotten out of a swimming pool. Sue felt a tap on her shoulder and turned around to see Rachel, unaccompanied, behind her in line; barely audibly, Rachel asked where the boy had been swimming—her own son, she said, loved to swim—and from there Sue coaxed it all out of her. The whole Hadi family, Philip too, was now living in Howland indefinitely. Philip, Rachel said matter-of-factly, had friends in very high places, both in government and in private-sector companies with strong ties to national defense; and the inside word suggested strongly that another terrorist attack on New York City was not just possible but imminent. There had been that anthrax business but Rachel said no, that wasn't it, what her husband had been warned about was something much bigger. What struck Sue was that there was no shrugging or eye-rolling on Rachel Hadi's part at all, none of the hedging two wives in conversation would normally exhibit when describing the impulses or confident opinions of their husbands. She wasn't happy about it but she clearly believed that her husband was a very well-informed man. And maybe he was. Who knew how these echelons worked.

Anyway, the Hadi family, for safety reasons, was now living here. The only point of contention seemed to be how long they planned to wait before returning home to Manhattan; Rachel's face, Sue said, clouded a bit at that question. "When it's safe," Rachel answered finally, and then Sue was at the front of the line paying for her sons' smoothies and Rachel withdrew from the store with a quick, borderline rude goodbye, as if concerned that she had said too much.

A few months earlier, there might have been some skepticism in town about the pretensions to secret knowledge of rich summer people from New York, but now no source of dire information seemed safe to dismiss. Rachel's own paranoia might have been strengthened if she knew the speed at which people in and around Howland shared with each other the details of their every encounter with her. Not just the bit about the terrorist attack: it got around quickly that she'd asked Sue Scoville about nearby indoor swimming pools, and that she'd asked the pool director at Simon's Rock about good local schools, and that she'd asked the nervous admissions director at Mullins Day School—who was now Karen Firth's boss—if she knew any good local contractors.

Mark had a rudimentary web page for his business—strictly informational, not much different than a Yellow Pages ad—and of course he was listed in the Howland phone book as well. But when he stopped in at Daisy's one morning for an egg sandwich and a coffee—mostly just to get out of the house; he had no job site to go to afterwards—Chase mentioned to him as she was handing him his change, "That New York fella was in here looking for you earlier. Asking for you."

"Asking for me?" Mark said. Earlier? It was ten minutes to eight.

"That rich fella," Chase said, with lips maybe slightly more pressed together than usual, and turned to walk the three steps to the counter to take the next order. Daisy's staff in the early morning was just Chase and the cook, Horace, who was only ever visible through the thin slot where hot plates and foil-wrapped takeout orders emerged, and with whom the settled rumor was that Chase was sleeping. The fact that you never saw him gave him a troll-like aura that made the rumor, if you knew Chase at all, somehow more plausible.

Next morning Mark got to Daisy's at six forty-five, and there in the little triangular lot, between the dumpster and the fuel tank (Daisy's sat at a three-way intersection, with nothing but fields surrounding, so every part of its little operation was just as visible as every other part), was some kind of black SUV that looked like it might have been part of a presidential motorcade, conspicuous amidst the other salt-stained, rust-nibbled vehicles in the lot, Mark's truck among them. He parked a respectful distance away, mostly because the SUV's heavily tinted windows made him unsure whether Hadi, or someone else, might still be in there.

But he was inside, sitting alone at one of the two-tops, facing the door. Mark had seen him once or twice before, in the summers in town, but even if that weren't the case he would have recognized him right away—partly because he knew by name every other red-eyed working man in Daisy's at that hour, and partly because Hadi was wearing a new-looking gray sleeveless Patagonia fleece over what appeared to be a white oxford shirt. Also, he did not look the least bit tired. An untouched cup of black coffee sat next to him like a prop or camouflage, like the fleece.

"Mark Firth?" Hadi said. "I mean of course it's you, I just watched you get out of a truck with your name on it. Very simple that way! Maybe everybody should do it. Have a seat. I'm Phil."

Right away Mark felt a sort of natural ceding of control, one that went beyond the canny deference you'd normally show a prospective client, if that's what this meeting was even about. It was more like the respect you'd show an older man, which Hadi was, though not by much—surely he was no older than forty. His hair was thinning. He was not loud but he had a certain preemptive command.

"I heard a remarkable story about you," Hadi said. "You were actually in New York on 9/11?"

Mark nodded. "Same as you were, I imagine," he said. "It was nothing, really. I was never in any danger."

"Yes, you were," Hadi said. "We were all in danger. But I lived there—what brought you there?"

Mark's instinct, oddly, was that this question was a trap or a setup, that Hadi already knew the truth about why he'd been in New York, for no other reason than that guys like Hadi made it their business to know everything, and had the means to do so. But that was insane. "I was showing some plans," Mark said, "to a client who's thinking about building up here."

"Of course you were." Hadi finally went for his coffee, then seemed miffed to discover it was cold. "So, I know you're a contractor, and I know your work is well thought of. Which is why I was hoping to catch you here. Do you have a few minutes?"

That last was just barely a question, but the truth was that Mark had nowhere to go today until Haley's school pickup at quarter to three.

"So my family and I have this house in Howland, off Route 4 but I mean way off, kind of built into the hill that looks back toward town, it's hard to describe but if you're driving—"

"I know just where it is," Mark said. "We're neighbors." He was smiling, but Hadi was not. "I mean," Mark said, shifting in his chair, "we're a couple acres apart, but we can see your house from our place, which is back off 4 also. Since you're on the hill and all."

"I didn't know that," Hadi said, and it was clear to Mark from the way he said it that that's what irritated him—not that he and this middle-class contractor were, relatively speaking, next-door neighbors, but that he'd shown up for this meeting not knowing something relevant that the other guy knew. "Well, good, then you know the location. We built it as a summer place, but between you and me, my family and I are staying up here full-time."

He paused, and something in Mark, the thing that made him successful with prospective wealthy clients, made him understand that Hadi wanted to be asked why. "Why?" he said. "If you don't mind my asking."

"Not at all. It's a reasonable question. Let me start by telling you about my work. I used to be an academic, a professor at the Columbia Business School, but I had an idea, an algorithm, and I was able to get some acquaintances to let me make them some money with this algorithm, and in the end I started what's known as a hedge fund. You know what that is?"

"More or less," Mark said. It was important to let them condescend to you a little at the beginning, if you could see that was the tone they wanted to set.

"When you get to a certain level in my field, which is basically the investment field, you start to meet people, powerful people, much more powerful than I could ever hope to be. They give you their money to manage, that's an intimate thing. People drop their guard with you. You get let into those conversations where the line between business and government starts to blur a little bit. Anyway, without—"

Chase came by and dropped a paper bag in front of Mark without a word. In it, he could smell, was an egg sandwich, which he hadn't ordered, but which she knew he wanted. She'd wrapped it to go, he realized fondly, as a prop, in case he wanted to pretend he had somewhere to be. He took it out of the bag, opened up the warm foil.

"Without getting too specific, I am sometimes privy to information earlier than most people. Information that might cause problems if it spread too widely."

"Classified things?" Mark asked.

"Not on that level, necessarily. I wouldn't go that far. Anyway, in a nutshell, New York City, my hometown, is not a safe place to be right now, or for the foreseeable future. There are more events coming, of different sorts. Imminently. Good men and women are working around the clock to try to head some of these events off, but they may not be able to, even they acknowledge that much. I mean part of the problem is that you're called upon to imagine, and prepare for, things that are outside imagining. Turning passenger jets into missiles, for instance. Who imagined that one?"

Mark shook his head.

"I mean, that's one of the reasons these people call me in," Hadi said. "Seeing the future. Gaming it out. It's not a bad description of what I do. But anyway. First things first, which in this case means getting my family out of harm's way, out of the target zone. What's her name?"

Mark looked back over his shoulder. "Chase?"

"Thank you. Chase? I'm afraid I've let this coffee get cold. And could you also bring me whatever it is you brought Mr. Firth here? It smells amazing."

"It's called an egg sandwich," Chase said mirthlessly. "To go?"

"Yes please. I mean I won't lie, I don't consider it some great hardship to move up here. It's kind of what I wanted to do anyway. I love it here. I grew up in a town like this. I've loved it ever since I first saw it. I'm always trying to drag the family up here for weekends. My wife is still pissed that we didn't build somewhere closer to the good skiing. But that's what I love about this place, it hasn't gotten all precious. It isn't near enough to anything to be attractive to outsiders in that way. So it stays what it is, which is exactly how I like it. Anyway, my wife hasn't skied for years, so I'm not sure what she's on about. How long have you lived here?"

All this was taking longer than Mark had expected, and he still didn't understand where it was going. He was more accustomed to rich people who wanted every meeting to be over in five minutes or less. "All my life," he said. "Well, not right in Howland. I grew up closer to Pittsfield. My folks still live there."

"No kidding. What was that like?"

Mark wasn't sure about the spirit of the question, but figured Hadi had probably never been to Pittsfield. "It's bigger than Howland, but it's not exactly a city. It was nice enough. It can't have been too bad, because none of us moved too far away in the end. I have a brother who lives here in Howland and works in Stockbridge, and a sister in Great Barrington."

He could see all this was hitting Hadi in some emotional sweet spot (which was why he'd left out the sister who'd moved to Colorado). "See, that's so great," Hadi said. "And do you have a family of your own?"

"A wife and a daughter, who's almost eight."

"Eight. I should probably ask you about schools, then, but that's really Rachel's department, she will want to figure that one out on her own. Anyway, you're probably wondering why I'm lying in wait for you like this. I have some upgrading I need done on the house, now that we'll be here full-time. I've asked around a bit and your work was recommended to me. Of course I imagine you might be booked up at the moment, and I'd want to get started right away."

"I could move some things around," Mark said, without trying to put on too much of an act about it. "One thing to bear in mind is that if any of this work involves breaking ground, winter's on its way and conditions are hard to predict. If you're not in a hurry I might even suggest postponing the job until spring."

Hadi thought. "I see your point," he said. "But I don't want to postpone hiring you and then maybe risk losing you to a bigger job. Maybe we can work out some kind of retainer-type arrangement, so that I'm paying to make sure your schedule is clear, so that you can go right to work whenever conditions permit. Exclusivity. Is that kind of thing done in your business?"

More and more effort was going into trying to suppress the physical symptoms of his excitement, his relief. "I'm sure we could sketch out something like that," he said.

Hadi took a moment to look around Daisy's—the old Formica counter with cake-stands at either end, the thin, frilly curtains, the sign by the register identifying the credit manager as Helen Waite—with a little smile on his face, as if it were all just exactly what he hoped it would be. Another customer got up to leave, and Hadi smiled and nodded at him, not minding in the least that he got nothing in return.

"I guess I'm sorry to hear the place needs work already," Mark said. "Since it's a relatively new construction." He couldn't possibly want space added onto it. It was already more than enough for a family of however many kids he had.

"It's nothing like that," Hadi said with a smile. "It's about security. Certain changes, certain installations. Mostly outside the house itself."

"Security?" Mark said. "I'm not sure I—"

"I know that probably isn't the kind of work you customarily do. I understand that. I'm not assuming any sort of special expertise on your part."

"It's not that. Well, it is that, in part. But what I was going to ask is, why go to the trouble? I assumed you were moving up here full-time because you thought it was safer here."

"It is," Hadi said, "relatively. But to a certain extent, I—" He paused as Chase, without breaking stride, dropped a white paper sandwich bag on the edge of the table near his elbow. "Look. I am fortunate enough, in this day and age, to be able to do the work that I do pretty much wherever I want to do it. I need a fast, protected internet connection and phone service and not too much more than that. But a lot of money flows through me, or past me at least—other people's money, I'm talking about, not mine—and disrupting that flow is going to be one of the potential goals of our enemies. In that respect, I bring the sense of diminished safety with me, unfortunately, wherever I go."

"Ah," Mark said. He wasn't sure how much of it to believe. He reminded himself that he wasn't here to discuss the state of the world, but a job, a job he very badly needed. "As to what you were saying before," he said. "Don't get me wrong, I can put in a bollard or run wires underground as good as, or better than, the next guy. You don't have to be an expert. But can I ask why me? Why not get someone who is an expert to come up from the city and do it?"

"Because," said Hadi, "I don't want this to look too much like what it is. How much are these egg sandwiches, by the way? Couple of bucks?"

He was starting to stand up. "A buck seventy-five," Mark said. "More with meat."

"So why don't you come to the house," Hadi said. He pulled out three singles, dropped them on the table, and pulled up the zipper on his fleece. "Tomorrow morning, maybe six thirty? I'm up very early." He smiled warmly but did not shake Mark's hand before heading out the door, holding the bag with his sandwich in it. Mark watched him through the window; he climbed into the black SUV—the driver's side—and rolled out of the lot. A tad bit full of himself, Mark thought. But clients' egos could be gold mines. And there was something else about Hadi specifically—an obliviousness, like an anti-charisma—that Mark felt paradoxically drawn to as well. These were the guys who ruled the world. They didn't care what anybody thought of them. Maybe that was part of what separated Mark from that class of man: he knew he lacked a certain ruthless-ness, but maybe it was even simpler than that, maybe he just put too much stock in the idea that everybody had to like him.

He figured he'd go back home and do some quick internet re-search on high-tech home security and what could be charged for it. Hadi seemed like a money-is-no-object guy, and why wouldn't he be? On the other hand, with all his millions he apparently couldn't buy a neighbor an egg sandwich. Mark pulled out his wal-let, gathered up Hadi's singles, and headed for the register.

———

The southern Berkshires were green most of the year, lush even, the low, wavelike foothills tightly canopied; so when the foliage-tourist season was over and the leaves turned brown and fell, it was inva-sive, like an x-ray, like the nerves of the earth were exposed. Winter seemed to shrink the area's geography. People's sense of where and how they lived depended on seclusion, on privacy, which nature generally provided for free, and then seasonally reminded you to appreciate by taking it away. Neighbors' properties seemed aggres-sively close all of a sudden. The grass turned brown as earth and everything felt reduced. The river looked like it was in as bad a mood as every place else, opaque in the dull November sunlight, visible all of a sudden from roads that ran right by it in the summertime without suspecting. Your car smelled like its heater again. You felt wrongly dressed.

Howland differed from neighboring towns in that almost a thousand contiguous acres of it were undeveloped—a land trust dating back to the seventies, when a lawyer from Boston, in the course of preparing his will, was dismayed to hear his ungrateful son express a desire not to be burdened by inheritance of the land his father had lovingly bought up over the course of forty summers. He made those acres a gift to the town instead, on the condition that they never be built upon. Since then the trust had become a favorite charity of the summer people; the old man's will perversely named the ungrateful son as trustee, but he was a lawyer himself and managed to dump the whole bequest onto a local group called Citizens for Controlled Growth. Even the woods preserved by the trust seemed thinner and less formidable in the weeks before the first snow, or would have if any of the locals bothered to decelerate and glance into them. If you lived there, and saw them every time you drove to town and back, they didn't register as Controlled Growth, they just looked like nothing.

Two weeks before Thanksgiving, if you got away from Route 7 and drove the winding county roads where the year-rounders mostly lived, you didn't have to go too far before the only colors falling outside the spectrum of brown were on the flags that still scrolled down from porch eaves, or stood at sharp diagonals from brass pole-brackets screwed to support beams. Some people had taken their flags down after a few weeks, but many had not. They knew the flag couldn't just stay out all winter without getting damaged or ruined, but folding it up and putting it back in the closet seemed too much like forgetting, too much like going back to the indulgent state of mind they'd all enjoyed before, where they took their freedoms for granted, where they weren't alert to the predations of enemies. The fact that a part of them longed shamefully for just that—for the old life, in which they were not asked to defend the way they lived—helped guilt them into leaving the colors up. The nation was at war; the invisible nature of that war made it both harder and more important to be vigilant. Some even preemptively delighted in the symbolism of allowing the canvas flag to be battered all winter—of spring returning to find Old Glory, bought at the True Value, in tatters, in ribbons, but still there, still flying, evoking something more than just the elements and time.

The Berkshire tourist institutions—Tanglewood, Jacob's Pillow, The Mount—were closed for the winter, but the restaurants and shops, even the high-end ones, stayed open, sometimes with signs in the window announcing reduced hours. The Mass Pike, running from Stockbridge to Boston, bisected the region west to east; from south to north the towns—Sheffield, Howland, Stockbridge, Lee—were mostly strung along Route 7, itself shadowing the path of the Housatonic, a river that once drove the paper mills whose gorgeous architectural shells still straddled it, some of them restored and tricked up into gallery spaces and shops, others sitting empty, waiting for a buyer, their material decline poignant and picturesque until it was not.

Howland still had its own post office, although every few years there were rumors that it would be shut down or folded into the similarly sized post office in Sheffield, six miles away. Usually this rumor came up around election time; whoever was running in the primaries for western Mass's congressional seat would try to say more stridently than his or her opponent that he or she would fight the bureaucratic fat cats in Washington to protect Howland's PO from the budgetary reaper. Whether this was in fact a fight that required any cunning or courage whatsoever, or merely a matter of one phone call, one exchange of routine legislative favors, the people of Howland had no real way of knowing. But it remained, for any local candidate, a baseline campaign promise, so the tiny square brick building with the flagpole out front operated on Mill Street much as it had since 1922.

The job of postmaster in a town that size was not a demanding one, but for some reason—its claustrophobic nature, the little uniform you had to wear, the shame attached to government work—no native of Howland had applied to fill it; the position went to a young man named Glenn Brooks, who commuted all the way from Springfield and charged the government a fanciful markup on his travel reimbursements. That markup, though it stayed the same, turned all the more fraudulent after Glenn took up with a Howland woman named Penny Batchelder and, after two dates, started staying over with her on the three nights a week when her sons were with their father. On Monday he'd leave his rumpled Springfield apartment in the morning and return to it in the evening, but Tuesday after work he'd park his car in Penny's driveway about three miles from town, and unless the weather was bad he wouldn't so much as turn over the engine again until Friday morning. Penny didn't give a shit how many people saw his car parked there. In fact that was both the good and the bad thing about Penny, from his perspective: she didn't give much of a shit about anything, starting from the moment she got back from dropping the boys off at their dad's on Tuesday afternoon. She never asked anything of Glenn, or criticized him, or told him his facial hair was stupid, like his last two girlfriends had done. Sometimes she wouldn't talk at all, for long stretches; sometimes you'd ask her a question and she wouldn't even answer, like she didn't hear you, even when she was sitting up in bed next to you, smoking with the lights off and the window open. But she'd come back eventually from wherever her thoughts went to. And when she did, she was crazy. She would let you do anything.

In the mornings she gave him a ride to work, since it was on her way to her job with the medical practice in Stockbridge. He gave her his credit card to use to buy gas, so he could submit the receipts to make it look right with the USPS. Not that he had reason to believe they cared. They might have thrown all his receipts, the legit and the bogus alike, in the shredder for all he knew. It was all so corrupt. But the corruption of it made him feel good somehow: smart. He'd found his way inside it. Corruption was a fact of life, on the governmental level especially, and if you didn't find your own little way to make it work for you, then you'd be a victim of it. Either or. Maybe he was even undercharging them, just in terms of what he could have gotten away with. It was like paying taxes: there was a line you had to be careful not to cross but you felt like a coward if you didn't inch as close to it as you could. Still, at the end of every month he felt like a boss of sorts, collecting money for miles he hadn't traveled, on nights he'd actually spent in the bed of an arguably hot divorcée who didn't seem to want anything from him except just to be there, to make her not alone, and who in exchange for that would let him do whatever he liked, without making a huge deal about whether she enjoyed it or not.

The first morning the temperature touched single digits, in early January, he went downstairs while she was still in the shower and walked barefoot—terrible idea—through the door that led from Penny's kitchen into her cement-floored garage. It was a two-car space but half of it was covered by crap that belonged to her sons: skateboards, old lumber they thought they could make a ramp or a half-pipe out of, an outdated Nintendo console, a kind of junkyard of boyhood enthusiasms. All of it was already discarded, but he moved it gingerly anyway, stacking it against the walls or putting it on the sagging tool shelves, his feet freezing. The boys were a blank to him. Penny didn't answer questions about them, not that he had many. Looking at all their broken or abandoned gear didn't spark some desire in him to be a father or anything like that; what he felt, if anything, was a desire to hang out with them, to be like a step-brother or something. It was an incriminating wish, at his age. Building a ramp out of scrap lumber was one of those dad-things a man Glenn's age probably ought to know how to do, but he didn't. He wouldn't have the first idea, actually.

"What are you doing?" Penny said.

He looked at her in the doorway, holding a coffee cup, dressed for work. She was a few years older than he was; when she was dressed up, he felt it more. She had a little bit of a strong jaw for a woman, but her body was perfect for him, a body that most of his guy friends probably would have dismissed as bony. She had her hair up, which on the one hand he didn't like, but on the other, there were few things he liked better than watching her take it down.

"Just moving some of the boys' stuff," he said. "Ice on the cars this morning. I want to be able to pull mine in here."

"Okay," she said, "but you'll have to put everything back where it was before you go on Friday."

So just re-scatter the junk across the floor, then? But he knew what the point of that was: she didn't want her sons to know that he existed, that anyone had been in the garage or the house at all.

"Seriously?" he said.

"Seriously," she said, but not unkindly, and she turned around to pour out the rest of her coffee.

Candace lived just off 7 south of Great Barrington, in a former tool-and-tractor storage shed that had been converted into four cheap but very modern-looking apartments; hers was on the second floor, facing the road, which meant it also faced the windows of the packie, whose owner—a congenitally suspicious fat man who sat every day in a sprung swivel chair behind the register, standing with difficulty whenever somebody came with their bottles to the counter—owned her building too. She sat drinking coffee at her little kitchen counter, on the living room side of it, as if someone else on the kitchen side had served her. She was listening to NPR, on very low volume, because even though none of her neighbors on either side had ever complained, she was conscious of them there. The radio was murmuring war news, protest news. She didn't catch it all. It wasn't that she was incapable of understanding; but the barely audible tones of the radio at dawn were really more about gently waking up her mind, about hearing a voice, any voice, originating outside that little apartment, than about learning anything.

When she felt ready, she put on her coat and walked downstairs to the parking area. The February cold made her take a deep breath, painful and invigorating at the same time. There was a little runoff ditch behind the square of macadam, with a layer of dirty ice on it as thin as the top of a crème brûlée. The worst part about Candace's home was how it looked from the outside. Like a storage shed, basically, surrounded by curtain-thin lines of trees and uncut grass and mud. Either the landlord ran out of money before he could fix up the building's exterior, or it just never figured into his vision at all. Most likely, she thought, he considered caring about such things to be a vanity, an affectation. These towns were full of men like him. Not just cheap and simple, but proud of it, superior about it. She was probably in her late teens before she figured out that her dad was one of these men. Every story he told was a story about how he'd outsmarted somebody. Her brothers had more than a little of this quality in them too.

Five minutes later, before the interior of the car was even warm, she was at work. Then another day of filling out evaluations, going through discretionary-spending reports submitted by the teachers or, more often, the custodians, and scrolling through emails from parents that had come in at odd hours the night before. She tried to do a conspicuously good job precisely because she knew that her job wasn't entirely necessary, that the main reason there was a vice principal at Howland Elementary at all was because there was a lot of shit work that the long-tenured principal, her boss, had been able to negotiate his way out of having to do. She needed to make herself look essential even though she knew, better than anyone actually, that such was not the case.

There was an endless email chain—nominally among the parents, but she was looped into every Reply All—that particularly bugged her, as it had for going on two weeks now. A subset of the parents was concerned about security measures at the front door of the school. And there was no gainsaying their basic point, which was that there were zero security measures at the front door of the school. The chief custodian unlocked that door every morning (teachers and others who got there early had a separate entrance anyway), and he locked it again at the end of the day, unless it was an evening when the auditorium was being used. Candace happened to know that there'd been a few nights when some auditorium group had stayed later than agreed to and the custodian, who wanted everybody to pretend that his name was Ace, had gone home for the night without locking up at all, out of boredom or pique. Certain parents would probably stroke out if they knew about that.

So security concerns were fine and dandy, as her father might say. They probably ought to be more careful. But the email group was talking about something else, or so it seemed to Candace. They were concerned that the school, the elementary school, was vulnerable to attack.

What are those things called? The cement things that stick up out of the ground?

Bollards?

Yes thanks! Those. Come on, how much can those cost? Just some cement and four or five holes in the ground.

Exactly—the school admin is always crying poverty but I'll bet you anything we could get somebody patriotic to donate the labor.

And the cement!

Shouldn't have to donate it—isn't this what we pay taxes for??

Candace's irritation was hard to separate from the fact that one of the thirty-eight email addresses in the chain belonged to Patrick Kimball, patk86@yahoo.com, the married father of a sixth grader, with whom Candace had had an affair for a period of eight or nine months. It was now longer than that since the affair had ended, but it made her agitated just to see his name. Like her, he never contributed a post to the chain itself, he was just roped into it, silently complicit. Still, technically they were back to exchanging emails, which made her feel exposed and hopeful and furious.

She still saw Patrick's daughter in the hallways, nearly every day in fact. She didn't like her all that much, never had—socially the girl was ruthless, a little monster, and none too bright either—and it was hard for Candace to be unconscious of the bureaucratic sway she had over this brat's life, and would have for another couple of years. Not to mention that, in some alternate universe, Candace was her stepmother. The universe of lovestruck saps, maybe.

She hit Reply All. *Of course I understand the general concern,* she wrote, *but the issue isn't just the cost of cement. School construction, of any kind, requires approval on the district level. I know from bitter experience that the first thing they require is an extensive description of why the work is necessary to the operation of the school. If anyone wants to take a preliminary whack at that question, I'd be grateful for the input.*

She hit Send, knowing that the discussion, the ginned-up outrage, would just flow right around what she'd written like a stream around a rock, not to mention that it was too long a message to expect most of them to read to the end anyway. But now she could at least take some pleasure from guessing the panic Patrick would feel when he saw her name in his inbox. She should have erased the subject line. That really would have put a scare into him.

For lunch she had a Diet Coke and most of a pack of wintergreen Life Savers. She wasn't concerned about her weight or anything like that—she loved to eat—but some days she couldn't bring herself to eat in the cafeteria, not even at one of the designated faculty tables; and bringing her lunch to work in a little brown bag just made her feel like she might as well adopt a few cats and get the whole transition to spinsterhood over with. Plus there was no fridge in her office; she'd been told she could share Ace's. No thanks. Dinner at her parents' tonight, so she could pig out there. That would make her mother happy.

She sat in on a science department guest presentation about lab safety, and then when she got back to her office there was an email from her principal: *Great idea about the security proposal. District is giving out funds like candy for anything with the word security in it. Look forward to seeing proposal you come up with. Don't be afraid to think big!*

Everything was tied together, everything was connected. That was the problem with a small town like Howland, and also with the inside of her head. Part of what galled her about all this security nonsense, like they were hiding military secrets in the basement of Howland Elementary along with the gym mats and unfixable A/V equipment, was that on the fateful day itself she had actually broken down and used the tragedy as an excuse to contact Patrick: she'd written to him on his Hotmail account to try to get him to leave work and meet her, on the grounds that it seemed possible that the world was ending. She'd actually used the fact that her brother Mark was missing in New York City to cajole him into seeing her again. She felt like a psychopath afterwards, like a person incapable of knowing which of her own feelings were the real ones. The world was exploding and all she could think of was that there was no way he could refuse to see her now. And it hadn't even worked. He hadn't checked that Hotmail account until the next day, or so he said, not that there was ever any way of evaluating the truth of anything he said.

She drove the rolling back roads past the bare trees and rock-hard fields to her mom and dad's house just outside Pittsfield, her headlights on though it wasn't yet five thirty. Only the kitchen light burned at their place. Since selling their old home—the home in which Candace and her three siblings were raised—ten years earlier, the two of them had become phenomenally cheap, and would turn the lights off every time they exited a room. Candace dreaded visiting in winter because they would rather get through it, it seemed, by wearing every article of clothing they owned simultaneously than by turning up the thermostat even one degree. She didn't remember anything like this from her childhood. They were on a fixed income now, it was true, but they weren't that badly off; Candace gave them some money every few months and she was pretty sure Mark did too. It wasn't about money, though. She wasn't sure what it was about.

"Drink?" her dad asked. She'd started to take her coat off but then thought better of it.

"A short one," she said. "I'd love a tall one but I have to drive home in the dark."

"Well, now that you're here, we can eat," her mother said. It was quarter to six. "For goodness sake take your coat off! You can't sit at the table like that." This despite the fact that she wore at least two sweaters that Candace could see. "I'm glad you're here. You have to talk to your father. I would love it if someone could get him to stop watching the news sixteen hours a day."

Her father scowled. Candace said, "We can talk about current events all you like, but first please let me eat something. I'm starving to death. Is it lasagna?"

"Manicotti. I got it at Sam's. Frozen but it's pretty good."

"We know that," her dad said, "because we've already had it twice this week."

Candace, after briefly, discreetly warming her hands over the baking dish, was already serving herself. "That's better," she said after a few bites. "Sorry. I couldn't wait."

They didn't talk much. There wasn't a great deal at the moment, in any of their lives, that seemed worth sharing, except for whatever it was her father was watching on the news, and that was a subject she didn't want to open up until she was through her first glass of wine, if at all. As the oven cooled, it grew frigid in the kitchen.

"So are you part of these protests?" her father finally blurted out. Her mother theatrically sighed.

"What protests, Dad?"

"You know. Please let's not hurt that poor misunderstood Saddam Hussein."

"You see any protests like that going on around here? No. I've seen stuff on TV, like you. In the big cities, New York, London, Paris, wherever. Far away from here."

"In New York. That's the capper. New York of all places. In my generation New York would already be emptied of able-bodied young men, they all would have reported to the draft board on the spot."

"You see?" her mother said.

"Dad, I do not have any strong feelings about it one way or the other."

"Well, that's just dandy," Dad said.

"All I can tell you is that there are many, many channels on your television, and if whatever you are watching makes you this upset, you should change it. It cannot be good for you. I mean physically. Speaking of which, Mom, I will give you twenty dollars right now if you will turn up the thermostat five degrees until I leave."

Her mother looked at her skeptically. "You're cold?" she said.

. . .

69

The first Thursday evening of every month was the Town Hall open meeting, a proud anchor and vestige of classic New England–style democracy and a huge fucking pain in the ass of the usually humanity-loving First Selectman. It was supposed to be a general forum to discuss, in a transparent setting, some of the current challenges pertaining to the rather simple government of Howland; the problem was that only the most passionate, committed, crazy people, the ones who had something specific they really, really wanted or did not want, ever bothered to attend, and then they had zero interest in talking or hearing about any grievance other than their own. They all wound up yelling, even when it mostly sounded like they agreed with each other, and then they all wound up irritated at Marty for not resolving everything. They'd voted him First Selectman three times now, which was an honor and a responsibility (a full-time one, even if the job itself was only part-time); still, his role at these town forums was just to listen, and they didn't seem to get that. So these quaint little monthly meetings inevitably turned into a collective failure of patience that sent him straight to the Bushmills bottle pretty much the second he got home, even though the doc had advised him not to eat or drink in the hour right before bed. Doing anything just once a month couldn't be too dangerous, though. Sometimes he fantasized that the stress of it actually would give him another heart attack and he'd die in his office, and then everybody would be sorry for how they'd taken everything out on him, and then they could all go to the next Town Hall open meeting and get into a big fistfight about putting up a memorial to him.

Because that's where the January and February monthly forums had ended up—arguing about memorials—and that's surely where this one was going as well. Often the attendance was in the single digits, but tonight it looked closer to fifteen, and that couldn't be good. Marty sat at a card table between his two fellow selectpersons, who were flanked by the town's treasurer and its recording secretary. Rows of folding chairs sat facing them. Everyone was too close together. There was a stage behind them, but they never used it—too imperious, Marty felt; the space on the floor was more democratic but also more cramped.

Of course he sympathized. He knew he was too practical by nature, even in his heart. And if putting up some memorial to 9/11 victims meant they'd have to hope like hell it didn't snow too much next winter because they'd have to cut back on their advance purchase of road-salt reserves, well, they were all adults—his neighbors and friends and customers, a lot of them—and he was their elected instrument, and it was not for him to command them that one consideration should outweigh another. Even if no one from Howland or any of the surrounding towns had died that awful day. Even if their closest connection to it was that Mark Firth happened to have been in the city that day for undisclosed reasons, in a hotel room no less, probably shacking up with one of the rich summer wives that hired him to redo their kitchens. Or that was the rumor the recording secretary couldn't stop herself from sharing with Marty, anyway.

It was all the posturing that got to him, the wasted time, the passion contests. Right now, it was already eight forty-five and a couple of the regulars were just starting to hit their stride. Daisy Scoville, who apparently had too little to occupy her now that she'd turned over the day-to-day of her little café to her daughter, wanted to know if they could get an actual piece of one of the towers, a steel shard; she'd heard of some town in Pennsylvania that had gotten such a relic, and built a little park around it. She was fat and wore stretch pants and he felt guilty for how hard he found it to look straight at her when she was talking.

"So can we check into that?" she said.

Marty raised his head. "Any idea," he said gamely, "of the associated costs?"

Daisy scowled. "I hardly think that's the issue," she said.

"Well, all due respect, it's always the issue to some degree. You know, because you're a regular at these meetings, that our last assessment—"

"The memorial should go at the school, I think," Daisy pushed forward, "so maybe the county or the state will pick up whatever costs you're so worried about."

"The school," Marty repeated. "Where at the school?"

"I was thinking between the upper and lower athletic fields."

He knew he should just stop there and say something to make her feel validated, something to tide her over until April at least, but he was tired and couldn't check himself. "You'd like to stick a large shard of steel," he said, "into the ground in the sideline area between the two children's athletic fields?"

"Obviously not," she said. "It would be part of a fenced-off memorial garden there."

Hands shot up. God damn it, Marty thought, god damn it, I will never get home now. I will miss *CSI* again. I will never be any good at this politics shit, never ever, I don't have it in me to learn.

"This is a national tragedy!" Daisy was shouting back at the parents who were shouting at her. Her eyes were red. She was rolling now. "It doesn't matter where it happened! It happened here too! Do you just not care that we have enemies, who hate us? You think if you forget about them, they'll go away? Please, the athletic fields! You want to raise your kids to get lacrosse scholarships or to believe in something? Either we're a part of this country or we aren't!"

He hated the gavel, but he finally used it; and then, even more brazenly, he proceeded straight to the prayer that had closed every one of these meetings since November, the prayer for the safety of William Nagel, Evvie Nagel's only son, who'd graduated from Howland Regional High three years ago, who'd been a junior at Berkshire Community College, and who'd dropped out to join the Marines. Nobody was going to bicker after Will's name had been invoked. Marty felt bad for using it that way, to shame people into shutting up, but enough was enough. A lot of them had children of their own they ought to get home to.

Marty installed furnaces and hot water heaters, a business he'd expanded to include air-conditioning systems about twelve years ago—too soon, in retrospect, or anyway too quickly, which had led to some money problems and some lean years and ultimately the end of his marriage. But that marriage wasn't a keeper anyway. Probably a good thing, in retrospect, that all the yelling and hard feelings about money had exposed the cracks in that relationship sooner rather than later. Before there were kids. His life might have gone very differently otherwise. In fact Kelly had gotten pregnant at some point during their last few months together, and it got back to him, much later, that she had driven to Pittsfield and aborted it. She never knew he knew about it. Possibly it wasn't even his.

The expansion had meant opening a second store, in Ashley Falls, but he was in over his head from day one and wound up selling it off for a loss just to service his debt. It left him feeling pretty stupid. And that's because he was stupid, back then, about certain things. He had a sort of American image of himself as a man of ambition, someone who wasn't happy unless he was dreaming big, growing, conquering. Conquering what, though? He'd thought it was important to his self-esteem, somehow, to become the Heating and Cooling King of the Berkshires, but when he failed at it he found out that it hadn't really changed his estimation of himself after all. He was a small-town guy. He made a fine living with the one store, and he didn't miss the stress of having two and always wondering what your employees were managing to fuck up or steal, what easy sales they were failing to close, in whichever store you weren't at that day. He liked being able to walk down the street to the Undermountain Café for lunch, and he liked it that if anybody happened to drop by the store while he was still eating, they generally knew where to find him. His life had a lot less negativity in it

73

once Kelly moved out and he no longer had that voice in his head, putting him down for daring to be happy where he was.

And people liked him; that was indisputable. He did not put on airs. He didn't mind in the least being in the same neighbor's house at different times in very different capacities, first as the guest of honor at some dinner in his role as First Selectman and then two weeks later wearing waders in a flooded basement. There were worse ways to get to know your constituents. Sometimes if he couldn't get to sleep he did a local house-tour in his head, or made a mental list of the homes in Howland he'd seen the inside of and those he hadn't.

The heating and cooling business brought in decent money—he lived alone, the house was paid off, he didn't have expensive tastes or hobbies—but you never knew for sure the pace at which that money was going to come, and that's where the modest $22K salary the town paid him really came in handy. It was pitched to him initially as a half-time job, but he had it down to where it usually took up much less of his day than that. Though he had an office in the Town Hall, he found it easier to organize his time if he kept all of his work in one place, so a lot of the Howland government's pending business could usually be found on the metal desk in the rear of his store, which was only about half a mile from Town Hall anyway. Beyond five or six somewhat tongue-in-cheek ceremonial duties a year, the job mainly required balancing a small, pretty simple budget, most of it revenue that flowed down to them from state or fed and was already earmarked to be spent in certain ways. There was some property tax collection too, which had sometimes led to incidents, but not for years. Marty was aware enough to see that some relatively hard times were coming—the economy was just bad everywhere, and the housing market locally was certain to take a bath. But there was always a waxing and waning to these things. The city money, the summer money, moved in and out like the tide over the course of ten or fifteen years, but it never receded entirely. You just had to be patient. In the meantime the electorate both trusted him and failed to take him all that seriously, which was just the way he liked it.

"Your sister called" was the only message on Gerry Firth's desk when he got in at about 9:30, "about" being his own estimation of 9:48. He was hoping for some other messages, work-related messages, to help justify the fact that he was quote-unquote late. He'd gotten into a kind of negative loop at work lately: the worse things were going for him commission-wise, the more tenuous his position felt, the more compulsively he screwed up in meaningless little passive-aggressive ways like failing to get to his desk on time. Of course, there was a scenario in which showing up late might turn out to be a shrewd office-political ploy, because if a buyer called while he was out, instead of going straight into his ear the message would have to be taken by the receptionist, Alina, and Alina would have to write it down and walk across the office to put it on Gerry's desk, and anybody who knew the first thing about Alina knew that she could never perform such a task without describing out loud to everyone in earshot what she was doing. Which would make Gerry look good to his colleagues and his boss. But that only worked if calls actually came in, calls that weren't from his sister Candace bugging him again about going out to visit their parents and fixing their fucking storm windows while he was out there, like he had nothing better to do, like his own time and labor were worth zero.

He tried to look busy immediately; when he could, he raised his gaze to Alina, who was waiting for it and gave only a little conspiratorial frown in return. Kimbrough, their boss, didn't say anything to him but there was no way he hadn't seen Gerry come in late; the whole office was the size of a two-car garage, with five desks wedged into it, so there was no way for anybody to avoid seeing anything. The rule about being at your desk by nine thirty was moronic anyway, classic Kimbrough. Giving you a pointless rule to follow and then getting off on making you follow it. Meanwhile home values continued to tank, and their all being behind their desks at dawn, like a bunch of blazer-wearing farmers, wouldn't have done a thing to address that. The whole South Berkshire housing market was about to get good and fucked, like everywhere else in the country, only worse because around here so many of the homes were second ones, luxuries. All of their jobs were basically hanging by a thread, which would give Gerry some small vindictive comfort when he was inevitably the first to get let go.

Two hours crawled by somehow and then his phone rang—his desk phone, not his cell. He made himself wait for a second ring before lifting the receiver. But it was his sister again. "Did you get my message before?" she said.

"No," Gerry said, turning his back to Kimbrough's desk. "The girl here is terrible. But I've told you, why not call my cell?"

"I did. I have. So look, can you make it out to Mom and Dad's this weekend or what? You can't believe how cold it is in that house, and if the business with the windows goes on much longer, Dad is going to try to get up on the ladder. I would take care of it myself, like I take care of every other damn thing for them, but it's a kind of work I can't do, you know that. That's why God burdened me with brothers."

"Yeah, well, speaking of, why don't you ask Mark to go over there and fix whatever needs fixing?" He caught a reflection in the window and turned to see Alina putting on her coat to go to lunch, not looking at him or at anyone, as if lunch were already where she was. She had an unusual ass. There wasn't that sort of hourglass-style pinching-in at the waist, so when she was standing up, her ass looked kind of like a shelf.

"I tried. He's got some big job. Claims he's working weekends till it's done. For one of his neighbors, he says, some rich dude from New York."

Gerry, who had a good memory for property transfers, realized she was describing Philip Hadi; thinking of his brother in proximity to that kind of money made everything seem even more unfair. "Whatever his priorities are, I guess," he said. "Protecting your elderly parents from the elements or felching some billionaire."

That got a laugh out of Candace, at least. "He'd probably custom-order some reclaimed storm windows from Newport or something anyway, and they wouldn't get here until next winter." He knew she was only pretending to side with him against Mark to get him to do what she wanted. Why was she so into that family-obligation shit anyway? They both knew their dad would probably prefer a broken storm window he could complain about to one that worked fine. "But the other thing is, they ask me about you," she went on. "I don't know what to tell them. Just go spend a few hours with them and get it over with for a while. It's been too long. Suck it up, boy."

"They always ask me about Lindsey," he said.

There was a pause while his sister tried to think of what to say. "They worry about you" was what she settled on.

"Well, it's been two years, they should let it go. Okay fine, I'll go up Saturday. Okay? Gotta bounce, I have another call." He hung up. He was still facing Alina's abandoned chair. He hadn't done a great job of making that look like it wasn't a personal call.

He busied himself for a few minutes longer, reading through some recent listings he already knew by heart; as his eyes ran over them, another part of his brain was engaged with the mystery of why he found it so hard to get to work on time. It's not like nine thirty was so early. He knew it was self-destructive. He knew it was probably some Freudian expression of the fact that he hated his job, except that his problem with punctuality was chronic and extended to appointments he didn't hate at all, appointments he actually looked forward to, like right now. It was already 12:05. He got up, took his down jacket off the back of his chair (it never fit right anymore, over that stupid fucking blazer they had to wear), and started for the door, smiling pacifically at Kimbrough, who took that moment to tilt his chair back into Gerry's path with his fingers laced behind his head. "Lunch already?" Kimbrough said. "Well, I can't say I blame you. After all, you did come in early today. Oh no wait."

"Not lunch," Gerry said. "A showing."

"Good for you. Which place?"

"225 Valley Road."

"That dog?" Kimbrough sat back up and let his feet touch the floor. "Better you than me. Still, break a leg and whatnot."

"Will do," said Gerry, and went out to his car. The house at 225 Valley Road was indeed a famous dog. It needed foundation work and was an eyesore to begin with, painted brown with red trim; but the real issue was the owner, a cheap ancient Yankee who'd moved in with his daughter in Maine. He didn't hassle them, particularly, about the house sitting empty and drawing no offers, but he refused to spend one dollar to make the place more presentable and wouldn't come down on the asking price either. You couldn't talk to people like that. Which is why Gerry never talked to him. Thus the house had sat there, fully staged, for fourteen months now. He turned into the driveway, the shoots in its cracked asphalt just greening, and parked behind a red Mazda. He went around to the back door and pushed it open with two fingers. On the kitchen table by the drawn curtains were two Subway wrappers, one still rolled up and full and the other splayed open, little sesame seeds and bits of shredded lettuce spilling out of it.

"You're late," Alina said from the chair. "I ate."

"Of course I'm late," he said. "Kimbrough held me up."

"Well, my lunch hour's almost gone now," she said, her petulance half-real. "I don't think you're going to have time to eat."

"I've told you," he said, hanging his coat on the door hinge, throwing the accursed blazer on the tiled floor, "I like it when you start without me." And he stood across the room and held her gaze, smiling, until she understood what he wanted.

When there was a crisis, a tragedy, you wanted it to change you—or not change, but reveal you, show you who you really were when all the usual bullshit worries were stripped away. Show you your true, best self. And that had happened to Karen, for a while, anyway. On the day it seemed to everyone like the world might be ending, she bore the added fear that her husband—her handsome, sweet, feckless, stupid, thoughtless, naïve fuckup of a husband—was dead, caught in the middle of a terrorist attack of all ridiculous things, in a strange place where he knew no one, alone in some crowd, never coming back home. And for all her complex feelings toward him, for all the ambivalence and the difficult, tangled nature of her thoughts about their future, on that day, under that threat, her whole being had reoriented as simply as a compass needle toward one thought: Please, God, let him be safe and alive. Let him come home to his family.

She even thought at one point that she might be having a religious awakening. She could see in retrospect that she'd overreacted, although if she was overreacting then so was pretty much everyone else in the world, and if everyone reacted the same way, that meant it wasn't an overreaction, right? No one wanted to live in fear all the time; still, when the fear was gone she wanted its epiphany, its de-complication of herself, to last. But life just crept back in. You wanted to be changed, but change was very hard, so hard that even one of the major events in the history of the entire world was ultimately no match for the pettiness and impatience inside you, the mundane frustrations that ruled your average day, the tiny, aggravating reflexes that at some indeterminate point had just made your life what it was doomed to be.

Mark had no head for finance. His gifts were artistic, or at any rate had to do with beauty, with craft. Yet he fancied himself some deep thinker. He wanted to make a killing. His business, his actual business, could have been performing so much better. But instead of doing practical things, he was back to reading books at night about how to attain great wealth through a positive attitude. And this after his foray into online investing, which had pretty near destroyed them. His gullibility, which was really a form of sweetness, was a huge part of what had attracted her to him in the first place, back when they were young and dumb and flirting in various Berkshire bars, with their whole lives in front of them. Now that exact same quality, or her perception of it, had pickled into something that made her wonder seriously if she might be going crazy.

"When was the last time you checked in with that lawyer?" she said to him. He was lying on the floor playing Slaps with Haley. He was a little better at it than a man his age probably should have been.

"What lawyer?" he said.

"In New York City. That guy."

"Oh yeah. Back in March, I think? No news."

"What does that mean, no news?"

"The wheels of justice turn slowly, is I guess what it means."

"Don't you think you should maybe take a less passive attitude about it? It's a lot of money."

"The way I figure it," Mark said, "the lawyers are in the business of making money. In this case, he only makes money if the suit goes forward and is successful. So why wouldn't he already be doing everything he could think of?"

"Yeah, Mommy," Haley said, and giggled.

"We did my deposition by webcam. He doesn't need me to bug him. He's got bosses to do that. Besides, I wouldn't know what to tell him to do differently anyway."

Haley can't see it, Karen thought. She was going through a period where she was very close to him. The two of them had their little society, defined in large part by their rolling their eyes at Mommy. But she would grow up and figure him out. Then maybe Mommy would start to get some of the vindicating sympathy she deserved.

She felt no sense of control over her life; she could control the weeks, maybe, but not the years. He read his cockamamie books about success in bed at night while she lay awake beside him thinking about their proximity to failure, and somehow he didn't even feel the panic radiating from her. Her job at Mullins Day School was boring and menial but she couldn't quit—it would be like pulling her finger out of a dike. Karen could really only influence the direction of their lives, she felt, by influencing him. Which was both easy and hard. You could get him to do what you wanted, however resentfully, on a given day, but there seemed no way to change the course of the man he was.

There was no good reason Gerry couldn't just take Alina to his place for their lunch hours. He lived alone. His house was closer to the office—close enough that there was the risk of some other co-worker happening by and recognizing Alina's Mazda in the driveway; but no way could that be considered riskier than their basically using as a motel room a home currently listed for sale by their employer, an offense so inventive it would have ended both their jobs on the spot, not to mention, very likely, her marriage. It was all pretty raw and perverse, which he liked, not because he was into taking chances but because he was way into the idea that he could convince her to take them. That part was intoxicating. Anyway, there was something about his house, apparently, that women in general seemed not to care for.

Then one afternoon they were upstairs in the Valley Road place, defiling its fully staged master bedroom, when they heard a car pull into the driveway. Alina, on top of him, froze. Immediately the car backed out again and the sound of its engine receded. "Just some-body turning around," Gerry said. "Just lost, or missed their turn." But it got into Alina's head and stayed there. The next day she handed him a fake phone message saying his noon appointment was canceled, and at the end of the day after that, while he sat in the lot at work letting his car warm up before heading home, she came out and knocked on his window. He lowered it and saw that she was crying. Hurriedly, folding her arms against the wind, she said she'd decided she couldn't see him anymore. There was no future for them, so all this was doing was making her hate her hus-band for not figuring it out, for never noticing or suspecting a thing. He was such a fool. And she had to stop herself from feeling that way before things got completely out of hand. Plus she needed this job. She turned and ran back inside without giving him a chance to answer.

Damn right there's no future for us, Gerry thought, not without a little relief. She was just overreacting: nothing had happened, nothing had changed, they weren't at any greater risk of getting caught than they'd ever been, and the sex hadn't gotten old as far as he was concerned. But he had to be careful not to plead with her in any way that might encourage her to think he really was in love with her, that might lead to her showing up at his door some rainy night with a suitcase, beaming and saying, "Well, I did it!" The truth, which of course he could never tell her, was that much of her appeal for him, sexually speaking, had to do specifically with her being married. Turning out another man's wife—there was noth-ing on earth more gratifying. He didn't care why. He put the car in gear and decided to stop at the Ship for a drink, to contemplate these matters further.

But the Ship was dead that night, for some reason, and it dark-ened his thoughts. There was not much on his horizon. He lived in a small town, and worked in a small office, with only one woman in it, whom he'd already seduced. He was trying to hang onto a job that he didn't even like. What did any of these things mean? What was at stake for him? He and Lindsey had been engaged before he'd wised up/panicked and called it off, and in a weird way he'd feel better right now if he regretted that, if the foundering of his life was just a matter of his having taken an identifiably wrong turn; but he didn't regret it. Less today than ever. The problem was simply that the open space in himself—the one that it would have been a catastrophic mistake, in his case, to try to fill with marriage and kids—was still there.

Work in the aftermath was awkward. He thought for sure Alina would want him to treat her just like every other agent there treated the receptionist, but that actually seemed to offend her, so conspicuously that he was pretty sure her pouty demeanor tipped off everyone else in the office that there was something between them, ironic now that there wasn't. He did sell a house in Egremont, $40K below asking, but still, it was nice just to get off the schneid. He tried to widen his circle of bars, at least, but the farther afield you went, the farther you had to drive home drunk afterwards. His sister Renee in Colorado Springs had started forwarding various nutty links to him and Candace and Mark: stuff about PNAC, or Operation Northwoods. Too long to read to the end, even when he sat up late and tried.

He called his parents and asked if he could come over just for dinner, just to see how they were doing. He brought an hors d'oeuvre tray from Price Chopper. They seemed more suspicious than grateful. His father got onto the subject of immigration, and his mother went upstairs to bed. Gerry asked if his dad had heard from Renee at all recently, and he said no, why? The drive home that night was especially challenging. Heavy rain, and no moon, and three and a half of those Cutty Sarks the old man served.

He thought everybody on TV was full of shit—the pundits, the alarmists, the conspiracy theorists—but their very full-of-shitness was like a confirmation of what he felt inside: that things right now were off their anchor, that the decline of people's belief in something showed up in their apparent willingness to believe anything. Everyone he listened to seemed doubtful, edgy, ready for the worst. There was a drift from old standards, for which he forgave himself least of all.

Marty got another blow when he stopped by the Town Hall to check his mail the first Monday in June. With summer approaching it might have seemed like the First Selectman of a town like Howland would have more work to do, what with the population expanded and various festivals and entertainments going on to keep all the tourists and vacationers diverted. But he'd long ago learned that wasn't true. With all the extra workload local businesses had, and all the ingenuity they put into squeezing every dollar they could out of every day between now and September, people didn't find as much to complain to him about as they did in the long, stingy, crabby months of winter. The town pretty much ran itself at peak times, because the economy was flush. Sometimes he was asked to come cut the ribbon on this or that new shop, or to give a little thirty-second speech to open the Friday night concert series at the bandstand, but even in a ceremonial sense there wasn't that much call for his presence. He didn't mind a bit. He had a theory, which was that part of the fantasy the city folk were paying for was that a town like Howland had no actual government, that it just ran on small-town values and nostalgia.

At bottom he was a believer in Thoreau, that original Masshole, or at least in the quote a local woman had sent him in the form of a framed sampler after his first election: "That government is best which governs least." And it wasn't because he was lazy, or because he had central AC systems to install. But then that Monday he came in and found on his desk a registered letter from Boston—not even the courtesy or the bravery of a phone call—informing him that Caldwell House had been landmarked, added to the state's official Register of Historic Places, which meant that the mansion and its sixteen acres of grounds and gardens would all come off the town's tax rolls. Marty and most of his predecessors had borne this possibility in the backs of their heads for so long that at some point it had ceased to seem all that real. Whatever half-assed foundation ran Caldwell House applied for registry status every single year and never got it. But people eventually retired from the registry office, and new people got appointed to take their place, and you never knew, in the world of rich folk, who might be friends with whom. He was sure it was just somebody doing a favor for somebody else, which put the whole decision out of the reach of reason.

Caldwell House was one of the few actual tourist destinations in Howland, though it wasn't an attraction in the sense that people would build their Berkshire weekends around seeing it or anything like that. More often, they'd never heard of it until some rainy day on their vacation when they asked a local merchant or the woman who ran their B&B what there was to see around here, and were pleasantly surprised to be told about it. Winston Caldwell made millions in some corner of the railroad business, Marty thought it was, around the turn of the twentieth century. He lived on Fifth Avenue but in 1898 his wife Katarina developed chronic respiratory problems after a bout of pneumonia, and her doctors urged her to get out of the fetid city if possible and spend more time in the mountains. The southern Berkshires weren't quite "the mountains," even in Marty's view—you could have kept going a little ways to Vermont and done a lot better—but in any event Winston Caldwell built a gigantic, Vanderbilt-style mansion on some cheaply obtained land in Howland, where he and his wife spent the next eighteen summers. They had two children, a boy and a girl, both of whom died before the age of five, the girl from scarlet fever and the boy from falling under a wagon wheel. It was a tragic story. In order to keep the childless house from seeming too empty, they had friends staying with them constantly, from New York and from all around the world. Katarina Caldwell loved nothing more than to garden, but her lungs grew too brittle to allow her to do much of the work herself. So Caldwell, grieving, reached for what was at his disposal, which was money. He spent and spent in order to turn the grounds into a sort of horticultural paradise, or rather to hire others to do so, since he didn't know the first thing about flowers. Katarina supervised all the planting from the vast patio in the rear of the mansion or else from one of a series of gazebos built for the purpose, to allow her to watch while still seated and protected from the elements.

Katarina died at the age of forty-four; Winston lived on, childless, lonely, heartbroken, and rich, for another thirty years. Shopkeepers in Howland knew when he was or wasn't in town, but it was a rare occurrence to see him, and friends stopped coming around. His will was defiant: every cent was to go to the establishment of a trust to keep the house and especially the gardens in pristine condition, in perpetuity, and open to the public. Over time it became part of a Great Houses trail up and down the Berkshires. People loved the grandness of it, the opulent folly, the backstory of power dignified by sadness. The separate, round, stone playhouse, built for children dead a century. People didn't live like that anymore. The storybook wealth made both the romance and the tragedy seem larger than life.

Marty found in his Rolodex the number of the woman currently running the Caldwell Trust—Robin van Aswegen was her name: of course it would be something like that—and called her up. "Well, congratulations," he said. "You've screwed us."

"You should be thanking me less sarcastically," she said. They'd never met; she didn't sound as old as he expected. "This lets us upgrade the place a bit. It's not like we're turning a profit over here, you know. It's a fight to break even. Last year we had to raise the admission price to sixteen dollars, and you want to know what that did to our gate?"

"It's six percent of our tax base, almost. Gone. We have no way to make that up. We can't add land to the town. That's money for the schools, most of it. You want to be the one to call and tell them they're not getting it so you can grow flowers? You're sitting on millions over there."

"We can't touch principal. You must know that. Have you been here lately? It's like a haunted house. I had to lay off staff. I am trying to run a charity over here. Your budget problems are not in my purview. You've got a ton of nerve calling me greedy, sir. I'm just trying to maintain a little of this town's history, while you're out bending over for Walmart or whoever, offering them tax breaks to build here."

How did she know about that? "If your operation was a charity," Marty said, "then it would be helping somebody. It's a whim. Flowers! It's a tribute to his self-pity, not his wife. If he'd ever gotten laid again, that place would be a hotel now."

She hung up on him. He had to admit, even though the sense of catastrophe was undiminished, it did make him feel a little bit better just to have gotten under that pale van Aswegen skin. He had some bookkeeping to do at the store, and then he'd been invited up to Tanglewood for their season opener that evening. Nothing official, just a picnic with some friends. Now, there was a place that brought in some money. Half the Berkshires ran off of Tanglewood. Tonight they'd all spread out a blanket and eat some gourmet finger food, and when Marty's back started to bother him he'd get out of the camp chair and lie flat on the grass, half-hammered on white wine, and watch the sky change color over his head. That was something to look forward to. He'd forgotten what the program was tonight, not that it mattered. He didn't know shit about music, but that didn't mean he wasn't allowed to enjoy it anyway.

Joanna Whalen was a seventh- and eighth-grade science teacher at Howland Elementary, married, no kids of her own. Her husband Jack, married once before, was a farmer who had gone all-organic a few years prior and made a decent living, as he liked to put it, selling five-dollar tomatoes to weekenders who knew the value neither of a tomato nor of five dollars. There was way more to it than that, of course—he supplied restaurants all up and down Route 7, and some of the smaller markets and co-ops as far east as Springfield or Holyoke—but he was prone to modesty and was always faintly embarrassed by that turn to the "organic," even though it was a move born of economic desperation and had nothing at all to do with any political views.

Jo had taught at Howland Elementary for nine years, which didn't seem that long—Candace remembered being taught in the Pittsfield public schools by women who'd taught her parents—but when you looked at the school's payroll records, that made her the third-longest-tenured teacher there. Plus she seemed like a fixture, because everyone loved her. She was short, fiery, not pretty but magnetic, and seemed powered less by love of earth science (she'd originally applied for a job teaching math) than by love of a challenge, specifically the challenge of getting children to pay attention to anything long enough to get interested in it. The principal called her the Queen of the Field Trip—or Field-Trip Marshal Goering, which was less funny—because she was always petitioning them for money they didn't have to take a busload of hormonal kids to tramp around in some bog or other. Candace was formerly a science teacher herself—in fact she'd been promoted to vice principal from the teaching job Jo now held. She secretly suspected Jo wasn't all that smart—"secretly" only because she liked Jo too much to say anything unkind about her, and because the woman was an object lesson in the truth that intelligence wasn't profoundly connected to how good a teacher you made. A lot of fine minds had been brought low at the front of an eighth-grade classroom.

In June, barely two weeks before the end of the school year, Jo had the whole fifth-period class watching a film about the rain forest when she passed out. No one noticed right away because she was sitting in the back of the darkened room, beside the projector; it was only the sound of her sliding out of the chair and hitting the floor that caused any of the kids at their desks to turn around.

Two of them ran down the hall to the principal's office, a third to the nurse's office, but one girl who stayed behind in her seat produced from deep within her backpack an outlawed cell phone and dialed 911. Howland's resident trooper, whose last name was Constable—a joke he hated because not everyone got it, so he always introduced himself with a sort of pugnacious flinch—was the first on the scene; he had very limited medical training (Ms. Whalen was breathing fine and didn't need CPR or her airway cleared), but his presence was enough to calm the students, at least, many of whom were crying. When a crew from the Stockbridge firehouse got there, Trooper Constable let them push him out of their way as they stretchered her, put a mask over her mouth and nose, and wheeled her quickly through the dumbstruck hallways of the school.

She'd had a stroke, unlikely as that seemed, or maybe just unfair, in a woman so young and energetic. Her insurance was good—she was a government employee and a union member, so she was well covered—but money wasn't everything: her husband's farm suffered, and he wasn't the kind of man used to taking care of himself in the basic ways, much less taking care of someone else in the ways Jo needed taking care of. The fact that she was covered for a home health-care aide didn't mean she liked having a stranger there every moment, or ever got used to it; the nurses were helpful enough but she couldn't bear their matter-of-factness about her inability to walk or speak clearly or write or eat anything that required two hands. And it was too hard to give in to the urge to break down and cry, as Jo did about once a day, when she was never alone, when some strange woman was always a few feet away, a constant dispassionate reminder of the ordinariness of what had happened to her.

But this was the great thing about living in a small town—especially in those times, when everyone was still in the grip of an urge to show themselves in their own best light, looking for an outlet for their most charitable impulses. Everyone brought food, of course, until Jack had to politely start mentioning to people that their freezers were full, that there was no more room for anything. At which point two mothers with some computer savvy started an online Care Calendar, which quickly booked up through July. There was a separate calendar for driving Joanna back and forth to the doctor and to physical therapy, and a fundraiser to buy them a van with a wheelchair lift, and a turnout like an Amish barn-raising to help make the inside and outside of the old farmhouse wheelchair-accessible, and even a signup sheet for current and former students of Jo's to go over and mow their lawn. Jack uncomfortably accepted all of this charity, because he couldn't think of a way to reject such an outpouring of love for someone he loved too, and because, the shameful truth be told, he sometimes found it hard to be alone in a room with his paralyzed wife, whose physical needs, while sometimes humiliating to attend to, were nothing compared to the help-lessness and inadequacy he felt whenever she would look at him out of that half-frozen face, as if to say, is there really nothing you can do? Why couldn't you stop this from happening? You swore we'd be happy, and it was true, he had sworn that to her, and he felt so weak in her eyes that it was hard for him not to avoid her gaze.

As for Candace, she went back into the classroom and taught the rest of Jo's classes for those final weeks of the school year. The district and the union had both okayed it as an emergency measure. She didn't get much accomplished. Teaching kids anything in June was always a futile effort, and the fifth period in particular seemed to have gotten it into their heads that even trying to move on and learn something from somebody else was like an expression of disloyalty to Ms. Whalen. Still, she got them through their final, and graded it generously, to take into account all they'd been through. They had the whole summer now to find a replacement. But it wasn't easy—it was never easy—to find qualified teachers willing to relocate or even to commute to Howland. As the summer wore on it seemed more and more possible that they might ask Candace to keep teaching in the fall, if only out of necessity, just until Joanna could make it back, which everyone had firm faith she would do. It was technically a demotion: Candace didn't know how to feel about it. She didn't want to ask selfish questions. She was hoping that somehow the decision could be taken out of her hands.

Folks came to the window at the post office seldom enough that Glenn was able to buy himself one of those little bells, like at the front desk of a hotel, and put up a hand-lettered sign that said RING FOR SERVICE, and nobody took it amiss. He was never more than twelve or fifteen feet from that window anyway—the post office just wasn't that wide—but at least this way he could sit down out of sight, maybe flip through a magazine carefully before rolling it up and sliding it back into its addressee's box, and watch from behind the wall as the citizens of Howland came in to check their mail. There wasn't much to see from back there; sometimes he would make bets with himself about which tiny mailbox door would open. He got pretty good at it, because people were creatures of habit and he learned their routines. Sometimes one of the boxes on the lower rows would open and a child's eye would press up against the slot—they loved to do that—and when they did, Glenn would make a sort of pop-eyed face and give them a little wave. Then he would hear the kid trying to convince his mom that it had happened.

At around eleven thirty every weekday the half-sized local truck would pull noisily into the lot at the back, the truck that delivered the mail from elsewhere in the postal zone, rarely more than half a bag but the guy still had to make the trip, it's not like you could just let the mail pile up until you considered the trip worth your while. His name was John Francis, and Glenn wished he liked him more, because you didn't see too many people during Glenn's average working day, apart from those who rang the bell to summon him out of his chair to provide some service for them, which was obviously a less relaxed sort of interaction.

John Francis wanted to talk about sports, mostly, and for some reason was always frankly disappointed when Glenn couldn't offer much of anything in return on the subject, apart from sympathetic nods. Still, he'd always invite John to come in out of the truck and sit for a bit. Just for a bit, John would always say, and then after an awkward silence he would confess how worried he'd been all morning about the Pats. Or the Bruins or the Sox or the Celtics; but lately it was the Pats that troubled him.

"Have they started playing already?" Glenn asked. "Seems a little early in the year for football."

John stared at him. "No," he said, "they're in preseason now. That's my point."

John looked like the kind of guy who might actually be good at sports. He was probably still in his twenties, and in way better shape than Glenn was, but he never mentioned playing any sports himself, neither in the past nor in the present. It was more as if he were actually a member of the teams he was speaking about. The way he talked about the scouting reports on whomever the Pats were playing on a given Sunday, it was clear that in his mind he was preparing to play in that game. Glenn never understood guys like that. They couldn't feel embarrassed.

But John Francis never stayed more than half an hour anyway, because he had other stops to make, in towns all up and down the

92

Housatonic. Glenn waved to him as he backed out, then turned to box all the mail in the tied-off, half-filled bag John had dropped on the smooth concrete apron of the loading area.

On the Tuesday before Labor Day, Glenn made the drive from Springfield and unlocked the PO for business. He pulled open the loading-dock door and left it that way because it was a perfect day, and he liked seeing the strip of green on the other end of the lot. Not that pretty or anything, just some trees, but it gave a different sort of border to his tiny, solitary workspace, made it feel bigger and more varied. Fancier. Might as well enjoy it now, because in the wintertime, forget it. The front door had a metal slot cut into it where people could drop mail after hours; five or six envelopes of varying sizes were scattered on the linoleum beneath the slot. Glenn's first task, this and every morning, was to gather them up before some civilian could walk through the door and accidentally step all over them. At the top of the loose pile was one of those old-fashioned, stiff, waxy manila envelopes, a dark yellow that you rarely saw anymore, that he associated for some reason with childhood, slightly larger than the standard business-size. It was addressed to the Office of the City of Howland, MA. Which was odd because Howland wasn't a city per se, and had no office by that name, and anyone who lived here, anyone who would know the place well enough to bring a letter after hours to his front-door mail slot, would know that. It wasn't flat, either, not perfectly—there was something inside it.

So technically it was undeliverable? With no return address. His to do with as he would, though of course there were procedures to follow, but no one would ever know since, federal government or no federal government, he worked alone. Of course he knew where its sender had intended it to go, probably. The door opened and somebody came in, a woman, he could tell from the way the shoes hit the tile. She opened her mailbox, emptied it, and left again. No idea Glenn was so near to her, listening to her, on the other side of a wall with holes cut into it like it was a prison or something.

Whatever was inside the manila business-shaped envelope was loose and moving around. Like dirt or sand. He was within his rights, he was pretty sure, to inspect it; or, if it was legit, he could always just tape it back up and slap one of those stickers on it that said it had been damaged in transit. He held it sideways so that whatever was inside collected at the bottom, and then, as neatly as he could, he cut open the top edge.

Nothing happened. He bent his head and looked inside. There was some kind of grit or powder in there, maybe a spoonful, and a folded piece of paper. Carefully he reached in and pulled out the paper with one blade of the scissors. It too was waxy and stiff, more like a blank index card. Printed on it, in pencil, were the words WHAT YOU DESERVE.

He heard the door open again and without thinking he spun and ran out the open back door of the post office, across the pavement, and threw the envelope into the thin woods. He was panting, and not from the sprint. He'd seen the news. He checked the pads of his fingers for any residue; there was none he could see. Somewhere beneath the sound of the wind and the roaring in his ears he became aware of the bell ringing at the customer window inside. He headed back in, smoothing his hair. What was he supposed to do? Quarantine the post office? Based on what? He'd thrown the evidence into the woods, and it was probably a stretch to call it evidence anyway. White powder could be anything. It could have been cocaine. Most likely, though, it was a prank, intended to cause exactly the panicked reaction it had caused, only at the Town Hall instead of here, in the halls of government instead of in Glenn's own head.

He didn't feel sick or anything. He felt a little dizzy. He wasn't about to get the FBI in here to search the woods for traces of baby powder. No reason to put yourself on the radar that way. The bell again. By the time his legs were able to move him back to the window, whoever was there on the other side had given up and left.

He was pretty strung out by the time he closed up and headed back to Penny's. John Francis had come as usual but Glenn couldn't recall a single word of what they'd talked about. Just a prank, he kept telling himself. Somebody from the high school. It was the kind of thing Glenn himself probably would have found irresistibly hilarious back when he was in high school. And then he would have gotten caught. A criminal mastermind, in those days, he was not.

He kept hearing the click of the woman's heels on the tile. What did I ever do? he wanted to say to the woman. It was like he was having a dream while driving.

"You're here," Penny said. She never said, "You're home." Which made sense. It wasn't his home. "Another thrilling day at work?"

It was a joke they had. "You bet," he said.

"Did you pick up dinner?"

She'd asked him that morning and he'd said he would. "I forgot," he said. "My bad."

He looked at her and saw himself dead in her bed in the morning, saw the both of them dead and her kids getting out of their father's car in the driveway, wondering why there were two cars there, opening the front door. He saw the linoleum floor of the tiny, square post office overlaid with bodies.

"Whatever," Penny said, and smiled. He tried to smile back. "You don't look good," she said. She came over and felt his forehead, and shrugged. He stood motionless as she turned away from him, toward the refrigerator, opened the freezer door and pulled out an oversized bottle of white wine.

"Dinner of champions!" she said.

————

Beginning in late spring and all through the summer, Mark had kept on a crew of three to do the work in and around Hadi's house.

It was a succession of small jobs—bollards in the driveway, security cameras concealed in the birch trees around the house and wired underground, reinforcements to all the doors and windows, including bulletproof glass—but he did them serially so he could supervise each one, since none of his men had enough experience with this kind of work to be left alone to do it, as if it were laying tile or upgrading a bathroom. The big security measure—a panic room, though Hadi didn't call it that—had already been taken: it was part of the house's blueprint. So Hadi had thought of himself as a potential target for years—all along, really—and Mark figured he was probably right.

They did some work on the roof too. Hadi wanted short-wave antennas installed up there in case other forms of communication went out, and an extra layer of steel as well, under the shingles so as not to change the house's appearance, which meant taking all the shingles up and nailing them down again. From the roof, Mark could see his own house, looking handsome and unsecured. But any house looked pretty vulnerable from that angle.

Hadi's home was not as big as Mark had expected. There was plenty of space for a family of four—five bedrooms, a dining room, a media room, a huge living room with picture windows tinted on the outside—but somehow it wasn't all as excessive and opulent as Mark had assumed a guy like Hadi would go for. He thought a rich man wanted maximum wingspan, either just as a status marker or to make him feel his own limitlessness even in his downtime. If he were a billionaire, that's probably how he would have looked at it. But he learned a lot, those weeks and months, about how such people lived. Or how Hadi lived, anyway, and he had to have been somewhat representative, just because there weren't too many men like him in the world.

Hadi wouldn't sit in front of those picture windows anymore, he confessed. Looking into the woods made him feel too exposed. He didn't mean metaphorically. Even though the glass was now of a grade that would probably withstand a small missile, even though the woods were now full of high-tech sensors, in the trees and on the ground. He preferred his office upstairs, which was sizable and perfectly comfortable. He had Mark take the skylight out of it, though.

But he didn't seem nervous or paranoid—just endlessly calculating. He was pretty much like any other client. He just needed a certain peace of mind before he could enjoy his country home. He was one of those guys whose business it was to think of, and provide for, every scenario. Only then could he relax, or work, which in his case seemed more or less the same thing.

Mark's rate was substantial, and the job had gone on even longer than he'd hoped, because Hadi was always thinking of new measures, new precautions that might be taken: and if a thing might be done, then that thing needed to be done. Mark thought he'd clear maybe sixty-five thousand when it was all over, even after paying the crew, even after all the sometimes baroque expenses associated with making Hadi's vision of impregnability real. He'd had to send all the way to Maryland for the new window frames, for instance, to some place that did work for Fort Bragg. He cleared it first with Hadi, because the cost was borderline larcenous, but Hadi had just clapped him on the shoulder, delighted with the ingenuity he'd shown in finding the material at all.

He watched everything Mark and his crew did, from a not-quite-respectful distance. He wasn't critical, just interested—he never said a word unless it was to ask exactly how they were doing something they were doing—but it was still intimidating. When Mark got up the nerve to ask jokingly if Hadi didn't have any work of his own to do, he replied soberly that he was working mostly with Asian markets lately and so had been up since 2 A.M.

Mark was able to keep all three men on most days, a fourth whenever they were up on the roof. For this job he made a point of hiring only guys he'd worked with, on and off, for years: Hartley, a master carpenter even though mostly rudimentary skills were required for a job like this one, Dave, who lived in Becket and had five kids, and Barrett, who was great with any kind of machinery and technology, which made him ideal for the job even though his usual gigs involved hooking up home theaters and wireless climate controls. He'd also done some security-cam installations before, or so he assured Mark. That relationship was always a little fraught because Barrett had been a year ahead of Mark in the same high school. He had to be careful not to act too much the boss with Barrett, especially in front of other people, because Barrett was capable of going into some kind of prolonged sulk and working half-speed or even just calling in sick the next morning.

Once in a while, when the workday was over, Hadi would invite Mark—never the others—to stick around and talk, have a beer out on the porch. It was a little discomfiting to sit on that porch and see the lights come on in his own house, five hundred yards away. He might have expected a guy like Hadi to want a captive audience to sit and brag about himself, but it wasn't like that: pretty much all he did was ask Mark questions, mostly about his own work—the craft of it, the economics of it, how he first got interested in it.

"My dad, mostly," Mark said. It was the answer he always gave. "He was in the home-building business. I mean I wanted to emulate him and rebel against him at the same time. He took a lot of pride in his work but there was only ever one way to do things, and that was the cost-efficient way. The idea that a house could be beautiful, or that it had a history, never entered into it for him."

After a while Mark felt emboldened to tell Hadi that he had dabbled in the stock market, and even that he had suffered losses, though he wasn't any more specific than that. Hadi winced sympathetically. "Very tough for an individual to make any headway in that world," he said. "Or no. That's not quite right. I mean, technically I'm an individual. What I mean is that it's very tough for a relatively small amount of capital, such as an honest working man like yourself might have, to get itself taken seriously."

"What do you two talk about?" Karen would ask him when he came home.

Mark wouldn't articulate it to her or even to himself, but in fact he was looking for some evidence, some manifestation, of what set him apart from a guy like Hadi: a guy who had everything and from whom nothing could be taken away.

"Not much," he said instead. "It's a little old, at this point, actually. But he is a client. My only client right at the moment. So if he wants to have a beer with me, I'll have a beer with him."

Karen frowned. "Well, what's the house like, then?" she said. "Since you're the only person in town who's ever seen the inside of it."

Inside it he felt the contrast—or maybe it wasn't a contrast at all, maybe it was harmony, it was hard to tell with marriages—between Hadi and his wife: the whole place was decorated with vintage furniture and with antiques (Mark hadn't seen a single piece post-1950, though he hadn't been in every room in the house), while the house itself was ultramodern, conspicuously brand new. All the fixtures, all the systems. Not because Hadi was some sort of tech buff but because he could not stand it when things broke or wore out or otherwise failed to do what he expected them to do. The combination didn't look great, to Mark's own eye, which was a pretty good one for that sort of thing. It was a compromise, a shotgun wedding of a house. You could read a lot about clients, always more than they realized, in their design decisions.

Mrs. Hadi herself—Rachel—never hung around for long. He'd see her in the kitchen or in the driveway, and he'd smile, but he could tell that she didn't like having him and his men there, particularly not inside the house.

"She misses the city," Hadi said. She'd just opened the porch door, seen them sitting there having a beer, and withdrawn again. "Of course she understands why we had to leave it. But there's a mourning period." Mark nodded and looked discreetly away from the tinted door, toward the woods reflected in the dark windows of his own home.

One morning in September Mark came off the roof, backwards down the ladder, and found himself right next to her. She wasn't doing anything, just standing there, arms folded, looking at him as if he had just dropped out of the sky, which in a way he had, though the presence of the ladder really should have tipped her off.

She had a way of looking at him that suggested she knew that he knew he was good-looking, and that his hickish charms were beneath her. He never addressed her by her first name because he felt uncomfortable using it. But "Mrs. Hadi" didn't seem right either. They were probably about the same age.

"I'm sorry," he said. "Looks like I've got this ladder in your way."

She raised her eyebrows.

"What are you doing out here?" he said.

"Gardening." He looked around his feet, in a panic. "No, I'm just joking, for God's sake. I came out here to have a cigarette."

She was empty-handed.

"I forgot them inside, though," she said.

The silences were harder for Mark to bear than when she spoke. "I don't smoke," he said.

"Of course not."

"What do you mean, of course not?"

"You're the picture of country health," Rachel said. "How much longer will you boys be up on the roof? I mean how many more days?"

"At least a week, I'm afraid," he said.

"The noise is hard to describe. I mean the hammering, when you're in a house and there's hammering on the roof it's just like it's inside your head. The footsteps up there are even worse. I came out here to get away from it. I can still hear it, of course, but out here at least I can tell when it's coming from somewhere outside my skull."

She was pretty in a harsh way that had never done much for Mark. Very thin, very toned, lots of organized exercise, not at all a welcoming figure. Thin lips, or maybe she just kept them pressed together without realizing it.

He needed to get back to work, but he didn't know how to extract himself; he couldn't just walk away from her after she'd made what was basically a complaint, but he couldn't apologize either, not for doing what he was hired to do. His men were always as considerate as possible when the client was in the house. Mark insisted on it. Not his fault that this woman couldn't differentiate between the house and her own head.

"So our kids are in the same class now, I hear," he said. "My daughter Haley is eight. She says your son has the desk behind hers. Or had. I don't know about this year."

She smiled perfunctorily, the way you do when someone brings up children whom you don't know, but she seemed to think it was an odd remark.

"How are your kids liking it? I think Haley and your son have Mrs. Tuttle this year. Is that right? I think so. Anyway, everybody says she's great."

"They are having a difficult time," she said simply.

"Well, sure, it's a big adjustment," Mark said. "I mean, I can imagine. Especially joining mid-year."

"That is a first-rate observation."

He wasn't sure if he was being made fun of. "Probably a lot different than the school they went to in New York."

"You could say that," she offered. But then, in the ensuing silence, she seemed to warm to the topic. "It's a fine school," she said. "I'm sure. But it is hard to see your children do without.

Whatever the circumstances, for whatever good reason. You know what I mean? You must know what I mean. Every parent feels that way. You want the best for them. You want them to have everything. And you certainly do not want to give them everything and then take it back from them. And try to explain to them why. That is not a good feeling."

He was praying for one of the men to call for him, so he would have an immediate way out of this conversation. But all was silence except for the midday insect buzz, and the hammering.

"Well, kids are resilient," he said.

She stared at him. "Wow," she said.

He colored. "You know," he said, "my wife is an administrator at Mullins. If you or your kids ever needed anything, or whatever at all, she'd be happy to help out if you just say you know me, or I could mention it to her if you want. Just in case something comes up."

It was a lame offer, and he wasn't even sure how valid it was— Rachel Hadi was just the sort of person Karen was likely to hate— but it did provoke a glimmer of engagement from Rachel. Maybe he'd found the language of the world such people moved in, the language of connections and favors, of access.

"Thank you," she said. "That's nice of you. I may take you up on that." She paused, as if expecting him to say something more, and when he didn't, she laughed sheepishly, and he laughed too. "What was your name again?" she said.

Friday was a day set aside for Marty's own, nongovernmental, moneymaking work. It was kind of an artificial boundary between his two professional lives; he split his time between heating and cooling jobs and town matters on most days, at no great cost to him either financially or in terms of stress, but he liked to go into the weekend feeling he'd made some money, improved his lot, and he liked to have that Friday evening beer or three at the Ship with the mild soreness in his forearms and back that came, at his age anyway, with physical labor.

He did two easy estimates up near Lenox, charming some folks he'd never met who insisted on addressing him jokingly as Mr. Mayor, and then he stopped for a long lunch at a place he liked, down the street from the Red Lion Inn. The burger was good but what really got him were the Cajun waffle fries, a novelty that hadn't caught on, for some reason, in any of the other establishments he favored. The waitress at this place knew him well enough now to give him a slyly oversized helping of the fries. He gave her a little smile of thanks and then he reflected how much better it was to have that sort of woman in your life than it was to be married to someone who would probably feel obligated to scold you for eating delicious things the doctor had described as "not a good idea." Well, most ideas weren't good ideas. He left a tip to be remembered by, and got back in his van.

The Frasers were originally summer people, but ever since Joe Fraser had retired from AT&T in Albany, they'd spent more and more time in Howland, over half the year this year. They had kids, and grandkids, whom you'd see on holidays or on big anniversaries, but the nearest one lived in Philadelphia, so they weren't around a lot. The house was for Joe and Vivian. Marty admired older folks who didn't take the usual beaten path to Florida or Arizona. It seemed like waving the white flag, to him.

"Smokin' Joe!" Marty shouted as the old man came out on the porch to welcome him. "How's life treating you?"

"Better than this crappy secondhand water heater you sold me," Joe said, but with a grin. Like a lot of vacation homes built out there, Joe's hadn't been properly winterized, so he was having to lay out some money for improvements now. Such cases were a big part of Marty's business. The electric heater he'd installed in Joe's basement wasn't old at all—brand new, in fact—but according to

Joe he was having to hit the reset button constantly, sometimes five times a day. It would kick off and then fail to kick on again. Marty wiped his boots outside the kitchen and said hello to Vivian, who gestured toward a chair.

"Thank you, Viv, but no," he said. "I'd better get down to the dungeon there, so I don't bother you folks too long. Friday night, so I'm sure you're headed out on the town."

"Have they started work on the memorial at the high school yet?" Joe called after him as he descended the steep stairs.

"Well, that's a long story," Marty said without breaking stride. He liked the Frasers but he was pretty eager to declare the weekend officially under way. He had a thought about that first swallow of beer at the Ship, but then he pushed it out of his mind. Just another hour to focus between now and then. Maybe less. Besides, he had a sinking feeling that he might have installed the heater wrong. It was a new model—new to him, anyway; it was from Korea, of all places, and this was the first one he'd ever hooked up.

It was just about the most brightly lit basement he'd ever been in. Viv did the laundry down there. Otherwise there wasn't much to it except a wall of tools that had a suspiciously organized look to them, like they didn't get used too much. Or maybe Joe was just a neat freak. Marty took the screwdriver out of his belt and popped off the cover over the thermal switch. He stared at it for a while, but it wasn't as familiar to him as the Finney units he'd installed for twenty years and knew like the back of his hand. It's not like he'd gone to the Korean model because it was any better (it wasn't) or even any cheaper (it was, but not by much). He'd had to start pushing a new model on customers because Finney had gone out of business.

He straightened up and felt it in his back, a spasm, or more like a deep cramp—it didn't let go like a spasm did, but held on—that radiated along his side. He gave a little snort of pain and frustration. He didn't usually get it that bad, but maybe it had been a long week. Rather than bend down again, he pushed the reset button with his toe; the heater kicked on again just like it should. Nothing seemed obviously wrong, which was a bad sign in terms of his prospects for fixing it quickly. If he couldn't figure out what the issue was, then he'd have to install a new one, which would mean coming in over the weekend because of course you had to stand behind your own work. Or he could just stay down here in the Frasers' basement, kicking the button every few hours, until they moved away or died. The Marty Solomon Guarantee. He had a manual for this model out in the van, printed in English even, but he knew they would be watching him and he didn't want to be seen fetching the instructions for the thing like he didn't know what he was doing. It was unprofessional.

Why couldn't he concentrate? Why did things have to change? Why did a great American company that made a good product, one that worked, have to fail? Why on earth had he saved this job, which he should have known would be hard, for four o'clock on a Friday afternoon?

The pain stayed in his left side and started to make itself felt all the way into his arm, and it became a little bit harder to take a satisfying breath, and just like that Marty knew what was happening, because it had happened to him before. "Oh no," he said. He tried to straighten up calmly, to make it to the steps, but then it hit him like the house itself falling down on top of him, and he went to the floor, just like last time. All he could think was how close, how within reach, it all still was—the basement steps, the van, the beer—and then the pain swallowed those thoughts too.

The door opened. "Your Honor?" Joe called down gaily. "Vivian would like to know if you'd care for something to drink." But he couldn't answer.

She couldn't cook anymore, not really. She never was that great at it. But she was efficient—especially in the years when all four kids were running around, and the two boys ate like wolves—and efficiency was all he ever really asked for anyway. Asked for silently, that is, in his head, in terms of his expectations. Something filling and unsurprising and on time. He didn't feel like that was too demanding of him. Truth be told, if it had been purely a matter of what he wanted, he wouldn't have much minded having the same thing for dinner, or for breakfast, every damn day. He had plenty of other things to worry about, plenty of other surprises to adjust to.

But now he'd come downstairs, even on a Sunday morning like today, and another hour would go by and no breakfast would have appeared, nor any sign of its imminent preparation. He'd go into the kitchen when he couldn't stand it anymore and make himself a bowl of cereal with as much noise and banging as possible and sometimes that would get her attention and sometimes it wouldn't. He knew he shouldn't be angry with her—it was just old age coming to get them, it wasn't her fault—but by the same token, she couldn't simply have forgotten that there was such a thing as breakfast, so it was hard not to ascribe some mysterious hostility to it. Plus it was just a physical reaction on his part, a reaction to the hunger, and so he wasn't to blame for his irritation either, it all couldn't be helped.

It was damned hard to eat a bowl of cereal in a reclining chair. But she'd disappeared upstairs somewhere, so he sullenly went about it, trying his best not to spill milk on his shirt while also hoping spitefully on some level that he would, so she could see it. On the television was a story about how some kindergarten teacher somewhere had read a book to the kids about some girl who had two mommies.

She came downstairs, nicely dressed. "Where are you going?" he said, but he remembered the answer as soon as the question was out of his mouth.

"Church," she said. "I'm lector today." She paused on the landing behind his chair, where he couldn't turn his head to see her. "Would you like to come?"

Oh, the hostility in that question! No one else would ever catch it, not even if they were sitting right there in the living room and heard it. That was marriage. She'd stopped going to church years earlier, when the kids were young but old enough to start refusing to go, and she had only resumed in the last few years. He figured it was a good deal for her: two hours out of the week, in order to feel morally superior to him for the other hundred and sixty-six. She called it being "worried" about him.

He realized he'd forgotten to answer her question. He twisted around in the reclining chair to see if she was still standing there.

"Do you have to watch that?" came her voice. "It puts you in a bad mood."

"It's the only channel that covers the war," he said. "Every place else, it's like it isn't even going on."

She sighed theatrically, or anyway he knew her well enough to know that's what she was doing, and a few moments later he heard the garage door go up. On the television there was something about a mosque, and bin Laden, or maybe it was some other guy because they all seemed to be trying their best to look like bin Laden, and then bin Laden said to him, "Why do you even care? Nobody else cares. It's not like it was. Nothing will ever be like it was," and he realized he was dreaming, and when he realized it he could hear his wife making noises in the kitchen and it was already past time for the Patriots. He changed the channel. He fell asleep in that chair two or three times a day now, and then when he got into bed at night he had to take a pill. The days didn't have any structure to them anymore.

He should stay more active. He should get up and do something. There were things to be done to keep up the house, God knew. She didn't like him getting up on ladders and whatnot. But the real issue, which he dared not bring up around her, was his focus. It was baffling: he just couldn't pay attention to anything for too long a stretch, not anymore. And that's how accidents happened. He knew that better than anyone. He'd built houses for forty years. Now his son took money from the weekenders to make sure their second homes looked properly old and run-down. It seemed more like a scam than like building something. But Mark didn't invent that world. He just lived in it.

Well, anyway, it was Sunday. A day of rest. He still felt that rhythm in the week even though he didn't work anymore, even though every day was pretty much the same.

Dinner was some frozen chicken marsala thing from Sam's. The problem with Sam's wasn't that it didn't taste good; the problem was that whenever you ate it for the first time, you knew you were going to eat it four or five more times because it was just the two of them and everything from Sam's only came in bulk. Part of the problem was that she ate almost nothing. He couldn't understand how she got by eating as little as she did.

"How was church?" he asked her.

She took a while to answer. "Very nice," she said. "By the way, they need some help with the plumbing in the rectory. No water pressure, Father says. I told them maybe you could help them out, if you were willing."

"I could look at it," he said. She cleared the table and they went back to the living room to watch some of the TV she liked—*Murder, She Wrote*, or *Law & Order*. He didn't mind so much. It put you in the mood to go to bed, at least.

"I'm going to make a cup of tea to bring up," she said. "Would you like anything?"

"No, that's all right."

"Okay. By the way, they need some help with the plumbing in the rectory. I told them maybe you could help them out."

He started to get irritated, but he caught himself. This kind of thing was happening lately. Especially at night.

"I'll give them a call," he said.

In the middle of the night, he sat up suddenly. Nothing woke him. But he had a feeling of unease. He went downstairs, slowly, listening, waiting for his eyes to adjust. As soon as he reached the landing he could see an orange glow coming from the kitchen.

She'd left the burner on. He switched it off and stood there in the heat from it, in the air that darkened as the burner cooled. It was such a battle, within him, not to get angry. He knew he shouldn't. If he could just tell someone, that might help with the anger thing, but who was there he could tell? It would be a terrible betrayal of her. He couldn't say anything to the kids. Candace, that worrywart, would lose her mind. He couldn't even talk to his wife about it—no reason to shame her, it's not like she did it on purpose. He'd just bear it himself. What else was new? Nobody had the least sense of all he'd borne for their sake, to keep things going. Forty years.

She'd left every single drawer pulled out, too. He hated that.

2

The town of Howland was incorporated in 1748, and in accordance with its charter, the longer-serving of Marty Solomon's two fellow selectmen—a retired high school teacher named Maeve Brennan—succeeded him as First Selectman until the end of his term, which ran another fourteen months. There was no provision in the charter for anyone to replace Maeve herself on the three-person board: no authorization for a special election, nor any other, junior branch of town government from which someone might be promoted into her spot. Which meant Howland would technically be governed, for those fourteen months, by a voting body of two—Maeve and John Waltz, a former electrician who first ran for office three years ago after he broke his back on the job and went on permanent disability. The two of them had always gotten along well enough, but in the wake of Marty's death they became excessively polite to each other, almost formal, holding doors and offering to refill each other's coffee at meetings, so afraid were they of any voting issue coming before them that might produce a 1–1 tie.

Marty was unambiguously dead, the EMTs said, by the time they arrived to carry him up the narrow stairs of the Frasers' basement. It took a while, surprisingly, to figure out whom to contact: everybody remembered Marty's ex-wife but no one was in touch with her anymore. They'd had no children, and Marty's parents were deceased, his father of a heart attack at the same age at which Marty had died, fifty-four. His big metal desk at Solomon Heating & Cooling held only work-related records. Trooper Constable assumed the awkward duty of breaking into Marty's home; with his eyes cast fastidiously downward he checked desk drawers, file cabinets, and the like until he found an address book on a bedside table. There wasn't a Solomon in it, but there was, in the S's, a woman identified only as Bridget; Constable took a chance and called her, and she turned out to be Marty's sister, who lived in Rhode Island. Her last name was now O'Keefe. No one could recall Marty ever mentioning her, and by the time the funeral was over and she and her husband went back home, they had an idea why. Despite seeming not to know the first thing about her brother—not even that he had been voted by his neighbors into his hometown's highest office—she cried theatrically and almost nonstop. Whenever Maeve or the funeral director or some other dignitary sat down to try to console her, she would ask them, as indirectly as she could manage, about Marty's money. There couldn't have been much, but he did leave a typed will (in the drawer of the same bedside table where the address book was found) that left everything to her. He had no other family.

In another way, of course, the town was his family, and so the day of the funeral itself had an air of high emotion and fragile festivity. Services, kept simple, were held in the Episcopal church— likely the first time, a few of his friends allowed themselves to observe, he had ever crossed its threshold. The Undermountain Café put out a nice spread in the church's reception hall afterwards, of which everyone gratefully partook, but the real tribute came later at the Ship, where the drinking and the tearful toasts and the unusual physicality among the men would go on past the State of Massachusetts's legally designated closing time, because, as they kept grinningly reminding each other in loving memory of

Marty Marty the One-Man Party, there was no law in Howland anymore.

Mark stopped in early for one beer, which turned into two. He saw his brother across the room, which wasn't a shock even though Gerry had never had an especially kind word to say about Marty Solomon; he was surprised, though, when he turned back to say goodbye after that second beer and saw that Gerry was already gone. Mark shook a few more hands and drove back home. He'd thought he might see Hadi at the bar—he'd been at the church, without his wife—but Hadi didn't show, which was just as well, Mark figured, since someone in that roomful of drunk, sad locals would surely have tried to mock him into paying for a round, or for every round. The Frasers had been at the church too. They sat in back and skipped the reception. Mark had heard through Karen that Viv Fraser was so shaken up, still, that she wouldn't even go down to the basement to do laundry unless Joe stayed down there with her.

In his driveway Mark turned off the truck and before he even got to the top porch step he could hear Haley crying. It was her angry cry, her cry of injustice over not getting something she wanted, and so his real concern as he opened his front door was that whatever confrontation he'd missed would have put Karen in a touchy mood.

And it had. "You didn't drive home drunk, did you?" was the first thing she said to him. Of course not, he replied softly. "Well I hope you had fun. I didn't make dinner, because I figured we all got plenty to eat at the church."

"What's wrong with Haley?"

"Why don't you ask her yourself?" Karen said, and took a glass of wine out onto the porch and let the door shut behind her.

She sat on the swing—the vintage Nantucket porch swing he'd seen at an estate sale when they were on their way back from visiting her brother in Vermont, and had restored and hung as a birthday present to her—and pushed herself back and forth with her toes. He would make Haley feel better. He always made Haley feel better, because that's the only thing he was interested in, never the nature of the problem itself or what lesson a good parent might try to produce from it. When she went back inside, Haley would be smiling again. They would probably be watching TV.

He didn't mean to, she knew, but he undermined her. It almost would have been better if he had meant to, because then at least he wouldn't act so clueless and aggrieved every time she tried to call him on it. Mark didn't seem to feel that a parent's job was to shape or influence or improve the child in any way, but rather to entertain her, to appease her, to do whatever it took to make her happy. He couldn't see that Haley was in danger of becoming a classic only child: entitled, solipsistic, used to being the center of everyone's attention, unable to empathize. Not a sharer. Karen had seen that firsthand at school. This was not how it was supposed to be. The whole only-child situation was itself a product of their economic failure, mostly, which you could say made them even more responsible for correcting Haley's behavior. But you couldn't argue with him about a problem he insisted he didn't see.

Little girls were supposed to adore their mothers. But this was the thing about marriage: the way your spouse acted, the person he was, forced you to act a certain way in response, and vice versa, and over time those roles hardened and became exaggerated. You grew into a kind of cartoon of yourself. She suspected that her relationship with Haley would be a great deal less oppositional if Mark weren't there for the girl to appeal to all the time, if he weren't a sort of turf for mother and daughter to fight to claim. He fancied himself the Great Centrist.

A section of the woods across the field from where she sat suddenly glowed. It was one of those outdoor floodlights at the Hadis', motion-sensitive, so that every deer that walked through their property lit it up like it was the yard at Alcatraz. Mark had installed those lights himself. Maddening. But the money from that job, which was somehow still going on, was their lifeline. She drained her wineglass and went back inside. The TV flickered, but only Mark sat in front of it, watching *The Matrix* for the two thousandth time.

"It was just on," he said sheepishly.

"It's always on," she said. "Where's Haley?"

"Doing homework. Such as it is. She has to memorize the four-times table."

She finally sat next to him, on the couch. He rubbed her shoulder. "So what was the dispute?" he said.

"She didn't tell you?"

"No."

"You didn't ask her?"

He shook his head.

She bit her lip. "She was making fart noises with her mouth at the funeral," she said.

They were facing the television rather than each other. She could feel him trying not to laugh, and then he did laugh, explosively, through his nose, like a little boy. She got up and left the room.

Damn it, he thought. That's not good. He would have to apologize, but not now; if you apologized too quickly, she wouldn't accept it, because it was like telling her to stop being angry before she was ready. Anyway, *The Matrix* was back on.

He went up a while later to get Haley ready for bed, then he sent her in to say good night to Mommy, who was already in bed as well (another dark sign), and he went back downstairs and sat by himself a while longer. The quiet was relaxing. He needed to set aside some time to think about whether it made sense to refinance the house, and now was as good a time as any, but when he was tired, his brain wouldn't stay on track. He thought he'd only had two beers tonight, but then he remembered the other two at the Ship. It all added up. He turned out the lights and slipped into bed beside Karen, who was already on her stomach, asleep.

Next morning he was back at Hadi's place, and then for two more weeks after that. The job was winding down; Mark let Dave go when the reroofing was done, and then Hartley the carpenter the following Friday, so for the final few days it was just him and Barrett. What they had left was mostly cleanup work: replastering, replacing some baseboards and paneling, repainting the master bedroom where they'd opened up a wall for sensors and surveillance equipment. Barrett handled all the painting. For Rachel Hadi, the incursion into her bedroom had been the last straw: she'd checked into Asana, a yoga retreat built on the grounds of a former seminary in Stockbridge. The children agreed to ride the school bus in her absence. Hadi and Mark had a beer in the kitchen, on the last day of the job, while Barrett finished up. There was nothing left for Mark to do, no real reason to linger, but he didn't want to leave Barrett alone in the house with Hadi. You just never knew what he'd say. So Mark stuck around, somewhat awkwardly, for a second, and a third. Barrett, with typical perversity, was taking forever, but Mark knew that going upstairs to check on his progress might start an argument, a loud one. Hadi drank mostly in silence but seemed perfectly at ease. Mark wanted to leave; but then, as he got drunker, he didn't want to leave. He felt a door closing. He felt like someone better, smarter than himself would be seizing this unusual opportunity to learn from the brand of man Hadi was, the brand of man Mark longed to be. He had hoped all these months of exposure to Hadi—observing him, listening to him—might generate some kind of lesson about success, about boldness, but now time was up and that hadn't really happened, and Mark assumed the failure was his.

They sat at Hadi's cherry drop-leaf table. Mark looked him over with what passed, in his state, for discretion. It was, he thought, as if Hadi periodically went into town, made some notes regarding what kind of clothes the locals wore, then returned home and tried to find the nearest match online. Even when he got it right, he could never quite carry it off. Part of the sartorial issue was that Hadi was a man incapable of wearing a T-shirt as anything other than an undergarment. His Carhartt jackets and Wranglers and new-looking boots were always held together by a signature, discordant white dress shirt that looked like it cost two hundred dollars. Maybe he'd worn those shirts for so long that he wasn't comfortable in anything else. Or maybe at some point, years ago, he decided he'd found the ultimate shirt and bought a gross of them—that seemed like the kind of thing he'd do—and now he couldn't bring himself to throw them out and start over. The very rich, Mark had read, were sometimes thrifty in eccentric, unnecessary ways, just to keep in some kind of emotional touch with the actual value of a dollar.

Still, it wasn't that he was trying to fit in, exactly. That kind of social insecurity seemed foreign to Hadi. He wasn't concerned with being accepted, and he probably wouldn't have cared that much if he knew he was laughed at. It was more about learning a language, a system, mastering it in all its aspects. It was about making a study.

"Barrett's just cleaning up," Mark said, even though they could both hear him upstairs. He was singing. "I'm sorry for the inconvenience."

"No inconvenience," Hadi said.

"I'm sorry your wife was inconvenienced, then."

"Well, look, that's not such a bad thing every once in a while. It gives her an excuse to go someplace she likes, a place I can't stand. Good for her, good for me. A little fresh air."

He opened two more beers.

"You don't mind the solitude?" Mark said.

"Solitude has its potentialities," Hadi said. "Solitude is great if you know how to use it."

The kitchen was spotless. In his months on the job, Mark had sometimes seen the two Hadi children, but when they were not present, there was rarely any visible sign of their living there.

"And they kind of hold you back," Mark said. He was maybe drunker than he should have been. It didn't take much, with him. "Wives. Or at least you're most yourself when they're not around. Don't you think that's true?"

Hadi didn't look offended, or uncomfortable. "That second thing you said. That's probably true."

Mark tried to remember the second thing he'd said. "So what do you think?" he said instead. "What do you think of our little town?"

"It's a special place," Hadi said. "Unspoiled. Very serene. Of course, I see more now, living here, than I saw before. But that vulnerability just makes it more interesting to me."

Vulnerability? "Hey, speaking of," Mark said, "looks like that second terrorist attack in New York City you were predicting never actually happened."

Why were the things coming out of his mouth so disrespectful-sounding, all of a sudden? He didn't mean it. He was trying for camaraderie, actually, but then this other note was bubbling up from somewhere.

"Thank God," Hadi said.

"Yes, of course, thank God," Mark echoed, and held out his bottle, which Hadi touched with his own. "All I meant was, you told me way back when that you were moving up here to avoid that danger, and then the danger never came, so I hope that doesn't mean you think it was a mistake moving up here, or that you regret it."

Hadi went to the fridge and handed Mark another; the more nervous Mark felt, apparently, the faster he drank. "No, of course not," Hadi said. "First of all, risk is not binary. Just because something doesn't happen, that doesn't mean you were wrong to have protected yourself against the likelihood of it happening. You understand what I mean?"

"Sure," Mark said.

"And second, this place is home to me now. This is where I belong right now. The only thing I left behind in New York is the obligation to spend time with a lot of people I really never enjoyed spending time with anyway. Here I have no social obligations of any kind. People don't think of me in that way."

Mark heard an inexplicably loud noise from upstairs.

"And it's good for work in that sense too," Hadi went on. "I'm completely isolated. I'm in my head. No distractions unless I choose them, which I sometimes do, but usually not. It's like the home itself is my head."

Mark had heard that before, from his wife, but he thought it would be impolite to mention. Hadi probably didn't appreciate being told that any of his thoughts weren't original ones. Mark wondered why he didn't ever feel like his own head was his house, or his house was his head, or however it worked.

"So let me ask you something," Mark said. "Since the job is over today and I don't know when I might get to talk to you again, even though we're neighbors or whatever."

"What's that?" Hadi asked calmly. They heard Barrett's footsteps on the landing upstairs.

"What am I doing wrong?" Mark said. "I mean, in your opinion."

"In my opinion you're not doing anything wrong."

"No, I mean . . . I've been trying to think how to improve my position. To improve my lot. I know I'm never going to live like you. But so much of life seems so bound, so limited. I want to reimagine myself."

"You want to make more money," Hadi said.

"Yes. And I know that I don't possess the same skills you have. But it's more than that. I feel like something is lacking in me, in terms of personality, in terms of vision. So it may sound weird, but I was wondering if you had any advice, any words of wisdom, for somebody in my position."

First half of a ladder, then Barrett, then the second half of the ladder passed across the kitchen doorway behind Hadi's chair. The front door opened and closed, and they heard the sound of the ladder being tossed—probably from some distance, knowing Barrett—into the bed of Mark's truck.

"We can't be envying each other's positions," Hadi said. "Your role is as necessary as mine. If you were bad at what you do, or hated it, that would be one thing. But in my opinion we are both right where we belong. My advice to you would be not to be so dismissive of something you do so well. Easier said than done, I know."

"But this is America," Mark said, coloring. What a thing to say. Obviously it was America. If it weren't, a man like him wouldn't be sitting in the kitchen of a man like Hadi; a man like Hadi probably wouldn't have existed at all. But the America thing seemed to explain how he felt, or maybe he was just using it to defend who he was, what he wanted. "You're supposed to better yourself. You're supposed to think big. Right?"

Hadi sighed. "If you want to do something else besides restore houses, then by all means you should. Life's too short to waste time. I'm just saying, don't devalue what you do just because others make more money than you. We are parts of an ecosystem. It relies on you in the same way it relies on me."

Barrett let the door slam as he came back into the house; Mark turned around and saw him in the kitchen doorway, grinning. "All finished upstairs," he said. "Another two hours to dry, probably. Looks like I missed the after-party."

Hadi shrugged. "Still a beer or two left in the fridge, I think, if you're thirsty," he said.

"No," Mark said quickly, "thanks, but we should shove off." He'd seen Barrett after a beer or two, many times in fact, and it was not something he thought Hadi should be exposed to. Not to mention that he didn't want to let one of his employees drink a client's last beer. "All cleaned up upstairs?"

"Yes sir, boss," Barrett said. "Unless maybe you need me to clean up all these dead soldiers too."

"Dead soldiers?" Hadi said.

Barrett indicated the empty beer bottles.

"Huh," Hadi said. "Never heard that one."

Barrett turned and went back outside to the driveway without a word. Mark saw that he had pissed him off. Well, whatever, as long as he was pissed off outside the client's house. He took a deep breath and turned to Hadi.

"I know your wife will be glad to see us gone," he said.

"You'll invoice me?"

"Sure will. Within the week. And of course if there's any problem, you know where to find me." He jerked his head in the direction of his house.

"Could probably just shine a light in your windows if I needed you," Hadi said.

"Yes sir." They shook hands, and Hadi walked him to the door. Mark had the impression Hadi felt a lot more done with him than he felt done with Hadi. But then at the door the older man spoke again:

"One thing I will say, in regard to the whole thinking-big idea. Houses are an asset, whose value you understand, and know how to increase."

"Right."

"But it occurs to me that as long as you're working on the inside of them, you can only be engaging the value of them one at a time, if you see what I mean. An investor knows how to stand outside a thing, see it in its context. See it whole."

Through the front door Hadi opened for him, Mark saw Barrett pacing back and forth in the driveway. He hadn't realized Barrett was still there, so he thanked Hadi again, pulled the door shut behind him, and walked quickly onto the fresh gravel.

"Need somebody to drive you home?" Barrett said. "You seem like you might be impaired."

He had a hard cast to his mouth and eyes. You could never tell what was going to set him off. Mark was just glad they were outside Hadi's earshot. "It's like five hundred yards," he said. "I think I can manage it, thanks."

"Righty-o, boss." There was that edgy, fight-picking overexuberance in his voice. Maybe Mark should have just let Hadi give him a beer. Why not? Why should Mark sit and drink with the client but not Barrett? Because Mark was the boss, that's why not. He suddenly understood a truth that cast Hadi's attitude during their conversation in a different light: you expected those above you to welcome your ascension into their company, to root for it, but you wanted those below you to be happy in their place.

"Where's the wife today?" Barrett asked.

"My wife?"

"No, man, his wife. Rachel. Rachel Rachel I've been thinking. We don't even get to say goodbye."

"She's out. She doesn't want to be in the house when we're painting."

"When who's painting?"

"You know what I mean. She doesn't like to see people tearing up the place."

"Doesn't trust herself with me in the bedroom, eh?"

Mark stopped talking.

"I know what she needs. I doubt that geek does. Anyway, he's got you to suck his balls all day, so what does he care?"

"Okay," Mark said, putting out a hand toward the small of Barrett's back, but not touching him. "Let's just get on the road, we shouldn't be hanging out in their driveway like—"

"I would hit that," Barrett said. "I would hit it with great vigor. Maybe I still will."

"Okay, champ," Mark said, climbing into the cab of his truck.

"On the surveillance cameras," Barrett said cryptically, grinning like an idiot.

"Okay. Time to go."

"So when's our next job?" Barrett said.

Mark paused. "We talked about this," he said. "I don't have anything for you right now. Working on a couple of things. But this job's done and now we have a break before the next one. Thank God there was this one, the way the economy's been."

"Yeah," Barrett said. "Thank God."

They rolled single file down the long driveway, slowly because Mark's truck was in front, and turned right on Route 4, in the direction of Mark's house. He'd forgotten about Barrett already. He was trying to remember that last thing Hadi had said, about standing outside. He turned into his driveway; Barrett honked twice at him, jauntily, then floored it past Mark's house and down the empty road.

He slowed down in town but once he was across 7 he opened it up again. As if he really had been drinking, instead of being treated like a little boy. See? he thought. See, you smug asshole? I don't need a few beers to act wild. I can act wild at any time. He fucking hated that guy—Mark Firth—and particularly hated feeling dependent on him, like he felt right now, dependent on the money from this six-month gig that should have lasted Barrett and his wife through the winter but wasn't likely to. Tomorrow he'd go to Pittsfield and get back on unemployment. Tomorrow or the next day. He hit the radio but there was no good driving music on so he switched it off again and rolled down the windows and let the green roar fill the cab. The air was sweet and cold. It was still fall.

Fuck Mark. He thought the world of himself. And could he have

125

glued his lips any more firmly to the ass of that Hadi guy? Why, just because he was rich? That was exactly why. Mark worshiped those people. He thought they were like royalty. When the fact was that those people got rich precisely by looking at two guys like Mark and Barrett and seeing no difference between them at all. Yet Mark, that clueless douche, was afraid lest Hadi's hand be sullied by passing Barrett a beer. Barrett didn't really even want to do the guy's wife, she was nothing special, but he couldn't resist saying it just for the look he knew it would put on Mark's face, and boy, was he rewarded. Like he was some kind of commoner who'd suggested putting it to the queen.

He'd done Mark's sister, back in high school. Actually he hadn't, but he almost had, and he preferred to embellish the memory, just for imaginary revenge's sake.

Why not have a beer? Why not have one right fucking now? He pulled into the packie just south of Great Barrington and bought a six from the hostile owner who sat behind the register in a ratty old office chair on casters. He always looked like you were trying to cheat him somehow, even though he was the one counting out your change, so go figure that out. Barrett popped one, stuck it between his thighs, and put the bag down on the passenger seat.

Not going straight home was actually a gesture of consideration toward his wife, considering the mood he was in. If she could see him right now, she'd know: she'd give him her blessing to stay out until he could cool off and come home in a less volatile state. She'd give it as much for her own sake as for his. But of course she couldn't see him right now, she could only sit at home and get mad wondering where he was. And that meant she would be in an extra bitchy frame of mind whenever he did walk in. Which made him stay out longer. Life was like a loop, a Catch-22, a cycle you couldn't break in which the same things happened over and over, and yet somehow you got older anyway. How fucked up was that?

He had the idea that he was headed somewhere, like maybe up

to Adams or even the state line, but all he was really doing was driving in a wide, half-assed circle as he looked for safe places to throw the empties out the window. By the time he was ready to pop number five he decided that he might as well get off the road and see what was doing at the Ship.

The money: you might as well blow it, right? You might as well forget about making it last as long as possible, because there was no way to make it last long enough, and so all scrimping and saving did was put you in a shitty mood every day until the inevitable happened anyway, turn every day into a petty humiliation until the day finally came when you zeroed out like you knew you were going to all along. So why not zero out on your own schedule? Then at least you were living, you weren't some fucking Mark Firth out begging for rich assholes to hire you, making budgets and then asking permission to go over budget or whatever the fuck. And trying to restore some of your lost manhood by acting like the big condescending boss man with guys who'd agreed to do the actual work for you, guys who knew you when you were fifteen and could have kicked your ass as easily then as they could have now.

He was in enough of a state that there was another guy standing at the bar who he thought for a moment was Mark. He did look a lot like Mark, but fatter, less prissy-looking. The guy caught him staring.

"Tough day?" the guy said, and all of a sudden it hit Barrett who he was: fucking Mark's brother. How do you like that. Firths everywhere. He couldn't remember the brother's name.

"Laid off today," Barrett said. "Out celebrating the way of the world."

The brother smiled ruefully. "The rich get richer," he said.

"Like I said, the way of the world."

"Maybe not, though," Gerry said. "Maybe it wasn't supposed to be like this, but we just accept it. If you forget the past, then it's like hey, I guess things have just always been the way they are right now."

"Um, whatever."

Gerry smiled. "Things are fucked, is my point," he said, "so we un-fucked have to stick together." He summoned Slade the bartender with one finger, and put a twenty down on the bar. "That's for my tab," he said, "and a round for my brother here."

"I sure ain't your brother," the guy said, "but thanks."

Gerry walked out to the lot. It made him feel pretty good every time he got into his car at the end of the night still relatively sober. A small measure of control, but control nevertheless. By the time he got home he felt how much he needed to sleep—he hadn't been getting enough sleep, he hadn't even really been trying—but as usual he got online first and then before you knew it, it was the pit of the night.

It had started with just idly tooling through some of the websites whose links his sister Renee was always bcc'ing him—typical Renee-drama, like the list had to be secret, in case they were all rounded up and tortured for the names of the friends of Renee Firth Tomlinson, famous housewife-revolutionary. Some of the sites were flat-out insane. Tonight she'd sent him a link to something on InfoWars about how the Defense Department was suppressing evidence of bin Laden's whereabouts: leaked memos proved that they had a budgetary interest in keeping bin Laden alive, because as long as he was alive, they would get whatever money they asked for. Gerry didn't believe a word of it. But he was also aware of not wanting to believe it, and his not wanting to believe it made his disbelief seem suspect, knee-jerk. It was scary to open your eyes too wide to the world. He bookmarked it to read again later, when he was less tired, and logged in to Little Green Footballs for a while.

Renee emailed him again; it wasn't as late out there, but it was still pretty late. *Did u read it?* "U" instead of "you," like the nanosecond that saved her was so important to her day, like she was so busy that it was a big sacrifice just to stop what she was doing and write to you. *Not yet,* he wrote back. *Just got home. Hold your horses.*

"Warblogs" was a term he'd learned through her; the first time he saw it, he'd thought it referred somehow to blogs that warbled. They were interesting up to a point. I mean, America had real enemies, you could hardly deny that now, even if the notion that these enemies were swarming at the gates of Colorado Springs was a little bit laughable. Colorado Springs probably had even fewer Muslims in it than the Berkshires. Something was happening, though. You followed the links where they led and the sense you got—slowly sobering up in your living room, in the lamplight and black silence of the middle of the night—was of something weakening, giving way. The paranoia, the sense of helplessness, of being overwhelmed, was self-fulfilling. And when that happened, your weakness became apparent, and you really were ripe for attack.

And there was no better representation of the connectedness of things than the internet. It was a world inside the world, a counterforce to one's sense of events as random or uncontrolled. There were a lot of lunatics. You didn't have to engage with them, but in the aggregate all that lunacy meant something, was a symptom of something that couldn't be harnessed. You dismissed it at your peril. The best part was feeling that you were anonymous out there but had an identity at the same time. He'd started out as Baystater76, though lately he'd grown to worry that even that revealed too much; he was thinking about a new name.

You forgot the house was empty when you were in that other world; you forgot it wasn't fully paid for and not particularly clean. If he felt like he had a romantic or sexual prospect anywhere, he might have taken care of the place a bit better. But he didn't. Once, a couple of years ago, not long after the whole Lindsey thing, Candace had come over unannounced and, after an awkward ten minutes or so during which she didn't sit down, she started cleaning—his shower, his baseboards, his nasty fridge, everything. He was sort of offended at the time, and in fact they'd had a little fight about it, but now he hoped it would happen again at some point. In fact that could fairly be described as his plan.

Every once in a while the intimations of decadence and rot, though generated by solitude, would jump the borders of his virtual world and make an appearance in the real one, particularly the world of his work. There was a guy who drove a school bus in Ancram: in December he came with his wife to an open house for a four-bedroom modern on six acres in Egremont—which was fine, it happened all the time, people came to high-end open houses to gawk or to research property values or even just to act out a pathetic little fantasy that they were successful enough to be able to live in an upscale place like this, which was listed at $295K. No harm done, he didn't mind humoring them for a few minutes, supporting their play-acting questions about taxes and solar heat. Then two days later the bus driver shows up at Gerry's office and he's holding a check. Paid list for the place. Gerry thought for a moment that maybe the guy was literally, unamusingly crazy. He was reluctant even to ask Alina to print him out a contract.

But you couldn't discourage buyers just because you didn't know everything about them. Maybe the bus driver's wife had a rich aunt or something. Sure enough, the sale—and Gerry's commission—turned out to be real after all. When he told Alina, who was the only other person in the office that early (Gerry had found it in himself lately to start showing up on time), there was a little polite flicker of a smile but she didn't seem to share his enthusiasm. She was very weird around him now, even when, as on that morning, there was nobody else around to put on an act for.

A lot of that mid-priced housing stock that was such a bitch to unload—rich people didn't want it, locals couldn't afford it—was all of a sudden in play. Even 225 Valley Road, that legendary dud where Gerry and Alina had hooked up, found a taker. Gerry had his best quarter in . . . well, he hadn't previously kept track of such things too carefully, but it had to be one of his best quarters ever. One night in March he was sitting at the bar in the Ship, absorbed in his laptop—they'd just gotten wi-fi in there, which made it a little harder to leave some evenings—when a guy tapped him on the shoulder from behind.

"Are you Gerry Firth?" the guy said. He was young, maybe still in his twenties, a little soft-looking around the jaw, and he had an earring. Trying to be something he wasn't.

"I am," Gerry said, closing the laptop. He'd been flaming some guy on Daily Kos who wanted to talk about Al Gore and global warming.

"You work at the Century 21 in Stockbridge?"

"I do," said Gerry. He should have been more patient—a good salesman could turn it on and off in any situation—but he didn't feel like it now, and this was a pretty inappropriate time and venue for a business inquiry, let's face it. He was smiling as gamely as he could and reaching for his wallet to pull out a business card for the morning when the guy wound up and threw a punch at him. It was apparently the first punch he'd thrown in a long while, maybe ever—the windup went way behind his head—but even though Gerry had that instant to move out of the way, it still glanced off the bone right by his eye, and it stung like a bitch. Gerry put his hand to his face to check for blood but it was too dark to see, while the guy took an ambiguous step backward and Slade the bartender flipped up the counter and ran toward the action.

"Come on, big man!" the guy yelled at Gerry, after Slade was between them. "Fucking piece of shit! Putting your hands on another man's wife!"

Gerry put his hands up in front of him, trying to calm the guy down. He wasn't going to hit him. He couldn't get banned from the Ship, for one thing. "Who's your wife?" he asked, which he realized a second too late was not the best thing he could have said.

"Jesus!" the guy squeaked. Slade was facing him, holding him by the upper arms, but loosely, because it was clear now that the one punch was all he had come here to throw. "You're a fucking predator!"

"I'm a man," Gerry said. He was trying to gin up some testosterone, mostly because some of the people watching were people he knew. But the guy was such a weasel. Even if you pounded him in self-defense you'd be in the wrong. He looked on the verge of cathartic tears now. He was trying to be inconspicuous about shaking off the pain in his hand. What a fallen world this was, Gerry thought, in which this passed for a bar fight. A fight over a woman, no less. It had probably taken this poor wuss hours, or days, to work up the nerve to track down the man who may or may not have fucked his wife and throw a mostly symbolic punch at him; surely it had not gone at all like he'd imagined it. "Throw him out, would you please?" Gerry said.

"I'm leaving," the guy said, and Slade casually let him go. "But this isn't over, motherfucker."

"Better luck next time," Gerry said, and turned back to his laptop and his beer. He was positive the guy was just mouthing off, trying to save face on his way out the door, but about that he was mistaken. The man with the earring was, as Gerry had started to figure out toward the end of their encounter, Alina's husband; the next day, Alina wasn't at work, and the day after that she came in sporting a bruise on her face that, even covered in makeup, was way worse than Gerry's. Adrenaline hit him like a thunderbolt. She wouldn't meet his gaze, but when Kimbrough came over to her desk and whispered to her, she got up with him and the two of them went down the block to get coffee. There was no privacy for them in the one-room office, and whatever she had to say, she didn't want anyone else there to hear it.

She returned alone, red-faced, and walked to her desk, not holding a cup of coffee. Kimbrough, following her, did not allow the door to close behind him; he beckoned Gerry out into the parking lot, using just one finger. It was raining.

"Did you have a relationship, a personal relationship, with an employee of Kimbrough Century 21?" Kimbrough said.

Gerry made the mistake of smiling at the self-regard in the boss's super-serious demeanor, as if he were a lawyer, as if they were in front of an audience. Kimbrough didn't even seem that mad—just self-consciously solemn, like a bad actor.

"She's an adult," Gerry said.

"And did the two of you carry out this relationship in a home belonging to a client, a home listed by us for sale?"

Jesus. She'd held nothing back, clearly. So stupid.

"No," he said instinctively. "That's not true. She's lying."

Kimbrough nodded. "You're fired," he said.

Gerry's mouth fell open.

"You're seriously surprised?" Kimbrough said. "You can't go around banging the secretary. You have any idea what that opens us up to, in terms of liability? She could shut us down. I could lose my franchise."

"Did she say I forced her or something?"

"No. Well, arguably. She's the victim here, that much is plain."

"You're right," Gerry said, reddening. "You're right. She is the victim. So let's you and me get in your car right now and go find that impotent fucking wife-beating husband of hers and lay him out. Lay him the fuck out. That's what you and I should be doing, if you actually give a shit about her."

"Be serious," Kimbrough said.

"I've never been more serious. What kind of a world is this? What kind of men are we? We're fucking lost. Getting sued, that's seriously your first thought in this situation?"

"Gerry," Kimbrough said. "Look, leave aside for a moment how incredibly stupid it was to get involved with somebody you're technically in a position of power over, somebody younger than you. You guys did it in a home we were commissioned to sell. I'm not just worried about what she might do. If this gets out, the client could take us for everything, do you understand that? Not just you. I could lose my license. In fact I almost definitely would. You have put every single job here at risk. People with families. You cannot honestly be shocked that I'm firing you."

It was cold out there but Gerry was trying hard not to fold his arms. Unlike Kimbrough, he didn't have his blazer on. "Fine," he said. "Then fire her too."

Kimbrough laughed. "Sorry, no," he said. "If the idea is to keep her from suing for harassment, that wouldn't be such a hot maneuver."

"How is her offense any different from mine?"

"She's the victim here," Kimbrough said again.

"That is such PC bullshit. We're both adults. We both work for you, we both did the exact same thing at the same time, completely consensually. You could argue that she's worse than me, because she did it while she was married. But she's the victim and I'm the oppressor because, what, she's a woman?"

"Classy," Kimbrough said coldly. "Right under the bus with her. The marriage is over now, by the way, so she tells me. So good going there too."

"You're a spineless pussy, you know that?" Gerry said. He was starting to panic. "I should sue you, since fear of that seems to be what you have in place of a conscience."

"Knock yourself out," Kimbrough said. "That one, I'm sure I could get dismissed. In the meantime I'm giving you five minutes to go back inside and get your shit and go home."

The look on his face was unbearable; after the hard part, which was the firing, his nervousness had quickly given way to a smug sense of triumph. Gerry flirted with the idea of just dropping him with one punch, right there in the wet parking lot. What's the worst that could happen, now that he already didn't have a job? Unfortunately that question had a real answer. He'd call the cops and Gerry would get arrested. Guys like Kimbrough always hid behind the law. That's why there were so many fucking laws. Gerry walked past him and back inside, his hair plastered to his head by the rain. No one in the office was speaking; everyone stared angrily at him. Angrily! He couldn't believe it. This was not a world of men. That line popped into his head, from *Glengarry Glen Ross,* one of his all-time favorite movies: I swear to you, Machine, it is not a world of men. He loved that movie but he'd never understood that line until just now.

He'd had sex with her twenty or thirty different times, yet not only did that create no sort of bond between them now, it seemed if anything to accomplish the opposite, to make them intolerable to each other. He had no residual positive feeling toward her at all—only a derision he could barely contain, and then, as he scooped the few contents of his desk drawers into a small white wastebasket-liner whose previous contents he'd dumped onto the floor, he thought, Why contain it? Why be silent? For whose sake? "You're a cheating whore," he said to her from across the dumbstruck office, "and I wouldn't mind that, but you're a hypocrite too. You care about no one but yourself. Do the world a favor and don't have kids." She burst into tears and turned her back; one of the other brokers went over to console her. Smooth move, dude, Gerry thought, now she'll probably let you fuck her too. He grabbed the garbage bag and his yellow blazer. He was feeling a little of the high you were supposed to feel when you got fired and made a scene on your way out the door, but mostly he just felt isolated and small. What world were these people living in? Nothing made sense, morally. It used to but it didn't now. He dropped the whole trash bag full of his belongings into a different wastebasket, by the door. Outside, he spread the yellow blazer carefully on the puddled asphalt just behind his car and backed over it on his way out. He didn't have to turn his head—he knew they were all watching. He honked the horn twice and drove home.

Her, his victim? What had he done, raped her? Is that what he was supposed to believe now? This was the hilarious part: even though the reason the two of them had connected in the first place was that they were exactly alike, now he was instantly presumed to be the opposite of her, the bad guy. Why, because he was white and male? That was his supposed position of power? He thought that was pretty rich, as he stalked back and forth through the shabby rooms of his half-assed house, jobless, with no savings, nothing. Gerry the Powerful!

He went online and scrolled through Drudge for a while: illegal immigrants collecting welfare, the ACLU suing to get terrorists released from Guantánamo. Everybody shouting their innocence. He went to Daily Kos and got into it with some liberal clowns in the comments section. He was looking for catharsis but it didn't work, it was all just words. He told himself he wouldn't drink. Two days later, not having left home once, he was telling himself the same thing. Then he got a notice from the post office telling him he had to come in and sign for some piece of registered mail. He wasn't expecting anything, so it seemed unlikely to be good news, but he figured it couldn't hurt to get some air into his lungs other than the fetid air of his dusty home. He went to the counter with his little green notice and rang the bell, summoning that weird loser with the pretentious facial hair who worked there. The guy disappeared again for a moment and brought back a letter addressed to Gerry from the Assessor's Office of the Town of Howland and he ripped it open right there on the spot, letting the fragments of paper fall on the floor.

Gerry's home had been reassessed, mysteriously, anonymously, which suggested the outcome was a foregone conclusion; and, shocker, it was now magically worth more than it had been when he woke up in it that morning. Like the town government knew more than Gerry did about the value of his home, about the value of any home in the Berkshires! His property taxes had gone up by six hundred dollars annually. Just like that. Just because they could do it. There was a form letter from that idiot Maeve Brennan—who held power now not because the people had elected her but because fat old Marty Solomon had dropped dead in somebody's basement—explaining that this reassessment was prompted by the newly tax-exempt status of the Caldwell House, but he didn't do that bullshit excuse the honor of reading it all the way to the end.

"Sucks, right?" said the guy behind the counter, with the little US Postal Service emblem on the sleeve of his blue zip-up sweater. Gerry lifted his gaze.

"I mean not that I read it. Of course. But I've seen like twenty people open that same notice this week, so I know what's in there."

"Do you," Gerry said. "Let me ask you something. How much do you get paid?"

"I'm sorry?" Glenn said.

"What's your salary? I mean before taxes." That last bit was said with something of a sneer, Glenn thought.

"I think that's kind of private," he said.

"Actually it's not. It's public record, since I'm the one who pays it, me and everyone else in this town. That's where this tax revenue goes."

"Actually, I think it's earmarked for the school budget," Glenn said.

"I thought you didn't read it."

He'd read Penny's, when it came three days ago. But he couldn't very well say that. "Postal service salaries are federally mandated anyway."

"I'll bet they are. So what?"

"So it's apples and oranges," Glenn said, without quite knowing what he meant. He tried to smile, to keep it friendly.

"No, it's all one big fucking apple, is what it is," the angry guy

137

said, and he turned and banged the door open with the flat of his hand and was gone.

What an asshole, Glenn thought. Not for the first time that day, either. There'd been some woman in earlier who wanted to negotiate with him the price of sending a piece of certified mail, which was like, what? Did she think he had anything to do with it? Yeah, okay, lady, he thought as he drove back to Penny's at the end of the afternoon (his lips moving as he drove, to help him imagine his retort), tonight after dinner when I sit down for brandy and cigars with the Postmaster General, I'll be sure to bring up your complaint. Maybe you'll get a refund from him. How do you spell your name again?

In fact he was having dinner tonight with Penny's boys. It wasn't a regular occurrence but it had happened a few times now. It had all come about more or less by chance; one Wednesday afternoon earlier that winter, Penny's ex-husband had called her from the emergency room in Stockbridge to say that he'd been in a car accident, so could she please pick the boys up from basketball practice and take them for that night? She called Glenn at work—it was already past four—and told him he would have to spend that night in Springfield; and could he please leave work a little early and get his car and the rest of his shit out of her home, just for tonight, the boys' practice ended in twenty minutes, she wouldn't have time to go home first herself and do it. They got into a little bit of a fight about it—federal law, for one thing, prohibited his locking up the post office early on a whim—and then out of nowhere she just said, "You know what, fine, who cares," and that was the night he finally met Henry and Carl. They were wonderfully impolite to him— seriously, their utter lack of manners put him immediately at ease—asking him who he was and was he Mommy's boyfriend and where did he sleep and how come they'd never heard of him before. He answered all their questions while Penny sat eating quietly.

Then the three of them went into the living room and played Mario Kart while she stayed in the kitchen and smoked.

He knew she didn't really want all of them to get that close, and that was because she didn't see him as someone who would be around forever. It was a little insulting, but in truth he didn't really think of her all that differently. It wasn't only the certainty of rejection that kept him from ever suggesting that they take their relationship to some next level. In the meantime, he wasn't going to resist the boys' efforts to get along with him, to include him; what would be the point of that? He sometimes wondered how they described him to their dad. That's if they'd mentioned his existence at all. But, knowing them, he bet they had.

For their sake he did his best to put the trials of his workday behind him and walk into Penny's house in an upbeat frame of mind, but the atmosphere quickly soured anyway when it emerged that he'd forgotten, somehow, that tonight was parent-teacher conference night at their school, which meant that he'd be alone with Henry and Carl for a couple of hours. Penny couldn't believe that he'd forgotten, that it meant that little to him. She'd told him five times. He wasn't even aware enough to be nervous about it—his first time alone with his girlfriend's kids, ever. He was a kid himself. Same old story, she thought. There was the man you wanted, and then there was the man you got.

She sat in the car while it warmed up, looking at the bright windows of her home against the disappearing shadows of the woods and hills beyond. It was only about six o'clock. The house itself was an accident; it had belonged to David before they met, and then she got it in the divorce, and so now it was her house. She backed out onto Route 4 and took the county roads to the school, the shorter route, past ambiguous stripped woods and fallow farms, concentrating on the tunnel of light the car made through it all, never once meeting anyone coming in the opposite direction, so her brights stayed on. Every crack and pit in the asphalt showed up in the light as if being interrogated; the road itself looked hard worn, like it had been put together from pieces of other roads. The colors didn't even match. Stop signs glared at the intersections, and she observed them, though she didn't need to. You had to observe them, just as you had to stay between the yellow lines even when there was no reason to. Craziness was right there, waiting for a word from you, a nod. Another winter in the middle of fucking nowhere.

Penny rolled into the half-full parking lot (it was never more than half full; it had been built back in the sixties when they still expected the regional population to go up) and cut the engine. She gave herself an instinctive once-over in the mirror on the back of the window visor; she would likely run into half the town in there. She marched off across the dark lot toward the floodlit front steps of Howland Elementary.

It looked like they all do. A long, featureless rectangle, lots of windows, a sort of tower in the center where the steps led up to the main entrance, the whole edifice in the posture of a kneeling mother with her arms spread wide to keep you from getting past her. Or an eagle, maybe, or an insignia on a coat of arms. An institutional beige. No relation to the lot on which it sat or the landscape against which it had been built. Across the street were playing fields, but no more than fifty feet from any edge of the school building itself, the lot reverted to scrawny woods. You had to go pretty deep into those woods before you could consider yourself truly hidden, as each generation's edgy subset of middle schoolers learned anew. The structure's most remarkable feature was that it sat only about a thousand yards from the district high school, which looked almost identical and had been built at the same time, in some sort of orgy of public works. Thus there was no mystery, for the students, as to where their yearly promotions were leading them. Any time you were out front, waiting for the bus or crossing the street for sports, you could point right to it.

Inside, the light was mind-frying and there were three PTA moms at a card table, each cheerfully responsible for one-third of the alphabet. Penny recognized one of them, though all three seemed to recognize her. "Penny!" the one on the left said, and urgently waved her closer. "Come, come! I've got the B's!" She gave Penny an adhesive nametag, already filled out, and a schedule that granted her four minutes at a time with each of the boys' five teachers. So forty minutes in total—closer to sixty, because there were some breaks built in—but when it was all written out like that, it seemed like more than she should be asked to endure.

"Coffee in the teachers' lounge on the second floor!" Mrs. Stepford shouted. Coffee was the wrong instinct entirely. Having been to these perfunctory conference-nights before, knowing exactly what to expect, Penny would have shown up comfortably tanked for sure if she didn't have to drive. Her nervousness had nothing to do with her sons' academic progress or lack thereof. Here was the thing: listening to a series of other people, almost all of them women, women she didn't even know, talk knowledgeably about her children—give her advice, offer her their half-assed opinions about what was best for them and what was not—sometimes made her start to cry. Literally. It had happened before. "Carl is a good boy," some fat idiot with hair like Prince Valiant had told her, "and he can handle this level of material, but only if his study habits improve," and Penny had barely made it outside the building and into her car before she'd started sobbing. She did not like other people to talk about her boys. She did not like to be confronted with the fact that there was no way to hide them forever from the world, no way to keep them from being exposed to the soulless predations of smug grownups.

So by the time she reached the next-to-last appointment, in Henry's animal-bio classroom with the cloudy beakers stacked on the counters against the wall, she was already looking toward the finish line. The bio teacher was a somewhat mousy-looking chick whose nametag read Ms. Firth. Penny recognized right away that Ms. Firth was as ready to be done with this whole evening as she was. Anyway, she tried to read Penny's name discreetly off her left tit and then commenced flipping through some papers on her desk, her cheeks reddening.

"Henry Batchelder," Penny said helpfully. "Short, kind of a mullet, wears videogame t-shirts a lot."

"Of course," the teacher said. "I'm so sorry, it's no reflection at all on Henry that I had a little brain freeze there. He's a great kid. It's just been a long night."

"I can imagine. It's been a long night for me and I only have my own kids' names to remember. To be honest there's no way I would have come up with yours if you weren't wearing it."

The teacher stuck out her hand and smiled with what looked like relief. "Candace," she said.

"Penny. So you're a science teacher, there's no way you could build like a margarita machine with all this crap in here?"

Candace laughed. "If only," she said. She was happy to drop her formal demeanor, maybe unwisely; but it was not only because she liked this loose cannon of a mom, though she did. Her defenses were down. "Anyway, Henry is one of my favorites. He's funny but he's never disruptive; if he's not interested you can see him try his best to get interested. He's got a solid B and he works hard for that. I like him."

Henry's mother continued to stare at her, smiling, and Candace realized she had run out of things to say about the boy. Some kids were geniuses and some were nightmares, but if you were in that middle eighty or ninety percent, there just wasn't always four minutes' worth of stuff to say about you. Usually this wasn't an issue because the parents took over and did most of the talking. But here an awkward silence had taken shape. When Candace tried to think how to break it, she drew a blank.

"That's it?" the mother asked.

"Well," Candace said. "I do like to leave time for questions."

"Jesus Christ, you've made me so happy!" the mom said. "That's all I want to hear. That's all I care about. He's doing fine and nothing's wrong. To be honest some of these other teachers who go on and on about how they know your kid better than you do, for four solid minutes, it makes me want to pop them right in the mouth."

"Well—"

"Like that English teacher! What an asshole!"

"Well, okay," Candace said, worrying she'd let things go too far. Though she bet she knew which English teacher was being referred to. "I'm glad to give you a respite from all of that."

"I mean I don't mean to put it all on you teachers. I'm sure you get some batshit parents coming through here."

Candace knew she shouldn't answer. But it had been a rough night, for reasons she could never tell anybody, so she needed to talk about something else, just to redirect the thoughts in her own head.

"I had a mother in here once," she said. "Wanted to know if I was teaching her daughter about the theory of evolution. I wanted to say well, it's not so much a theory anymore, you may have heard. But I just said not yet, we haven't gotten to evolution yet, they won't start the human-bio unit until next fall, thinking that would pacify her, you know? Then she says, can you prove it? Meaning evolution. I said we only get four minutes, but if you'd like I could recommend some excellent scientific sources. She says, I thought so."

"Nice," Henry's mother said.

"So she says, if one explanation of what we're doing here on earth is a theory, and the other explanation is the word of God, then it makes sense to her that we'd only be teaching one of those, but you picked the wrong one. I said ma'am, I certainly respect your beliefs, and she said like hell you do, and they're not beliefs, they're God's word."

It had been pretty upsetting at the time, but they were both laughing now.

"You gotta be careful with those people, though," the mother said cryptically. "I work for a bunch of doctors. Ob-gyns, some of them."

Candace let her face compose. "How do you mean?"

She shrugged. "Some people really come to life when they have an enemy," she said.

"Excuse me?" said a voice from the doorway, and Candace started, though the mother did not. "I don't want to rush you. But they make this schedule so tight."

"Not a problem," Henry's mother said, and she stood up quickly, offered a brief smile that put Candace in mind of someone flicking their brights on and off, and left the classroom without another word. Past her came the woman from the doorway, trailed by her husband, who, like a lot of the husbands, wore a blandly cooperative expression that made it clear he had checked out some time ago.

It was rare to see fathers at these conferences at all—rarer than it should have been, at least, in this day and age. Which was why Candace had been so disarmed to see her former lover Patrick walk into her classroom, behind his wife, earlier that evening. He wasn't as surprised as Candace was; she could tell from the look of grim phoniness on his face that he'd known she was going to be sitting there. How could he not know? She was his daughter's science teacher. He couldn't be as remote from his own family's life as all that, despite his many past dishonest vows to the contrary.

"Ms. Firth," Patrick's wife had said. Candace damn well knew her name but was not going to use it, even in her head. She'd seen the wife plenty of times before, but they'd never actually met. Now she stood and the two women gingerly shook hands. The fact that Candace had been rehearsing that moment in her head all day—to be honest, on and off all semester, ever since she'd seen that Bayley Kimball was enrolled in her animal-bio class—did nothing to slow her heart or dull her panic, which she only hoped she was managing to keep off her face. On Patrick's face was a stricken, apologetic look Candace guessed was meant to convey that he knew how awful this was yet felt powerless to stop it. On the wife's face, a plastic formal decorousness. Candace did not worry that that look was concealing anything: she knew enough about that marriage to be certain the wife knew nothing, suspected nothing, had been told nothing by her husband. The mask of politeness was just a mask she wore all the time.

"Bayley enjoys your class so much," the wife said. "She talks to us about it constantly." From that ground-softening lie she went on to question a recent B-plus Bayley had received on a lab assignment. The truth was that the girl had deserved a B, but Candace was so guiltily conscious of disliking Bayley, both on her own sorry merits and because of her status as living reminder of what a fool Candace had been and still was, that she graded her more generously than any other student in the class. And then resented her for unknowingly receiving special treatment. God, Candace thought, while the wife yammered on, I am an awful person. Although at least when I was in seventh grade I didn't make other girls cry.

Patrick's childish fidgeting mirrored what Candace was trying to do invisibly with the entire force of her will: make four minutes go by. Anything, even this, could be endured for four measly minutes. He was very handsome. And stupid. The stupidity, the utter resourcelessness, was what made him so hard to turn away from. You just knew what you could reduce him to.

And then it was over; and at the end of it, she stood and he stood and they shook hands, while the wife watched. She got through the rest of her conferences somehow. Already she barely recalled most of them. She thought she might have said something a little inappropriate to Henry Batchelder's mother, but it was only a residual guilt, not a memory.

She drove home exhausted, taking Route 7 most of the way, which was slower and longer but the road was better lit. She pulled into the tiny lot across the street from the liquor store, which kept most of its interior lights blazing even when it was closed. She turned on all her living room and kitchen lights, and her TV, with the sound off. A triptych of heads, one yelling, the other two scowling, while scary reminders of the state of the world scrolled like stock prices beneath them. All in silence. She poured herself a glass of sauvignon blanc and watched the heads for a while. They were only moderately less alarming when you couldn't hear what they were saying. She poured another one. Like all her neighbors, she kept her shades down, not because there was nothing to look at outside, but because after a certain hour your windows just operated like mirrors anyway, and who wanted that?

She was glad she had no one to come home to. She didn't know why people were so sentimental about that. Oh, boohoo, poor Candace never married and has no one to come home to. But why was that something you wanted? To come home feeling like shit and then have to put on some act? She'd been putting on an act all night. Just let her quietly put herself to sleep with wine, thank you, without feeling all judged and self-conscious about it.

The heads gave way to a commercial. She could tell it was for some sort of drug by how long it went on, how protracted was the shot of the couple and their dog walking on a path through the woods. She was shaking, she remembered, after Patrick and the wife left her classroom. She held her hand out level in front of her: nope, no shaking now. She tried to think instead about all the other parents, but they blurred together, earnest, anxious, bored, ugly, ugly. Finally, when she was drunk enough not to question her own impulses, she stood abruptly, walked into her bedroom, and sat down at the little vanity table that just barely held her computer. She logged in to the old Hotmail account she'd used to communicate with Patrick, back in the day. She told herself that if there was nothing there, she would just close it again. But there was something there.

Hi Candy, I just wanted to say sorry about tonight, surprising you like that. Bayley's class schedule, which has been up on the fridge since August, still has Ms. Whalen's name on it for science. It wasnt until I got to school and they handed me the conference schedule that I saw your name. But at that point there was nothing I could do. I know you'll probably say I should know my own daughter's teachers names, but she's at the age where she doesn't hardly talk to us at all about school, or about anything. Anyway, I'm really sorry.

Candace let her eyes run over this communication a few times. There was nothing I could do, she thought: that's like your middle name. That'll be on your tombstone. Of course there was something he could have done, if he cared enough. Or if he really didn't want to see her. He just didn't have—well, she was going to say the balls, but he had balls, what he lacked was any imagination. Then, while she was still staring at the screen, his name came up again at the top of her inbox. Which meant he was staring at the screen himself, at this very moment. Probably because the wife had gone to bed. They were staring at each other, basically, through the medium of the screen, like two people on opposite sides of a darkened window.

I shouldn't have apologized so much—it makes it sound like I wasnt happy to see you. I was, just not about the circumstances. You look great. The situation wasnt ideal, obviously, but it was really good to see you.

Jesus, she thought. He was like a child. A big, dumb boy. He spent a lot of time apologizing for this or that, always had, but really he was ruled by nothing more than the balance of expediency and desire. You put him in front of something he wanted and he started wanting it, that's all. For instance, her. It was arousing, in the same way now as it had always been, to feel how incapable he was of being smart, of being prudent around her, even after all that had happened. Desire was desire: it did not learn.

You looked good too, she typed. *I mean, in a dead-man-walking sort of way.*

Lol, he answered immediately. *Yeah, I never did have much of a poker face. So here we are, back in touch again. Well, writing is okay, right? We can't get in too much trouble writing.*

She logged out of Hotmail and went back to the living room for another glass of sauvignon blanc, but she didn't get a third of the way through it before she fell asleep. She awoke in her chair, dawn glowing around the window shades; in front of her the news of the world silently flashed. She showered and dressed and went back to school. She taught the seventh graders about amino acids and proteins, the same dimly familiar lessons she'd heard at their age, the carboxyl group and the conjugate base. The only way to get through the lesson was to avoid looking at Bayley, or even at the side of the room on which Bayley always regally sat. Candace genuinely did not like that kid. Very phony and superior. A lot of her mother in her.

On Saturday she drove up to Pittsfield to pay her parents' bills. She didn't know for sure they had any bills to pay right at the moment, but she did know that they sometimes fell into a sort of mood or rut where they simply stopped opening their mail, letting weeks' worth of it pile up, going out faithfully to collect it from the box at the end of the driveway every afternoon but then just letting it sit in a neat stack on the dining room table, a development that baffled her utterly.

"I suppose I can take care of my own household," her father would say when she questioned him. "Been doing it since before you were around to save the day."

It made sense he'd react like that, lash out at her, scold her for her supposed pride because his own pride was injured. But other routines of the life they'd settled into were more alarming and harder to account for. Often when she opened the refrigerator door she was hit with the smell of rot—stuff had been left in the crispers and forgotten about. And he wouldn't touch it because, he said, "that's her job." A tangle of blankets on the living room couch suggested that he'd been sleeping there—how recently or how regularly, she didn't know. As for Candace's mother, she spent more and more time in the garden, and yet the garden looked like hell. He was so angry at her—for fading, basically, for growing older, which he seemed to see as disingenuous and a personal affront—and the angrier he got, the less she seemed to notice he was even there.

And the television. It was never, ever not on. She could remember being forcibly pushed outdoors, as a child, if she and her siblings got caught spending non-rainy daylight hours in front of the TV. Now it played so relentlessly it effaced whatever was outdoors, all sense of an outdoors. It used to be considered the opposite of the world, but now, in this house anyway, there was no outside world except that of the television, a world of outrage, calumny, tears and canned laughter, provocation, paranoia, sinister forces bent on taking away all you had worked for and earned, just because they wanted it, just because they said so. Why would you want to prepare to exit this life—for that was what Candace's parents seemed to be doing—to this harassing soundtrack of gloom? Maybe her father wanted to believe that it really had all been for nothing? Maybe that would make leaving it all behind seem less bitter somehow? He seemed pretty damn bitter nonetheless. She didn't get it.

"Daddy, I think there's stuff in here for a sandwich," she said. "Can I make you a ham sandwich?"

"I'd eat a sandwich," he said.

"Have you eaten yet today?"

He shrugged. She wasn't sure how to read it; he liked the drama of martyrdom.

"You have to eat," she said testily, her frustration getting the best of her. "What am I going to tell people, 'He died of malnutrition brought on by stubbornness'?"

"It's a wonder I can survive a whole day without you around," he said.

Her mother stomped the dirt off her shoes and came in through the kitchen's back door. She smiled happily. She took off her gloves, and hung up her coat, and then she stood in the center of the kitchen for a bit, still smiling.

"Pills," Candace's father said, between bites of his sandwich. The look on her mother's face was not that of having been reminded of something—of having heard, that is, another voice—but of having remembered it herself. She passed by them at the table and headed upstairs.

They all knew something was going on with her, but one of the things that made it easy to pretend otherwise was that her fogginess of mind was different only in degree, not in kind, from the way they'd always known her. She was never the type of mother who ran the proverbial tight ship. Their whole childhood was about reminding her of things: permission slips, clothes to be mended, games or parties to and from which they needed transportation. They took it for granted back then, they were protective of her—in large part because the flip side of her spaciness was that, provided Dad's attention was otherwise engaged, they could get away with murder. As teens they would fight over whose turn it was to sneak out of the house after bedtime, so little did they worry about getting caught. Now that impulse to protect her seemed gone in Candace's brothers—"That's just Mom," they'd say to her—and in truth it was not always easy to find it in herself.

"Work is getting me down a little lately," she said to her father, just to force a conversation with him that wasn't about him, and to cover the sounds of his chewing. "I had a whole curriculum for the spring, and then we're handed these new state tests and told the school's funding depends on how our students score. So anything you wanted to teach them that's not on that test goes right out the window."

"Thought you weren't teaching anymore."

"No, Daddy, I've been back to teaching this whole year. Ever since that Whalen girl had her stroke, remember that?"

He frowned. "Well, you know," he said. "That's government work."

"What?"

He pursed his lips as though he had said something self-evident.

"It's a job," she said. "They don't grow on trees, especially around here. We can't all be like Renee and just find some rich guy to marry."

"No, we cannot," her father said. Then, perhaps sensing from her silence that he had gone a step too far, he said, "But you're right. You can't take anything for granted. Look at your brother."

"Right," she said. "Wait, what?"

"Your brother Gerry got fired," he said matter-of-factly. He started in again on the sandwich, seeming hungrier now.

"Why? When?"

"A little while ago. I don't know. Not sure the why of it changes anything. So apparently he didn't tell you."

"But apparently he told you."

Her father shrugged. "He's been over here more. Helping out. You're not the only one who comes over."

When she'd washed her father's dishes she got back in the car and dialed Gerry's number while heading home. "Are you in your car?" he said. "I thought you didn't make phone calls in the car."

"Gerry, you lost your job? Why?"

"How'd you hear?"

"From Dad, I was just there. Are you okay?"

"I'm fine. Don't worry."

"You're on unemployment, I hope?"

He took a while to answer.

"Please tell me you're collecting unemployment," Candace said. "You're entitled to it!"

151

"What entitles me to it?" he said. "But no, I mean yes, I'm getting it. Not much choice. I don't feel very proud of myself. I just try to think of it as getting back some of what I've put in."

"But what happened? Dad said you got fired but of course he would put it that way."

"I just didn't fit in there," Gerry said. "I don't fit in that culture in general, that PC culture. I wouldn't play the game. You try to stand up for something and that is basically the worst thing you can do."

He went on in that vein for a while, but she couldn't get anything more specific out of him, so when she got home she called Mark. "Hey, Candace," Karen said. "What's up?"

"Not much," she said reflexively. "Is everything okay? I thought I was calling Mark's cell."

"You are. He's out—he forgot his phone here. I heard it ringing and found it in the bathroom." She paused. "So I'll just give him a message you called, then?"

She was so touchy, Candace thought, so easily slighted. Candace had never really figured out a path to intimacy with her only sister-in-law, maybe because Karen had seemed to take that intimacy for granted from the beginning. She'd talk about how they had to stick together as the only women in the family (leaving Renee out, though that seemed fair enough); and for the past year or two she'd go on about how they both "worked in education," which bordered on insulting, Candace thought, because education was something for which she'd trained and to which she'd devoted her whole adult life, while Karen worked part-time in a private-school admissions office. Bottom line, she seemed desperate for a sister, which was weird only because she already had a sister, though there was some kind of dark backstory there, which Candace had never really asked her about, which probably counted as a slight too.

"No, that's okay," Candace said. "How are you?"

"All right, you know," Karen said. "Haley's great. Kind of a handful, but she knows how to be charming when it suits her. Can't imagine where she gets that from."

"Sure. The thing I was actually calling to tell him, maybe you guys already know. About Gerry losing his job?"

Karen's eyebrows went up. "No, I did not know that. Shit. What happened?"

"He won't really tell me, so I'm going to assume he lost his temper and told somebody off. He's always this close to doing that, wherever he is."

"Wow. Is he okay? I mean does he need anything? If Mark knows about this, he hasn't told me."

Karen walked through the upstairs as she talked, in and out of the unholy mess of Haley's bedroom, in and out of Mark's office, full of furniture catalogues and old free weights. She headed down the back stairs that led to the kitchen.

"I don't know whether he needs help," her sister-in-law said. "He's apparently been up at Mom and Dad's a lot. But no way he'd ask Dad for money. Knowing him, things would have to get pretty bad before he'd ask any of us for anything."

"Well, listen, of course we'll do whatever we can do," Karen said, looking out the window, where their view of the Hadi house was filtered by spring again. "We're not exactly sitting on a pile of money over here. Not that that matters, I mean it's family. I'm really glad you called."

"Yeah, well, I have to run. But anyway, tell Mark to call me if he wants to. And to call Gerry, even though Gerry will probably hate that. Just wanted to make sure the family knew what was going on, since I only found out today."

Karen left Mark's phone on the kitchen table. Haley was at a birthday party. Some mom was taking eight kids to laser tag and then to Benihana. She still had an hour to kill—the pickup was right from the restaurant—and as the sun went down she really felt like a glass of wine, but not if she had to get in the car. Too windy to sit out on the porch. Television was a waste of time. She looked down with displeasure at the silhouette of her seated body. She should exercise more. But all the forms of exercise were so boring. Running was okay, but around there you really had no choice but to run along the thin shoulder of the road, struggling along past your neighbors' windows, listening for the hiss of cars behind you. No thanks.

Gerry had always seemed like the powder keg in that family; Karen didn't think he'd been quite right since he left that poor girl Lindsey practically at the altar, though wherever her erstwhile sister-in-law was now, Karen hoped she'd come to understand what a bullet she'd dodged. Not that she couldn't imagine what Lindsey had fallen for, since she'd essentially fallen for a version of that herself. A little gallantry, a little self-confidence, some well-muscled forearms went a long way in a small town like that, especially when you were young and dumb.

Six o'clock now and still no sign of Mark, and of course she couldn't call him because his phone was sitting right there. What kind of work could he be doing, at this hour on a Saturday? Maybe he was having an affair. It struck her as unlikely, even if she couldn't have explained why. She picked up his phone and scrolled through the call history, just for the hell of it, and there was nothing there to trip any alarms. Hardly even any number he'd called more than once. She tried to feel guilty for doubting him, but she hadn't doubted him really. If anything, she might have been a little excited to find something incriminating, to learn that there was something about him she didn't already know.

She got in the car and let it run. Then she had an idea and went back into the house for some CDs. She never got to listen to music anymore—certainly not loud music. And she used to love loud music. The drive to Benihana was only long enough for four or five songs; she put in the first Pretenders album, one her older sister used to play. In the bubble of the car she nodded her head and sang along lustily, remembering to keep her eyes open, skipping past the slow tracks, great though they were, to get to the harder ones, remembering how shocked she was not just by the lyrics but by her sister—back before their parents kicked her out of the house—daring to sing along with them, just as Karen was singing now, not me baby I'm too precious yeah fuck off!

She was one of the last parents to arrive even though she was exactly on time. Her ears were still ringing a little as she crunched across the Benihana parking lot. Haley of course did not have her coat on or even know where it was, so Karen stood by the door and chatted with Whitney, the mother of the birthday girl. Whitney looked like she'd just driven a hundred miles with the top down, but she was still smiling, she was one of those mothers determined to pretend that nothing was hard.

"They didn't tear the place apart?" Karen asked.

"No, they were great," Whitney said. "Everybody had fun. I should warn you that I don't know if I saw Haley actually eat anything, so she might be hungry later."

"Yeah, I don't know if she's ever had Japanese food before."

"Well, it's more about the show, of course."

"Sure. I remember loving these places when I was a little older than her. There can't be too many of them left now. Weren't they kind of a seventies thing? I'm surprised this one is still hanging on."

Whitney raised her eyebrows and leaned closer. "Funny you should say that," she said, "because it isn't. Hanging on. They sold the place and they're out of here in two months. The manager told me."

"No kidding? Please tell me it's not going to be another Dunkin' Donuts."

"No! Way better. Todd Van Dyke bought it!" Karen's game expression must have given away that she didn't know who Todd Van

Dyke was. "The guy that owns Iron and Wine, in New York City? Like literally a world-famous chef. He's opening a new restaurant right where we're standing."

"Why here?"

"I have no idea!"

"Well, that's exciting," Karen said, glaring at Haley to induce her to wait for her mother before sprinting out the door. "A little sad about old Benihana, though."

"Well, out with the old," Whitney said.

"What's sad?" Haley said.

"Nothing is sad," Karen answered reflexively. They walked to the car; she turned in her seat and watched until Haley had buckled her seatbelt, and a few moments later the sound of the restaurant's gravel driveway disappeared beneath them.

"Did you have fun?" Karen asked.

"Yes!"

"Did Kristine like her present?"

"She didn't open them."

"No? That's odd. Kind of more polite to open the gifts in front of everybody, I think."

"Maybe she was scared food would get on them," Haley said.

"Yeah, maybe."

In the dark the car became a bubble. You couldn't see out, only yourself reflected back in. Mom always talked more, Haley had noticed, when driving at night. Even though she was in front and could see out, because of the headlights.

"So was laser tag fun?"

"Laser tag was the best! I only got shot two times. Mom?"

"Yes, Bug?"

She didn't know why her mother sometimes called her Bug, but it always meant she was cheerful. "Can we do laser tag for my birthday this year?"

"I don't see any reason why not."

"Yay! Thank you, Mommy!"

"You're very welcome. I'm glad you liked it so much. Did you say thank you to Ms. Reed?"

"Who?"

"To Kristine's mommy. Whitney."

"Oh." She tried to remember. "I don't remember."

"Well, you have to do that. It's important."

"Okay."

"You have to remember. It's not my job to remind you every time."

"Okay."

"Do you hear me?"

"Okay!"

Sometimes—often when she was being picked up from somewhere—the mood would just flip like this, and her mother would start looking for something Haley had done wrong, or failed to do. She wouldn't stop until she found it. And there was always something; knowing that there was always some failure for her mother to unearth, that she was never in the clear, was what made Haley hate those moments so much. She wished Dad were there. "Where's Dad?" she said.

"Beats me. Working. He forgot his phone at home, so I can't call him."

"I'm hungry," she said, to change the subject.

"You're hungry? You just had dinner!"

They passed something in somebody's yard that looked like a scarecrow. Haley tried to turn her body to look back at it but she couldn't because of the seatbelt.

"How can you be hungry?" her mother said. One of those questions that had no answer, but then she always waited like she was expecting one.

"I don't know."

"You just ate, I thought."

"No."

"Why not? She went to all that trouble and expense and then you didn't eat anything?"

"I ate something."

"What?"

"Some rice. But it had stuff in it. Everything else I didn't like."

"Well, God forbid they fail to serve one of the five things on earth you like," her mother said as they finally turned into their driveway. "There, Daddy's home, so maybe he'll make you something."

"How can I eat it if I don't like it?" Haley said, hearing tears in her own voice.

"It's just good manners. You eat what you are served. You are not the Princess of Persia, as my mother used to say to me."

Haley, having unbuckled herself, was waiting for her mother to stop talking; when the pause was long enough to seem definitive, she opened the door and ran past Dad's truck into the house. He was in the living room, with the TV on, drinking one of those smoothies he made for himself: they looked like they would taste good but they didn't, and she had learned never to say yes when he offered her a sip. She jumped into his lap and burrowed quietly into him for a while. Then he made her a grilled cheese sandwich, and he ate the half she didn't eat.

The next day was Sunday-quiet—no playdates, a little homework, an hour on the computer, ninety minutes watching TV—and she mostly played alone in her room. She liked playing alone, particularly after a day of mayhem like yesterday when kids kept trying to impose their will on other kids. In solitary games your will wasn't even your will, it was just what happened, like Fate. Power made Haley beneficent, though. If one of her animals or dolls was sad, the others all rushed over to try to figure out why.

Recourse to that imaginary world of caring helped her bear the worst of school. Bad things happened to Haley herself only rarely—she was kind and nonassertive and had no qualities, good or bad, that made her stand out, and anyway boys, the source of most bad things, were easily and effectively ignored—but she suffered when others suffered, less from empathy than a sense of justice, heightened if not especially modulated. Kids made other kids cry all the time, sometimes in private and sometimes in front of everybody, and the teachers didn't seem to care as much as she believed they should. Group playdates were a thing now, and there were some girls who went on seemingly every one and others who never got included at all. Haley would report this to her mom and dad when they asked her how school was, and they would try to act all outraged, but she could tell that it was just for her sake, that they didn't really feel the injustice of it, and she could not understand why.

Her teacher, Mrs. Tuttle, listened to her more patiently than most adults and had offered the theory that if Haley had had brothers or sisters, she might have better understood the inconsistent operation of fairness in the world. Maybe that was true. She did not have siblings or even cousins, unless you counted the ones referred to as the Colorado Cousins because no one seemed confident about their names, of whom she had no memory. Aunt Renee didn't bring them to visit, and whenever she asked her dad about going to visit them, he said it was super expensive and anyway they couldn't just show up there, they had to wait to be invited. But in any case the trouble with Mrs. Tuttle's theory was that it made it all about Haley, and Haley knew it was not about her at all, it was about the meanness of people—again, boys especially.

Sometimes it happened that some boy or girl she stood up for in public decided that that meant they were friends now. The kid, or the kid's mom, would call up and invite Haley over, and then Haley's mom would get so annoyed at her for not wanting to go. She would have to make up some excuse why Haley couldn't do it and then she would be all stressed out. "Why don't you say yes for once?" she'd ask. "It would be nice of you. And it wouldn't hurt to get out of your room for a while." The charge of not-niceness stung a little. But nothing was as calming as her room, because all hurt feelings were redressed there. And when she felt like it she could stop playing and read, yet another thing that was apparently considered impolite if there was another child present, a rule no one had ever explained to her satisfaction.

Even at Thanksgiving or Christmas, when the whole family came over for dinner, she was the only child—which had an upside, certainly, in that all of the Christmas presents were for her, and her aunts and uncles and grandparents seemed to put a lot of thought into them. The grownups did get gifts for each other, but they were small and boring and everyone always joked about how bad they were and how hard it was to think of anything to give. It didn't make being an adult seem too appealing. But then they all took turns playing air hockey with her in the basement and she beat everyone at least once except for Aunt Candace, who was really good and seemed way more serious than the others.

She didn't like English class anymore because in preparation for fourth grade they were practicing something called Analytical Paragraphs, interpreting the things they read, and somehow it was possible to be told you were right and still not get an A, which she didn't think was fair at all. She preferred math, where you were either right or wrong and if you were right there was none of this B-plus nonsense. Social studies was somewhere in between, because their teacher, Mr. Sills, was always trying to trick you into giving what seemed like the right response, only so he could then tell you, in front of everybody, why that was actually the wrong response. The students caught on to this rhythm eventually, though, without quite understanding it, with the result that they would sit silently in the wake of one of his rhetorical questions even when, or especially when, they thought they knew the answer. By April there

was a tacit understanding that Mr. Sills, having been outmaneu-
vered pedagogically, would do all the talking.

"Why are there police?" he asked them. "In cities, in towns like
this one. Why do we have them?"

Silence.

"To protect us, right? To keep us safe from criminals, from bad
people?"

Outside the window there was a branch that only hit the glass
on very windy days.

"Actually that's not why," Mr. Sills said. "Policemen and police-
women are very brave, that's true. But bravery is—well, it doesn't
tell you enough by itself, does it? I mean, flying an airplane into a
building on purpose is pretty brave too, if you want to think of it
that way. I couldn't do it. No, the police are very brave but they are
also people, just like you and me. Somebody hires them, somebody
pays them, and somebody can take their jobs away from them, and
of course they need those jobs, they have families and children. So
they are not there to serve us, really. They are there to serve the
people, or the organization, that hires them. So who hires the police? Who do they work for, who's their boss? It's us, right? The
people?"

This, somehow, was part of their social studies unit about government. But Haley, like all of them, had learned to ride out Mr.
Sills's digressions by gazing silently at him and not looking too
conspicuously at the clock behind his head. If you looked too interested, he would call on you, and if you looked too bored, he would
call on you. Haley only remembered this particular class at all because a week or so later, her dad asked her about it. He was home
more often now, working in his office and on his computer. He met
Haley at the school bus, walked her up the driveway, made her a
snack of apple slices with peanut butter, and then sat down across
from her at the little table in the kitchen.

"Did you have social studies today?" he said.

"Today's Tuesday," Haley said. "So yes."

"Oh." He watched her eat. "Did he—maybe you don't remember—but did your social studies teacher, Mr. . . ."

"Mr. Sills."

"Right. Was there one class where Mr. Sills was saying something about how the people who killed all those people on 9/11, the men who hijacked the planes, were brave?"

Haley swallowed, unhurriedly, and shrugged.

"Huh. And what did—did you—" Mark realized he didn't really have a follow-up question. "Did you think that was weird?"

"Everything Mr. Sills says is weird."

Mark smiled. "You mean weird like unusual, or . . ."

"Or like what?"

"I don't know." Having started this conversation, Mark now wanted only to escape from it.

"Anyway it's true," Haley said. "Right?"

"What's true?"

"What he said. You can be brave and still be bad. How did you even hear about that, anyway? Why are you asking me about it?"

"Well, somebody from the school told me, actually. She asked me if you'd mentioned it, and I said no."

"Who from the school?"

"I forget her name."

"Why does she care?"

"I don't know." Of course he did know—it was Karen, who was still working part-time in the admissions office—but he'd probably said too much as it was. Some father of some other kid in Haley's class had heard about this episode and had flipped his shit. He was demanding Sills be fired.

"Can they do that?" Karen asked Candace on the phone that night.

"Sure," Candace said. "It's a private school. There's no teachers' union. They can do what they please."

And they did fire him. He'd taught at Mullins for twelve years. Karen pulled the file on the parent who'd complained and saw that he had three kids enrolled there and was paying the full tuition for all of them. So you knew he was loaded. She realized there was no one else at work with whom she felt safe questioning the wisdom of all this. It had been a dumb thing to say, for sure—particularly to a roomful of nine- and ten-year-olds—but that didn't mean the punishment shouldn't fit the crime.

So, what, this guy's a terrorist now? she emailed Candace. *You can't just be a weird old hippie with hippie ideas anymore? This whole area used to be full of them. Now it's like, let's just send them all to Gitmo. Have you had anything like this happen over there?*

A few years ago I would have said it's all about the money, Candace wrote back the next day. *But it's about something else these days. Just keep your head down and wait for it to pass. P.S. Note that I sent this from my personal email—please don't send any more emails like that last one to my school account. Never know who's reading!*

But Karen couldn't let it go. She tried sounding out some of her admissions-office colleagues about it; they just shrugged. She couldn't tell if they were afraid to talk or if they just didn't consider the unfairness of it far enough out of the ordinary to be worth their attention. She didn't want to work with people like that, and it wasn't a long trip from that conclusion to feeling like she didn't want her daughter to go to school with people like that.

"We should take Haley out of Mullins next year," she said to Mark a week later, when they were both staring into the bathroom mirror. "I mean don't freak out, I know we can't really do it. I'm just saying."

"What are you talking about?" Mark said.

"Forget it. I—"

"And send her where, to Howland Elementary? I thought you told me—"

"I said forget it. I just don't respect those people. Probably what I'm really saying is that I don't want to work there anymore, I don't want to be part of it, at least not in that way, but I know that's impossible."

"What is?"

"For me to quit."

"Why?"

"What do you mean, why?" she said quietly. "Because we need the money, or the break on Haley's tuition, same difference."

"We don't need it," Mark said. "Or we won't for much longer. I mean I don't even know what I'm arguing for here, because I want Haley to stay at Mullins anyway. I'm just saying that if you quit it wouldn't mean she couldn't go there."

"What are you talking about?"

And that finally opened up the discussion, which he had been trying to find a way into for two months, about taking out a second mortgage on the house, to give Mark enough ready cash to expand his business by buying up some of the distressed or foreclosed homes throughout southwestern Mass.

"The housing market's taking off," he said. "Especially around here. A big part of the reason is that the banks only want a few percent down. In some cases nothing down! So if you know where to look, and have a little patience—and let's say a little skill in the art of renovation—you can flip these places serially and make a fortune. Or just hold on to them and make a fortune down the road. The timing right now is perfect. Remember, it's how we got this house, and that turned out not to be such a bad thing, right? It just takes a cash reserve which might seem like a lot, but in terms of risk/reward, it's like nothing."

Karen was bent over the sink, the water running, so that Mark's was now the only face in the mirror.

"Give you an example," Mark said. "There's a place I bought at a government auction last weekend in Becket. The previous owner was selling drugs out of there, so it was seized. But it's the government, right, they don't know the real estate business and they just want this property off their hands. So I wound up buying it for about forty percent of what it was valued at four years ago. And that valuation is only going up. So we can sell it whenever we want, but the longer we can wait, the better, right? And that's like Haley's college tuition right there."

"We?" Karen said. "I don't understand. What did you buy this home with?"

"Cash," Mark said. "That's how cheap it was."

"The cash from where, like from our bank account? The money from the Hadi job, that cash?"

He didn't want to tell her why credit wasn't an easy option for him right now. Explaining it would mean going back and telling her about something that happened almost two years ago, when out of some weird post-traumatic compassion he'd let a total stranger spend the night in his hotel room in New York, something that he should have told her about at the time but it was too late now, she was upset enough as it was.

"You didn't even want to ask me first?" she said.

"Do I usually do that? My business is my business, I don't usually have to get my decisions approved by you or by anybody, do I?"

"And now you've borrowed against this house. Holy shit."

"No, I haven't. And technically I wouldn't be. It's complicated. But if you don't understand it then I don't know why you won't take my word for it."

"You don't?"

"The housing market is just like everything else. You don't have to be like some clairvoyant about it; if you don't panic when everybody else is panicking, you can clean up. I talked to Phil Hadi about all this. He said you have to take a step back from your work, see it whole, if you want to succeed, if you want to profit from trends rather than be a victim of them."

Everything he said was designed to reassure her, yet he could see her expression growing more and more horrified. He was tired of it.

"You know, it would be one thing if you disagreed with my business model, or my market analysis, or anything like that. Even though that would contradict people who do this for a living, by the way, who are paid to know what they're talking about. But you've made up your mind already. What are you so afraid of? You complain about this life and yet when I try to lift us out of it, you couldn't be more negative. Why?"

"You'll fail," she said, before she could think to stop herself, and she put her hand over her mouth.

This is who I'm married to? Mark thought. This is my partner in life?

"I mean I do not understand you at all," she went on. "It wasn't that long ago that we lost nearly everything."

"Okay, first of all, this is the difference between guys like Hadi and the rest of the world. He loses ten times what I did every single day, and makes it back again and more, and do you know why? Because he doesn't look back. He learns from his mistakes but he isn't frightened by them. The past stays in the past."

"Oh my God," Karen said.

"And second, there is a big difference between losing something and having it stolen from you. You do see that, right?"

"That's all that world is, people who want to steal from you. So what makes you think it won't happen again this time?"

"Because I'm smarter. I trust people a lot less. I don't let anybody handle what I can handle myself. I've changed. You do believe people can change, right?"

"Actually, no, I don't," she said. "I just get more and more like myself, every day, and so do you."

She was crying now, and there he sensed an advantage. "Would you really deny Haley what you want for her," he said, gingerly taking her by the upper arms, "just because you're so primed for the worst-case scenario? You say you want to change. So let's change. Let's dare to be hopeful for once. For Haley's sake."

There was nothing to do, no way to stop him. The following Monday, Karen gave notice at Mullins; they were surprised but not all that inconvenienced, since the admissions season was over, and perhaps for that reason they graciously agreed to extend Haley's tuition abatement through the end of the school year. Three weeks later, Karen took a different job, thirty hours a week, as a secretary in the development office of the Caldwell House, right there in town. It paid eighteen thousand a year, almost exactly the amount of Haley's new tuition, which mattered to Karen for some reason. It had all happened quickly, if not quite spontaneously; she'd read in the *Gazette*'s want ads that they were hiring, she called them up, she went in that same day, and she accepted the job, without even time to consult Mark. But that was half the point: to take an important step without consulting him. Of course he didn't even give her the satisfaction of getting mad. He thought it was great. Not because of the extra money, but so she would get out of the house more, stay occupied, you know, interact more with people. She could have punched him.

It was true that her salary didn't matter. Fifteen hundred a month, before taxes, was no protection from the disaster latent in however many tens of thousands of dollars Mark's business was now in debt—she didn't even want to know the figure. It was only a kind of hedge, a safety valve, an escape route. He would not take her down with him if he crashed again, which she feared he would do, so much so that she remade her daily life in order to be ready for it.

She'd been to Caldwell House exactly once before, way back when Haley was two and Karen was always searching for some new, safe outdoor space for her to run around in. They went with Whitney Reed and her daughter, on their recommendation in fact, since Whitney said she and Kristine went there nearly every week when the weather was nice. You could get a grounds pass then for just eight dollars; you couldn't go in the house, but who knew what manner of rare china or whatever was on display in there, too nerve-racking to approach with a two-year-old anyway. The whole trip had backfired. The inside of the mansion, of course, was the only thing Haley had any interest in seeing, especially after it was explained to her that she wasn't allowed. Real flowers turned out to be no more engaging—possibly less so, in fact—than her own drawings or paintings of flowers. She bolted across the manicured east lawn toward the flower beds and started yanking them out of the soil, as a present for Mommy she said, and as some angry skinny matron bore down on them Karen lifted Haley off the ground, carried her kicking the air back to their spot on a blanket in the middle of the lawn, and basically held her down while she squirmed and complained. It was a disaster. Kristine sat and played quietly, murmuring to herself, like a little angel, or a simpleton.

The house itself (she picked up quickly that no one who worked there referred to it as a "mansion") was erratically heated and in-termittently sunlit and very clean and deceptively gigantic; the daily operations of the trust took place in small rooms behind the kitchen, one-person offices originally used by the head domestics. Neither Karen nor her fellow employees—a Director of Develop-ment, a Head of Guest Services, a Horticultural Supervisor, the heads of housekeeping and groundskeeping—worked full-time, but schedules were staggered to make sure there was at least one person present to cover the phone during business hours. For stretches on some days, at least until June, when the grounds offi-cially reopened for visitors, Karen was the only one in the house, typing correspondence left for her, responding to email inquiries off the website. Some days, when the phone rang, she jumped.

She brought lunch and, after eating and washing her hands, if she had some time left—she observed the convention of lunch hour, even on days when she was alone—she would tour the empty rooms, staying behind the ropes only housekeeping was allowed to cross, admiring the vast canopy beds. The beds were stripped in the off-season, revealing anomalously modern mattresses encased in plastic; still, their naked condition was somehow suggestive to Karen of the fact that people had died in those beds. There was also Winston Caldwell's study, with two desks in it, old-fashioned rolltops, one left open and one forever shut. Other rooms were un-restored and always locked. The deeper Karen got into the vast upper floors, the more nervous she became, mostly for fear that the phone would ring while she was up there and she wouldn't be able to run downstairs in time.

She read all the brochures, listened at her desk to the audio guides, trying to internalize it all so that if someone asked her a question, she would have the answer at hand. She aspired to inti-macy with the place, even a feeling of semi-ownership, but that was mostly in the interest of doing a good job. She was not one to half-ass anything. She didn't find the history itself all that riveting. Just some rich folks with a big country house. She tried to work up some sympathy for their childlessness, but it seemed a bit much to treat as a tragedy the fact that these people who enjoyed almost every conceivable privilege had not lived lives completely free of misfortune. She looked out her window at the emerald lawns and the black-bordered flower beds, full of gawking strangers. If it had happened when old Caldwell was alive he probably would have had them all shot on sight. But what was property in death? She texted Mark to make sure he was there to meet the bus that brought Haley home from day camp. He worked mostly at home these days; he didn't need to be reminded but it made her feel better.

On it, Mark texted back. He'd invited his brother Gerry over for a lunch that was still going on; so he was grateful for the reminder, if also a little unsure how to get Gerry out the door before Haley came in. No more beer would be a good start, he determined.

"So to sum up here," Mark said, regretting it immediately when he saw the look of hurt belligerence on Gerry's face, "there's no capital you could bring to the business, which is frankly what I need most right now. But you do know more than I do about the housing market here in general."

"A lot more."

"And your credit is solid? If we needed to do transactions, like bank transactions, in your name?"

Gerry squinted at him. "You asked me that before," he said. "I don't get it. It makes me nervous that there's some kind of risk you don't want to expose yourself to, but you're happy to expose me to it."

"That isn't it," Mark said. "Look. This is between you and me. But I've been a victim of a kind of ID theft. I haven't lost any money but in terms of credit and bank accounts and whatever, it's been a nightmare. I've been trying to change my cell phone plan and I can't even do that."

"You're shitting me."

"Nope. But it's temporary. At some point soon all these restrictions get lifted."

"Do you have any idea how it happened?"

Briefly, Mark imagined himself telling his brother the story. "None," he said. "So but anyway, I don't have the cash flow to pay you a straight salary until we get enough money coming in. So we'd have to agree on some percentage of the business you'd own."

"Like partners," Gerry said, just to be provocative.

"In a sense. A family business."

"Mom and Pop."

"No, Christ, I wouldn't bring them in on this. It's just you and me."

"I was kidding," Gerry said, "it's just an expression. Like a family business, a mom-and-pop operation. I guess you'd be the pop, in this setup, and I'm the mom? What do you say," he said, waggling a beer bottle back and forth by its neck, "one more?"

"You know, Haley gets off the bus in a few minutes, and I don't really want to be any deeper in the bag than I am."

"Ah."

"In fact," Mark said, "it's about time for me to go get her."

"You have to go get her? From where? I thought the bus—"

"Just from the end of the driveway."

Gerry raised his eyebrows. "You mean the end of the driveway like a hundred feet from here? What, she can't walk it?"

"Obviously she can walk it. But she likes seeing me there, and I like it too, so bite me."

Gerry rolled his eyes and held the door for his brother and the two of them walked down to the road. It had rained all morning, and though the light was strong enough to cast their shadows now, the invisible life that surrounded them, the birds and insects, remained silent. Gerry wished he'd worn boots. At the same instant they both caught, on the leftmost edge of their vision, the flashes of yellow through the green canopy as the school bus downshifted to make the turn at the intersection a few hundred yards away.

"So, you know," he said, "if you really want to make some money, the thing to do with these distressed properties you buy up is to rent them."

"Yeah?"

"Yeah. Otherwise it's just lost income, for as long as you hold on to them. Plus taxes. And there are all kinds of tax breaks and such you can get if you rent to certain people."

"No shit? See, I knew this was a good idea."

And there's a classic Mark moment, Gerry thought: instantly turning someone else's good idea into his own. He wished Candace had been there to hear it.

His niece was happy, and oddly unsurprised, to see him; they walked her back up the drive, swinging her by the arms over the puddles, and by the time they were back inside the house Gerry felt his buzz had pretty well worn off. He grabbed his jacket, said good-bye, and got back in his car to head home. Something in him kept warning that it was a mistake to get involved in any business venture with his brother, not because Mark wasn't a smart guy but because it would inevitably revive, and exacerbate, all that was worst about their relationship. Which was to say, what was worst about Mark himself: he was condescending and superior and never, ever troubled by the thought that maybe he was wrong about something or that maybe someone else might know more about a given subject than he did. On the other hand, Gerry needed the money, even the prospect of money. Plus he didn't want to be a hypocrite: he'd been reading a lot lately about the decay of traditional nuclear-family structures, so if he found that idea troubling, he couldn't be so cavalier about it in his own life.

He'd been spending most of his time lately on the blog, which of course was not a moneymaking venture, at least not yet. He'd heard of instances where it had become that. The Little Green Footballs guy had ads all over his blog now. Of course, that site's concerns were national, not local, so its audience was national too. Gerry stuck mostly to local politics, for now—not that he was afraid to call out other figures in Washington and elsewhere when necessary, but you had to distinguish yourself somehow, and if you went after, say, Michael Moore, or Dan Rather, you were one of a million people saying the same thing. You wanted that—to be part of a movement—but you also had to be distinct from it. It wasn't simple. You had to find a niche and try to make it yours, a basic principle of business, even though this was not a business. It occupied some sort of strange netherworld between journalism and diary. It was cathartic but you couldn't let it get too cathartic. It was hard, sometimes, to decide whom you were speaking to. Gerry was anonymous—he went by the alias PC Barnum, and he called the blog Workingman's Dread, which was a Grateful Dead reference he kind of regretted now, but you couldn't just go changing your blog's name if you wanted people to be able to find it in the vast steppes of the internet. More than once, he'd deleted entire posts because they'd morphed into angry rants so fringed with personal detail that a savvy local reader might have deduced who PC Barnum was. Personal exposure was something he did not want, at least not yet. Part of it was simple internet convention, but part of it was his feeling that if you didn't have a name, to which people could attach their various judgments and preconceptions, then you were more credible as a voice, a voice of the people.

The town government's job was so simple that nobody even paid it enough attention to notice how badly their elected representatives were fucking things up, simple things. That was the paradox Gerry wanted to address. And if it was Gerry Firth versus Maeve Brennan, then everybody just treated it like gossip, but if it was Maeve Brennan versus the voice of the citizenry, that was a more substantial matter. That's why he kept his name out of it. Not cowardice, as some of his commenters had it. A few of his blog's twenty or so regular visitors were such internet novices that they used their real names; he had to fight the urge to say something to them, or to ding their car or commit some other form of petty retribution, when he ran into them in town.

Calling himself PC Barnum gave him license to go a little overboard, sometimes, in his personal attacks on various Howland officials. But why shouldn't he go overboard? The white noise of people's indifference was itself loud enough that you had to shout over it in order to make yourself heard. Besides, Maeve Brennan really got under his skin. He knew her, but only in the way everyone knew everyone in Howland. He'd never really forgiven the unscheduled bump in his property taxes, which came at the worst possible time. It just seemed like organized crime to him. And taxes were thievery, in a sense: you paid whatever you were told to pay, in response to threats, to implied muscle. Somehow it was more humiliating when there was less muscle. He paid more to Uncle Sam than to the town of Howland, way more. But the Howland taxes were what made him feel like a weakling, like a man who would put up with anything.

First he checked the comments on his previous post. It had only been up two days. Still, four comments was an embarrassing number, especially when one of them was some robot urging people to make money by working at home and another was from his sister Renee, out in Colorado Springs. She was a loyal reader, that was for sure, and she was also the only member of his family he'd told about the blog's existence. Their politics were similar—though she was way more caught up in what he considered Anita Bryant–style bullshit about NAMBLA and other phantom nonsense—but more than that, it was just easier to deal with her via email and blog posting; because she lived far away, because he hadn't seen her in almost five years, she was more like the idea of a sister.

Tell it! she wrote in her comment. *Lack of border protection is the shame of the nation, all the more so now with the constant terrorist threat. But liberals would rather risk our lives than stop recruiting future voters. Fast-tracking citizenship is next—you watch.* He'd never had to ask her not to out herself, on his site, as his relative; she knew instinctively that he was trying to be taken seriously. Still, reading it, he knew that this support came not from some stranger whom his words had inspired but from his sister who loved him, and it made him feel frustratingly small-time. He would tell it, god damn it. If people didn't hear you then you weren't speaking loud enough.

Threat Level Red! he wrote. *That's pretty much the situation right now in Howland, as this fall's pseudo-election approaches. Oh, I know, the whole Threat Level color wheel thing is a classic piece of governmental fear-mongering in the first place. It's a ploy they will use to keep us docile whenever they want to take another one of our freedoms away from us. Hey PC, you've written about that before! you're saying. True. But that's the irony I'm trying to wake you up to: they get you into such a lather over the supposed Muslim hordes with bombs in their underwear that they blind you to the real threat, the actual threat, right in front of you, and that threat is them.*

It was a little convoluted, but when he read it over again it made sense to him, so he pressed on. He tried not to revise too much. Correcting yourself, apart from things like misspelling, was just a manifestation of fear. Everything came out most honestly the first time.

The State is Washington, sure, but the State won't rest until it reaches all the way down into our lives, and the way they do that is on the local level. And let's face it, readers: we are not going to take some bus down to Washington and march around in a circle on the National Mall and accomplish anything, except maybe giving ourselves the illusion of having fought back. No: the fight back begins on the local level, right here. So let's look at this election. We only elect six officials in this little town: the Town Clerk, the Treasurer, the Tax Collector, and the three selectmen (no, I will not say "selectpersons," thank you very much), including our Dear Leader, the First Selectman of Howland. And folks, though it beggars belief to say it, in all six of those "races," the incumbent is running unopposed. No, wait—five, not six; we will be allowed to elect one brand new dummy Selectman, but that's only because the other incumbent died. Lucky us!

They're running un-opposed because nobody else in town really wants those jobs, and who can blame them? I mean, who in their right mind would want to stop working for a living in order to be-

come the Tax Collector? Who loves the State so much they want to devote their labor to supporting it, to becoming part of it? Not me! This is why we get the incompetent stiffs we get. It's a vicious circle: the worse job our government does, the shallower the pool of morons that wants to go to work for it.

But the time has come, people of Howland! This is a call to arms! We have to get ourselves inside the machine in order to start sabotaging and dismantling it from within. And the place to start is with the current First Selectman, that old pile of incompetence, that hag-bride of the State, that schoolmarm who has spent her life bearing out the truth of the maxim: those who can't do, teach! In less than half a term, this matron saint of incompetence has run the town's modest finances into the ground, and has responded in the only way her ilk knows how: by raising your taxes. She let Caldwell House escape through some government loophole, so that they don't have to pay to be here even though we have to pay to go there, and that cut the revenue that goes to the town's few simple, basic services, like snow removal or elder care, not that elder care should really be the province of the State but that's a subject for another post. In fact, plowing too would work much more efficiently and cheaply in private hands . . . But anyway! She secures her salary and makes up for her financial mistakes by arbitrarily revaluing your homes. Where do you think that one is going, citizens? They will revalue your home until you can't afford it anymore, and then they will take it from you and maybe consent to rent it back to you.

Out with her! Send her to the old folks' home where she belongs! She can run the Social Committee there, maybe overspend on Bingo, in a place where her constituency is too demented to notice what her mistakes are costing them.

Citizens, literally a Driver's Ed dummy would have done a less destructive job this past year. We need someone to step up and oust her, just for one term, because surely one term is long enough to

176

start dismantling the useless, self-justifying apparatus these appa-
ratchiks continue to build and to solidify. Then let the state, the
nation, the world take notice of the fact that we can, indeed, sur-
vive without it! Let Howland be the bathtub in which it drowns!

He read it over quickly, shaking his cramped fingers, and hit
Post. Two weeks later a link to the blog post was forwarded to the
tax collector by a buddy of his, with the subject line *"this isn't you,
is it? Tom Paine in the ass lol";* and the tax collector, after reading
the post once quickly and then a second time more carefully, refor-
warded the link to Maeve Brennan, whom he did not like. Maeve
read it at her desk in Town Hall, got up, closed the door to her office, and sat down to read it again, dabbing her eyes.

It was a small town, and everybody was constantly in everybody's business despite a deep Yankee presumption of self-
sufficiency. Surely it was possible to find out who was writing this
hateful drivel without even the courage to sign their name to it. But
she didn't really have the urge to pursue it, to seek out and confront
her enemies or even to know who they were. The truth was, she
agreed she wasn't doing a particularly great job. It was hard. It was
hard to apportion the town's budget to everybody's satisfaction, to
provide services and also pay for them, even in good times, and
these were not especially good times. The job required bonhomie
and ruthlessness, neither of which she possessed. She knew this.
What hurt her feelings was the level of invective. She'd thought her
neighbors, regarding her struggles in a job she'd never sought,
might actually have sympathized with her a little bit. But tough
times brought out the bad side of people, it seemed, and this internet was like some giant bathroom wall where you could just scrawl
whatever hate you liked.

The election was three weeks and change away. If she was voted
out of office she'd be disappointed but also, in her heart of hearts,
a tad relieved. There was no actual campaign, of course. There
were, to her embarrassment, lawn signs with her name and face on

them, a box of which had shown up unbidden from some party-affiliated headquarters in Boston. Half a dozen of them were brought home by Town Hall employees and stuck in the grass on the streets where they lived, but most of the signs remained in the box. After Maeve saw one of them vandalized, she refused to let anyone take another. She stayed in her office when she could. She had to negotiate the road-salt contract for the coming winter, with a really unpleasant, red-faced old bully from Pittsfield who hadn't even heard that Marty was dead, and he left Town Hall with a smirk on his face suggesting he'd ripped her off, which he probably had. She didn't even like going across the street to the Undermountain anymore, because while the cook and the waitress still smiled at her, their smiles weren't the same.

"You know," the tax collector said to her one sunny, freezing morning in late October, standing in her office doorway chewing a breakfast sandwich from the Dunkin' Donuts on 7, "you don't even have to do this job if you don't want to."

"Why would you say that to me?" Maeve asked him.

"It's just I've never seen anybody who dislikes her job quite so much," he said. "And here you have an opportunity to get out of it. If you're not careful, you'll be on the hook for another four years."

But who would take my place? she thought, and then all of a sudden she got it. "You want to do it," she said. He shrugged, and grinned, his teeth full of egg.

People and their ambitions made her weary, too weary to take much offense. "I'll think about it," she said to him. "Still time, legally, to get your name on the ballot?"

"Oh yeah, plenty," he said. "The charter says we can accept nominees right through the town meeting." The town meeting was held the Thursday before the election, in the auditorium right down the hall from where she sat and he stood. Maeve went home that night and watched *Survivor,* without much caring, for once, about the outcome. The shame of it was that she knew she was hesitating only because she needed the salary. She was sixty-one and there was nothing to take its place. Damn Marty Solomon for dropping dead anyway. A little more restraint in the fried-food department and her problems would all still be his. The next day she phoned Abigail Bogert, who edited the *Howland Gazette* and also wrote at least two of its front-page articles every week, and said that if Abigail would buy her lunch at that fancy place that had just opened up where the Benihana used to be, Maeve would have a scoop for her.

Abigail was more worried than excited. Scoops, generally, were not what she was looking for; she ran the *Gazette,* which had published weekly since 1887, in a fragile coalition with the town and its steadier businesses. She was a booster—the *Gazette* existed to promote the town, to stimulate it, to fuel it, rather than to criticize it. Still, the paper itself survived on the thinnest of margins. Abigail's imperative was to please her audience, enough so to hold off the doomsday withdrawal of one or more regular advertisers. But while all this was stressful for her, it was in no way ethically difficult. She wanted the town to do well, and she wanted to show it to itself in the best possible light. She had no taste whatsoever for confrontation, neither on the page nor in person.

So her heart raced a bit as Maeve shared with her, a little tearfully, her decision to throw the town's government into relative chaos. The election was two weeks away—twelve days away once the next issue of the *Gazette* came out, which was how the news would reach almost everyone. Abigail would have to finesse it, so as not to alarm people.

"I never ran for the job in the first place, Abby, you know that," Maeve said. Abigail put down her pen and her notebook, and tried to eat whatever it was they had been served. It had ferns in it. "I never said I was best qualified. I was just the one who volunteered.

179

I did the best job I could. I don't deserve to have everybody mad at me. It's not my fault the town's finances are going to hell in a hand-basket."

Abigail looked around to be sure no one had overheard. The dining room was about half full, but she didn't recognize a soul. "How is your soup?" she said helpfully. "Or not soup, right, they had some other name for it."

"People are good at complaining," Maeve said. The two women had been comfortable acquaintances for more than ten years; neither had grown up in the area, but both their late husbands had. "I mean, it's affecting me too. Here I made you take me to this hoity-toity restaurant just because I wanted to try it, but the bill will probably be outrageous."

"The paper can afford it," Abigail said, even though the paper, effectively, was her, and she had made a point of ordering the second-cheapest item on the menu.

"Anyway, I was saying people love to complain, but you don't see any of them volunteering to serve. They want to cut my salary. Twenty-four thousand dollars a year! Hardly extravagant. I don't sleep in the Town Hall, you know, I have heating bills just like anyone else."

"So there's no one else running?" Abigail said. This was going to be the hardest story she ever wrote.

"Well, no, of course there's always one ambitious person. Tom Allerton. He says he'll run. Nobody seems to like him that much, is my impression. But then who likes the tax collector? I'm sure he'll do fine."

"Can I say that you're endorsing him? That you're, what's the expression, handing over the reins to him?"

"Say whatever you need to say, Abby. I'm not looking to make your life any harder."

That calmed Abigail a little bit, and she went back to the office and wrote the story in a manner that was truthful but calibrated not to excite. She fretted over the front-page layout—she wanted not to treat the story like some catastrophe, but also to give Maeve the respectful sendoff that was her due—and in the end she went with a three-column headline, but not a banner. Four days later the paper was in every subscriber's mailbox. Even Gerry Firth had a subscription, because the *Gazette,* twenty years out of date in all ways, had no website. When he spread the paper out flat on the kitchen table, his face flushed, because his first thought was that he'd made this happen. But he quickly got ahold of himself. Just because you write down your thoughts and hit Post doesn't make you Thomas Jefferson, he thought. You're just a guy with no job trying to get his thoughts together. Gerry was trying, as part of a general campaign of self-improvement calculated to bring his own life in line with his political principles, to be humbler. The problem wasn't excessive pride, though—it was that the distinction between humility and self-loathing was, in practice, a slippery one. He read the story again. Tom Allerton, he thought. I sold him his house. He's a moron too. Change doesn't come all that easy.

He resolved to go to that town meeting on Thursday, the meeting that was usually a pro forma adoption of the slate of candidates for the election five days later, but that promised to be more lively this time. A lot of other people in Howland resolved the same—among them his brother Mark, who kept thinking about something the *Gazette* story didn't even mention: this was the first election since Marty Solomon's death, so if Maeve Brennan was quitting, and this Tom Allerton was running to take her place, that still left one selectman position open. Mark wouldn't even let the thought fully formulate, but it seemed logical that those in attendance would have to nominate someone for that third spot on the board, someone, very likely, present at the meeting itself.

It wasn't an overflow crowd by any means. Where in most election years they might get twenty people at this meeting, this year they had thirty-five or forty, but there were still folding chairs enough for everybody, and then some. The five current officials of the Howland government sat together at the heavy folding table. There was coffee in the back, and some Pepperidge Farm cookies on a platter; they didn't have enough of those to last even until the meeting was called to order, but then they never did—however many cookies you put out, that's how many people ate.

They opened with the Pledge, then with the moment of silence for the town's war dead, whose names were all on the obelisk that stood on the center island of Howland's main intersection. The town clerk asked for and received approval of the previous meeting's minutes, then proceeded to the reading of the slate of candidates for Tuesday's election. The man who currently worked as Tom's assistant was named as the sole candidate for the tax collector's job, Tom was named as the sole candidate for First Selectman, and Maeve's name was not spoken. Tom was smiling calmly, reassuringly, though he also had a white handkerchief he touched to his forehead a few times. In just a minute or two, he would be asked if he wanted to give a speech, a formality that in past elections he'd waived, but tonight he had prepared a few remarks to help put the town, in this time of sudden but still orderly and democratic transition, at ease.

It was not unusual, at these town meetings, for people to blurt out jokes to undercut the rickety, mostly pretend formality of the whole ritual. But tonight everyone was still. Even if all the candidates were running unopposed, it was nonetheless democracy in action, the very essence of what set them apart from so many other nations of the earth, some of whom hated and resented and wanted to rob them of exactly this; and they were solemnly aware of that opposition, they absorbed and then reflected it. Before granting time for voluntary statements from the candidates, the clerk asked if any other candidates for town office wanted to petition for a spot on the ballot before the process was officially closed.

"I do," said a voice. Everyone turned in their seats to locate it, and the clerk said rotely, "Will you stand, sir?" The speaker stood and about half the people in attendance recognized him as Philip Hadi.

There was a long, uncertain pause; everyone gradually turned from Hadi back to the clerk, waiting for some kind of procedural rule to be invoked so that everyone would know what happened next. The clerk knew the rule, but was a little too intimidated to enforce it. "Yes?" he said finally.

"Okay, well, I wrote down a few things," Hadi said. He still wore the black fleece vest over the white dress shirt; it had come to seem less ridiculous, Mark thought as he watched from the back row, as if Hadi had waited it out, until it had become not the way in which he tried to look like others, but the way in which he looked precisely like himself. Plus it was cold in that gym. All those years with Marty in charge and they never even upgraded the heat. "The town of Howland, which I have come to regard as home, is vulnerable," Hadi read. "Its economy is shrinking, its tax base is eroding, and it is not, with due respect to those present who have done their civic-minded best, professionally managed. After much consideration, I have decided to volunteer my name as a candidate for First Selectman." He folded the paper but remained standing. He didn't seem nervous exactly, Gerry thought. Irritated? That wasn't it either. He didn't relish doing this—commanding the attention of a roomful of people—but he didn't doubt he was capable of it.

Two or three people started clapping, but they couldn't get anything larger going, so they stopped.

"Well, it wasn't really time for statements yet, but okay," the clerk said. "Are you willing to answer any questions this meeting's attendees may have?"

"Sure," Hadi said. "Should I come up there?"

"No. Folks, let's try to do this in an orderly fashion. If necessary we—"

"How can we afford you?" someone asked. "We can't possibly pay what a guy like you is used to."

"I will forgo a salary," Hadi said. "So that's, what, twenty-four thousand back into the town's operating budget right there."

"What about the property tax hike? Will there be any more of that, in order to get us out of that vulnerability you think we're in?"

"Right, that. We can roll back last year's tax increase right away. It wasn't really necessary."

"It wasn't necessary?" Maeve blurted out.

"It was made to keep the government itself going," Hadi said simply. "It did nothing for growth per se. A government's nature—and this is by no means a problem unique to Howland—is to eventually become both means and end, self-sustaining, self-justifying. There is a lot of it we can simply get rid of."

"And replace it with what? You?"

"And replace it with nothing. I don't want to be all sentimental and say that the people of a small Massachusetts town like this have historically been able to take care of themselves, and of one another. But I will say that where a genuine, common need arises, hardworking, exemplary American citizens will seize the opportunity to fill that need."

The old gym was dead silent. From across the aisle Mark exchanged a wide-eyed look with his brother; had they been sitting together it would have been hard to resist the vestigial, loving urge to express his excitement by punching Gerry in the arm. He'd thought about running himself, but this was so much better.

"Part of that budget you think we don't need," Maeve said, trying to control an emotional tremor in her voice, "is a reserve in case of emergency. Some years it snows twenty times instead of ten. Last year the septic overflowed right by the bandstand. What happens in a case like that? You want people to come together on their own, but sometimes things happen where you can't wait around for that."

Hadi seemed to think about that one for a moment. Then he lifted his head and shrugged. "I'll pay for it," he said.

"What do you mean, you'll pay for it? How do you get paid back, if you're cutting all our taxes?"

"I know every detail of what Howland spends, in good times and in bad, and frankly, it's not that complicated. I want this town to succeed without losing its character. I want it to thrive. In order to see that happen, I'll meet temporary or emergency needs with my own money if necessary. I can afford it. This place means that much to me. But of course this is a democracy, and it's up to you."

He sat.

Somebody elbowed Abigail lightly in the side and said, "Shouldn't you be writing this down?"

One person let out a sort of celebratory whoop, and the clerk overreacted by shouting, "If we do not maintain order here, I will instruct Trooper Constable to remove any protesters from the hall. Trooper?" Constable, in the back of the gym by the door, separated his shoulders from the wall and stood up straight but otherwise remained where he was. Just as he did so, his pager went off. He had his radio with him, volume off while he was in the meeting; he held up an apologetic finger even though no one was looking at him anymore, and left the room, still hearing the clerk's miffed voice as the door swung shut on him in the hallway.

The page was from 911 dispatch in Pittsfield. There was a report of a domestic incident within the Howland zone, out on Route 155, which figured. He pushed open the gym door again, just to make sure things weren't degenerating, and heard the clerk, his evening now totally off track, saying something about a petition; people were already noisily pushing back their folding chairs to stand in line to sign it. Tom Allerton looked like he'd been kicked in the nuts, Constable thought. Couldn't happen to a nicer guy. He let the door close again and went out to the parking lot. The clerk would be pissed at him, but so what, he was no security guard, sometimes he had a real job to do.

The cruiser roared up the empty roads. He could have put the siren on, or the lights, but there was no need, his path was clear. The trees were at the moment in the season where one good, windy storm would bring most of the leaves down in one shot. Soon he hit the flat, exposed stretch of 155 that was all locals—no country cottages or hidden manors out there. Just regular houses, barely set back from the road, lit by the flicker of oversized faces on TV screens.

Rich people, he thought. The world shaped itself around their impulses. This would be something new under the sun, for sure—if the town voted basically to let some sentimental billionaire pay their bills, so they wouldn't have to—but he was not immune to its attractions. He was tired of what he had to go through for the simplest things: a new roadside-assistance kit for the cruiser, for instance, after he'd used up the flares in the old one. That one had taken months. The forms he had to fill out, the begging, the dismissal. Maybe this would work better—just knock on a door and say, Hey, Rich Guy, the town's one cop car is on bald tires, can you peel me off a couple hundred bucks? Thanks a lot! Simpler, for sure.

He rolled into the driveway and got out of the cruiser. He stood still for a moment, and heard nothing from inside, and then just as he took a step forward he heard a loud thud. He trotted up the steps and knocked loudly; he put his ear to the door, heard nothing, and took a step back. He wasn't yet fully engaged but adrenaline had pretty well vaporized anything he might have been thinking about a few seconds before. "Police!" he said. The knob turned and the door parted about a quarter of the way. A man stood there too calmly, with a look of which Constable had learned to be wary. "Help you?" the man said.

"Evening. I'm Trooper Constable. Sorry to disturb you but I'm responding to a 911 call at this address."

"Oh yeah? I don't think the call came from here, though. Did it come from here?"

He'd been drinking. In his head Constable went through the checklist. The man's left hand, on the doorjamb, bore a wedding ring, so he said, "Sir, is your wife home?"

"I like being called sir," he said.

"What is your name?"

"Barrett Taylor."

"Mr. Taylor, is your wife here with you? I need to see her."

"You need to *see* her?" he said, smiling. "What kind of a perverted game are you running here?"

And suddenly it fell into place for Constable, with the instinct that came from having responded to a couple dozen of these calls: while this was probably not a big deal, the guy was trying to goad him into making it one. Confrontations like this escalated, for no good reason, all the time. "Mr. Taylor, I just need to see that your wife is here, confirm that she's unharmed, and then I can go and leave you alone, all right? I'm sorry but we all have rules at our job and those are mine."

"I love the way you guys talk," Barrett said. "Hey, honey? Come here and let Officer Friendly confirm that you are unharmed."

He opened the door another two inches and his wife's head appeared under his arm. Her face was red, but that could have been from a lot of things.

"Man, go the fuck away," she said. Her husband smiled proudly.

"Ma'am, did you place a call to 911—"

"That was our bitch neighbor. You should arrest her, you're so hot to arrest somebody. See, that's the problem with our world today. Everybody's gotta be up in everybody else's shit."

"Ma'am, have you been drinking?"

"How is that any of your fucking business!" she screamed. "Aren't you ashamed that this is your job?" Her husband let his hand fall lightly on her shoulder. Constable tried to peer around them, into their living room, such as it was. He saw clothes and dirty plates and a gym bag but no drug paraphernalia and nothing that indicated the presence of children.

"As you can see, she's peachy," Barrett said.

"I fucking hate cops!" she yelled, and she wrestled the door's edge away from her husband and slammed it in Constable's face. He stood there. He had reasonable cause to enter their home, without a doubt. And without a doubt that would end with his cuffing and booking one or both of them. Which would take him hours. And accomplish what? They were right: Why did he need to be there? On whose behalf? Screw these lowlifes. Let them stay behind closed doors and drag each other down in private. The idea that their personal problems were somehow his problem was a magical idea, a construct, some Mayberry shit, and it stopped being true the moment you stopped believing it was true. In the cold moonlight he radioed dispatch that the 911 call was resolved, and got home to his own family before the kids' bedtime.

3

M*arch: Turnips, carrots, javelin parsnips, arugula, mâche, rainbow chard, Finn Dorset lambs, Tamworth pigs, Belgian endives, cardoons, honey.*

The restaurant was rarely more than two-thirds booked, but that was the way Todd liked it. Better atmosphere in the dining room, better pace and attitude in the kitchen. More of a learning atmosphere, like a teaching hospital as opposed to a battlefield, a MASH unit. He had the time and the patience to explain what he was doing, not only to the diners but to the young sous-chefs and line cooks and culinary students who cycled through. Students at CIA, forty or fifty miles down the Hudson, could sign up for a full-credit internship with him now, and why wouldn't they? Cutting-edge work was being done here—not in terms of technique, which had become a sort of louche dead end anyway, but in terms of philosophy—and the countryside was beautiful, even in winter, especially for those unused to it.

As for the economics of a two-thirds-full dining room, that was not a concern. Pricing wasn't something they needed to worry about. The restaurant had no dinner menu, just a nightly prix fixe for whatever Todd felt like preparing; right now it was $195, but he could have doubled it if he wanted to. He didn't want to price the locals out completely. Let them come for a special occasion. Still, he knew from his nightly tour through the dining room—talking to them, although he could have told just by looking at them—that he was serving mostly out-of-towners now. The restaurant had become a destination. The maître d' had a list of local hotel and B&B recommendations for people who called for reservations from the city, people who maybe didn't realize how hard it would be to make the long drive back home after being fed like that.

And the writers were starting to sniff around, the journalists and critics, from the *Times,* from *Gourmet.* Once word got out that way, they'd be booked solid every night. He should enjoy these easy servings while he could.

April: Ramps, shiitake mushrooms, fiddlehead ferns, watercress, asparagus, rhubarb, Swiss chard, beets, French fingerling potatoes, Finn Dorset lambs, Toulouse goslings, Tamworth pigs, leeks, horseradish, mâche, dandelion greens.

Diners were given, in lieu of a traditional menu, a booklet listing by month the local, seasonal ingredients from which the courses of the evening's meal would be assembled. They were also given a small pencil, in case they wanted to record, for memory's sake, any details or impressions. The dinner was usually sixteen or seventeen courses, so he found people appreciated the thoughtfulness of leaving space for notes.

You wanted to give them what was seasonal, what was local—to restrict and awaken them, as most high-end restaurants did not trouble themselves to do, to the specific place that they were in, and to the revolutions of time—but then it was also a matter of educating local suppliers about what else they might be growing: produce that would thrive up here, in every natural sense, but that few Berkshire family farms were familiar with. The stuff he got from Jack Whalen, for instance—the beets, the asparagus—was fantastic. Todd knew enough about soil to know that purple kohlrabi would do well there too. But Jack didn't know from kohlrabi, because no one up here ate it, and he acted like it was some sort of hybrid or modern genetic experiment. Todd didn't push him. He went over to the farm once a week or so, to be neighborly and to check on what was coming in. Even that much felt like an imposition; Jack's wife Joanna, who'd had some kind of a stroke and walked and talked with difficulty, insisted on serving him coffee every time— they were very old-school that way—even though her efforts to get around the kitchen provoked visible agony both in her and in her husband. Finally one day Todd blurted out, and then was forced to maintain, the outright lie that he'd given up coffee. He worried that Jack might spot the travel mug that was always in his car.

Now, in April, he brought them a plastic container full of a kind of turnip candy—he didn't know what else to call it—that he'd made using liquid nitrogen and the crate of turnips Jack had loaded into the bed of Todd's truck the week prior.

"I served it Saturday for one of the dessert courses," he told them. "People went crazy for it. You can't even tell what it is until you bite into it."

Jack tried one, with a strange, preoccupied, businesslike expression as he chewed; Todd thought he was trying to work out the flavors, but then he looked at his wife and shook his head, just barely. "Too hard for Jo to chew," he said. "But it's interesting. Thanks."

The men went out to the fields. Todd squatted down and crumbled some of the soil between his fingers. Lightly he touched one of his fingertips to his tongue. Jack looked off toward the foothills as if embarrassed. The sky had that great quality of early spring, cold whenever a cloud crossed the sun, raw and promising, scoured by the wind. Todd talked up the kohlrabi, gave some stats off the top of his head about the pH balance it left in the soil, said he knew some other restaurants in western Mass would probably come for it too if they knew it was locally grown, and he wouldn't stand in the way of that even though he would have loved exclusivity. He understood a farmer needed to make a living.

"'Twas ever thus, as my dad used to say," said Jack.

Todd said he would assume the costs of the first planting, if Jack would tell him what they were. Just as a gamble that he was right, that it would thrive up here.

"If you say so," Jack said.

Todd beamed. "Glad you're as excited about it as I am," he said teasingly.

"Well, it doesn't much matter what I grow here anymore," Jack said. "Money is money."

Which Todd found a somewhat disappointing attitude. There was nothing more exciting, more fundamental, than what he and Jack were engaged in together. He left the farm feeling, as usual, a strange combination of energy and sorrow. It was a sad scene, the old farmer and his younger, disabled wife. She tried to come out to the porch, at least, to wave goodbye to him, even though it was clearly hard for her to do. Not painful, he hoped. She always had the same expression on her face, a sort of petrified alarm or confusion; he didn't know if it was the stroke that froze her features that way or if that was just the way she always felt now. He knew that on some level they hated having him there, hated having company of any kind. But he couldn't help it. He and Jack were like partners at this point. And Todd's real dream, which it still seemed too soon to mention, was to buy the farm itself and operate it exclusively for the restaurant—turn it into a sort of transparent farm-to-table operation, a teaching center for children and for chefs and just for people with an interest in the whole approach he was pioneering. It was too sensitive a subject to bring up with Jack for the moment, and yet every time he rolled back down their driveway to the road, Todd imagined that conversation in his head, and every time he did, the look on both their faces—Joanna's too—was one of relief.

May: green garlic, asparagus, rhubarb, beets, butter chard, flint corn, tomatoes, peppers, orazio fennel, soybeans, leeks, eggplants, poussins, mustard flowers, pea shoots, Dutch belted milking cows,

Normandy milking cows, Tamworth pigs, stinging nettles, Mokum carrots, butter.

The philosophy was this: We, meaning Americans—others too, but you had to keep it close to home, to instill a sense of pride and identity in your audience—are estranged from our food. Where it grows, how it's made, how it gets to us. Just because I can have bananas delivered in the middle of winter, and can charge what I want in order to make up for the cost, doesn't make that a good or productive idea. We are alienated from the most basic, defining experience of being alive, of being human, of knowing what it means to survive. Todd would build a place that would show the world what was possible within the confines of this idea—a restaurant infatuated not with the narcissism of technique, but with its own harmonic relationship to the land, the weather, the seasons. He could cook anything he wanted, anywhere in the world, at this point in his career; but he would let the specifics of this time and place dictate what he did, and from that commitment to humility, others would learn what was possible. A new way of cooking, of eating, of achieving beauty and refinement while still surviving in harmony with the earth, before it was too late for any of that to make a difference.

And this spot in the Berkshires was perfect. It couldn't have been more rural—New England was America, if you had any sense of history at all—but it was still close enough for New Yorkers to get there, if they were committed enough. So far the coverage had been rapturous. He expected a Michelin visit before the year was out.

By the end of May the dining room started to fill up in a serious way. It was the high season around there; people came up for the summer, people who could afford to dine there semi-regularly. The occasional celebrity, which as a restaurateur you wanted a little of, but not too much. If there was one conspicuous absence, it was Philip Hadi, arguably a celebrity but more pertinently the First Selectman of the town in which Todd's operation was putting down its roots. Todd didn't want or need to schmooze him, he just felt that they were partners of sorts, kindred spirits who had seen the promise in this unspoiled little place; but Hadi had never come into the restaurant, not once. Not even when Todd invited him. He was famous for his frugal habits, Todd knew, so he tried not to take it personally. When Hadi did eat out, it was usually at the Undermountain, the diner just down the street from the Town Hall. He'd always order the patty melt. Every day the same. Just like he wore the same clothes. He was a little obsessive that way, people said. After the first ten or fifteen times he ordered the patty melt, they'd just renamed it after him—printed a new menu and everything—but he never asked for a menu anyway, so they weren't even sure he knew about it.

Foreclosures, though there weren't that many of them in the immediate area, seemed like a safe place to start—less money up front, more profit potential down the line—and when Mark mentioned that to Gerry, Gerry had a clever idea. Bank-auction listings were published first in the *Gazette;* the *Gazette* came out every Thursday, which meant Abigail Bogert had the information a few days before that. The two Firth boys took her out to lunch, to plead their cause: local entrepreneurs, not speculators from who knows where, and if by chance the *Gazette*'s published bank-foreclosure listings were shorter by a line or two, that only made Howland look better, right? Mark had assumed he would have to do all the talking at this lunch—older ladies loved him, and he had a lot of experience charming clients—but he had never really seen his brother in work mode before. By the time that lunch was over, tiny old Abigail was so red-faced from the attention that she probably would have let them rewrite the front page if they wanted to. They thought differently, spoke differently, the two brothers: all Mark's life that had been a frustration, but now it was an advantage. In

June they flipped their first property, for a modest $20K profit, and he gave Gerry twenty percent of it.

One August morning there was a bank-owned house in Egremont Mark wanted to check out. He drove over right after breakfast, but maddeningly he couldn't even see inside: someone—the crazy decamped owner, most likely—had taken the extraordinarily hostile step of painting all the windows black. Mark drove back to Howland and met Gerry at Daisy's for lunch, expecting some sympathy, but Gerry just laughed at him. "They have this thing now," he said, "called the internet?" Sure enough, when Mark got home it took him all of five minutes to find photos of the interior and a floor plan too. In his head he still heard the mocking voice of his brother, who loved to make him feel stupid. But this was his business, and when you paid people to work for you, that meant their good ideas were your good ideas.

They picked up the Egremont house by borrowing against their three others, and those internet pictures, while structurally accurate, proved woefully out of date. Some kind of private or personal disaster had unfolded in that house. There was water damage everywhere, including most of the living room floor, which was warped. One of the toilets was cracked almost straight down the middle—puzzling, but not so bad—but then the waste pipe had been damaged too. The closets were ripe with mold, the window sashes looked like someone had been cutting at them with a knife or a scissors. Why? He knew nothing about the previous owners except that they had stopped paying their mortgage. Maybe their sad tale was somewhere on the internet too, like everything else seemed to be, but if so Mark had no desire to read it. A house was an asset, not a story.

The Egremont place was more spacious than it looked from the street, with an exterior upstairs entrance and a capped gas line that could be used for a second kitchen; Mark thought the smart thing to do was divide it into two units. More rentable that way—

certainly to the type of tenants they were looking for. It was work he could have done himself, but he would have lost a month to it, maybe more, depending what he found under that living room floor. He still had Barrett Taylor's number in his contacts, so he reached out. Barrett said he'd take the job, since he could get the clock to restart on his unemployment after it was over. Mark thought he sounded drunk. He was a headache, but also one of the few guys Mark knew who could do more than one thing well. And this was the perfect job for Barrett, because when he felt like trying he did excellent work, and when he didn't feel like trying, there'd be no homeowner there to get in his or Mark's face about it. Barrett had a knack for offending clients—a compulsion, maybe. Mark had once had to fire him on the spot. Rich people disliked him, was Barrett's own take on it, because he called them on their bullshit.

Five weeks later Mark summoned Gerry over to the house to check out Barrett's handiwork, before they started advertising for tenants. Gerry was great at knowing what the local market would bear. Mark introduced them and they shook hands.

"You bought me a beer once," Barrett said. "At the Ship."

"I sort of remember that," Gerry said.

"Yeah. It was right after the last time your brother laid me off."

Mark rolled his eyes. "Well, there'll be steady work now," Gerry said. "These floors look great, by the way."

Barrett grinned. "Amazing what you can get accomplished when the boss is off site," he said. "Like way off site."

"Yeah, hilarious," Mark said, "so look. Here's the thing I wanted to ask you. Those exterior stairs in winter will be like a lawsuit waiting to happen, plus it looks like a servants' entrance, so I'm thinking there's room for a staircase right inside the front door. What I want to know from you, Gerry, is whether cutting off the view of the street from what's now the living room, in order to put in a front staircase, would affect it—"

"Plus whether the construction is even doable," Barrett said. "That'll be a narrow staircase."

"It's doable."

"Who says?"

"I say. By which—"

"Oh, well, excuse the fuck out of me then. I just thought you might want to check the code for the width of the stairs—"

Mark's cell phone rang. He pulled it out of his pocket; it showed a 212 number. "Hold on," he said.

"Yeah, it'll definitely devalue the house," Gerry said. "For resale down the road, I mean. But no reason—"

"I did check the code," Mark said, "that's all I—"

"Resale?" Barrett said. "Then why would you—"

"Just hold on," Mark said, "I have to take this," and he went through the front door and down the steps onto the overgrown lawn. "Mark Firth," he said.

"Mr. Firth? Hold for Greg Towles."

Mark walked across the lawn, toward the road, as he held. A semi—technically illegal on this county route, trying to bypass the slow traffic on 7—lumbered odiferously past. Across the street was a two-car garage, doors wide open and packed to its rafters with junk; beyond that, the autumnal trees waved in the shade of the valley.

"Mark! It has been a long, hard road, and you have been very patient, but I am happy to say I am calling with good news. There's a settlement. The judge in the case has appointed what's called a Special Master, a kind of overseer in charge of distributing every recoverable nickel our friend Mr. Spalding tried to hide. In return, we've agreed to a formula for compensation, which is to say, basically, how many cents on the dollar you'll recover, in terms of your original claim of loss."

"And how much is that?"

"In your case, about forty-three cents on the dollar. Which is pretty good compared to yesterday when you were getting bupkis, right?"

"That's before or after your commission?"

"Before. If you don't mind my saying so, I think we earned it on this one. You have no idea how satisfying this is. We're all jumping up and down over here."

"What happened—I mean, I'm not saying any of this out of ingratitude or anything like that, but just totally out of curiosity, what happened to the rest of the money?"

"Guys like this—which is to say, thieves—they're pretty good at hiding their assets," Towles said. "You cannot believe how much work this represents, finding even this much of it. It's all over the world. We've gone into his children's IRAs, for Pete's sake. We've been ruthless. The rest, he spent, or lost, or gave away."

"What do you mean, gave away?"

"Like to charities. Lots and lots of money to charities. Go figure. Very hard to recover that money, even if, you know, we wanted to."

"Wow," Mark said. "I would not have guessed that."

"I know, right? Bad conscience, maybe? Or maybe he knew we were coming and just wanted to put it out of reach. Well, even if he was doing it for bad motives, which who knows, at least we can console ourselves that the money's doing some good in the world. Right? So anyway, what would be best, if you could see your way clear, is to make a trip to the city, look over the entire agreement, sign an affidavit of your consent, and we can begin the process of getting your money back to you. When might that be possible?"

"Pretty much any time," Mark said. "I've got a lot of flexibility right now. I can't believe this is happening."

Towles laughed. "That's always the way, right? Nothing happens, and nothing happens, and then everything happens."

Back in the empty living room, Gerry watched his brother

through the window, fuming as the minutes dragged on. This Barrett guy would not shut up. He kept wanting to talk about high school, which then morphed into some strange rant about how much he hated working for Mark but every other general contractor in the Berkshires had a vendetta against him.

"I say things," Barrett said. "I can't seem to be quiet when I should."

"Oh yeah?" Gerry said.

"Political things, sometimes. Like, forbidden things." Gerry turned to look at him. "I mean it's this environment where you can't say anything. Sometimes I just can't help keeping it real. But you can't even say what's true, sometimes, because it's suddenly not allowed."

"Well, that's for sure," Gerry said. He watched his brother put his phone in his pocket and then give what looked like a little fist pump before turning back toward the house. Take your fucking time, your highness. "Yeah," he said, "people do not want you to speak, unless it's in a certain way. Somebody can announce he intends to kill us all, but God forbid you should say anything offensive about him."

"People will suck up to their enemies," Barrett said. "Every time."

Gerry looked at him with a sudden awakening of interest. "That's right," he said. "That's exactly right. Why do they do that, though?"

"Damned if I know," Barrett said.

Mark walked in and told Gerry that the remaining design and construction decisions were entirely up to him. Whatever he thought was best, Mark would go along, and Barrett should get right to work on it. They could work out the pay. In the meantime he was taking the rest of the week off. He smiled and clapped them both on their shoulders and went off to his truck.

"Douchebag," Barrett said. Gerry thought about reprimanding

him, to remind him of the hierarchy that Mark himself had just undermined by giving them both the same peremptory order; but even though he knew he should, he couldn't bring himself to disagree. "Got any siblings?" he said instead.

"Yeah. I'd chew my arm off before I'd work for any of them. Hey, can I ask you something?"

Gerry couldn't tell if this guy really thought they were pals now, or was just testing him. Sometimes guys like Barrett were aggressively friendly, intimate, like they were trying to push you to the point where you'd reveal that you thought you were better than them. Usually this happened in a bar, where it could be a delicate situation to get out of. "Ask away," he said.

"What are you two doing? Buying up these shitty places. I thought Mark fancied himself some kind of a fucking artist. I mean whatever, I don't care what he does except I can't figure out how this is more money than doing renovations for rich assholes you can charge whatever you want."

Gerry sighed. "If we rent to people below a certain income level, the federal government will subsidize that rent. On top of which we get these properties, which we bought for nothing, at zero percent interest. So they're assets we can borrow against, assets worth two or three times what we paid for them. We borrow against them to buy more houses. If you just do it with one house, the revenue stream is pretty small. But mo' houses, mo' money, basically. And thanks to the feds, it's all rigged, we can't lose."

"Huh. And here I thought the rich people were where all the money was. But it's the poor folks, eh?"

"The government is where all the money is," Gerry said testily. "You can't beat them. But you can exploit them."

"Fucking Mark," Barrett said.

Mark drove home and packed a bag. He didn't even bother to look at a train schedule; if he got to the station in Wassaic and had to wait, he'd wait. On weekdays there was a train every two hours or so. Karen was in her office at Caldwell House; he sat in their empty kitchen and phoned her with the news.

"What about Haley?" she said.

"What about her?"

"She gets off the school bus at four. I'm working."

"So leave early. What are they going to do, fire you?"

"Maybe, yeah! But the point is I'm not just going to leave—"

"You don't need that job anymore anyway. That's my point."

"Don't tell me what I need. It makes no difference if you wait one day to go down there. Right?"

It didn't. And now that he was doing the math in his head, he wasn't sure it was still possible to get to Towles's office by five o'clock anyway. He'd been so excited he hadn't thought through a single detail. But he wasn't going to admit to a mistake like that. "Fine," he said. "I'll go tomorrow, then. Just wanted to share the good news."

The next day he drove down to Wassaic and boarded the early train. He could have just driven the whole way into the city, but he'd tried that once many years ago and it hadn't gone well: he'd gotten lost and honked at and ticketed for parking somewhere even though other cars were parked there too. He looked out the window at the pale blur of greenery for two and a half hours. At some point an idea took hold of him. That guy, that sketchy little guy, fellow victim of Garrett Spalding, the one he'd met in Towles's office his last time down there—three whole years ago, now—maybe he'd be there again today. Why not? If they needed Mark's signature, they'd need his too. The longer the whole nightmare of Mark's compromised credit and ID theft had dragged on—and it still wasn't over, he'd had to explain to an angry woman from some collection agency just a week or two ago that there was a real Mark Firth and a fake one—the more firmly he'd convinced himself that the little guy was behind it, that that whole strange day and night in the hotel room, with the guy going on about how traumatized he was, had been conceived as a scam, a con, from the very beginning. When he replayed those hours, remembered what they said to each other, he felt like a fool.

So what would he do, if he ran into this guy again today? "Did you steal my credit card out of my wallet?" "No." "Then I suppose you didn't also take the photo of my wife and daughter I showed you?" "No, why the hell would I do that? I thought you were a decent guy, I thought we had a special moment together, like a connection, but I guess I was wrong, huh?" And then where were they? The only move remaining would be to try to beat a confession out of him, or at least threaten to; that wasn't really the kind of thing Mark could pull off, and anyway the truth was that he could never be completely sure, there was no way to prove any of it, not even to himself. The little guy would probably just laugh at him.

Still, the fantasy consumed Mark as the train cut through the suburbs, slowed down in the Bronx, slipped into the tunnel: the fantasy of scaring the guy, menacing him, which gave way to the image of actually doing it, laying hands on him, hitting him, until he confessed his wrongs. Mark got confused exiting Grand Central and had to walk all the way around the station once before he was confident he was headed west toward the law firm. The city was a grid but he could never get oriented in it unless the sun was almost down. The streets were so crowded. It wasn't even rush hour. People got irritated with you just for standing still. He'd carried with him his last memory of the city, stunned into suspension, seemingly empty; so the ordinary landscape of a workday, the endless blaring horns and the wave of pedestrians bearing down on you without seeing you, undermined him. He'd always disliked it here, really, all the more so for the feeling it gave him of being surrounded by people who knew something he didn't.

The grand Rice and Powers office looked just the same as it had three years ago, though the faces at the security desk and the receptionist's station were all different. Mark's own business had always been synonymous with him, but then there were businesses like this one, greater than the sum of the people who occupied the desks and chairs: institutions more than businesses, people-proof, so substantial they didn't really depend on you at all. It was a relief to see Towles and to be escorted back to his burnished private office. "You're looking great!" Towles said. "All that country air! So isn't this amazing news? The arc of the moral universe is long, or however that goes. But I told you from the start we just needed to be patient, and now here we are."

"How much was recovered total?"

"Well, it's ongoing. We're finding new little holes in the baseboard all the time. New victims too, actually, which means all the percentages have to be recalculated. But that's the Special Master's job, thank God, not mine. So once I have your signature here, the whole process can get started."

Get started! Mark's face reddened. He thought he'd be carrying a check home, a check to hold up in front of Karen and produce a capitulatory smile. "So you're not actually handing me any money today," he said, trying to keep it light, trying to keep any anguish out of his voice.

Towles laughed. "Not today, but it's coming. Restitution is a long road. Not for the faint of heart. You and the other plaintiffs have been extremely patient."

Mark sighed. "Hey, speaking of the other plaintiffs," he said, "I'm curious about the guy I met when I was in here the first time. You remember?"

Towles cleared his throat. "Well, I wasn't actually present that day, so—"

"Oh, right. I don't remember his name. Funny little guy, lived here in the city, worked in some kind of lab at Columbia, I think?"

"Doesn't ring a bell," Towles said. "Oh no, wait, I know who you're talking about! Because we were all just talking about him. You wouldn't know how to get ahold of him, would you?"

"Me? No, no idea. We didn't exchange numbers or anything. It was just that day."

"Yeah. We can't find him. It's weird. None of his old contact info is good. We're trying to get him in here to sign off on the agreement. But no worries, he'll turn up, you can't just disappear these days. Even if he's dead, God forbid, we'll find him. My best paralegal is on it right now. Why do you ask, do you want to get a message to him or something?"

"No," Mark said. This was it. He was going to have to let it go, forever—even though it would never let go of him: the credit agency people had told him that at this point, short of changing his own identity, there was nothing definitive Mark could do—and that was because the story itself was too humiliating to tell. Taking the pen Towles had been patiently holding out to him, he said, "I was just curious. We met that day, that's all. It was a pretty strange day. I actually think he might have stolen something from me."

MINUTES OF MEETING OF
BOARD OF SELECTMEN

Oct. 28, 2004, 4:00 P.M.

Present: Mr. Allerton, Mr. Waltz, Ms. Burrows (sec.)
Absent: Mr. Hadi

Meeting began with recitation of Pledge of Allegiance. Mr. Waltz asked for summary of revenue collection. Mr. Allerton presented data demonstrating that collection for water and land revenue was at 72%, with two months still to go before official arrears declared. Mr. Waltz asked if list of those in arrears was likely to remain the same as in past years. Mr.

Allerton conjectured yes, but that the list was likely to grow somewhat, owing to the general increase in "anti-tax sentiment." He went on to say that even with no such increase in delinquency, direct town revenue was likely to be down between 12-15% owing to cuts in the tax rates as "decreed" by the First Selectman. Mr. Waltz corrected Mr. Allerton on use of the term "decreed," and Mr. Allerton said he "[stood] corrected."

Mr. Waltz reported that the town's reserves for paying its snowplow and road salt contractors were the same as in 2003, even though those contractors' prices had increased. Mr. Waltz said that forecasts for the coming winter were mild. Mr. Allerton said he had spoken to Mr. Hadi and had received assurance that any emergency shortfalls would be covered.

Mr. Allerton asked for further business. Mr. Waltz brought up the proposed Railroad Days celebration, and said that the Chamber of Commerce had requested the dates September 16-18. Mr. Allerton asked why the proposed date was after Labor Day, when obviously many fewer out-of-towners would be present. Mr. Waltz said that the local merchants had specifically wanted a boost during a traditionally down time for town commerce, and that the Railroad Days celebration was more a local matter anyway, as it celebrated the Town of Howland's history and had little to do with tourism per se. Mr. Allerton asked what the Chamber was specifically requesting from the Town. Mr. Waltz said it would require only a waiver of parking regulations, overtime for Trooper Constable, and approval of signage. Mr. Waltz added that the dates had already been approved by Mr. Hadi directly, in conversation. Mr. Allerton said that in that case, discussion of the matter might as well be brought to a close.

The meeting concluded with an official resolution of support for our troops overseas.

Respectfully submitted,
Anne Marie Burrows
10/29/2004

On a rainy, raw day in November, the kind of day that in retrospect seemed to explain and excuse everybody's bad mood, Candace lost her composure and said something she shouldn't have to a student. It was all very well to say they were just kids and you shouldn't let them get to you. But Candace wasn't arrogant enough to expect perfection in herself; when she slipped up and made one of the girls in her eighth-grade human-bio class cry, she apologized at the first opportunity, admitted that the fault was entirely hers, and suggested that they just put it behind them and move forward. Which of course the girl refused to do. She was so intoxicated by the rush of victimhood that she kept coming up with ways to prolong it.

That the student was Bayley Kimball was not Candace's doing. The whole incident was sparked, indisputably, by the girl, who should have and certainly could have said nothing when she noticed that Ms. Firth had her shirt on inside out. When she called attention to it, the class laughed, which was evidently something Bayley enjoyed, because she then called attention to it three more times. Candace smiled and tried to laugh along; that seemed like the only choice, since she wasn't about to take her shirt off and put it back on again in front of a room full of eighth graders. Bayley, in order to get the laugh again, had to keep upping the ante, because others were tiring of the joke too; so she said—to her teacher— "You oughta live with your mom or something so she can check you out before you leave the house looking like that," and Candace turned around and said, "At least my mom wouldn't let me out of the house with the word 'Juicy' across my ass," and the whole class made a sound like "Ohhhh" and Candace knew she'd stepped in it. Bayley, to her credit Candace supposed, held her tears in until the bell rang.

It wasn't even that bad, Candace thought but couldn't say, except maybe for her injudicious use of the word "ass." Her own teachers had said meaner things to her; the fact that she couldn't recall specific instances just went to prove that a little smackdown from your teacher wasn't such a big, life-ruining deal. But Bayley's mother went to the principal; the principal met with her, then with Candace, then with her and Candace and Patrick, and, as the principal later took pains to remind her, that was a total of three extra meetings he shouldn't have needed to have. The principal had always shown flashes of being a decent guy, Candace thought—he probably even had a sense of humor, outside of work—but in his professional life he was interested only in whether you were the type of person who made his life harder or the type who made his life easier.

Bayley's mother wanted Candace fired. The principal said he couldn't do that. The mother asked if that was some union thing, and the principal said no, it was more a thing of there being literally no one to replace her, this deep into the school year. The whole time, Patrick just sat there beside his wife, looking miserable and weak. No one seemed interested in his opinion. I could alter the lives of everyone in this room, Candace kept thinking, with one word, one fact. It sickened her to imagine what might await her when she went home that night and got drunk enough to check her Hotmail account. In the end Bayley's mother settled for a vague promise that Candace would be formally disciplined, and a written apology to the girl.

It was all resolved, but now Candace was the one who found herself unable to let it go, and so she went unwisely into the principal's office without an appointment, at lunchtime.

"Bill," she said, "I've been thinking. I was a good soldier about going back into the classroom when Jo Whalen—when that whole thing happened. But it was supposed to be temporary and I want to ask formally for my old position back."

Bill was eating cafeteria food, off a cafeteria tray, in his office. He wiped his mouth. "You don't like teaching?" he said.

She wanted to try opening up to him, to someone—to say no, not really, not anymore, which is probably why I'm not very good at it—but she reminded herself where they were, and what their relationship was. "I like it fine," she said. "That's not the point. It's a demotion, which I took temporarily to help the school out in a crisis. I don't want it to become permanent. I have every right to ask for that."

"Yes, you do," he said. "I'll put in the request with the district. You'll have to ride out the rest of the semester, though. You understand that, right?"

She did. There was no further issue with Bayley but Candace found herself counting the days anyway. Junior high was mostly a time of suffering, and it was a terrible thing to admit but she didn't want to be around it, it depressed her. They were so compulsively mean to each other. You could see them learning everything they would need in order to be insincere, selfish, status-conscious adults, and there was nothing you could do about it, you might as well try to keep them from getting taller. She tried to feel sorry for them, but mostly she just didn't like them. She was seeing some guy—they went out for drinks or dinner and then back to her place once or twice a week—but she couldn't talk to him about any of this. When she tried, she could see that he thought she was just joking.

It was helpful, at least, to have sex on the regular: she couldn't imagine how pissy her mood in general might have been if it weren't for that. Andrew, second-generation owner of the sporting goods store in Howland where Candace bought running shoes and the like, was a classic local type. He thought he knew everything: he was overconfident and condescending and maybe two-thirds as good-looking as he thought he was and he had always gotten what he wanted because he was too dumb to understand how much else there was to want, outside of the life he was living, the life he'd always lived. The less he knew about something, or someone, the more superior he felt. She longed to undo him. She teased and provoked him to the point of cruelty—sometimes past that point, for sure, though not on purpose. The politics of her own arousal were complicated. Her goal, always, was to make him lose it, make his composure crack, make him try to overwhelm her, try to shut her up. It was like child's play, to get him to do that. She felt in control of him and, at the same time, doomed to him.

It was warm for December but they had to keep the windows closed because of the neighbors. She climbed off of him and lay with her head and one hand on his stomach, while they caught their breath. She didn't like to look at his face after she came, at least not right away. It was good of him, she reflected, to keep that stomach as flat as it was. She knew it was about vanity more than any desire to please her, but still. You didn't have to make much of a tour of Howland to appreciate that masculine vanity of that sort wasn't to be taken for granted.

"That was amazing," he said unimaginatively.

She opened her eyes and looked up close at his cock, which was kind of perfect, though she gave him no credit for that, it was just serendipity. He had a whole elaborate workout routine, but it's not like that was part of it.

There was the sound, in the sealed room, of a vibrating phone. "Yours or mine?" Andrew said. "If it's mine, fuck it."

Candace lifted her gaze and saw her phone skittering across the laminated surface of the dresser. "I'd better get it," she said as sincerely as she could. It was her mother. "Hi, honey," she said. "Haven't seen you in a while."

"I was there three days ago," Candace said.

"You were? Well, there are a few things around here we could use a hand with."

"I'm a little jammed up today," Candace said. She looked at Andrew on the bed, willing him to move, to swing his legs onto the floor and head for the shower. "Can I call you later?" She hung up. Andrew smiled at her and laced his fingers behind his head. "So this morning I had this guy come in, from New York City," he said. He always said those words—"New York City"—in a mocking, pseudo-intimidated voice that Candace had stopped finding funny a long time ago. "Tells me he's very up on carbon-fiber downhill skis, because he's done a lot of internet research."

Her heart sank. There was only one direction in which a story like this could go. This was the essence of the males in her life: They were always the smartest character in their own stories. They always came out on top. Self-deprecation was a quality unknown to them.

Her phone vibrated again. The screen said *Mom*.

"Hi, honey!" Mom said.

"Mom," Candace said. "You just called me."

"What?"

"Five minutes ago. How can you not remember that?"

"Well, whatever you say," her mother said indulgently, as one would to a child. Andrew swung his legs onto the floor and lumbered off to her shower. "Anyway, I just wanted to say that there are a few things around here we could use a hand with."

She waited until Andrew was out of the bathroom, said goodbye to him, showered him off of her, and got in the car to head to Pittsfield. It was unseasonably warm and mud was everywhere. She took the back roads as far as she could, to avoid the rat's nest that Route 7 would be until New Year's. At the rare stop signs, with her windows down, she could hear the bare trees creak in the wind, before her engine drowned them out again.

Nobody wanted to admit what was wrong with Mom, not because they were emotional or scared or in denial, but simply because admitting it would oblige them to do something about it. "Hi, honey!" her mother said when she walked in the kitchen door. "What a pleasant surprise!" Though she was overweight, she'd aged well physically. Her face was largely unlined, and its penumbra of neat white hair had become a sort of accent to its perpetual expression of gentle, resigned, good-humored passivity, an expression not startlingly different from what it had been twenty or thirty years ago.

"I told you I was coming, Mom," Candace said, not irritably, but coolly. "We spoke about ninety minutes ago. And about two minutes before that."

This notion brushed across her mother's face like a headlight from a passing car, then she said, "Have you had any dinner?"

Dinner was a broad aluminum pan of chicken marsala; it finally drew her father from within the depths of the house, even though he must have known that Candace had been there for some time. Anyone who didn't know them would have assumed, just from their appearance, that he was the one who needed taking care of. He seemed to assume this too. His sullen, martyred affect suggested that he was being chronically neglected, that his wife, along with pretty much everyone else in the world, had abandoned her post. He could have taken care of her—he could have done for her nearly everything that Candace did—but he wouldn't. He saw his own home, as he saw the wider world, as fallen, irredeemable.

"So, Mom," Candace said, "you mentioned there were some things you needed some help with around here?" Her father looked up sharply from his plate.

"Did I?" she said.

When nothing followed, Candace said, "For instance I noticed that the fridge is almost empty. Do you need me to go to the store?"

"That's because your mother lost her cards again," he said. "ATM and credit. Again. So we have to cancel them, and then they

213

make you wait however many business days for the new ones to show up."

His wife smiled as if this were a story about people she didn't know.

"Jesus," Candace said. "Well, look, if you like, I can hold on to that stuff for her, since it's hard for her to keep track of it. Give her, you know, cash as needed."

"That'll be the fucking day," her father said.

"Honey!" her mother said, looking reproachfully at him. One day, Honey would probably be her name for all of them.

"Yeah, Dad, that's my master plan," Candace said. "To get my hands on your millions."

After dinner there was moonlight enough for her to go out and clear the brush that had overgrown their mailbox. Then she washed the dishes. On a hunch she went upstairs and into her parents' bedroom, and the sheets clearly had not been changed in some time. Or maybe Mom had started to change them and had just lost track and put the dirty ones back on. That had happened before. Candace's father certainly could have dealt with it. But it was women's work, and his life was full enough of humiliations without starting to take that on.

He followed Candace into the bedroom, not liking it that she was in there at all. The news still blared from the oversized TV downstairs. "Been sleeping on those same sheets since Labor Day," he said. "She doesn't give a damn."

"Dad," Candace said, "she forgets."

He snorted. "Believe me," he said, turning to leave, "there's things I wouldn't mind forgetting. But that is a luxury I don't have."

She drove home slowly in the dark, on the same back roads, quiet now. Her lips moved silently the whole drive. How had all of this—not her share, but her brothers' too, her absent sister's, all of it—fallen on her? How was that fair; more perplexingly, how and when had it happened at all? These people who had dogged her

214

childhood, who'd reflexively smothered every manifestation of self-esteem, who'd poisoned her against the very idea of marriage (and that was still true, she never wanted it, the thought of dying alone was in no way scarier than the specter of dying trapped in the embrace of someone you hated and blamed for everything): how had these people become her problem? Whenever she called Gerry or Mark and told them to call their parents, or to go over there, they did it. If there was an expense, they would ask her how much and then write a check and mail it to her. Otherwise, she knew, they didn't even think about it. She, too, longed not to think about it, to forget all about them as if they had died. But that was impossible now, and of course it was impossible to go back to the moment this whole unspoken arrangement had taken shape, whenever the hell that was.

The next day, the principal had his secretary summon Candace to his office. He told her that her request to be promoted out of the classroom and into a job as assistant principal had been denied by the district.

"I wasn't asking to be promoted," Candace said. "I had that job, I voluntarily stepped down from it to help everybody out—to help you out—and now I want it back."

"Well, they don't see it that way. When you gave up that job, the job technically stopped existing, so now approval for an assistant principal has to be obtained all over again. They've conducted a review and they've determined that it's not necessary, which is code for there's not enough money in the budget for it. Which means a lot more work for me, by the way. I'm as unhappy about this as you are."

She stood in his doorway; she could see, even when he was sitting still, how every fiber of his being strained toward wanting this meeting to be over.

"I quit," she said.

And she did it; her seventh-grade animal-bio class started in twelve minutes, but she didn't go. She just didn't. She walked out of the building and into her car and drove away from there.

She thought about sitting in a bar—that seemed like what one did, right after doing what she'd just done—but they weren't open yet and anyway she wasn't truly in the mood. So she went home, and lay down on her bed, and her adrenaline went out like the tide.

How was this her life? She hadn't made the necessary effort to get away, as her sister had; she'd stayed and taken a job that forced her to pretend that the sons and daughters of people she'd known since her own childhood had it in them to be improvements over their parents. She was haunted by her unlived lives, by the various corpses of possibility. It didn't matter what they were. Nothing about her life could be said to be temporary or provisional or experimental anymore. This was it.

Whatever it was that had given Renee the escape velocity to get out of there and live a life that had nothing to do with Howland—the narcissism, the oblivious self-confidence, the shameless talent for ingratiation with men—Candace understood that these were terrible, unlikable qualities, yet for the first time she caught herself wishing she had them too. It must be nice to have so little to worry about that you can spend your days forwarding emails about Agenda 21 or whatever the fuck.

She was thirty-four years old. Once in a while she would have this insight that she should really get into therapy, that her actions were being determined by some part of her that she didn't even understand; but it never took more than a few minutes' thought to come down from that idea. Because what kind of shrink were you liable to get up here, in the middle of nowhere? The kind not good enough to make it elsewhere, that's what kind. A bitter, defensive washout, like her, like most people she had to talk to every day. She was going to ask such a person to explain her to herself? No thank you.

Anyway, she could forget about such louche concerns as mental health now. Now the question was, where am I going to find another job around here?

She waited until five o'clock, when she would normally be home from work, then she walked across the street and bought a liter of Chardonnay from her landlord. He didn't meet her eyes.

She got drunk and had a revelation. She wanted to do some good in the world. That was why she'd tried public school teaching in the first place. In her mind she eliminated anything further to do with kids, but there were plenty of adults who needed help, right? She should go to work for a nonprofit or a charity. Feeding the hungry, helping the poor. Even in the Berkshires you had your hungry and your poor. When she Googled such things, though, all she got were charities affiliated with various local churches, and that—working for a church—she would not do. Her mother's mother had tried to indoctrinate them into the church when they were kids, with the bribe of a trip to McDonald's afterwards, but that arrangement hadn't even lasted a year before Mark and Gerry got kicked out of Mass for spitting at each other and Grandma said they could all continue on their path to hell for all she cared.

So you had to think big—or not big, necessarily, but just outside existing structures. If what you wanted didn't yet exist, where would you go to make it exist? Sometime during the night she had a thought. She was pretty drunk when she had this thought, but when she woke up the next morning it still seemed like a good one. When she got out of the shower her phone was ringing; it was the school, and she ignored it. Instead she called the main number for Howland's Town Hall. When her call went to voicemail she checked the time and saw it was still only eight twenty. She left a message requesting a meeting with the First Selectman, to discuss a proposed new project; she spelled out her name, and said that she believed her brother was a friend of his. When five hours passed with no word, Candace just got in her car and drove over there. Bureaucracy was a state of mind, in a town that small.

She'd been in the building before, but only a few times, when school budget meetings were held there. In the hallway, just where it cornered toward the old gymnasium, was a strange feature, no less strange for having always been there: a "Food Bank," more literally a card table holding up a display of donated canned goods and supplies for the town's neediest. It looked temporary but Candace remembered it from previous visits. Maybe it was always the same food, like in a fallout shelter. It wasn't enough to last a family more than two or three days. Not to mention that any local would sooner starve than accept public charity of that kind.

Hadi had brought his own former personal assistant up from New York City—had persuaded her to move to Howland, the story went, husband and children too, by offering her a salary too life-changing to refuse. She exuded an intimidating professional bearing even behind her undersized desk in the anteroom outside the closed door of the First Selectman's office. Candace asked to see him, and thought she would outflank the secretary by adding, "I have no appointment."

"I'm afraid he's not in," the secretary said. Her little desktop nameplate said Ms. Burrows. She had maybe five or six years on Candace, eight years tops.

"It's kind of a local custom, a tradition, to see the townspeople on a walk-in basis," Candace said, making this up on the spot. "The whole my-door-is-always-open idea. Transparency in government."

"That's interesting to know," the woman said. "Still, unfortunately he's not in."

Stymied, Candace walked back out into the empty hallway. She was starting to understand her own behavior as symptomatic of some kind of breakdown. Less than twenty-four hours ago, she had a job, she was a schoolteacher. She stood by the weird, lonely Food Bank and drummed her fingers on an unoccupied corner of the surface of the card table. The food there was horrible, unwanted, like a punishment for failing. Canned asparagus, a jar of pimentos, a six-pack of flavored water. It's like they knew it was all for display anyway, so they figured, why waste something tasty? Just gather up the stuff no one wants, and it'll stand for whatever it is that we want this Food Bank to stand for.

Candace left the building and walked down Main Street to the Undermountain, to sit and have a cup of coffee: no point in rushing back home. She took a stool at the counter, beneath the faded Christmas decorations, and when she lifted her eyes from the list of specials clipped to the top of the napkin dispenser, there he was: Hadi, sitting alone in a booth, holding half of a patty melt in one hand, scrolling down on his BlackBerry with the other.

For some reason he hadn't taken off his bright red Canada Goose down jacket. Candace thought it looked like something no guy would wear unless his wife bought it for him. With a start she realized that he was now looking up at her, and that was because she had been staring at him. The diner was mostly empty—it was an odd hour for lunch—so she was able to speak to him in a normal voice from where she sat.

"I hope you don't mind if I ask for just a minute of your time," she blurted out, and stood up and slid into the sprung booth seat across from him. He stopped chewing. She felt like she had breached security, even though the waitresses and the cashier ignored her. There was an aura that came from Hadi, for sure. He didn't have that prickliness, that layer of self-protection, the locals usually had. He didn't need it, she supposed—he lived a life in which things happened because he made them happen.

"I'm eating," he said simply. "Who are you?"

"Candace Firth. Until—until recently I was the assistant principal at Howland Elementary School." There was an inconsequential pause. "My brother is Mark Firth?" she said, wincing internally. "He's your neighbor on Route 4, did some work on your house a few years ago?"

Hadi smiled. "Sure," he said.

"Just so you know, I did try your office first, I had no idea you'd be here, but since you are here . . . I wanted to run an idea by you. Howland doesn't have any kind of facility for women, a shelter, a safe haven for victims of domestic violence primarily. The nearest one is across the state line in Hillsdale, which creates problems in terms of public assistance, what with the two different states. The closest one in Massachusetts is all the way up in Pittsfield. For women who work, or have children, that shelter is too far away to be practical. It just occurred to me that such a shelter, for people who have nowhere else to go, is something that a town like this needs."

Hadi put down the sandwich half he'd been holding and wiped his fingers. "Where would this shelter be?"

"I'm not sure," Candace said.

"I mean, it would have to be a place where a number of people could sleep. Right? A house. An existing house, probably."

Candace willed herself not to turn red.

"And is domestic violence a particular problem in Howland?" he said—not meanly, but very rationally, almost as if Candace were no longer there. "Of course I understand it's a terrible problem everywhere. Absolutely. But I mean are there any numbers, is there any way of measuring the proposed need?"

"This idea," Candace said, "is really just in the preliminary stages at this point."

He looked at her, not impatiently, but for an uncomfortably long time.

"The public school system is a horrible mess," he said finally. "Is that why you left?"

"I'm not sure," she said. Her face felt hot. Who was this guy? She had the illusion—she recognized it as an illusion—that he could see right through her. Something about his money—for that's what it was, of course: the money—seemed to put him out of reach of the usual run of social concerns, to lend him a sort of impartiality. Or maybe that was just a different way of acknowledging that he had no reason to care one way or the other about her. Which made him into a judge of sorts. She could offer him nothing.

"When did you leave?" he said.

"Yesterday. You're right, I came to you too soon with this. Plus I don't actually live here, I live in Great Barrington. But I thought you . . . I'm just at kind of a crossroads right now, and I'm trying to think of some small way to make the world better. Which doesn't seem like it should be hard, at all, because the world is mostly a pretty terrible place. Right? Ironic. But anyway, it was a pleasure to meet you and I am sorry to have interrupted your lunch."

She walked slowly back along Main Street to where her car sat in the Town Hall lot, and she drove home, feeling calm, submissive now to ruin. She Googled "how do I apply for public assistance" and the next day she drove to Pittsfield to fill out the first of the forms. She did it that way, rather than asking Gerry, because she didn't want her family to know until she was ready to tell them— ideally after she'd already lined up another job—but that didn't work, her school phone number and email account were disconnected, so first Renee and then her brothers figured it out right away. They all consoled her and then they all got used to it. She applied for a few jobs she didn't really want and she didn't get them. Every day she tried to make herself leave the apartment at least once, unless it was too cold. She told Andrew, in an email, that she didn't want to see him anymore, and his reply to her was so cruel she couldn't even laugh at it. Thirty-nine was the number of weeks her benefits would last; that worked out to sometime in August or maybe September. She told herself she wouldn't do the math until she got closer to the end. But then, before she was even halfway there, she got a call from Hadi's secretary in the Howland Town Hall. The First Selectman was out of town on business but he wanted to invite her to apply for a job running Howland's free library, on Mill Street. The current librarian had just announced her intention to retire.

A librarian? That's not what she had in mind back when she'd talked to him, back when she'd still had anything in mind at all. The Howland library was tiny, just two rooms and an office. Candace had only ever seen it through its windows. She wasn't sure who used it. Maybe it was like the Food Bank, there only because it seemed unflattering for it not to be there. But what did it matter, she had no choice. And she had to admit it made a nice, ironic fit with the small-town, old-maid lifestyle to which it was now time for her to grow accustomed.

Caldwell House stayed open to the public each year until November 1; after that, only the offices were heated, in the renovated warren of rooms off the kitchen. Karen was warned that a little stir-craziness could set in then, particularly on days when no one came in to work but her. In fact her predecessor in the job had been fired for having work calls auto-forwarded to her home number; it wasn't that she was lazy, she'd said, but that she kept hearing scary noises upstairs.

The house and grounds reopened after Memorial Day, but that was still a few weeks off; in mid-May there was the annual board meeting to prepare for. The board members, who were all from Boston or New York, liked to schedule it to coincide with the return of spring warmth and visual pleasantry. It made the drive there and back less onerous. Karen coordinated overnight accommodations for those who wanted them, arranged the catering, saw to special dietary needs or requests, printed out annual reports and quarterly revenue projections—it was a lot of work, and her understanding was that these society types were particularly impatient with mistakes. But what really stressed her out was when she asked the director, Ms. van Aswegen, who would be in charge of taking the meeting's minutes, and Ms. van Aswegen answered her with a smile and a raised eyebrow. Karen had zero secretarial skills, and it's not like she'd lied about that on her résumé. But her boss just told her to do her best and not worry so much.

She was so worked up about it that she couldn't sleep the night before the meeting, but the task turned out to be undemanding. The six old folks on the board—four men, two women—talked slowly and tended to say the same things over and over again; and then there were long stretches when they weren't discussing anything foundation-related at all, just vacation spots and real estate and how the government was now totally out of control. Mr. Peck, who wore a bow tie, went on for almost ten minutes about the estate tax alone; Karen put her pen down as discreetly as she could. They went over the operating budget, asking only a couple of cranky questions about one-time expenses. Mr. Peck wanted to know why they'd paid for a new sign when they'd just paid for the last new sign two years earlier; the director cleared her throat and explained that the old new sign had accidentally been taken out by the town snowplow. Well, the town should pay for it, then, Mr. Peck said, and the director gently answered that the town had indeed agreed to reimburse them, but these things took time. Mr. Peck sat back and scowled, all his views confirmed. Then, just when it seemed like the afternoon was wrapping up, and Ms. van Aswegen was congratulating them all on another year of wise and excellent stewardship, her voice drifted to a stop as she and everyone else noticed Mrs. Elliot, who'd been driven from Brookline, raising her colorless hand in the air like a schoolgirl.

"I have some new business," the old woman said, "if everyone else is quite through." Karen took the cap off her pen again, flexing her fingers, disappointed but also curious.

"I have decided to retire from the board," Mrs. Elliot said, her hand still floating slowly back down toward her lap. "Effective immediately. I wanted to wait until the end of the meeting so as not to disrupt."

There was a confused pause. "But why?" Mr. Peck finally asked, in a tone of genuine concern.

"I have the cancer," Mrs. Elliot said. "I don't care to discuss what kind."

Karen did not know whether any of these people ever saw or spoke to one another apart from this one day every year. That still added up to something, since she knew that at least three of the current board members had served for more than twenty years. Mr. Peck looked absolutely stricken. For a moment the dark-paneled room took on a quality that stirred and conveyed all the bad news that had ever been delivered there.

"Please let the minutes reflect," Mr. Peck said hoarsely, without once looking at Karen, "the board's unanimous resolution thanking Deirdre Elliot for her years of devoted service, and expressing our confident prayers for her speedy and complete recovery."

"Yes, well," said Mrs. Elliot. "Thank you for that. Now the new business, obviously, is the appointment of my successor."

"I don't think there's any need to be in a hurry about that," Ms. van Aswegen said with great feeling, but a look from Mrs. Elliot silenced her.

"I would like my replacement to be female," she said, without elaboration. "With that in mind, I think there is an obvious candidate right here in town."

She paused a few seconds until everyone, Karen included, understood she was talking about Rachel Hadi. The prospect was approved in principle; Karen could tell the others were enthusiastic about it but didn't want to appear so, out of respect for Mrs. Elliot, even though she was the one somewhat impatiently moving the whole plan forward. "Now, I don't know her personally," the old lady said, "but someone here must."

Yet no one did. They all looked at one another sheepishly. Not even the New York contingent seemed able to claim a social acquaintance with her; "different generation," Mr. Peck said with a rueful frown. Karen almost raised her own hand—they'd met, they'd spoken, their kids went to the same school—but she had a sense this would not be embraced as a solution to their etiquette problem. In the absence of a more socially graceful option, Ms. van Aswegen said she would make the inquiry herself, discreetly, on the board's behalf. The meeting was adjourned. Mr. Peck slowly walked Mrs. Elliot to the portico, her arm through his, to wait for her car.

Karen went to the fridge and unpacked her lunch at her desk. Her window faced the grounds, not the parking lot, so she couldn't see everyone depart, but in another half hour or so the huge house behind her was silent. From her desk she could watch one or two of the board members strolling the lightly roped garden paths, reading the brochures, folding and stuffing them in their back pockets. She'd rewritten parts of that brochure herself. It was a sunny day, one of the first ones. Some of the flower beds were still under tarps.

Back in October, Haley's fifth-grade class had come to Caldwell House for a picnic. Haley had visited her mother's office before, and she remembered where its window was; so she waved at it when the line of kids passed by, but they had agreed in advance she would not come inside the mansion that day, nor would Karen go out. Too embarrassing. Karen ached for Haley nearly all the time these days. She didn't seem to have many friends anymore. There was no good way to talk about it because even bringing it up would seem cruel. Not that Haley seemed outwardly unhappy or anxious; she was self-sustaining in the way she had always been. She talked less, though. It was the dawn of the middle-school years, the age of self-consciousness, for girls especially, and it was hard for Karen to watch her only child learning to keep her inmost thoughts to herself.

A week after the board meeting—with the house still closed for the season, and a deep chill in every room that made it seem colder inside than out—Karen was asked to accompany Ms. van Aswegen and Rachel Hadi on a tour of Caldwell House. The director was beside herself with nerves. She'd asked Karen along mostly in case her mind went blank and she forgot some detail about the history of the house. When Karen appeared in the office doorway with her overcoat on, her boss practically hissed at her. "Suck it up," she said. "We are trying to impress somebody here. We don't want her to think we are in some kind of ruin."

It's not like she's looking to buy the place, Karen thought. Or maybe that was somehow the plan? Anyway, fine, she left her coat in her nice warm cubicle and made sure at least there was coffee for everyone. Rachel Hadi showed up on time, in her black SUV, and she walked across the gravel of the parking lot without so much as a jacket on; she was a slight woman, though very fit, but she did not seem to acknowledge the weather at all. "I know you," she said to Karen. Not in an especially friendly way: more like miffed that she couldn't remember from where. She was carrying a tote bag from Asana, which was some kind of high-end meditation center or spiritual retreat in Stockbridge. It was right smack in the center of everything but Karen didn't know anyone who had even seen the inside of it.

"This is Karen Firth," Ms. van Aswegen said, "she's my assistant here. So I thought we'd begin with the house and then move out briefly to the gardens, is that all right?" Karen noticed, not for the first time, that something about the house itself seemed to make people more formal, more obsequious, yet also ruder. The director was normally pretty nice to her.

"The Caldwell Trust was established in 1938, the year of Winston Caldwell's death," she intoned as they walked up the curving main staircase to the second floor, where it was even colder. "The house and the legendary gardens have been open to the public every year since. Prudent investment, by the board, of the interest on the original endowment has enabled us not only to maintain the grounds as they were when Mrs. Caldwell was alive but to keep them open to the public for the lowest possible admission fee."

Rachel Hadi didn't look at the director as she spoke, which was probably what enabled her to get through her speech so smoothly, Karen thought. They walked into the master bedroom, with its stripped, magnificently scrolled wooden bed, its two wardrobes and one spare, uncomfortable chair. "This is the master bedroom," Ms. van Aswegen said compulsively.

Rachel stepped over the low thin rope meant to prohibit visitors from lying on the bed and ran her finger appreciatively along the wood. "I've heard the basic story," she said. "They couldn't have kids, is that it?"

"Well, it wasn't that they couldn't," the director said. "This bed was the one they slept in on their honeymoon in Venice. Mr. Caldwell had it shipped here at great expense, after his wife fell ill."

But their guest had already turned away from the bed and was heading back toward the upstairs hallway.

"Many of the flowers, too, were shipped here from Europe," Ms. van Aswegen said, her voice a little more shrill now, at least to Karen's ear. "Some of them, the perennials, bloom here to this day. The whole place is—well, I like to think of it as a love story."

Rachel had paused at the small, cathedral-style window at one end of the long corridor, the window Caldwell had added so that his wife could look at her gardens, and signal instructions to the gardeners, when she was too sick to venture downstairs. Karen hung back discreetly. She was freezing. She thought of asking if anyone needed more coffee, but the silence just then seemed difficult to violate.

Rachel turned around with a genial, patient smile that seemed to fix the director where she stood. "What else do you want to show me?" Rachel said.

They toured the ground floor: the dining room with its ornately painted ceilings and impossibly long table, the modest ballroom where visitors danced and where later townspeople came to see Mrs. Caldwell's body lying in state (though the director omitted that detail), the modestly ugly offices, the old kitchen in which only a refrigerator now functioned. Something had gone wrong, though Karen was not sure where or when; she was aware of it mostly via the tremor in the director's increasingly loud voice. Maybe it was the absence of visitors, or maybe it was the weather outside, where the daylight was already faltering even though the day itself seemed only half over, but the whole place, which Ms. van Aswegen tried so hard to portray as a sanctuary of beauty and taste and a vital part of the Berkshires' link to its own history, just seemed redolent of death. The three women went out and shivered for a few moments on the vast rear patio, where in the old days parties of up to a hundred were entertained and which for years was rented out for wedding receptions until one unfortunate incident about a decade ago.

"Well, thank you," Rachel said abruptly. "It was a privilege to meet you, and to have a private tour of this beautiful home."

The director's eyebrows soared. "Of course," she said, "the real jewel of the place, which we have yet to tour, is the gardens."

"Oh, sure," Rachel said. But she didn't move. "Listen, I don't want to lead you on. I've asked around and this place seems to run pretty smoothly—you got full tax-exempt status back in 2002, is that right?"

The director smiled gamely.

"As you can imagine, I'm already somewhat overcommitted. We left our full-time home in New York but I didn't think it would be right to abandon our charitable commitments there as well. I am so sorry to have to decline your very kind invitation, but I'm sure you'll have no trouble finding someone else willing to take on such a prestigious responsibility."

The director had begun nodding about halfway through this

speech and, now that it was over, seemed unable to stop. "Well, of course we thank you," she said, "and we understand completely, of course. Karen, will you walk Mrs. Hadi to her car?"

"What?" Karen said, but it was too late, her boss had already taken Rachel Hadi's hand in hers and released it and was disappearing through the patio door.

They watched her go. "Jesus," Rachel said. "Do people never get said no to up here? I thought I was pretty nice about it." She turned and stared at Karen, as if for the first time. "Firth is your name? I've seen you at school things, I think. Your husband's the hunky contractor."

"Yes," Karen said icily. She felt a prick of loyalty, though she wasn't quite sure to whom or what. "Our children are in the same class."

"We should be wearing coats," Rachel said. "It's freezing in here. You don't smoke by any chance, do you?"

Karen shook her head.

"Of course you don't. Nobody around here does. Stupid question. Well, look, you really don't have to walk me to my car, I'm sure I can—"

"No, that's okay," Karen said, not really in control of what she was saying. She went to the entrance hall, opened the door, and gestured through it.

The two of them walked across the parking lot, a light rain now on their faces. Karen didn't completely dislike this woman—in person she was dominant, unafraid, much different from what Mark had led her to believe—but at the same time she had an impulse to harass her, just a little bit, by walking so conspicuously beside her, as if they were friends. They reached the car and Karen pointed to the Asana bag. "What's that place like?" she said baldly. "I've always wanted to check it out, but it's too expensive."

Rachel stared at her. "It's very spiritual," she said finally. "You'd probably love it."

She edged out into traffic and was gone almost before Karen realized she was still standing there watching. She went back inside and put her coat and gloves on; van Aswegen had apparently already left. It was true that Caldwell House didn't really need money. Maybe it was more about wanting the whole operation to be taken seriously, to be seen, from above, as socially worthwhile. In any event, Karen and her boss never spoke of that afternoon again—to each other, at least—not even a week later, when a check arrived in the mail, signed not by Rachel but by the First Selectman himself, for twenty-five thousand dollars, payable to the Friends of Caldwell House.

IS EVERYBODY HAPPY?—
POSTED 07/05/2005 AT 12:49 A.M.

There was an old jazz bandleader named Ted Lewis who was famous for saying that. He was a huge star at one time—there was a movie made about him. He wore a battered old top hat onstage. He called himself the "High-Hatted Tragedian of Song." He was just an okay clarinet player, and he couldn't really sing that well either, but people loved him, partly because he wasn't afraid to be as corny as hell. All through the Depression, he would play these hard-luck tunes—he once had a #1 hit with a song called "In a Shanty in Old Shanty Town"—and onstage, between numbers, or sometimes even during numbers, he would turn to the audience with a big smile and shout,

"Is Everybody Happy?"

This line has been going through my head non-stop. I think about it when I walk up and down Main Street in Howland; I think about it when I stop in at Daisy's for a coffee; I think about it when I drive around the county for my work, and see the Berkshire range looking so green and inviting, just as it probably looked a hundred or two hundred years ago. And I think about it when I open up my annual property tax bill. I think yours probably looks about the same as mine, if you live in Howland anyway. It's smaller. Money that I worked hard to earn stays in my pocket where it belongs. I spend that money in town, and it boosts the local economy, and everybody's better off—that simple, simple truth that tax-and-spend liberals have to jam their fingers really deep into their ears not to hear.

And I ask myself: Is everybody happy?

The answer seems to be yes, but I wonder. Let's not forget what's making it all possible. We have basically allowed ourselves to return to colonial times: we serve at the pleasure of King Philip. King Philip pays for the shortfall in the school budget, he pays for the shortfall in road maintenance, he pays for the shortfall in the recreation budget. I don't think the town of Howland necessarily runs any better—or even has less government, really—than it did before we elected him King. I just think we don't notice it as much, because we don't have to pay for it ourselves anymore. We've sold it to him. We've sold him the town.

And if we've sold it to him, then it's his to do with as he wants, right?

Maybe he doesn't want anything. Maybe he truly is a good guy, with all of our best interests at heart. I mean, billionaire hedge fund operators are famous for having the little guy's best interests at heart, right?

That was sarcasm, in case you missed it.

231

My point is: what looks from the outside like it might be some kind of libertarian paradise is actually the ultimate nanny state. Don't believe me? The scuttlebutt already is that King Philip is planning to impose a town curfew, one that would override the state law that forbids bars from serving drinks after 2 A.M. So what, you say. I don't even hang out in bars, what do I care? Well, ask yourself what your recourse will be if he decides to extend that curfew to all citizens of Howland. Because he could do it. He controls everything here now. Not because he took power, but because we gave it to him.

Remember, Citizens: When it comes to government, taxation is not the enemy.

Dependency is the enemy!

—PC Barnum

Comments (6):
—First!
—Jeez you libertarian assholes are never satisfied. This sounds like Ayn Rand's wet dream?
—I don't know PC . . . he cut taxes . . . everything's running smoothly . . . not sure what you're complaining about
    —have you seen this douchebag in his sweater vest tho? Eating by himslf in the diner every day? rotflmao
—Meet hot singles in your area!: [link]
—I totally agree, PC. I love this whole mindset about how billionaires are morally incorruptible! How the F do you think they got to be billionaires? Quid pro quo, baby!
—You keep telling it like it is, PC! We here out in Colorado are following your every word!

RAILROAD DAYS A FULL-STEAM SUCCESS!

Unseasonable Weather Leads to Crowds Greater Than Expected

BY ABIGAIL BOGERT

Howland's local commerce received a huge pre-season boost from the first annual Railroad Days Celebration last weekend. A spokesperson for the Board of Selectmen said the event was a great success and will certainly be repeated next year.

The revival of Railroad Days, a Howland tradition through the 1950s, was conceived by Andrew Durning, who owns Mountain Range Sporting Goods on Melville Road. "This area has a lot of history that even longtime residents don't know about," he said. "I thought we should celebrate that. At the same time, I thought it might be a nice way to give some locally owned businesses a lift, during what's usually a down period between Labor Day and the ski season."

At the old depot building, which runs behind the parking lots on the west side of Route 41, local volunteer re-enactors took children (of all ages) on a ride to the siding and back in a genuine, refurbished steam engine. The old Berkshire railroad ceased service to Howland in 1977; the late First Selectman Marty Solomon saved the depot itself from teardown in 1995 and oversaw its conversion into an indoor mini-mall. Staffers in the Depot shops wore historically accurate 19th-century garb while at work. The attention to detail, courtesy of Corinne Butler and her staff at the Berkshire Historical Society, was remarkable!

Elsewhere in town, nearly every local business held some kind of outdoor event or sidewalk sale. It was a delight to see the street looking much as it must have a century or more ago, with Main Street—closed to vehicular traffic for the day—a pedestrian mall and social gathering place. Events went on well after dark, with a concert by the high school orchestra at the bandstand, and a screening of *Meet Me in St. Louis* projected onto the wall of the old Foster mill, courtesy of enterprising minds at the Library!

The only black mark on the weekend came when official festivities were over. Several store windows were broken by one or more vandals on Main Street, and some graffiti was left. The affected stores included Berkshire Wine & Spirits, Diabolique, and Creative Kidz. Trooper Constable said the police would investigate thoroughly.

Still, all in all the first Railroad Days was an at-track-tion like no other! With crowds swelled by the curious from neighboring towns, the local economy got a much appreciated boost and a history lesson at the same time. One local merchant estimated his receipts for the weekend at "maybe two hundred and fifty percent" of what they were the weekend prior. Full steam ahead into the Holiday Season!

In order to qualify for the government backstop, which the banks required before they'd let you claim the maximum when you borrowed against the property, you had to rent to tenants whose income fell below a certain line. Mark did not like to stereotype people, but there were stereotypes and then there was direct experience, and he learned the hard way that there was a connection, there just was, between the amount of money people made and their responsibility as tenants. Not in every case, but in a lot of cases. And the issue wasn't always with the rent itself. There were noise complaints from neighbors, there were tickets for trash-pickup violations when they didn't put their stuff in the right-colored bin, or in any bin at all. There was damage to the mechanicals that they would demand to have fixed even when they were clearly responsible for the damage themselves. Basically they—or some of them, not all of them—refused to treat the place like it was their home, which of course, in a certain light, it wasn't.

A fellow named Gage moved into one of the two new units in Egremont; he was a single father with two boys, he had a decent job at the transfer station, and Mark liked him right away. Not even two weeks later, Gage called him at ten o'clock at night to say that the bathroom faucet was dripping. My kid can't sleep, he said. How one could be an adult male and not know how to fix a drip-ping faucet was something Mark could not fathom. Not to men-tion that those fixtures were brand new, which would strongly suggest that Gage or his sons had been screwing with them some-how. He told the tenant he'd come over tomorrow, the tenant said fine, and then half an hour later he called back. The worst part was that Karen was livid. "Did you even meet this guy before you rented to him?" she said. "You couldn't tell he was a crackpot?" No, I couldn't, Mark thought, but there was no point in saying it, because if it interrupted the whole my-husband-is-easily-taken-advantage-of narrative in her head, then she wouldn't hear it anyway.

It wasn't about income, it was about what you were worth; and he was now worth a lot. She didn't want to concede that it was true, because, he felt, that would mean conceding that she'd been wrong about him. He'd been swindled by a con man, but that was one time, it could have happened to anybody, indeed it had hap-pened to numerous other people, some of them with much more of a background in finance than he had. Why wouldn't she *want* to be wrong about him? If you love someone, how can you not want that person to justify your love by succeeding? He didn't get it. A couple of times, things had gotten so heated that he was pretty sure Haley must have heard them. He didn't know for sure, but he thought so. Sound traveled in that house. It would certainly explain Haley's distant attitude toward him lately, which Karen claimed was just about her getting older, learning to see her parents not as heroes but as they really were. Still, he vowed to keep better control of himself.

An offshoot of success, in his new field, was that he didn't always have a great deal to do, day to day. It was the opposite of what he was used to; in his old life, success equated with keeping busy, with being overwhelmed by demands on his time. Minor maintenance he referred to Barrett. He could have handled these requests on his own and saved a bit of money, but he just couldn't see himself unclogging a drain or fixing a door hinge at this stage. He still fielded all the initial complaints himself, though. He could have just given his tenants Barrett's phone number but that struck him as risky.

He offered to drive Haley to school, but apparently the bus itself was now a sort of social scene that she couldn't miss. He left for Daisy's in the morning just as early as he used to when he was on his way to a job site, but then he hung out longer, and returned home when he was sure Karen had already left for work at Caldwell House. He made the mistake of remarking once—just trying to make conversation—that he had no idea what she did all day over there, and she replied that that was her favorite aspect of the job. One morning he invited his sister to meet him at Daisy's for breakfast, just to catch up with her, and that didn't go so pleasantly either.

"I can't understand why you like this place," Candace said. "It's horrifying."

"It is not," Mark said, looking around to make sure no one had overheard. "It's fine. It doesn't change, that's what I like. Why do you have it in for old Daisy?"

She pointed, not subtly, over his shoulder; he turned and figured out that she was indicating a new hand-lettered sign, hung among all the other corny signs, that read IF YOU'RE NOT OUTRAGED, YOU'RE NOT PAYING ATTENTION.

"I mean what is that shit?" Candace said. "Outraged about what?"

"I don't know," Mark said. "What, do you think it's political?"

"Jesus Christ," she said.

"So how is the new job? Still hard for me to imagine you as the kindly small-town librarian. I mean, I could tell some stories."

Candace frowned. "It's fine," she said, "it's a job. Mostly pretty simple stuff. More paperwork than you'd think. But I don't have a boss, at least not one I have to see every day, so that's a nice change."

She looked at him appraisingly. "And you?" she said. "Settling into life as a slumlord?"

They all made light of him, disrespected him. His own family. It was galling because they were all unashamed to depend on him too: his wife, his brother, who'd be who knows where if Mark hadn't invited him into the business, his father, whom he gave money every couple of months to tide them over in return for some sarcastic remark. Even Candace: he'd given her some money when she was between jobs, money she'd never hinted at paying back. He was effectively the patriarch, the head of the family, but no one treated him that way. Happy to benefit from his success as long as they didn't have to acknowledge it. Hypocrites.

Back in his home office he was on the internet, toggling between real estate listings and extreme-sports videos, when his phone buzzed in his pocket. On his screen was the name Philip Hadi. He'd never deleted the contact; he always maintained business contacts, even after a job was over. He took two deep breaths before answering the call.

"Mark? It's Phil Hadi. Listen, I have something I want to talk to you about, and I wonder if you could come over and see me. At Town Hall, I mean."

"Yes, sir," Mark said, and winced at his own response. "Of course. When's a good time for you?"

"I was thinking of right now," Hadi said, sounding confused.

Mark had a moment when he started, or wanted, to take offense at the idea that he could be summoned without notice in the middle of the day, or indeed at any time. But this was just Hadi's manner, more a guileless absence of social grace than some arrogant power play. And Mark truly did have nothing else going on that day. And of course he was curious.

"I'm finishing up some things," he said, "and I'll come over as soon as I can."

Despite the summons, Mark was made to wait ten minutes to see the First Selectman once he got there. There was no waiting room per se—the place had not been built for that—so he sat in a weak chrome-and-plastic chair up against the wall in the main hallway, near the Food Bank. At length Hadi's secretary, the one he'd reputedly lured up here from New York with an astronomical salary, stuck her head into the hallway and gave him a tight little smile to beckon him inside. The door to the inner office was open. Mark walked through it and she quietly pulled it shut behind him.

A rendering of the town seal hung in a frame on the wall. Otherwise there were no pictures or objects of any kind, nothing of a personal nature on the desk—only an open laptop and several neat stacks of paper. Hadi had not personalized the space in any way, which was admirable, Mark decided—like it was more about the office than about the man. The desk itself was unlovely, indestructible, metal and gray and not much smaller than a pool table. The only two objects in the room that looked as though they dated later than the Eisenhower years were the laptop and Hadi's ergonomically sophisticated chair.

"Mark," Hadi said. "You're well?"

"I am. I have to tell you, a little exchange we had, the last time I saw you, really made a huge impression on my life, for the better. I'm not doing general-contracting work anymore."

"You're *not*?" Hadi said. He looked crestfallen. "Why not?"

Mark grew flustered. "I'm dealing more in properties now. Local properties. You said I needed to look at them as assets, more in the abstract. Houses, I mean. And you were right."

"Oh. Well, that may change things, although maybe not. You're not doing construction work of any kind, then? Construction or installation?"

Mark suddenly felt embarrassed, and the unexpectedness of that feeling put him in a somewhat defensive posture. "Not really, no," he said. "I'm past that."

"Because what I wanted to offer you was a fairly simple job. I need two security cameras installed. They have to be above a certain height."

"This is at your house?"

"No. At either end of Main Street, basically. Two should be enough to cover the length of it, unless there's something, some obstruction, I'm not thinking of, in which case, I guess, there'd be a third. Not that different from what you did at the house, which is why I thought of you. What would you charge for that kind of work?"

"I don't understand," Mark said.

"Remember the vandalism back in September? Railroad Days? Just in case something like that happens again. Howland's only got one assigned trooper, he can't be everywhere. So this is just a cheap law enforcement tool. Having a second policeman would be overkill, and way more expensive besides. I mean, I'd be paying for it, not the town, but still."

They sat for a few moments in a silence from which Hadi seemed to expect something.

"Why ask me?" Mark said.

"Because you're my guy," Hadi said.

Mark pictured himself in a cherry picker on Main Street, wiring and affixing surveillance cameras. He imagined his neighbors driving by, standing underneath him, asking him what he was doing.

"It's kind of you to think of me," he said. "But, as I say, I've kind of transitioned out of that line of work. It's been really time-consuming, getting the new business off the ground. I don't think I'd have the time to do it even as a favor."

"Oh. Okay," Hadi said. "Too bad. I'll find someone else. Thank you for coming in."

Mark might have mistaken Hadi's abruptness for anger or rudeness if he didn't know him. He smiled generously at the secretary on his way out, got in the truck, and was home before the school bus. He didn't tell Karen about the meeting; in fact he didn't tell anyone about it, which helped him to forget about it himself, and when the cameras went up at either end of Main Street—one on a telephone pole, the other on the cornice of the old Holbeck mill—he didn't notice them there for a long time.

LARCENY

GREAT BARRINGTON—A 17-year-old from New Marlborough turned himself in on a warrant Feb. 8 to troopers at the Troop B barracks and was arrested for fifth-degree larceny, criminal mischief and interfering with an officer. The juvenile was released on a $10,000 surety bond and later appeared in Pittsfield Superior Court Feb. 10.

DUI

STOCKBRIDGE—Brendon Davis, Stockbridge, was arrested Feb. 4 and charged with driving under the influence and improper use of high beams. Davis was arrested after following the arresting officer with his high beams on for several miles. Davis was released on a $500 non-surety bond and is scheduled to appear in Pittsfield Superior Court Feb. 27.

BREACH OF PEACE

STOCKBRIDGE—Molly Clayton, 418 Lime Rock Rd., New Marlborough, was arrested Feb. 3 for an incident that occurred Jan. 14 and was charged with breach of peace. Clayton was released on a $1,000 cash bond and is scheduled to appear in Pittsfield Superior Court Feb. 27.

DUI

LENOX—Kenneth W. Novak, 38, 255 Newfield Rd., was arrested and charged with driving under the influence, evading responsibility, failure to obey a stop sign and reckless driving in a school zone during a Feb. 7 incident. Novak was released on a $500 non-surety bond and is scheduled to appear in Pittsfield Superior Court on Feb. 21.

DUI

HOWLAND—Penny Batchelder, 38, 711 Melville Rd., was arrested and charged with driving under the influence, evading responsibility, failure to obey traffic signal and disobeying an officer's signal after a motor vehicle accident on Feb. 4 in front of Applebee's. Batchelder was released on a $500 non-surety bond and

is scheduled to appear in Pittsfield Superior Court on
Feb. 14.

DUI

GREAT BARRINGTON—Richard Morey, 53, 52 Clark
St., was arrested and charged with driving under the
influence, failure to illuminate lights, operating
without a license and interfering with an officer, during
a Feb. 11 incident. Morey was released on a $2,500
bond and is scheduled to appear in Pittsfield Superior
Court on Feb. 21.

His "job" was so nebulous, and the work it required of him so spo-
radic, that Gerry's hours online began to seem more real to him.
When he was off his blog (where traffic never really grew the way
he'd dreamed of, but held steady), and off HotAir or Pajamas
Media or other sites he loved or hated with equal passion, his
thoughts drifted toward women. There were different ways to encounter women on the internet: the simplest and most immediate,
of course, was porn, which he looked at once in a while, more in a
spirit of amazement than arousal. Thank God, was all he could
think, that he'd grown up in the previous century and not this one.
The lengths he had gone to in those days, the risks he had taken,
just to get a look at a *Penthouse* or a VHS tape! One of the bloodi-
est fights he and Mark had ever had was over an old *Hustler* they
kept stealing from each other, because it was too shameful just to
come out and ask to borrow it. Their father got so mad when they
wouldn't tell him what they were fighting about that he made them
clean the floor of the garage. And it was worth it. Now, the most
extreme or specific pornography was available to you for free as
fast as you could type a request to see it. His parents wouldn't have

been able to get him out of his room, were he a thirteen-year-old boy of today. The fire department couldn't have gotten him out of his room.

There were other avenues, less extreme, though their luridness was closer to home. A local Craigslist knockoff called soberklive.com mostly offered junk for sale or trade but also had an "Encounters" tab where anonymous women were offering massages. Massages! They were hooking, was what that meant, right there in the southern Berkshires, in Howland itself perhaps. Gerry had no desire at all for a massage, euphemistic or otherwise, but he almost replied to a few of the ads anyway just because he was dying to find out if he recognized one of these women who had a secret life. Maybe he'd gone to high school with her, or once had a beer with her husband, or sold them their house, back when he did that for a living. The idea that someone he knew, some respectable local, might be driven by kink or by hardship into the netherworld of whoredom: now, that was titillating.

The same went, in a less lascivious way, for the dating sites. The fun part was breaking the code of people's online identity; sometimes they didn't even bother to make it hard. Some of the women used real photographs, and once in a while, in his browsing, he would see a woman he thought he recognized. Did they realize they were exposing their own need in this public way? Maybe they didn't care. He recognized one woman who used to work as a bartender at the Ship. Short, with frizzy hair. He'd never really given her a thought at the time, but if he'd known she was that hard up he might have given it a whirl.

He thought about joining the site, creating a profile—he even had a thumbnail photo picked out, an old, black-and-white, crazy-eyed picture of George Orwell—but in the end, even with that to hide himself behind, he couldn't go through with it. He was too afraid of getting some reply saying "Gerry Firth, is that you?" He told himself he was an old-school guy, with a pretty damn impressive record in the area of women, depending on how you chose to measure it, and if he was feeling the need to meet someone—not necessarily a one-night thing either, but with the object of maybe spending a little less time by himself—all he needed to do was get out into the world. First stop was the Ship, naturally; he knew the frizzy-haired bartender didn't work there anymore but he found himself checking behind the bar for her anyway.

He told himself to be patient, to watch and wait and not get too drunk to drive to one or two other places; but then it was ten thirty and he was talking to some woman named Penny, from right there in Howland, who was out by herself because she said she got too depressed on Tuesday nights, when her two sons went to their dad's, to stay home alone. She was a mom, and had been living in that whole world of moms and kids, which would account, Gerry thought, for his not having seen her before.

"Did you grow up here?" he asked her. It was a sensitive approach to figuring out how old she was. It turned out she'd moved west from Chicopee at the behest of her ex-husband, who was looking for a likely place to open a wine store. He thought money just fell off of rich weekenders like fruit off a tree, she said. But at the end of the day it's still a business, and you still have to know how to run it. He'd had no idea at all what he was doing. He didn't even like wine. Gerry asked what happened after that, and she just smiled and put down her glass to make a gesture with her two hands, a simulation of something blowing up.

She asked what he did for a living and he said he had a real estate business going with his brother. Older or younger brother? was all she asked about that. He didn't tell her how he'd gotten into real estate in the first place or how his previous experience therein had ended. When she asked if he'd ever been married he didn't tell her the story of his backing out of his wedding. It crossed his mind that there was very little, in the way of autobiography, he would choose to share with any woman whom he cared about impressing.

But she seemed to have a good sense of which questions not to ask. She was thin, a little thinner than he usually liked. She wore a thin dress—calico, he wanted to say, though he wasn't sure that was the right word—and old boots and a jean jacket. Don't do it, he was surprised to catch himself thinking. Not the first one you meet, the first place you go. You are making a joke out of yourself.

"I'll tell you the truth," Penny said, as if she were reading his thoughts. "And it's the God's honest truth. I don't want to go home. Because I don't like my house. In some ways I like it least of any place in the world."

"I feel that way too," Gerry said, so softly he wasn't sure she heard.

"I mean it's different when the boys are there. Don't get me wrong."

"Sure. Of course."

"But then when they're not there. When I'm by myself. Sometimes I'm a little worried about, you know—" She turned to look at him, a small smile pulling at her mouth, and she opened her lips to form an O. Then she stuck her index finger in it, her thumb in the air. She flexed the thumb and her head jerked back.

Gerry watched her until she turned back to her wine. "Me too," he whispered. It seemed true, even though he'd just that moment thought of it.

She laughed, not cruelly. "So what do you do when you feel scared of yourself?" she said. "Come here?"

They were sitting at the bar side by side, facing in the same direction rather than toward each other. Gerry looked past the bartender's bearded face to the mostly empty wooden tables, and the backwards Narragansett sign and his own rusty car in the parking lot. "Nothing I do means anything," he said suddenly. "I just want to mean something. To stand for something. But it isn't just me either. I feel like it's all been, what's that word? Like with gas?"

"Pumped?"

"Siphoned! Siphoned away from us. But by what? Or who, or whom I guess. I want to lead a life that's more . . ."

"Like your dad's?" she said teasingly.

"God, no. But it is back there somewhere, yeah. In the past. It's not here now but I know it existed. Because otherwise how would I miss it?"

She was looking at him wearily, but she was looking at him. He couldn't tell whether she took him seriously or not.

"Nobody wants to look inside themselves for what's missing," he said. "They all want to act like victims. But your first obligation is to yourself, isn't it? I mean, that's your first obligation to *other* people is to look after yourself. That seems like such a simple idea."

"It is not a world of men," she murmured, and his eyes went wide.

He paid her bar tab, and then he drove behind her—slowly, in case the trooper was out—until she pulled safely into her driveway. He was all set to leave at that point, but instead he stayed. There was sex, technically, but it didn't amount to much; they were too bombed. Anyway, he was feeling something he didn't want sex to distract him from. Not love—obviously it couldn't be love. After she fell asleep he vowed to stay awake until the sun came up, just to watch her and to think, but he held out for about five minutes before he was asleep too. In the morning, thank God, she seemed like the same person. She came out of the bathroom and he thought for a moment she'd put pajama bottoms on by accident, but they were scrubs—she was a nurse or something.

In the hallway between the kitchen and her front door hung photos of her sons, lots of them, in no particular order. He stopped to scan them, looking for the ones that were most recent. She watched him, her hand resting on the door latch.

"There was a guy I was seeing," she said. "The boys got to like him. That was another mistake I made."

"What happened?"

"He hurt himself at work, and he went on disability. It made him so happy. To not have to work anymore, and still get paid. I couldn't look at him the same way after that."

"What did he do?"

"He had a government job," she said evasively.

He looked at her and put his hands in his pockets; his coat was already on. "Do you ever feel angry?" he said. "Like at people like that, who just skate by?"

Penny shrugged, in a way that meant yes. "It's just that nobody ever lifted a finger to help me," she said. "And I wouldn't want them to. I'd say no if they asked."

"I write this blog," Gerry said. "It's mostly for myself, I guess, though a bunch of people read it. Anyway, I write about this kind of stuff sometimes. The stuff I think you're talking about."

"Oh," she said, smiling. "A blogger."

"I didn't mean it like it was any big—"

"No, that's interesting. So I can just Google you and find it?"

"No, actually," he said, "my name isn't on it."

"Why not?"

Gerry shrugged, but a warm feeling was coming over him; he worried he was blushing.

"I was reading something the other day, in some blog some-where, about privilege," Penny said. "The idea of privilege. Appar-ently, we have all of it."

"Who's we?"

"White people, I gather. You and me. Although you more than me, of course, because you're a man."

"You don't say. Do you feel privileged?"

She laughed. "Hell yeah, I wake up every morning feeling privi-leged as shit."

"I'll tell you what I feel," Gerry said, trying to keep his tone as light as hers, but feeling himself fail. "I feel like the world is trying to get rid of me. I feel threatened, but that's not the bad part, the bad part is that everybody keeps shouting that I'm the one doing the threatening, that black is white, that up is down. It's like Orwell. They think if they say up is down often enough, and loud enough, then we'll believe it. And they're pretty much right. It's only recently I feel like I'm starting to understand what's really going on."

"Well," Penny said, and she stroked his arm, at the same time as she seemed to maneuver him closer to the door. "You can't fix the world, right? But you can damn well protect what's yours."

That night—that same night—he found himself putting an X through every Friday, Saturday, Sunday, and Monday on his wall calendar, for the next two months. Those were the nights Penny's children were with her. The X's were so he would remember not to call her then. In the middle of the week, they went out. Historically, for Gerry, taking a girlfriend out to a local bar, instead of staying in, would have been a sure sign that that relationship was spiraling toward its end. But this was something different. It was a good feeling, to show up someplace as a couple, and to know that they would leave that same way. They were drinking a lot, that was true, but at the same time, something about it felt dead sober, and safe. She was almost as good a drunk driver as he was, but after he found out she had a DUI he wouldn't let her take the wheel at the end of the night anymore. They resented their fear of Trooper Constable, a fat-faced douche with a crew cut and a government-endowed power to ruin their lives. In the car, they would make fun of him until they were both in hysterics. It didn't take long before the sex reached the kind of edgy pitch Gerry liked, and then it went beyond that. He felt unsettled, nervous, but in a good way: on the verge of something. In the mornings he would meet Mark at his home or at a site, too hungover to pretend otherwise, and even though he knew Mark assumed he was just getting hammered at home alone on a weeknight, like a pathetic alcoholic loser, Gerry didn't say a thing to correct this impression; he would rather Mark think of him as death-bound and hopeless than expose to him any of what he was really feeling.

He felt that there was some better, more disciplined version of himself, not far out of his reach. But it was difficult to get there. He even thought about going to church, giving that a try, but he would only have gone with Penny, and he could never see Penny on the weekends. Showing up at church by himself would have felt like walking into an AA meeting or something.

One morning Mark asked Gerry's advice about a problem with a tenant in Egremont. The cops had been out to the house twice in the last month. Mark thought there might even be some damage to the place, but the tenant was refusing to let him inside. Refusing? Gerry said. The tenant had changed the locks, which was a violation of his lease. But evicting people was hard, even when the grounds were unambiguous. The laws were rigged against it. Gerry suggested letting Barrett have a little talk with the guy, and Mark said that didn't make much sense since Barrett was likely to side with anybody against him. When breakfast at Daisy's ended, Mark handed his brother an envelope, inside of which was his quarterly dividend, seven thousand two hundred dollars. It wasn't much, but then he hadn't done much to earn it.

In bed things went pretty far. Verbally too, which he'd never really been into before. It felt right to him, that was the weird thing: not like role-playing, but more like role-dropping. He loved it but then when the weekend came he welcomed time away from the intensity of it.

One Saturday night in June, hot as blazes, there was another episode of vandalism on Main Street—two storefront windows broken, at the newsstand that sold cigarettes and at Creative Kidz. Three local teens were arrested within twenty-four hours, and the story about it in the next week's *Gazette* was how Gerry, and most other people in town, first learned of the existence of the surveillance cameras.

595 Housatonic Rd., Howland, 4.2 acres, 5 BR 2b modern. Asking: $1.4m. Sold: $1.5m. Time on market: two weeks. Broker: Reynolds & Ives, New York City.

1080 RR #7, Lenox, .6 acres, 2 BR 1b ranch. Asking: $140k. Sold: $121.5k. Time on market: 15 months. Broker: Al Kimbrough, Kimbrough Century 21, Stockbridge.

228 Bluebell Lane, Howland, 1.1 acres, 2 BR 1.5 b Colonial. Asking: $249k. Sold: $194.5k. Time on market: 9 months. Broker: C.J. Glassberg, Glassberg Realty, Stockbridge.

2080 Route 343, Becket, 4 BR, 2b ranch. Asking: $310k. Sold: $45k. Time on market: 6 mos. Broker: none (bank foreclosure auction).

9 Red Lion Rd., West Stockbridge, 11 acres, 8 BR, 3.5 b modern. Asking: $2.9m. Sold: $3.3m. Time on market: 3 days. Broker: Thomas Gibbons, New York City.

MINUTES OF MEETING OF
BOARD OF SELECTMEN

July 17, 2006, 4:00 P.M.

Present: Mr. Hadi, Mr. Allerton, Mr. Waltz,
Ms. Burrows (sec.)
Absent: none

The meeting was called to order. Mr. Allerton suggested the assembled settle in for what might be an unusually long session. Mr. Waltz moved that the board order out for dinner; the motion carried unanimously.

A proposal was put before the board for an annual Howland Film Festival, to be held in the fall, as a way of extending the tourist season, increasing off-season revenue and expanding Howland's regional and national profile. Similar festivals in Long Island and New Jersey had generated tens of thousands of dollars in local revenue, according to the proposal. Discussion centered on the fact that such festivals typically have multiple screening venues, while Howland has only one, the Movie House, which has only one screen. The proposal originated with a summer resident who offered his home for opening and closing night parties. The challenges of securing the participation of some of the neighboring towns was discussed. The board agreed not to vote on the proposal. Mr. Hadi, who knows the summer resident who submitted the proposal, said he would convey the board's findings to him directly.

Debate was proposed by Mr. Hadi on the question of opposition to a cement plant being built in Hillsdale, NY. The plant is environmentally controversial but promises, according to Hillsdale's Mayor, the establishment of 78 new full- and part-time jobs. Mr. Allerton questioned the efficacy of debating an issue over which the BOS had no jurisdiction. After some discussion, the issue was tabled.

The food arrived, and a half-hour adjournment was declared.

Mr. Hadi introduced two items of new business pertaining to the two taverns operating within the town's limits: first, a midnight closing time, and second, a ban on smoking therein. Debate followed. Mr. Hadi raised the point, apropos of the curfew, that of Howland's 17 reported crimes to date this year (three instances of vandalism, four home burglaries, ten moving violations including six DUIs), all but three had taken place after 1:00 A.M. on the day in question. Mr. Waltz stated that if you closed the Howland taverns at midnight, people would simply drive drunk to other bars in surrounding towns, then drive home when those bars closed, leaving Howland with even more inebriated persons behind the wheel. No further action on the proposal was taken. The BOS took up the proposed smoking ban: while the common health benefits were unanimously acknowledged, Mr. Allerton spoke in favor of the tradition and importance of personal freedoms, and asked to have read into the record the observation that "this is not New York City." Mr. Hadi indicated his intent to explore whether he could impose these new measures, whose benefits no one formally disputed, unilaterally.

Mr. Waltz reported that town expenditures for the previous quarter were the lowest in more than ten years, mostly owing to the sharp increase in private giving to the town's various institutions. Mr. Allerton proposed the surplus be returned to the town's taxpayers in the form of a rebate. Mr. Waltz proposed to read into the record the fable of the Ant and the Grasshopper. He then withdrew that proposal. The measure in favor of the rebate was approved by a vote of 3-0.

The meeting concluded with an official resolution of support for our troops overseas.

Respectfully submitted,
Anne Marie Burrows
7/18/2006

Candace needed to talk to her brothers, so she asked them to meet her for breakfast; she didn't get lunch hours anymore, and there wasn't really room for the three of them at her place for dinner. Fine, Mark emailed, and suggested Daisy's; no, anywhere but there, she said. When he asked her to please tell him that it wasn't because of politics, she said you bet your ass it's because of politics. That old lady's a savage, and her ugly-ass daughter is worse. Seriously, have you seen her Facebook page?

He had not seen it; he couldn't imagine why his sister had, unless she was actually in search of things to feel offended by. He called her and said, "You have got to be kidding me, Candy. It's an egg sandwich. Eating an egg sandwich is not a political act." But she refused to budge on the vital issue of who would prepare their breakfast; just to get her to change the subject he agreed to go all the way to Great Barrington, to someplace called Grindhouse. "I know where it is," he said. "It's the lesbian coffee shop, right?"

"For God's sake," Candace said.

Her workday didn't start until nine; his started, these days, when he chose to start it. When she arrived he was already seated unhappily in front of a cappuccino with a floral design in the milk froth on top. "Nothing to eat?" she said.

"They just have scones," he said. "Zero protein in a scone."

The walls of the dimly lit café were hung with wood-block prints, all of them in identical frames, all by the same artist. Near the kitchen, a piece of paper was taped to the wall with the titles of the prints and their prices, which varied, for reasons Mark could not fathom.

"It's a gallery," Candace said, reading his expression. "I mean it doubles as a gallery. It rotates every few weeks. A way for local artists to get their work seen, maybe even by somebody from the city."

"Local artists," Mark said.

"Oh my God, you sounded so much like Dad just now," she said.

Whatever it was she wanted to talk about, she wanted to wait for Gerry to arrive. But he didn't. She pulled out her cell phone and left him a voicemail. They sipped at their coffee until it was gone.

"I'm gonna have to go soon," Candace said. "God damn it."

"So the library opens a few minutes late," Mark said. "Will anybody really notice?"

"Yeah, well, you might be surprised, actually," she said. But she didn't feel like describing it to him. Much of her daily clientele consisted of small children and their over-it mothers, who somehow had the idea that once their kids were inside the library door, they could close their eyes and take some mental time off. Like she was the town nanny or something. Some kids were sweet, others were little engines of annoyance and destruction. There was an irony to it that she didn't particularly savor and that her brother was unlikely to miss: wherever she went, whatever job she tried to do, she somehow wound up in charge of other people's kids.

"How about you?" she said instead. "Any place you need to be this morning?"

He seemed stung by the question, though she hadn't meant anything by it. "Well, I have to figure out what to do about this one tenant, in a house down in Egremont, who's doing his best to make my life miserable," he said. "He called me the other night at eight fifteen because he wants me to repaint his kid's bedroom. His kid says he can't sleep because he doesn't like the color."

"So why doesn't he just paint it himself?"

"Well, actually he can't, because it says in his lease he's not allowed to. I got so sick of him that I gave him Barrett Taylor's number, but he won't use it, he insists on calling me even for the most routine thing."

"Barrett Taylor? The same Barrett Taylor?"

"Yeah, remember him? He's kind of like my super now. Anyway, it drives Karen a little crazy that the guy calls all the time, and so I'm trying to come up with some way to just evict him without having to spend all my time in court. I've had it. You can just never do enough for this guy."

"Well," said Candace, "maybe you aren't."

"Maybe I aren't what?"

"Doing enough."

Mark colored. "You don't get it," he said. "The problem is that whatever you do, as soon as it's taken care of he's immediately on you about the next thing. There's no end to it."

"He's got a son, you said?"

"Two sons, actually."

"And the first one, the one who can't sleep, what's his problem exactly?"

Mark sat back and crossed his arms. He could see where this was going. "I don't know what his problem is," he said, "because his problem is not my problem."

"Ah." She tried to tilt another drop out of the coffee cup she'd already drained a minute ago. "Well, you know what they say, with great worth on paper comes great responsibility."

"What are you talking about?"

"Let's talk about something else, then," she said calmly. "Been out to see Mom and Dad lately?"

"Is this why you asked me out for breakfast," he said, "to try to make me feel guilty?"

"Kind of, yeah," she said.

In the silence between them the ambient sounds of the coffee shop asserted themselves: the hoarse gargle of milk being steamed, the dim mumble of insular one-on-one conversation, and the music, just audible, aggressively obscure and unlovely and never not playing.

"They aren't doing that badly," Mark said. "That's in your head."

"They aren't taking care of themselves. You don't see it because you don't want to see it. You live in that huge house with all those empty rooms—you should take them in."

"No. Are you kidding? No! Karen's head would explode, for one thing. And they'd never agree to it anyway. And to be honest I wouldn't want that kind of negativity around Haley every day."

"Well, I'm not taking them. And Gerry's not taking them. And you know they're not moving to Colorado. And they don't have any money. So if you're not thinking about where that's going, it can only be because you're trying not to think about it."

"Keep your voice down, please," Mark said.

"You used to talk so much about family," she said. "It used to make me kind of sick, to be honest. But it was all just bullshit, I guess."

"You know what, I've got to run," Mark said.

"Me too. I have to make an Autumn Leaf display. I'll let you pay for the coffee." She drained her cup a third time and stood and left. The bell on the door tinkled behind her.

He drove home with his lips moving angrily, pleased that he'd find his house empty at that hour. He'd dared to do the one thing that none of them could bear, which was to succeed. In Howland he stopped on Main Street just to pick up the paper. He was getting back into his car when something caught his eye, some slight change in the backdrop so dimly but deeply imprinted on his sense memory, a streak of white. He looked up, at the corner of the old Holbeck mill. Someone had climbed up there—it couldn't have been easy—and painted the word CAMERA, with a helpful directional arrow pointed at the spot where the surveillance camera was bracketed onto the cornice.

BIG BROTHER COMES TO HOWLAND—
POSTED 10/1/2006 AT 1:04 A.M.

Citizens, if there's one thing that history has taught us, it's that the more we're told to look across borders, across oceans for our enemies, the easier prey we are for the enemies within, the enemies right under our nose.

Did anybody notice that at some point—I'm not sure when, could have happened any time, because we weren't told about it, much less asked for our approval—the Benevolent Billionaire who rules us has put up surveillance cameras over our heads in town? Well, yes, somebody apparently noticed, because there was some protest graffiti up there for a day or two. One word—literally one word of protest—but of course that was too much for them, and the power-washers were up there practically the next day.

The cameras themselves aren't gone, though, of course. Two that I know of, probably more. (Why not a hundred more, if that's what he wants? He can afford it.) They're at either end of Main Street. They're not hard to spot if you just have the mindset to look for them.

So look for them. And then ask yourself why they're there. At whose behest? To look at what? Where is the information collected by these devices, information about you, being stored, and for what purpose? If you can even get anybody at Town Hall to answer these questions, I'll bet you a hundred bucks I can predict their answer:

"Security!"

People, don't you get it? This is what we've been hearing for years now, while they chip away at our rights: Security! Our enemies are coming for us! You have to do what we tell you, you have to give up whatever autonomy, whatever

constitutional protections, we tell you to give up! Because:
security!

Meanwhile, your real enemy is the one who claims he alone
can protect you. He's right beside you. Maybe in the next
booth at the diner . . .

It was easier to ignore the whole invasion of your personal
privacy when it existed mostly on TV. Or on your computer.
I mean, we know our emails are being read, but it still seems
too abstract to be real, it's happening in some place we can't
see and probably can't even imagine.

But now it's come home, folks. It's on Main Street. Not some
abstract "Main Street USA," but Main Street right here in
Howland. Next time you're buying a quart of milk, or a six-
pack, or a book or a magazine, remember that you're being
looked at—recorded—and think about why you let that hap-
pen.

I am so tired of the whole narrative about how billionaires
are so morally pure, how they can't be bought! First there
was Ross Perot, then Bloomberg in New York . . . The rich
are incorruptible, because the rich don't care about money!
Have you ever heard anything more Orwellian in your en-
tire life? No one, people, is more of a slave to money, and to
moneyed interests, than a billionaire. And there's no power
trip like using your money to buy people. "What's his mo-
tive?" his defenders will say. "What would he have to gain?
We can't make him any richer than he already is." The altru-
istic billionaire! You answer your own question about what
he has to gain when you defend him like that, because YOU

are what he has to gain. Power is its own end. And what's a billion bucks on paper compared to the thrill of owning a place, a town, a citizenry? It's all about control. The cameras seal the deal. He won't be happy until Howland is a kingdom.

Are you willing to be his subjects?

There are rumors, too, of a curfew in town (favorite tool of dictators everywhere: the curfew!), of a ban on smoking, not just in Town Hall but everywhere, in restaurants, in bars, in your own homes. Think I'm kidding? When it happens, remember that I warned you and you blew it off.

Or: Show me that you're out there. That you hear me. That you're alive, and not willing to roll over for those who would consolidate their own power by taking everything from you. And I do mean everything.

Show me you haven't given up!

Rally to Demand the Immediate Removal of the Howland Government Surveillance System

WEDNESDAY, OCT. 11, 5 P.M.
MAIN STREET, HOWLAND, MA

Some will call this an overreaction. What's a couple of cameras, they'll say? It deters crime! Two things: one, "security" is always the false flag under which the powerful expand their reach into your lives; two, why wait until the Dear Leader's security apparatus is even stronger, more extensive, more deeply embedded? Why not let him know now that this is unacceptable, that we're still Americans?

Because let's not forget that we live in Massachusetts, which is the proud cradle of American freedom from tyranny. Not revolution, despite the name attached to that war, but simple refusal—refusal to let a small, powerful class enrich itself by stripping the common man of his rights, his freedoms, chief among which is the inalienable, God-given right to be left the fuck alone. What business of yours is my business? That is the principle upon which the country was established, and if that principle is taken away, what reason is there for this country to exist anymore?

WEDNESDAY, OCT. 11, 5 P.M., MAIN STREET

Be there. Show the world your number! Stand up and be counted! It may be that your humble correspondent will be there as well, walking among you!

—PC Barnum

As had happened on just one or two other occasions, he was actually crying a little bit by the time he hit the Post button. He rarely edited or even reread what he'd composed. It was private and public at the same time. It was like imagining yourself a famous person, an immortal, keeping a diary: the diary was private but also for posterity—you knew it would live outside of you even if you couldn't see exactly how. The internet was like posterity moved up to your time frame. Like going to your own funeral. You took your passion, stripped it of any kind of social inhibition, and launched it into the dark, populated void. There was a little hit-meter you could access that told you how many people were visiting your blog, but he never looked at it anymore. He didn't want to know.

Constable pulled over four or five cars a week on suspicion of DUI, "suspicion" being more of a legal nicety in this case, since he wouldn't go to the trouble of turning on his lights unless he saw someone driving in a way that left no real room for doubt—in the wrong lane, or bumping the guardrail, or stopping at a stop sign for a full minute. He usually let them go with a reprimand unless they were repeat offenders. Just seeing the cop lights in your rearview had a pretty sobering effect on most people.

He tried not to let other feelings influence his judgment, for instance whether or not the driver was someone he knew, or whether he liked or disliked them or whether they were decently respectful as he performed his sworn duty or whether they gave him shit about it. In his own good judgment, he felt, there was fairness, and he tried to maintain that equilibrium even when people made no sense. You'd pull a woman over after you saw her backing down an entrance ramp to the Mass Pike, and then you'd tell her you were going to let her go with a warning, and instead of thanking you she'd scream at you about the police state and then give you the finger as she rolled up her window. But lately everybody just seemed chippier about everything. He'd been reamed out the other day by a weekender whose house had been broken into and defaced; Constable explained that the perpetrators were probably kids and that home surveillance video (which this bald posh city dude could obviously afford a thousand times over) was really the best bet in terms of preventing it from happening again, and the guy just went off on some rant about his tax dollars. Where were all his tax dollars going?

And once in a while you'd get the opposite, where somebody you'd let go, or even somebody you didn't, developed a weird attachment to you, like they went out of their way to thank you for your service and to act submissive when they saw you again. Nothing wrong with that—Constable was all for anything that made his job easier—but people took it too far, trying to act as informants, giving him a tip about a neighbor who was down at the Ship getting hammered, or about someone getting paid off the books at the Price Chopper, stuff he had no jurisdiction over, nor any interest in.

A man he'd popped for his third DUI—it was the middle of the day, he'd had his kids in the car, in the end the guy did ten days in the Pittsfield jail awaiting trial and lost his license for a year—forwarded him, at his work email, which he'd thought was a secret, some anonymous blog that claimed there was going to be a rally or a protest or something on Main Street in Howland on October 11 *"Have you seen this???"* was the guy's subject line. Constable hadn't seen it, and it didn't strike him as something to worry about. It had a sad, homemade look. Probably just some local crackpot. He was mildly curious who it was, from a gossip standpoint more than as a matter of law enforcement. The blogger was ranting about the security cameras, which Constable had told the First Selectman were a bad idea to begin with. Actually, no, he corrected himself, he hadn't told anyone that, at the time; he'd only thought it. He'd taken it as a sort of passive-aggressive message that the Board of Selectmen thought he wasn't doing his job well enough. Well, he couldn't be everywhere. They should try doing it, even for one night, if they thought it was so easy.

He Googled this so-called rally to see if any other websites or newspapers had picked it up, but he found nothing. Before he went home for the night he repeated the search and got the same negative result.

It was only after he left work that night, when he was home with his family, that he found the whole idea a little harder to dismiss. He didn't think it was real, but how could you tell when anger was real and when it was not? If you were any kind of cop, you knew, or felt, the difference between intuition and simple paranoia. He called up the blog and read it again: reading it in his home rather than at work made the language of it seem more ominous some-how. In the end he decided to kick it upstairs—to show it to Hadi, so he couldn't be blamed, at least not exclusively, if this supposed protest materialized into something he should have been better prepared for.

In his full uniform, which normally he might not wear when he wasn't patrolling, he went to Town Hall and asked that turtle-eyed lady whom nobody knew if he could have a few minutes with her boss on an urgent police matter.

"I'm sure that's no problem," the lady said, unsmilingly but calmly. He preferred it when phrases like "urgent police matter" ruffled people a little bit. "But he isn't in yet this morning."

"When do you expect him?"

That, for some reason, brought out a smile. "I'm sure I don't know," she said. "He has no appointments today, so he'll be in when he chooses to come in."

"Should I just wait, then?" Constable said.

"You mean wait here? Oh, I wouldn't. There's no telling how long it might be." She made that type of eye contact that profes-sional people made with you when they were trying to signal po-litely that their encounter with you was done.

So he went across the street to the Undermountain and had a coffee and a western omelet. He picked a stool at the counter where if he leaned back a little he could see the entrance to the Town Hall parking lot. People came in and out, pretty briskly that time of morning, and every one of them stared curiously at him in his full uniform, wondering if something was wrong. The uniform was al-ways like that: both magnet and shield. The crowd at the diner was pretty mixed, in terms of locals and tourists, mostly because of its prime location; there were places where you could get an omelet at less larcenous prices, but the tourists didn't know how to find them.

It was becoming a different town, Constable thought. Just the way the people looked. The locals geared everything toward attracting the moneyed people and then resented them when they came. The rich folks came looking for some country vibe but then seemed to want to protect themselves, to wall themselves off from whatever it was they meant to enjoy or absorb. Those feelings had always been there but now it was like they were rising to the surface. I mean just look, he said to himself, at that white-haired couple there, with their wind-burned faces and pastel clothing and Tanglewood tote bag, arguing quietly about how much to tip on a shared muffin. Constable himself experienced a reflexive contempt for them. Yet God help this place if they went away and never came back.

Just then he saw a black SUV pull into the Town Hall lot and disappear behind the building. He signaled for his check to the waitress, who smiled and discreetly waved him off; he left a five-dollar tip. Trying not to rush, he made his way back across Main Street.

The secretary directed him right in, and he stood in front of Hadi's desk waiting for him to look up from whatever was absorbing him on his laptop screen. Constable was at attention but he was pretty sure this was lost on Hadi. Oddly checked out for a leader, Constable had always thought. The fact that he had a lot of money—something fundamental about him that you couldn't see but still knew—gave even his leadership a behind-the-scenes quality, a sense of his operating on some level other than what he showed you, like a spy.

Finally the First Selectman glanced up. Constable explained the reason for his visit, and he watched as Hadi called up the Workingman's Dread blog on his laptop. He read it rapidly. "Okay," he said, and turned on Constable a patient look.

"So I don't think there's anything to this," Constable said. "I mean the internet is basically all talk. People can say whatever they want. Doesn't make it true."

"I suppose that's right," Hadi said.

"I just wanted you to know it was on my radar," Constable said. "And of course to ask for any instruction on how it's to be handled, if it turns out to exist at all."

"There's nothing to handle, that I can see," Hadi said. "People are allowed to assemble. Is there some question about a permit or something? Do we even have those here?"

Constable said he thought not, though he could check.

"Forget it," Hadi said. "Obviously if there's any destruction of property or anything like that, you'd have to make an arrest, just as you normally would."

"I'm a little concerned they'll go after the cameras," Constable said.

Hadi waved his hand. "Those cost nothing," he said.

Then there was a silence, in which Constable could see, or feel, the engine of Hadi's cognition.

"Why did you come to me with this?" Hadi said at length. "Was it just, you know, ass-covering?"

"Sir?" Constable said.

"It's okay, I can understand that. But why do you think this guy flatters himself that I'm watching him? Why does he need a fake name?" His tone was colorless and calm. "Projects come and go, you know. Interests come and go. I took this on because I have a genuine affection for this place, and because frankly democracy doesn't really work anymore—that's something I guess you're not supposed to say in polite company but it's objectively true. I wanted to help it out if I could. I have the means to do that, but that doesn't make me some kind of mad dictator. It just means I have means. You know?"

Constable made a noncommittal face, since he wasn't really sure what his boss was asking.

The First Selectman sat up a little straighter in his chair. "How selfish soever man may be supposed," he said, "there are evidently

265

some principles in his nature which interest him in the fortunes of others, and render their happiness necessary to him, though he derives nothing from it, except the pleasure of seeing it."

Whatever that meant, he delivered it in a different voice: slower, almost theatrical. There was another long pause, so long Constable grew worried he was expected to say something.

"So thank you for seeing me," he offered, and feinted toward the door.

"Remind me what you make?" Hadi said.

"I'm sorry?"

"What's your salary? What do we pay you?"

Constable's mouth worked soundlessly.

"I'm asking because I'm wondering about the feasibility of hiring more of . . . you," Hadi said. "Just thinking out loud about the cost."

The door to the outer office was open, had remained open the whole time. "Thirty-nine thousand four hundred dollars," Constable said, feeling humiliated, though not by the amount. "Plus benefits."

Hadi looked relieved. "Okay then," he said, "good. Good to know. I mean not that you aren't doing an excellent job on your own. But should it come to that. Thank you."

Constable saluted and went back to sit for a while in the little office—really just a desk and a chair and a door that closed—the Town Hall provided for its resident trooper.

When the eleventh came, he made sure to position himself in a spot on the Main Street sidewalk with good sight lines to either end, so that he could see the cameras, and the cameras could see him. A few people smiled and stopped and asked him what he was doing there. Every moment, as the afternoon wore on, he waited for the appearance of some homemade sign, or the sound of a chant or a megaphone, or the advent of some group of locals or outsiders marching in an organized fashion around one or the other corner.

The foot traffic in town seemed the same as it always was, on a weekday, in the off-season, after work. You couldn't tell what was in their hearts, of course, not even the one middle-aged guy who came up and asked him, sort of hopefully, if there was anything unusual going on. Maybe the curious had come out and been warned away by his own presence there, by the authority of his uniform, like a scarecrow. Or maybe it was all a phantom, this whole notion of unrest, and as afternoon turned to evening no one was registering Constable's presence there at all, except of course the cameras.

Evidently one of Gage's sons had plugged up the kitchen sink and then let the water run overnight. The cabinet and the floor beneath it were ruined, Barrett reported, and the subfloor might be a goner too. Did Mark want him to start tearing stuff out, or to go to the new property in Sheffield, as previously planned, and work on the renovation there? Mark sent him to Sheffield and drove to Egremont to inspect the water damage himself, trying unsuccessfully to calm down the whole way. What was wrong with people? That was the bug in his business: he had built-in protection against their being financial deadbeats where the rent was concerned, but not against their utter lack of personal responsibility. How could you let your kids get so out of control? It's not like Mark knew nothing about this subject. He had a kid. She didn't vandalize his house. It wasn't so hard.

He knocked on the door and Gage opened it about an inch. There was a chain on it that Mark had not ordered to be installed. Belatedly Mark was surprised to find him there; why aren't you at work, he wanted to ask him. "Good morning," Mark said civilly. "Mind if I come inside?"

"Why?" Gage said.

Why? Mark, who often struggled for authority, in this case felt the authority of ownership surging through him quite naturally. "I understand you've damaged—further damaged—this property, and I need to see it. Let me in."

"I'd really rather not," Gage said. "I mean, this has become a situation now. And you're, you know, the landlord."

"You let Barrett in, right?"

"Who's Barrett? Oh, that dude. Yeah, he came in. That's different."

Mark wanted to ask why this was, but the tenant was not the one setting the terms of this discussion. "Look, this is ridiculous, just open the door, please. I can't possibly make a decision about repairing the damage you've caused until I see it."

"I didn't cause it. My son caused it."

"Well, aren't you responsible for your son?"

"Well, aren't you responsible for me? I mean you rent this place to me, to my whole family, we have no other place to go, you have the power to put us on the street, or to not do that. So you're responsible for us."

"What the hell are you talking about?" Mark said. "I'm talking about you being a father, man, about looking after your own child."

"My child has problems," Gage said. "I'm sure your kids are perfect."

"You know what?" Mark said. "I don't give a fuck about your kid's problems."

"And there it is," Gage said. He sighed and licked his lips. They stared at each other through the crack in the door.

"I'm going to ask you one more time," Mark said.

"Nope," Gage said. "I mean you can bring the sheriff back or whatever. If you want to go next-level."

"This doesn't make any sense!" Mark said.

"I know it doesn't. But I got my pride, still."

What Mark wanted to do was break the door down. The impulse was almost overwhelming. He felt that the clear moral rightness of his case should endow him with the necessary strength. It was his house, and the guy wouldn't let him enter it. He knew enough to know the law was on the tenant's side. The law was always on their side.

He took a deep breath. "The next time I come back," he said, "will be with the trooper. You'll be served with an official eviction notice, and you'll have a set amount of time to vacate the apartment completely or the trooper will enter the premises and put you and your family and your belongings out on the sidewalk." He wasn't sure about any of this, never having gone through the process, but it all sounded right. "Do you understand?"

"I thought you were a good guy," Gage said sadly. "I thought you were looking out for me. Think about it, man, what it means to have the guy who owns the roof over your kids' head to be, like, your enemy. But hey, you do you." He softly shut the door, and then locked it.

Mark got back in his truck. He was due in Sheffield to check on Barrett's progress in dividing the units there. On the drive over, he tried to think about the necessary steps for eviction—figuring out which court had jurisdiction in Egremont, calling the lawyer he'd used to incorporate his business to see if he handled this type of work or knew anybody local who did—but he couldn't: instead his mind kept returning to fantasies, detailed daydreams in which the encounter just ended had ended instead with a physical confrontation, and Mark, left no other choice, took the house back by force. In his mind's eye he saw the tenant taking a swing at him, which he ducked, backing away, saying "You don't want to do this," then Gage maneuvering him into a corner or against the porch railing and raising his fist again, at which point Mark dropped him with one punch to the chin. He saw this so clearly he ran a Yield sign and got honked at by someone in a Lexus merging onto 7 just north of Great Barrington. He could see the driver cursing at him. It was completely Mark's fault but Mark gave the guy the finger anyway.

The wall Barrett had put up to divide the living room in Sheffield looked good enough; it was never going to look great from a design standpoint, it was completely inorganic, but it was sturdy and Barrett had done the best, probably, that anyone could have done. Barrett seemed to see in Mark's gaze that he was not thrilled, but he took that to be about the quality of his work: "I mean, we could do crown moldings there or something," he said.

"No," Mark said.

"Make the eye follow the new line, you know. Not that much more labor, really. I should have asked you before."

"No," Mark said. "Fuck it."

He went out onto the still-handsome porch and sat on the top step. Barrett followed. He sat with a loud groan of relaxation, cracked open a can of beer at ten thirty in the morning, and said, "Fuck what?"

Mark looked at the beer and put his chin in his hand. Part of him was offended Barrett didn't offer him a beer of his own. He told the story of his trip to Egremont, and how Gage wouldn't let him through the door. Barrett listened sympathetically while polishing off the can.

"I can't calm down," Mark said, "is the weird thing. I just keep fantasizing about beating the shit out of this guy. But I know violence isn't the answer."

"People always say that," Barrett mused. "But what if it turns out violence actually is the answer?"

Mark ignored him. "I mean where do guys like this come from?" he said. "Where does that come from, that sense of entitlement? Were you raised that way? I wasn't raised that way. Just no respect for anything. Total self-interest."

Barrett appraised him. "Respect," he said. "That's the key. You've hit the nail on the head, dude. The thing people forget is that there is a physical component to that, you can try to deny it but it's always there. It's the bottom line. Instinct, man. Instinct. It still controls us."

Mark's brow furrowed. "What are you talking about?"

"I'm back to the idea," Barrett said, "that you should have hit him."

"Come on."

"Why not?"

"Why not? Because for starters I'd get sued, or arrested, or both."

"And is that really what rules you, even in a man-to-man moment like that? Fear of the law? Are you thinking about the law right now, this moment, while you and I are talking?"

"No. Hey, just out of curiosity, was that your first beer of the day?"

"Because I think you are more of a man than that. Even I, who don't really like you all that much, can see that there's a real man somewhere deep down inside of you, that's just been suppressed by this, by this modern world. Stand up."

He took Mark by the arm, not roughly, and Mark, too baffled to resist, stood up with him, on the top step of the porch.

"Tell you what, man," Barrett said. "You clearly need to go at someone. And I know how that feels. I've been there. I'm there all the time. So go ahead. Hit me. Take a free one."

"What?"

"Go ahead," Barrett said kindly. "It's okay, I swear. I know it won't hurt."

"What the hell is the matter with you?" Mark said. He turned and stared across the road at the garage there, the undergrowth, the wildflowers. His eyes stung.

"I'll make it easier for you," Barrett said. "Look at me." Mark turned to look at him, and Barrett slapped him hard across the face.

"It's okay," Barrett said supportively, his arms down at his sides. "You know you want to. Come on, let it out. I promise it's okay."

Mark couldn't speak right away. He could feel the redness

spreading across the left half of his face. Gingerly he walked down the porch steps, where he was out of Barrett's reach, then turned and stared back up at him.

"You fucking lunatic," he said, "you're fired."

Barrett sighed and shook his head. "Yeah, that's disappointing," he said. "I actually had my hopes up there for a second."

4

Part of the internal mythology of Mullins Day School was that it was always about to get much harder. Every year you'd hear, from upperclassmen and teachers alike, how the following year was the academic watershed, the year your homework load would turn overwhelming and stay that way, so you'd better enjoy your childish paradise now, while you could; but for Haley that transition never really happened. Not that she was some prodigy or runaway genius. Her grades were always good. They had an Honor Roll there, which wasn't that hard to make, but she was never first in her class, or even close. She hated class rankings anyway. They seemed designed to encourage the kids to compete, but the kids would not be outfoxed by such tactics. It had become fashionable to mock the class rankings (the middle-school office had even stopped posting them on the main bulletin board, because they were so routinely defaced) and there were rumors that Grace Waltz would refuse to accept the Top Scholar award at the Prize Assembly that year, as a protest. Top Scholar hadn't been determined yet—it was still only March—but everyone knew it would be Grace.

By seventh grade Haley suspected that the promised descent into drudgery was never going to come, that the increase in what was expected of you academically was incremental and not overwhelming and that that must have been by time-tested design. And then she began to understand a central truth of Mullins Day School, which everyone said was one of the three best and most prestigious and certainly most expensive preparatory schools in the Berkshires, which ran K–12 and sent some of its grads to Ivy League schools every year (if not as many as in the old, pre-diversity days): the whole point of the school was not to go there, but to have gone there, to be from there.

So in a way, the important work was already done. This changed how everything looked to her. After the school's Holiday Concert back in December, after she'd taken her place in the Middle School Chorus and sung songs from a conspicuous variety of cultures to a group of parents and teachers with maybe one or two nonwhite faces in it, she and Tom Kerrigan and Boyd McDowell and Amy Andersen and Dustin Cates slipped through the fire door behind the theater building and shared a joint in the freezing cold. They only had the one: it had come from Tom's older brother, who was a junior. Haley was pretty sure Tom had stolen it from him. Maybe he had some fantasy that it made girls take their shirts off and thus was worth the almost certain beatdown whenever his brother next counted his stash and figured it out.

They were passing it around, burning their lips, trying and failing to inhale, when an amazing thing happened. An adult opened the fire door, maybe thirty feet away; the light from behind him kept his face in shadow, but it seemed, from his stillness especially, like he was looking right at them. They all froze—Boyd tried to hide the lit joint in his pocket, which under different circumstances would have been hilarious—and then after a few seconds, the man just turned and went back inside the theater and let the door click shut behind him without a word.

Amy started crying. "It's cool," Tom said, "everything's cool," but the frightened way he said it made it worse than saying nothing. Haley got a ride home, as planned, from Amy's parents, and spent a sleepless night; winter break began the next day, so she wasn't sure what to expect or when to expect it. She was too nervous to call Amy or Tom or the others, even though she knew it was crazy to think they were being surveilled or anything.

They waited through the break, through Christmas and New Year's, and through the first day back at school in January, and the next day was the first day they allowed themselves to accept that nothing was going to happen to them.

"He had to have seen us," Tom said at lunch, smirking, but speaking in a whisper. "There's no way he didn't see."

"And so?" Amy said.

"And so he decided he didn't see it," Haley said, trying to understand the ramifications of what she was saying. "He saw it by accident, he wishes he hadn't seen it, he's going to pretend he never saw it."

They didn't want to deal with problems, at that school. They didn't want problems at all. They didn't want to be a school where seventh graders got expelled for smoking pot at the Holiday Concert. And so they weren't. Poof! It was all about seeing what you wanted to see in order to make happen what you wanted to happen.

"It's just like Iraq," Haley said.

They stared at her and burst into relieved laughter; they were used to her and her non sequiturs. "What," Tom said, "the everloving hell are you talking about?"

The more she tried to explain the comparison, the harder they laughed. She wasn't a political person, but it did amaze her how little interest her friends had in the world outside their world. It was like you had to make an actual, conscious effort to be so unaware.

That whole attitude, that sense of innate achievement and proud ignorance of whatever did not affect them directly, was tolerable when they were all at school, but whenever she got together with even her best friends from Mullins on a weekend or over vacation, out in the real world, it embarrassed her and she lost her taste for it. In any group of more than two, it never took long for their elitism to emerge. In their body language, in the things they said. Even if they were sitting in Boyd's TV room, or in Allegra Durning's house, where her parents barely seemed to live. Even just watching a movie, or pretending to enjoy some drink somebody had tried to make, a Negroni or a Black Russian or whatever else you could make from a bottle that didn't get checked that often.

"Oh my God, the lady that works in the post office now?" Amy said. "She is so fat! She is seriously so fat that she was breathing hard just standing there. She has like no wrists."

"She doesn't have wrists?" Boyd said. "I'm sure you're wrong about that."

"One thing about me," Amy said, "is I'm never wrong. You should have picked up on that by now."

Without ever really making up her mind to do so, Haley started finding excuses for not hanging around with them outside of school. First they acted like it was nothing, then they acted all weird and hurt about it, and then they went back to acting like it was nothing again. It meant more time at home: more Saturday nights, more lazy vacation days where she tried her hardest to sleep as long as she could. Her mother couldn't accept that nothing was wrong. "What's the matter with you?" she said. "I don't mean it like that; I mean what's wrong, what happened? Did you and your friends have a fight? Did something happen with some boy? Why don't you want to see your friends anymore?"

She did want to see her friends, just in their right context, in their friendship's particular ecosystem. Her mother claimed she was worried about depression—everybody knew what crucial, fraught years these were for kids, girls especially—and she annoyingly monitored Haley's every meal, to make sure she was eating normally, whatever that meant. Haley knew her mother's anxiety was real, but she also knew it had more than one source. She understood that imperfectly, though still better than her mother did. Her mother did not want to be the mother of a child with problems. Not that she was superficial, not really, no more than anyone else at least. More that she felt like Haley was the face their family showed to the world. It wasn't that she was one of those mothers for whom everything had to be perfect; it was more like, if we aren't raising a happy child together, then what are we doing together at all?

Because they argued a lot. It made them feel bad but they could no longer seem to help it. Dad complained that he had to do everything, be the breadwinner and do all the domestic household stuff too; Mom said that was because he worked at home and had lots of time on his hands, while she had a job; he said that if that was the problem then she could certainly quit her job since they didn't need the money and he didn't understand why she held on to it anyway; she refused; at some point one of them would complain about something that happened years ago, the other would say, "I cannot believe you're bringing that up again," and then they were off to the races.

Sometimes, just to get out, she would go to the Howland public library and hang with, or near, her Aunt Candace. It was usually pretty dead there, but in a good way. There was a Children's Room with a soundproof door, often crowded on weekdays, especially if the weather was bad. The mothers sat in there, amidst the noise, looking weary. Out in the main reading room Haley mostly looked through magazines, or bounced around on the internet. Candace sat behind the checkout desk, reading a book, looking up from it and out the window, sometimes, to watch the people walking by. On occasion she'd give Haley a five and send her down the street to a new place called The Beanery to bring back some decent coffee.

The attraction to Aunt Candace was hard to explain. In terms of female role models in the family, she was Haley's only alternative to her mother, but that wasn't really it, Candace wasn't a role model exactly. She exuded a vague dissatisfaction. She was sarcastic but did not complain. She didn't, or didn't seem to, give a lot of thought to how she looked. Only once did she ask Haley what she was doing in the library in the first place.

"Nothing," Haley said, a little defensively.

"I can see that." Her aunt examined her. "Everything okay at home?"

"What? Yes. God. If it's a problem for me to be here, I can go."

But she didn't move. At length Candace shrugged and said, "Well, look, if you're going to hang out here, you have to at least read something. I mean seriously. Read the paper or something."

So Haley read the paper. It caused her some anxiety, not because of what was in it, but because it was impossible to read all of it and so you always felt like you were being lazy and missing something important. The *Globe* was a little less stressful in this regard than the *Times,* but not by much.

One Tuesday in March she came back with two large Americanos and there were two kids roughly her age, a boy and a girl, sitting in the Periodicals section, not because they were reading periodicals but because that's where the softest chairs were. "Nothing for me?" the boy said to Haley, smiling, and the girl slapped him on the arm. There was still an empty chair right next to them but she thought it would be too weird to sit there when the whole rest of the library was empty, so she walked up and down the stacks for a bit, discreetly staring over the lid of her cup. Occasionally they said something to each other in a whisper but mostly they just sat in silence, as if the silence were what they had come for. From some angles Haley thought she recognized the girl and from others not. They certainly didn't go to her school. They didn't appear, from their body language, to be more than friends. He wore a knit ski hat and an old green fatigue jacket. She had very short hair and four earrings and fingerless gloves that she never took off.

The next day they were back again. Now and then they checked their phones but mostly they just sat together, calmly, like brother and sister, though they looked nothing alike. "Friends of yours?" Aunt Candace whispered to her. Haley shook her head no.

"There's six chairs over there, you know," Candace said. "You don't have to feel like they marked the territory."

Her aunt seemed strangely at home inside the library, Haley thought. It was warm and quiet, narcotic, and there didn't seem to be much actual work to do. Haley mouthed the word "Coffee?" to her and Candace smiled and reached for her purse. On her way out, Haley slowed as she passed the Periodicals section and said, trying for sarcasm, "Anything for you?"

The boy and girl looked up. "No thank you," the girl said, and the boy said, "Large latte?" Haley waited until he reached into his pants pocket and pulled out four dollars. "This is the coolest library ever," he said.

She returned with three coffees, handed one to her aunt, and then returned to the Periodicals section.

"You're here a lot," the boy said.

"So are you," said Haley, "but you don't read anything."

"It's a free country," he said, and for some reason the girl laughed, like this was some inside joke. "You and the library lady seem tight, what's up with that?"

"She's my aunt."

"No way. What's her name?"

"Candace."

He nodded. "Very cool," he said.

"If you guys want to talk," Candace said from her desk across the floor, "maybe go in the Children's Room?"

They stared at her.

"I mean it," she said softly. "I have to maintain a certain atmosphere around here. It's not out of the question that somebody could walk in."

So they went into the Children's Room and let the heavy door swing shut behind them. Awkwardly, there was a mother in there, sitting on a window seat watching her son fit together some Duplo train tracks. She had earbuds in.

"I remember those," the boy said about the train tracks. "So you just come here to hang out and get your aunt coffee?"

"Yeah. And to get out of my house," Haley said, thinking that might make an impression on him, which it did not. "What about you?"

"Just killing time. I mean we like it here, it's very chill. But basically we're just waiting to meet some people." The girl glared at him. "Chill," he said.

"Where do you guys go to school?" She cursed that as a dumb question even as she asked it.

"Regional." They did not ask Haley where she went to school. It was probably written right on her, she thought.

"So killing time until what?"

"Progressive dinner," he said, and this time when the girl glared fiercely at him he leaned further forward and avoided her eyes. "It's like a semi-weekly thing. You know what a progressive dinner is?"

"I think so. Like a different dish or course or whatever at each house, right?"

"Correct. See, Becca? I've told you before, I am an excellent judge of people. I'm Walker, by the way."

He said he couldn't invite Haley that night because it would be too rude if people hadn't been told in advance she was coming; but there was another one scheduled for next Wednesday. She wasn't sure she knew what he was talking about. But she asked her mom for permission to go out Wednesday and her mom seemed relieved to say yes, even though it was a school night. She had to walk a long way to meet them, almost to the triangular intersection where Daisy's was.

Only Walker was there, which was odd and, for a moment,

frightening: what kind of horror-movie scenario had she been naïve enough to walk into? But he smiled his stoner smile and said, "Come on, everybody else is in the woods," and he slipped between a pair of trees onto what she supposed was a path and it was already so close to darkness she had no choice but to follow him. When her eyes were fully adjusted he stopped and she saw they were in a kind of circular, trampled clearing. There were four or five other people squatting or lying there but it was too dark to make out their faces. Again she had a kind of flash-forward where she saw herself being raped or killed. She almost turned and ran. She heard the sound of someone crushing a beer can.

"Okay," Walker said in his ordinary voice, which startled her. "Progressive dinner?"

With a few muted noises of assent they all rose. The moon was out by now, and she was able to follow the shoulders of the silent kids in front of her and even to differentiate the one other girl (who was not Becca) from the boys. They walked confidently between the birches and the pines and then it grew vaguely lighter in front of Haley's eyes as they started to emerge from the woods again.

They were behind a house, a fancy one, silent and moon-shadowed. No lights were on and the driveway was empty. It was a summer place, undoubtedly. The lawn was raked and neat but that was something the people who owned this kind of a house would pay locals to do for them, until the weather warmed enough for them to return.

She wanted to ask who lived here, but everyone had gone silent. The six of them walked quickly from the woods across the grass to the house, where they flattened themselves under the eaves as if to protect themselves from rain. Walker reached up and removed his hat, with such solemnity that Haley almost expected the others to do the same, but then he briskly put the hat over his fist and punched through one of the small panes beside the door. They all listened for a moment and heard nothing. Walker shook the hat off his hand, reached carefully through the hole he'd made, unlocked the door, and they were in.

Though spacious, it was certainly not as large as the house where Haley lived. Still, it was like a portal to some other world, a world of casually limitless means, indulgent of limitless attention to detail. Every piece of furniture, every plate, every fixture matched and shone. Decorated, she thought, or designed, more than lived in—yet people did live in it sometimes; framed photos of them hung from the triangle of wall between the staircase landing and the second floor, photos Haley could not bring herself to look at. She was terrified to think what they might have come there to do—steal, destroy things, set fire to the place—but the answer turned out to be nothing much. They just hung out there; and indeed, a few of them opened up their backpacks and brought out food to share for dinner. Somebody opened the fridge and hissed "Fuckers!" when it turned out to be empty, but in the brief automatic light from the open door she got a look at most of their faces, and they seemed like normal faces, grinning kids' faces. A couple of them pulled out of their backpacks cigarettes, a pipe, a bottle of Jager. They sat in the living room of these wealthy, absent strangers and got a buzz on and talked. Laughing, almost like play-acting; Haley thought how incredibly violated these people would feel when they came back, around Memorial Day probably, and saw that their home (well, one of their homes) had been entered, walked around in. They'd search frantically for what was missing. She almost felt like leaving them a note, saying no, don't freak out, it wasn't like that.

When all the dope and liquor and food were gone, they took a little mock-formal tour of the house. "Here we see the bones of our ancestors," Walker said in a sort of British accent, "and on your left is the crapper, designed specially by Frank Lloyd Wright."

But nobody defaced or damaged anything. Their presence, they understood, was the defacement. In high spirits they went back out the rear door, their boots crunching on the glass, and closed it behind them.

When they were back on the path and deep enough into the woods that she felt it safe, Haley said, "So, it is just one house in a night, right?"

Walker laughed. "Yeah," he said. "'Progressive' in the sense of, like, a lifetime."

In the light from her own porch, exhausted, Haley checked her boots and cuffs for mud. She entered her house through the kitchen; it was late, but her dad only asked if she'd been warm enough, and her mom didn't say anything to her at all.

Daisy's, a business whose margins had been thin for two generations, began to take on the look of an enterprise that was struggling to stay afloat. There had always been something aggressive in their relationship to their customers—the service was surly, and the menus bore a sarcastic warning that if you wanted to complain about how long it took your food to arrive, the Golden Arches were just a mile and a half up Route 7. But the arguably charming timelessness of the place had started to look more like decay. Coffee cups and saucers with chips in them were still in service, and broken ones weren't replaced. The thin curtains were fading from white to yellow. Daisy's daughter Chase moved even more reluctantly, and they seemed to view the mostly empty tables and chairs more with relief than as cause for alarm. As for Horace, half-visible through the serving window into the kitchen, even the loyal regulars like Mark could only guess whether and how time was having its way with him too.

One winter night the heat failed and the pipes froze and repairs kept them closed for two weeks. The construction triggered a visit from the state health department, and while Daisy asked for and received a grace period that kept her from having to close again, the upshot was that they would need to replace both their deep fryer and their grill. In March a For Sale sign appeared, hammered into the hard ground by the Route 4 entrance to the parking lot. None of the regulars, Mark included, said a word to Chase about it. It seemed unlikely that she'd get an offer. To put a sign up at all, on a road traveled lightly and mostly by locals, seemed hopeless. It really was, or over the decades had become, a terrible spot for a restaurant.

Then one day in April the sign was gone. Mark found himself locking eyes interrogatively with the four other local workingmen silently eating breakfast, but no one said anything. Chase came to Mark's table and refilled his coffee without a word. He sipped it and looked out the window, at the thin threads and buttons of green pushing through the mud in the lot across the road, maybe part of the land trust since it had sat there untouched for as long as he could remember. Ten minutes later his egg sandwich arrived. He tried discreetly to search Chase's face but he could detect no change in it. When he was paying at the register, his coat already on, he had a moment where he thought, This is ridiculous, and he said out loud, "I see the For Sale sign's down."

"Yep," Chase said.

"How come?"

"I guess because we're not for sale anymore."

"Well, yeah, I—" People did that around there, it was an old Yankee thing, they played word games with you to make you feel dumb when they knew there was something you wanted from them. His father was a master at it. "Did you find a buyer, Chase?"

"Nope. Five eighteen's your change."

"Five eighteen is always my change. Jesus. You can keep it if you'll just tell me what's happened."

Finally she looked up at him and sighed. He could see the relief in her, even though she was trying to hide it. "It was your friend there," she said. "Your rich friend. The Benevolent Billionaire."

"Hadi? He bought the place?"

"Nope. He just gave us some money."

Mark was aware, without looking, of the others seated behind him who had stopped chewing in an effort to overhear them.

"Gave it to you?"

She didn't feel the need to confirm something she'd already said.

"What," Mark said, "like a grant?"

Chase laughed. "If you like," she said. "He just said that we were important to the town and he wanted to do what he could to keep us going." Mark could hear a bit of pride in her voice; it was clear she was quoting him directly.

"I won't ask how much," he said, pocketing his change, "though I'm curious."

"Not enough for him to miss," Chase said.

Mark couldn't really absorb it until he was back in the car heading home. He wondered if great wealth allowed your more generous nature to emerge, or whether it was possessing that nature in the first place—that magnanimous understanding of the common good—that led one to wealth. The house was empty, as it always was at that hour on a weekday. The emptiness and the silence made him contemplative, and at some point that morning it dawned on him that maybe Hadi had nostalgic feelings for Daisy's for a more sentimental reason: it was where the two of them had met, where the first arrangements were made for the work on Hadi's house that made it possible for him to become a local, a full-time citizen of Howland and ultimately its leader. Not that their friendship was that important to Hadi—Mark didn't deceive himself to that degree—but it had been a signal moment in both their lives, for sure, and it had happened right there.

As Hadi's term came to a close, he did not campaign for reelection in any way, and his profile in town did not increase. He came into Town Hall less and less; there were weeks when he wasn't spotted there at all. His secretary sometimes said that personal business had called him out of town, or that he was working from his home office (which was, after all, the way Marty Solomon used to do it, and no one back then had found that alarming), or, on occasion, she would smile genially and admit that at the moment she had no idea where he was. She herself was at her small desk outside his office every hour the town was officially open for business. She even brought her lunch.

In September the *Gazette* published a front-page interview with Hadi, in which he said that he would be happy for his four-year term to be renewed, should the people of Howland desire it. (Readers who knew the timid Abigail at all found it difficult to imagine the circumstances of this "interview" and surmised that it was really just a press release Hadi had composed in Q-and-A form and had instructed his secretary to deliver to the *Gazette*.) He had some ideas for the future health and prosperity of the town that he would welcome the chance to implement. But he would not campaign as such—he wouldn't be giving any speeches, or showing up in restaurants to shake voters' hands. He thought it sufficient—he thought it proper—to run on his record.

And what was that record, in Hadi's own view? "All of the town's services are running smoothly and are fully funded. The property tax rate has been reduced to historic low levels. The rate of local business failure has been reduced. Is it a new way of governing? I suppose, but you have to admit that the old ways of governing stopped working some time ago, not just here in Howland but nationwide."

At the traditional pre-election town meeting, which Gerry attended, Hadi did not appear; and when the floor was opened to challenge the nomination of the current slate of selectmen and town officials for reelection, no one stood or raised a hand. The following Tuesday, Hadi was reelected by a vote of 231–79. Voter turnout was the second lowest in Howland's history.

One weekday afternoon back in October Haley had emerged from her usual school-bus zone-out and realized that the bus made a stop on Melville Road, just a few hundred yards off Main; this would put her a two-minute walk from the library, with The Beanery in between. So the following Monday she just stood up and got off at that stop, rather than ride for another ten minutes to wind up at her own house. She told the driver she was going to the library, which was good enough for him and also technically true. She squeezed past two bewildered little kids and their mother, who met them at that stop every day, and picked up two Americanos, one for her and one for Aunt Candace.

She just felt drawn to the place, she didn't know why. It wasn't like she and her aunt talked a lot—they were in a library, after all. Maybe it was the silence itself she liked, not others' silence but her own; in most situations you could only stay silent for so long before people started asking you what was wrong. It felt like a pocket in time, like one of those indoor, couch-cushion forts you'd build for yourself as a kid, a place to hide even when no one was looking for you, just for that feeling of hiding. She definitely wasn't there hoping to run into Walker and Becca. They still came in now and then, and various of their friends came in too, especially when the weather was bad. It was a tad awkward because Haley had politely opted out of further progressive dinners, if that project was even still going on, which she imagined it was. She couldn't figure out what the goal might be, other than to not get caught, which meant that there was only one way for it to end. She so wanted to tell Candace about it—she had an idea her aunt would find the whole thing funny, or even actually approve of it, approve of her for daring to do it—but she couldn't risk that. She read the news of the outside world assiduously, always with the expectation that Aunt Candace might ask for her informed position on this or that, even though that had never once happened.

But her new after-school routine survived less than a month: one Thursday night at dinner, Haley made reference to the next day's math test and her mother asked her why she hadn't been studying from the time she got home. "She got home like five minutes before you did, leave her alone," said her father, meaning to defend her, and her mother said, what are you talking about? By the time that conversation was over, she'd admitted to spending her afternoons at the town library but had made up some school research project to justify it, which meant the whole thing would have to come to an end anyway, sooner rather than later.

"So they'll just let children get off the bus wherever they want?" Karen was still raving as Haley cleared the table. "Hey, who cares where they go, not our problem!"

Of course it wasn't really about the bus, and though Karen tried her best to calm down over the next few days, she couldn't. She suspected Haley was lying, but not strongly enough to risk coming right out and accusing her, and anyway why would she lie? Why make up a reason to avoid coming home? Things weren't that bad: she could hear how she sounded saying that, even to herself, but objectively it was still true, things weren't that bad. Unless Candace herself was getting in Haley's ear for some reason, stealing her away, so to speak. She might not even have realized she was doing it; she might be drawn without knowing it to that kind of intimacy, a woman her age with no child of her own. A solution seemed to be to confront Candace directly, even though there was never a moment when Karen decided specifically to do so. The impulse came from some other level, where none of its drawbacks could develop in her thinking because she didn't really let herself think about it at all. She left earlier than necessary for Caldwell House, stopped for coffee, and then, as if surprised to find the time on her hands, dropped by the library at 9:02, two minutes after it opened.

Except it wasn't open. Karen knocked and put her face up against the glass of the door. She knocked again, and this time the interior door stenciled PRIVATE swung inward, and Candace walked briskly toward the entrance, frowning, and then raising her eyebrows without quite dropping the frown when she saw it was her sister-in-law at the door. One of Candace's shoes was unstrapped. Her shirt was out, though that could have been how she would wear it in any case, and her hair was flying everywhere.

"Karen, hi, what a surprise," she said muzzily. "Sorry, didn't think anyone would be here quite so early." She turned away and began flipping on the lights.

Karen was disarmed. Candace had clearly slept in the library. She'd been too groggy to close the office door behind her, and Karen could see the corner of what looked like a cot or a folding bed in there.

"What can I do for you?" Candace said, somewhat flippantly, Karen thought. "A particular book you're in need of?"

"Candace?" Karen said.

"Is that coffee, by the way? Because I will give you five dollars for it. For half of it."

"Candace, are you okay?" Karen said. "What the hell is going on?" Just then the door to the Children's Room opened, from the inside, and a teenage boy wearing a brown ski cap stuck his head through it. Karen, too disoriented by now to take this in, actually screamed.

"Jesus, Karen," Candace said.

"Everything all right?" the boy said calmly.

"Yeah, sure, but you guys need to get your stuff together and get out of there, like four minutes ago," Candace said without looking at him. "There's Story Hour this morning." She regarded her sister-in-law sternly. "Just go have a seat in Periodicals," she said, "and I'll come talk to you in a couple of minutes."

Karen did as she was told. She did not pick up a magazine. A few minutes later, the door to the Children's Room opened and the boy in the ski hat exited, accompanied by a short-haired, sullen-looking girl. He smiled amiably and waved, and the two of them went out into the street. Candace emerged from her office with her hair brushed and sat down in the other good club chair.

"So what can I do for you?" she said.

Karen, at a loss, just stared at her.

"Look," Candace said. "Not every family is the picture of domestic bliss, okay? That boy's father gets drunk and cleans his guns while yelling at the TV. Did you recognize him? I should have asked you that first, because if you recognized him then I just really betrayed a—"

"No. I have no idea who that was."

"Good then. Anyway, some of the local youth started hanging out here at one point, I think in part because they thought it was funny. And legit, in the sense that who's going to say it's a suspect thing, right? Teenagers hanging out at the library? And they talk to each other, and I overhear things, and eventually they wind up telling me things. They can trust an adult who's not a parent, who doesn't have any skin in the game."

She stared calmly into Karen's face, bravely even, like someone determined to make a good death. For a horrible moment Karen thought all of this was some oblique reference to herself. What had Haley been saying about her? She tried to remember the last time Haley had spent a night away from home, and where she'd said she was.

"So they know that this is a safe space, if things get rough," Candace said. "Last night things got rough in that kid's home, and he called me."

"But why were you sleeping here?"

"I only sleep here when somebody else is sleeping here. I'm not going to leave them alone. They're teenagers, they're animals, they'd burn the place down."

"Do people—does anybody know you're doing this?"

"You do. Nobody else as far as I know."

"I just—" Karen let her hands flutter above the arms of the chair. "You don't think these kids should be with their parents? Where do their parents think they are?"

"Family is a nightmare for some people," Candace said. "Family is something some people need to be protected from. You think this kind of thing doesn't happen around here. But everybody thinks that. Not everyone can enjoy the kind of traditional domestic bliss you do." Karen couldn't tell how sarcastically this was meant; it didn't sound sarcastic at all, but she assumed it had to be. "But listen, there has to be some reason you happened to come over here so bright and early this morning."

"Why has Haley been spending so much time here with you?" Karen said, and to her frustrated surprise she started crying. "And not telling us about it?"

Candace looked around for a box of tissues; when she didn't find one, she leaned over and patted Karen on the knee. "I actually don't know why. But I like having her around. And you flatter yourself, Karen," she said softly, "if you think Haley's problems are anything, anything like real problems. Don't worry. I think they're supposed to be a little bit of a mystery at this age. She doesn't come over here to complain about you or anything."

Karen, with little confidence that this was true, nodded, and stood up to leave. She drove to work and sat staring through the window behind her computer monitor, thinking of other things she might have asked, probably should have asked: If the boy was the one who called you, what was the girl doing there? How do you know when they're telling the truth and when they're lying? Was she sure they weren't just having sex in there? It seemed like a hysterical question but you thought differently about these things when you were a parent, especially the parent of a girl. Outside, the ground was brittle, and mist had pooled into spots of ice on the black tarps staked over the flower beds.

That night at dinner she announced that Haley would come with her to Caldwell House after school the following Monday, for Take Our Daughters to Work Day.

"Wasn't that in April?" Mark said.

"Mom, no," Haley said.

But she insisted. On Monday she picked Haley up outside school and drove straight to the mansion. She had a bag of picnic food she'd bought at the fancy épicerie in Stockbridge; it was raining lightly, though, so they had to eat inside.

"So this is my office," Karen said.

"Mom, I've been here," Haley said.

"I'm in charge now of the payroll for all of the employees here, and I help out a lot with fundraising, and I organize board meetings, and I also am on call to answer any questions members of the public might have, by phone or email."

"Why are you telling me all this?"

Karen felt the tears pushing at her eyes again. So you'll respect me, she started to say, but that was not a thing you could say out loud, it showed too much weakness.

Haley had picked up a flyer for a Berkshire Historical Society talk being given at Caldwell in a few weeks' time: Horticulture and Feminism in Fin de Siècle New England. "This is *such* a bizarre place to have a job," she said.

The housing market was through the roof now, locally just as nationally. The first property Mark had bought, in Becket, on foreclosure, had risen in value sixty percent in two years. Now the conservatism that had seemed so vital at the beginning of this venture seemed not just unnecessary but stupid—sitting on the sidelines was like losing money, like giving it away. But getting in deeper required a larger outlay. Prices were up, and as for bargains, there'd been no foreclosure sales in the Howland area for nine or ten months. It took some knowledge, all of a sudden, to know what constituted overpaying. He could try to convert some of his own properties into cash while they were at the top of the market. But there were renters living in most of them.

He sat with his brother at Daisy's, weighing these matters, allowing Chase to silently refill their coffee cups over and over, as they discussed the future.

"The hottest market in all of western Mass right now is here in Howland," Gerry said. "Know why?"

"Because of the publicity about Hadi?"

Gerry shook his head, then amended, "Well, yes and no. The reason prices are going up is that the taxes here are so low, which he lowered them, it's true. The increase in home prices actually more than offsets the taxes you'd pay on the same house in Lenox or Stockbridge or wherever, much more. But people hate paying taxes. They fucking hate it."

"You kind of have to hand it to him," Mark said. "He said he was all about protecting the character of the town, and he kept his promise. I mean, this place is a perfect example."

Gerry scowled, half-listening. He was staring at another one of the stitched samplers that had been framed and hung on Daisy's wall, behind the register: a hand-sewn reproduction of the old Gadsden flag, with the snake saying DON'T TREAD ON ME.

"Wait, what?" Gerry said. Mark looked around to make sure Chase was out of earshot and more or less whispered the outline of how Hadi had stepped in to keep Daisy's from going under.

"So he owns the place now?"

"No, he just gave Daisy the money."

"What do you mean, 'the money'? The money for what? How much?"

"No idea," Mark said. "Does it matter? Jesus, is there nothing you won't shit on? Maybe he just did it, you know—"

"If you say 'out of the goodness of his heart,' I swear to God my head will explode."

"Why, though?" Mark said, a little louder than he meant to. "Why? Why is that so impossible for you to imagine?"

"Funny," Gerry said, "because that's exactly the one question you won't ask yourself. Why?"

"It's not to look good, that's for sure, because he'd never say a word about it. Which makes you wonder if maybe this isn't the only time he's helped somebody out like this."

"Exactly," his brother said. "Ex fucking zactly."

"Jesus," Mark said. "Let's talk about something else."

There wasn't much other business to discuss. Mark was now back doing most of the occasional maintenance and repair work Barrett used to do, not to save money but because there was too little of it to justify hiring someone full- or even half-time. They didn't yet have a court date for evicting Gage and his vandal sons. There seemed no way to hurry that process along.

"Okay then," Gerry said. "Do I still need to pay for this omelet, or should I just charge it to Town Hall?"

"You can pay for me too," Mark said, "just to avoid any appearance of corruption," and they walked out to the lot and drove their separate ways. It was a Wednesday, and Gerry got home with nothing to do until he could meet Penny at her house after work. He slapped the space bar on his computer to wake it up, spent a few hours on the internet, took a nap, then made himself a sandwich. He had never been one of those guys who needed to work—he'd always particularly hated working with his hands, which used to drive his dad into rages—and in most respects the life he was living now was the life of which he used to dream: making a few savvy decisions and then sitting back and collecting the income from them. He had more in his savings account right now than he'd ever had in his life. Yet something felt off, there was something still between him and what logically should have been happiness or at least a more profound sense of satisfaction. Probably it was his brother, so naïve and so self-righteous, so confident and ignorant at the same time. Gerry kind of wanted to see him fail, yet their fates were now so completely intertwined that Gerry felt like he had nothing uncomplicated to wish for anymore.

How many other places in town, or in the surrounding towns for that matter, was Philip Hadi taking over? Was he doing it because it amused him, or for some other reason that was harder to fathom, assuming you were curious enough to want to fathom it at all, which most folks around Howland apparently were not? And what was the difference between working hard and not working hard, between succeeding and not succeeding, if what lay at the end of either of those roads was a guy with a checkbook to bail you out, to guarantee all outcomes?

He took Penny to the movies, and then they went down Route 7 to the Snack Shack for dinner. It was full of families; they were the only ones there without kids. He was willing to spend money on her—he wanted to, especially now that he had some money for a change—but she wasn't interested. Once he took her to that fancy-ass new place where the Benihana used to be, back when he thought such things might impress her. It was hard to get a reservation, even though no one he knew had been there more than once; supposedly people from New York or even further away would travel to the Berkshires and stay overnight, just to have a meal. Gerry dropped four hundred bucks on dinner for two and that was without any wine. They fed you stuff that looked like it came from the woods behind your house, served to you on things that weren't plates. One course, he still remembered, was stuck onto old pitchfork tines. The cherry on this sundae of pretension was that they gave you a little notebook and a pencil, in order to write down God knows what. Toward the end of the meal, a deadpan Penny had held up her open notebook to show him that she'd drawn with her little pencil a picture of a slice of pizza and a martini, complete with olive. At such moments he wished he could just risk asking her to marry him.

He thought he could put the whole Daisy's matter aside and then he attended Howland's annual Founders' Day ceremony. It was a gimmicky little celebration tied to the day the town's original charter was signed, just for locals really because it was too early in the holiday season for weekenders; the First Selectman read a tongue-in-cheek proclamation and the brass ensemble from the conservatory up in Lenox played a march or two and that was it. Marty Solomon used to wear a sort of Ben Franklin costume, even though that didn't make any sense. They held it outdoors at the bandstand if the weather was good enough, or in the auditorium at Regional in case of snow, though it hadn't snowed that early for several years now. This year the weather was so warm that some people brought blankets and coolers and made a little picnic out of it. Penny was there, but because it was a Saturday, they weren't there together; she and her sons sat on a blanket eating out of deli containers with plastic forks and generally having a good time while Gerry stood and watched, holding a cup of coffee, about twenty feet away. In truth he was there mostly just to get a glimpse of them—of the boys with their mom. He hadn't been to one of these ceremonies in years.

The conductor of the brass ensemble shouted "Hello, folks!"

and then shouted it twice more, until the crowd understood that he was trying to ask them to be quiet. There were still two weeks until Thanksgiving but that didn't stop him from welcoming them to what he hoped would be another joyous Christmas season in the Berkshires. He thanked the members of the ensemble, and their director, and the Friends of the Bandstand. He asked those who were sitting to please rise for the national anthem; after that was played, with some people singing and others not, the ensemble went right into one of those Sousa marches that everybody recognized but no one knew the name of, that instantly put you in a good mood.

Except for Gerry, who was scanning the faces on the bandstand and in the crowd for any reflection of what he was wondering. Where was Hadi? He didn't even show up? What kind of leadership was that? If you wanted to run things, in this part of the world, you had better start with a little humility, with a willingness to acknowledge that you were no better than anyone else and didn't harbor any delusions to the contrary. What better proof would you want that Hadi thought himself too good for all of them than that he would just blow off one of the town's oldest traditions? Running a town was about more than writing checks. Gerry glanced at Penny, who was so absorbed in the boys—even when they started punching each other for no reason, out of sheer restlessness, just like he and Mark used to do—that she almost seemed not to know or care where she was. The band started another number—"Stars and Stripes Forever," he was pretty sure it was—and he edged his way politely to the back of the crowd and walked to his car.

A couple of his windows needed new screens, so later that week he went down to the True Value, and ahead of him at the register he saw Tom Allerton, the selectman, the guy who was going to succeed Maeve Brennan until Hadi came forward, the guy to whom Gerry had sold a house way back when he worked for Century 21, back in century twenty. He felt a surge of nerves, like this was an opportunity, though for what exactly, he didn't know. "Tom!" he said. "I don't know if you remember me."

"Sure do," Allerton said, and shook his hand. There was a pause.

"Gerald Firth. I was the broker on your purchase of your house, on, was it Beacon Road?"

"Still is," Allerton said.

"Beautiful place. Good investment too, the way things have turned out."

Allerton smiled distractedly, waiting for the return of his credit card. "I've had two people in the last six months," he said, "just come up and cold knock on my door and offer to buy the place. Insane."

"Irrational exuberance," Gerry said.

"That's the phrase." He tucked his card back in his wallet and picked up his bag; Gerry resisted the temptation to lean over and see what was in it. Something in him urged him to be bold, as this encounter, or at least the seeming naturalness of it, was a second from being over.

"Listen," he said, "I need to talk to you about something. You free for dinner tonight?"

Allerton looked confused. He was a tall guy, a good six inches taller than most men, Gerry included.

"You know Talbot's Inn over in Hillsdale?" Gerry said.

"Hillsdale, New York?" Allerton said incredulously.

"Yeah, I know," Gerry said, "but no one will know us there."

Without breaking their eye contact Allerton had started for the door, and so Gerry felt he had no choice but to follow him, laying his window-screen rolls on the floor before crossing the threshold onto the sidewalk. Allerton put his True Value bag on the roof of his car and fished around for his keys.

"If this is town business, or government-related business," he said, "you know there's an open town meeting first Thursday of every month. I'd recommend you bring it up there."

Gerry shook his head, feeling the weakness in his own smile. He could see himself, reflected in Allerton's downward gaze, as a nuisance, as a crackpot. But he was neither of those things. And the window of this chance, unofficial encounter was closing.

"I just have this sense," Gerry said, "that you and I think alike. That we're not drinking the Kool-Aid."

"What Kool-Aid would that be?"

Gerry waited impatiently for a couple of strangers on the sidewalk to pass by them. "I just wonder," he said, "if you know, if the other members of the Howland government know, that Hadi personally bailed out Daisy's Restaurant when it went up for sale. His own money, the town's money, what's the difference at this point? I don't know why he'd do that. He says he wants to preserve the place, like it's all some kind of country-bumpkin theme park we live in, but there's still such a thing as a free market."

He paused, and when the pause was long enough for Allerton to recognize that that was all Gerry had, he laughed, not too kindly. "Daisy's," he said. "I didn't know about that one."

"That one?"

"Buddy, there are people in his office every week," Allerton said. "Businesses. Charities. Individual homeowners even. It's not a secret. I mean, whether or not they consider it shameful I don't know. But it's not a secret."

Gerry said nothing. He felt his face darkening, not from anger but from embarrassment.

"What's he doing?" Gerry said. "What's—what's his angle? His endgame?"

"Beats me, and I don't really care," Allerton said. "He is what he is. It's the people who go to him who baffle me."

He opened his car door and began folding himself inside.

"I don't know," Gerry said absently, quietly, looking down, almost as if Allerton had already finished fleeing from him. "It's like you can't stop it. The control gets taken away from you, but not even by force, you let it happen, you give it to them gladly and then thank them. How do you wake people up? I used to have this blog where I complained about things. It seems so childish now, that I thought ideas would make any difference. I called myself some cute fake name, PC Barnum. I ranted about Hadi like that would make any difference, like words would make any difference. Naïve! But whatever, right?"

Allerton took his hands off the wheel. "No shit," he said, looking more interested now but also, unmistakably, disappointed. "That was you?"

Dependency was the virus. What you were dependent on—that didn't matter, that was a red herring. The land underneath Gerry's tires was invaded and tilled and consecrated by men who believed that only the pursuit of one's own interest might multiply into the common good.

Barrett hadn't worked since August, more than five months now. His unemployment would run out soon. Calculating exactly when would only depress him and wouldn't change his situation in any way, so he didn't do it. His wife Stevie was picking up shifts now at the old folks' home in North Adams, which was a hike, but she did it without complaining, and occasionally there was a little bonus involved in the form of some prescription drugs from the dispensary. She could have stolen from the old people as well—it was so easy, she said, they were so out of it, if you told them they owed you twenty bucks they would just hand it to you, a lot of the night employees did it—but she considered that beyond the pale. Stealing from the company was one thing. She believed in karma, and so she left the residents and their useless assets alone.

It was enough for the two of them to get by on as long as Barrett didn't go out, so he didn't. He mostly just stayed in the house, in front of the TV, and he stuck to beer. His friend Kurt down the road let him have an incomplete set of free weights he'd picked up somewhere, and Barrett used them for a while so he wouldn't turn into too much of a fat turd just sitting on the couch all day, but eventually that motivation petered out too. He inquired about jobs, but there wasn't much new construction around, and it always seemed to come back to the same five or six guys doing all the hiring. He'd burned a lot of bridges, some he hadn't even remembered.

The sun reflected so brightly off the snow some afternoons that he had to get up and close the shades, in the middle of the day. Then the snowpack melted and on the afternoon he noticed that even the parts of the property that never saw sunlight were dark with mud, he put his boots on and went out and cleared the yard. He was still out there when he heard and then saw Stevie's car pull into the driveway, at two in the afternoon. Not good.

Her expression was so angry when she walked across the driveway to the house that he let her have a minute. When he went inside, she was at the kitchen table, halfway through a beer, her green hooded parka with the fake fur trim still on.

"They said I stole," she muttered. "Those fuckers. I mean I did steal but never what they said."

"So you told them you didn't do it, right?" Barrett said calmly, trying to generate an atmosphere wherein he could safely touch her head or her shoulder.

She pursed her lips. "Things got a little heated," she said.

They went on state assistance, but it couldn't last. It wasn't until their checking account went below zero for the first time that Barrett allowed himself to understand it might wind up costing them the house. If only he hadn't hit Mark Firth in the face that time. Over nothing, and not nearly hard enough to be worth it. But Barrett was pretty good at steering his thoughts away from the past. The future too. When he and Stevie fought, he'd sometimes go down the road to Kurt's, and drink Kurt's beer, which was a form of economizing. On one of these visits Kurt asked him if he'd been over to Town Hall yet.

"What the hell for?" Barrett asked.

Kurt told him that the mayor or whatever he was called, Hadi, was giving people money to keep them from losing their houses, when times were tough. You had to tell him your sob story and then he just laid the money on you, like that.

"Like a loan?" Barrett said. Kurt shrugged his shoulders and smiled gnomically.

"What the fuck?" Barrett said, mystified, and then belatedly he recognized the name. "I worked on that fucker's house," he said, "five-six years ago. He's nuts."

"Nuts and loaded," Kurt said. "Cool, so you already have a connection with him, even better. You should definitely try hitting him up."

But it didn't sit right. He had more pride than that, for better or for worse. And it went beyond pride, because he knew that if he'd had, say, a father, or a brother he still talked to, he would have borrowed money from them to get by or maybe even just accepted it as a gift. Nothing wrong with family helping each other out. It could bring you closer, make you humble. He'd even have taken help from Kurt if he didn't happen to know that Kurt too was just scraping by. No: he hated that Hadi guy, and nothing

304

would have made him feel more worthless as a man than acting in violation of his own avowed hatred. Way worse than just accepting charity. There was being humble and then there was betraying yourself.

For similar reasons he would never have accepted a handout from Mark Firth, not that any such thing was on offer. Still, that job was the last steady job he'd had, and he was good at it, and it was not impossible Mark might have cooled off since the whole episode that led to his firing. He couldn't bring himself to go straight to Mark, but he thought maybe the better approach was through the brother, Gerry, who was a little weird and hostile but not so superior-acting and who'd never had any real beef with him as far as Barrett could tell. He'd lost Gerry's number but he knew where his house was, so he folded up a note with his own number on it and stuck it in Gerry's screen door. Gerry called him and suggested they meet for a drink at the Ship.

That place never changed, and neither did the people you found in there at three in the afternoon. They got a couple of Narragansetts and sat at a table instead of the bar, at Gerry's suggestion. Barrett came right out and repeated what he'd said in his note, which was that he was hoping bygones could be bygones and he could get his old gig back.

"I doubt Mark would go for it," Gerry said, "but to tell the truth, it's kind of moot anyway, because he's actually trying to cut back on the renovating, on the renting too. He's going to stop renewing leases. All about buying and selling right now."

"Oh." Barrett slid his index finger up and down the beer bottle. He felt his mood blackening, the way it seemed to whenever he had to put his fate in the hands of these guys. "Well then, why didn't you just tell me that on the phone?"

"Because it sounds like tough times for you, so I thought I could at least buy you a beer and commiserate," Gerry said. "And because maybe there's other ways I can help you."

"Is this the Hadi thing?" Barrett asked glumly. Gerry raised his eyebrows. "Because I'm not fucking doing that."

"No, of course you wouldn't. Why not?"

"I don't know."

"Yes, you do," Gerry said.

"Rich people," Barrett said. "They think their money, like, purifies them. That's what they believe. And if I go to him for a favor, and he says yes, then I'm a part of it. I'm enabling it, I'm buying into it. I'm sure he doesn't give a shit what I think of him, but still, that's different than making him think I believe he's my daddy, even if it would help me out to let him think that."

"What will you do instead, though?" Gerry said.

"I don't know, man. Starve. Go under. I know it's stupid. But I'm like the scorpion, right? It's my nature."

"You married?"

"Why do you want to ask me about that, man?"

"Kids?"

Barrett shook his head no.

"Let me tell you something," Gerry said, "something I think you already know. Nobody believes in heaven and hell anymore. So there's no check on rich people, powerful people, doing whatever the fuck they want to do to the rest of us. No check except what the rest of us do to resist them. You know what I mean? You won't be bought, and that's admirable. But as this whole plan of his goes forward, there might be more to do than just passively opting out of it. You know what I mean?"

"Not really," Barrett said. But he stayed at the table.

At length Gerry took out a checkbook from his inside coat pocket. "I made some money off this scheme of my brother's," he said. "I've come to have mixed feelings about it, about the shit I had to eat to get it. I'm going to get out of it. He'll buy me out, I'm sure, and when he does I'll have even more money, so look, will you accept this from me? Just to help out your family? No strings. I just . . . we have to help each other out, we have to stick together, against outsiders. Against one outsider in particular. There is something about him we don't know."

Gerry folded the check in half and searched for a dry spot to lay it down. Its presence on the table was compromising, so before too much longer Barrett slid it off and stuck it in his jacket pocket without looking at it or unfolding it. They stayed and finished their beers without a further word.

Allerton was in his Town Hall office, feet on his desk, bouncing around various sports websites, when he got a text from that ball-buster secretary of Hadi's, asking if he was in the building. He couldn't very well say no. Even if she hadn't seen him come in, his car was right out there in the lot next to Hadi's. She summoned him to a meeting in the conference room in fifteen minutes. God knew what fresh enthusiasm had occasioned this summons; the only real way to avoid them, and him, was to stop coming in to Town Hall at all, but then you were removing yet another speed bump between the First Selectman and whatever the hell he felt like doing.

He'd never cared for Hadi, and in his own memory this distaste long preceded that night four and a half years ago when Hadi had stood up at the pre-election town meeting and high-hatted Allerton out of his rightful job as First Selectman. Everything about him reeked of the city. It wasn't that he was fake, exactly—Hadi was pretty authentically, unapologetically who he was—but people from Manhattan in particular seemed to operate under the misapprehension that the life they were living was the real one, the important, consequential life, and everybody else was provincial and out of touch. When the exact opposite was true: there was no earthly specimen more out of touch with reality than a New Yorker. People who lived on an island and paid a million dollars for a bedroom and spent all day creating computer programs to trade each other things that didn't exist—those were the unreal people. Like most Berkshire folk, Tom had a highly attuned radar for condescension, and he felt Hadi's patronage in every remark, every friendly glance, in his very residence in the town.

He strolled down the hall and around the corner to the conference room, the last to arrive. Hadi didn't even wait until he was in his seat to start talking.

"Got an idea to run past you," Hadi said. "A town in Massachusetts called Westhaven, you know where that is? I didn't know it, I had to look it up. Anyway, they've banned the sale of tobacco products within the town limits. It makes a lot of sense. I'm thinking of passing that ban here. What say you?"

They all stared at him, Waltz included. Maybe Waltz and Hadi had already discussed it, while Allerton was petulantly waiting in his office in order to be late. "Wow," he said. "That's a bold move." He was trying frantically to game it out. His neighbors and constituents, he was certain, would turn on Hadi in an instant if this ban were passed, and so he felt a strong desire to pass it. His own vote would be enough to do so; but then, if he voted for it, he'd be associated with it too. His path would be easy if he knew Waltz would vote yes, but Waltz would never vote for such a ban in a million years. The man smoked like a furnace, for one thing. And he was too dumb to be persuaded by any kind of Machiavellian argument about the long-game wisdom of passing a law that would adversely affect their superior whom they wanted to unseat. Besides, he wasn't completely sure unseating Hadi was Waltz's goal. Not because Waltz liked him—they had way too little in common for that—but simply because Hadi's governing style, lazy and autocratic at the same time, made the other selectmen's jobs so much less demanding.

"Maybe bring it to the next town meeting?" Allerton said finally. "People will want to hear your thinking."

And then came the moment when Allerton realized that he'd been even more right about Hadi all along than he realized, that all his worst, most ungenerous instincts in the matter of human nature were always to be obeyed.

"I don't think I'll do that," Hadi said. "Let's just pass it in session. I don't think a lot of opinions, people's opinions, on an issue like this are going to be all that productive."

"No?" Tom said.

Hadi shook his head and smiled. "Consensus really isn't all it's cracked up to be," he said. "This is what I felt going in. And I think our results these last few years have borne that out, don't you? If you let everybody vote on everything, some really destructive compromises and half measures are going to come out of that."

Allerton looked at Waltz to see if they'd both just heard the same thing, but Waltz wore the look he always wore, a look that said he longed only for this meeting, like every meeting, to be over. As for the secretary, pen stilled by the momentary silence, she probably would have made an outstanding Nazi.

"I have to point out something obvious," Allerton said, "which is that your lack of interest in popular resistance itself creates popular resistance. I know, for instance, that there's a popular local blog dedicated to opposing, well, you. I heard someone in town referencing it just the other day."

"Anonymous," Hadi said. "I've seen it."

Waltz's interest was stirred. "Do you know who it is?" he said.

"No," said Allerton a little more dramatically than he meant to, "I do not."

"I'm concerned with the real," Hadi said, "and blogs are what God gave the world to keep morons occupied. So can we leave it, then, that we'll vote on this measure when we reconvene in a week?"

"Awesome," Waltz said. Allerton nodded, just to acknowledge that he'd heard, and walked back to his rear-facing office and closed the door. His strength, he'd always felt, was that he wasn't an especially political guy. Political in the sense of ideology, that is, Republican or Democrat, conservative or liberal. But that didn't mean he had no core. On the contrary: he was a man and he expected to be treated like a man. Maybe that little toady real estate salesman, Firth, was onto something. They were under attack; and the way to come together was to refuse to be herded together. The best way to protect each other was to make sure everyone was free to make whatever stupid fucking selfish decision they wanted. He didn't smoke but he felt like taking it up just to prove a point.

Still, he had to be smart about it. The Town of Howland kept a database with all its citizens' vital statistics and contact information; Allerton copied Gerry Firth's phone number onto a Post-it he stuck in his wallet, and that night, from home, he called it. "I thought about our talk the other day," he said, "and I have to let you know something. Hadi not only knows about your blog, he knows who you are, he knows you're the author. Don't ask me how, I have no idea how, and I'll bet you don't either. But anyway, he sees you, he knows you're out there, so there doesn't seem any reason for anonymity anymore. Not to mention that I think the people need a leader. The opposition to Hadi needs a face. Because there is a battle coming. Let me tell you what we heard in the board meeting today." And he briefly outlined the proposed plan to ban the sale of cigarettes and all other tobacco products in the town of Howland.

Gerry hung up. It was a Tuesday, which meant it was a Penny night. His instinct was to try to keep from her what was on his mind, but whether or not that instinct was a gallant one, he couldn't obey it, the weight of it was too much. She cleared their plates from her kitchen table and lit a cigarette and asked him what was wrong.

"Remember that blog I told you about?" he said. "What did you think about the fact that it was anonymous?" She cocked her head at him. "I mean," he said, "did you think that was, like, cowardly or anything?"

"I never really gave that much thought to it," she said.

"I'm trying—I'm trying to do the right thing," Gerry said, twisting his napkin, "and if I'm honest with myself I'm trying to find the thing that will make you respect me more, that will make you let me into your life a little more. Is that stupid?"

She shook her head no, but apart from that her face showed nothing.

"Maybe you think it's pathetic not to stand up for what you believe in. Maybe you think it's pathetic for a man to just take potshots without identifying himself, while the world goes to hell around him. Maybe that's why you won't let me meet your sons. That's kind of how I'm thinking."

She sighed, and then patiently worked her way to the end of the cigarette before stubbing it out. Then she put that hand on his hand.

"Not really sure what the hell you're talking about?" she said. "But listen, just so you know: I made myself a promise. No more men in the boys' lives, at least until they become men themselves and I can't do anything more about it. It's got nothing at all to do with you. Or with hating men, for that matter. It's I don't trust my own judgment of who's a good guy and who's not. Historically you would have to say that my judgment on that is terrible, and my sons have already paid enough of a price for it. So the fact that you seem like a good guy to me is actually something of a red flag, you see what I mean?"

He spent the night, and when she went to work the next morning he drove home, made a pot of coffee, tapped the space bar on his keyboard, and waited for the light of the monitor to bathe his face. He kept it short and sweet: he described the proposed ban on tobacco-product sales in Howland, and then he identified himself as Gerald Firth, born and raised in the South Berkshires, and called for a petition to hold a vote to recall Philip Hadi as First Selectman. He didn't trouble himself with the question of whether the town's charter had any sort of provision for recall votes. He was more worried about the fact that it had been nearly a year since his last post; his followers, however many of them there were, had likely wandered off, and so perhaps he was speaking to no one.

He did still have Allerton's cell number in his phone, from yesterday's call; he left a voicemail. Allerton listened to it in his office after lunch and then frantically deleted it. He waited until he got home to look up the Workingman's Dread blog and read the new post. He read it again to make sure it contained no reference to him or mention of his name. Not since high school, probably, had he so successfully maneuvered someone else into doing something risky that he wanted them to do. He felt like he'd missed his calling, though he wasn't sure what that calling was. In the morning, at Town Hall, he called up that citizens' database again and spent the day copying by hand all six hundred–plus email addresses, every taxpayer and property owner in town except for the handful of

seniors and technophobes who weren't online. He carried the addresses home with him; after dinner, he set up a brand new Gmail
account and spent the hours until dawn typing every one of those
addresses into the Bcc bar of a new message containing a link to
Gerry Firth's blog. When he heard his wife moving around in the
kitchen, making coffee, he hit Send. He'd done everything he could
think of to keep his involvement hidden, but still he thought it
likely that it would all be traced back to him somehow in the end.
He was no computer expert. He'd read that nothing was really private on the internet, nothing was truly deleted, everything you did
or wrote or even looked at left a digital trail right back to you, and
it was precisely because he didn't understand how any of that
worked that he believed it.

Gerry himself was slow to realize what had happened; when he
saw in his inbox that someone had anonymously forwarded him a
link to his own blog, his first thought was that someone had blown
his cover as its author. Then he remembered that he himself had
taken care of that. He sat in his desk chair, drinking a cup of mi-
crowaved coffee from that morning, and thought. Then he went
online and checked the posting there. A hundred and twenty-two
hits. He hit Refresh and the number went to 124.

The comments section, which had never before hit double digits,
was now at twenty-eight, but a lot of those, he was disappointed to
see, were negative—taking him to task either for thinking that anyone in town would care what he had to say or for spamming up their
inbox without permission. They all assumed he'd forwarded the link
himself, even though it made no sense that he'd do so anonymously
just to distribute a post where he dropped his anonymity. "Where did
you get my private email address?" was a common theme. It was
depressing and hurtful. Some of the people telling him to shut up
and mind his own fucking business used their real names too.

Then emails began dropping into his inbox, and one of the first was from his brother Mark. *Can I ask you*, Mark wrote, *what the fuck you think you're doing?*

He drove over to Mark's house after dinner. Haley was still up, and for whatever reason Mark didn't want Karen to overhear them, so they took a couple of beers and walked down the porch steps out onto the lawn, even though the temperature had dropped into the forties. Hadi's house, with its security lights, shone through the trees like a prison yard.

"What have you done to us?" Mark said.

"How do you mean?"

"How do I mean? Well, first off, just from the point of view of self-interest, is it a great idea for our business to come out and make an enemy of the guy who runs the town? Why would you do that? How do you imagine that's going to be good for us?"

"I didn't imagine—"

"And second, and maybe more to the point, who gives a fuck what you think about him anyway? What do you know about the politics of the town, about politics period? What gives you the right to, to . . ."

"What gives me the *right*?"

"You've always been like this," Mark said, almost in a hiss, to avoid being heard inside. "You've always had some idea about yourself, like you're the great rebel, the unappreciated genius. But you're not. You're a fuckup. A fuckup with a persecution complex. You think you know so much more than you know. And now you're going to fuck this up too."

There was a tremor in his voice as he said all this, almost as if he might be about to cry, and Gerry could feel more than anything else how afraid his brother was, how panicked.

"I'm glad it's all coming out," Gerry said softly. "That's all I wanted, really. An end to happy talk. Everything out in the open."

"You haven't even lived in Howland all that long. You moved here after I did. What makes you the, the guardian of it? Your problem is that you can't trust anybody, you can't believe in anything. You can't believe that this guy might actually just be the guy he says he is, because if there really are guys like that in the world and you aren't one of them, then what does that make you?"

It was too dark now to see Mark's face very well. Just the lights burning in the windows of Hadi's house in front of them, and Mark's lights behind them. Gerry had rarely seen his brother like this, though when they were kids he had often wanted to see it, dreamed of it, worked hard to provoke it. But now he didn't feel any great satisfaction. People really showed themselves when you threatened their beliefs.

"I guess now is a good time to bring up something else," Gerry said. "I've grown uncomfortable with this business, with what we do, you and I. I don't think it's honest."

"Oh, you don't? What's—"

"Well, no, that's the wrong word. Not 'honest.' 'Honorable.' It's too dependent on the government, for one thing. Anyway, I want out."

"That's totally fine," Mark said. "You're a liability to me now anyway. The only reason you're part of it in the first place is that I thought I was doing something generous for you, something to help you out when you had nothing. But of course I get zero credit for that. Instead I have to apologize for making you feel dirty. Well, my bad for expecting anything different in this fucking family."

"You don't have to apologize for anything," Gerry said. "You just have to buy out my current share in the business."

"That is totally not a problem," Mark said.

It was actually a little bit of a problem, in terms of cash on hand, but Mark did it anyway; he could hardly go back to Gerry after that conversation and ask for more time. After some painful deliberation he decided he would have to warn Karen that their account balances would be temporarily low; it would lead to an unpleasant conversation, but the conversation that would ensue if she unwittingly bounced a check somewhere in town would certainly have been worse.

"So now it's just you?" she said, not unkindly, but he didn't like her saying it at all.

"It was always just me, really," he said.

"What will we do about money?"

"This alters the timetable a little, in terms of selling off some of our holdings. But it has to be done, so I'll do it. And also, in the short term, we have your salary." He said that because he thought it would make her feel better—more involved, more empowered—but it didn't seem to have that effect, judging by her face and by the fact that she didn't speak to him for the rest of the morning.

The comment thread on Workingman's Dread was now far longer than the final post itself. A number of commenters asked, often quite rudely, where was this recall petition Gerry was on about? Why no link to it? He didn't post again but he inserted his own comment, linking to a simple petition to which people could attach their names. Very few did, even though he'd left the grounds for Hadi's recall purposefully vague. Part of the reason for that was that he sensed there were now actual, legal considerations involved, which he hadn't fully researched. He intended to ask Tom Allerton for some help with that aspect of the effort before composing the petition, but Allerton, for whatever reason, was not returning Gerry's voicemails, even though Gerry was careful enough to call his cell and not his Town Hall office.

Not even a dozen virtual signatures. Upwards of two hundred comments on the post itself. Gerry was disappointed. People really did not like to put their names on the line. Which made him feel foolish and sullen for having done exactly that.

Some of the names he didn't recognize, which might have meant that they were fake. Penny's name was not on there. He was afraid to discuss it with her. He assumed that she knew about it, that she'd been part of the original email blast, since she was a property owner, and a taxpayer.

He felt people's eyes on him when he went into town, felt them talking about him in his wake. So he pretty much stopped going. Even the Ship wasn't that comfortable a place anymore. It was easy to do his rudimentary food or liquor shopping a few miles away, in Stockbridge or Great Barrington, where he was nobody and his name meant nothing. One afternoon he came back from the Price Chopper and someone had written SHUT THE FUCK UP in brightly colored chalk on the cracked asphalt of his driveway. He hosed it off and never said a word about it, to anyone, but it didn't matter, something was in the air.

A week later, Mark was in his living room watching a documentary about K2 when faint, revolving lights, so faint as to be shadows, started washing across the wall behind the TV. He couldn't figure out where they were coming from.

He opened his front door and saw the same lights flickering on the underside of the leaves, above the ryegrass that bordered his lawn. All was silent, except for the wind, as he walked toward the woods. Maybe kids had taken up some kind of residence in there? He'd heard stories—everyone in town had—about groups of local kids who met up in the woods and drank and took drugs and broke into people's houses. As he crossed the tree line and parted the branches Mark heard the sharp electronic crackle of a two-way radio, and then he saw the lights more clearly: there was a police cruiser parked in Hadi's driveway. Rather than turn back, get his car keys, and drive over there, Mark just pushed on through the woods, a route he'd never taken before, following the silent, revolving light.

Constable, who was standing in the driveway, was startled to hear and then see Mark emerge from the woods—startled and a little offended, because how did people know he wouldn't reflexively reach for his sidearm in a situation like that? "Sorry," Mark said, raising his hands, "sorry, I'm his neighbor, I saw the lights, it was just the quickest way." He knew Constable's first name, had used it many times, but was self-conscious about using it now, when there was apparently some official business going on. Neither, though, could he bring himself to address him as "Trooper," or "Officer." It would have sounded almost sarcastic. "What's happened?" he said. "Is everyone all right?"

"They're not here," Constable said. "They're traveling, in Europe or somewhere. I called the First Selectman's cell and they're all fine."

"Then why are you here?"

"Alarm went off."

"Which one?" Mark said, and Constable looked at him. "I mean, I actually installed some of the alarms here. He hired me to. Years ago. Did somebody break in?"

Constable started to walk around to the front of the house and waited for Mark to follow him. They turned the corner and Mark felt the gravel of the driveway underneath his feet. Constable's cruiser, its roof lights flashing, was parked there, but it wasn't until Constable reached through his driver's-side window and flicked on his headlights that Mark could see someone had vandalized the front door and the wall surrounding it. Across the facade of the house, in black paint, were the words LEAVE US ALONE.

Mark's face flushed the way it always did when he saw someone mistreating something of value. He thought instantly of his brother: not that he had done this, but that he was somehow responsible for it nonetheless.

"There are security cameras," he said to Constable. "They record."

They recorded directly onto Hadi's own hard drive, and they wiped every twenty-four hours. Constable explained this to the First Selectman and asked permission, in light of the situation, to gain entry to his home, and to access his hard drive. Hadi said no. Constable stated the obvious: that this meant whoever had vandalized Hadi's home would not be caught, and Hadi said that was okay, in the end they were just talking about a new coat of paint. Constable hung up the phone in his little cubby of a Town Hall office. He'd come there in the first place because he figured Anne Marie might have a key to Hadi's house. He considered driving to Pittsfield to find a judge who might issue him a warrant. But that was an impulse, he knew, born of pride rather than pursuit of justice. In the end he would lose his job over that, and for what? For the arrest of some kid, who would do community service for it anyway. He let the twenty-four hours elapse, and he wound up acceding to Hadi's other request as well, which was that Constable leave the incident off of the official weekly police blotter.

It had all worked out better than Allerton could have hoped. The proposed tobacco ban was public, which meant that he could cast the vote to kill it and look like a hero. They had their monthly BOS meeting in the Town Hall conference room—the three of them and Hadi's secretary, Anne Marie. Even after the meeting was called to order, she sat patiently with her pen raised half an inch above her steno pad as they talked about nothing—mostly about where Waltz wanted to order food. Tom tried not to let his impatience show. He was determined not to bring up the ban before Hadi did. After a half hour or so in which they mostly discussed repainting the bandstand, his patience was rewarded.

"If there's no new business," Hadi said, "there's one other important piece of news we need to discuss."

"The no-tobacco thing," Waltz said. "You know, I know you'd like a unanimous yes on that, but frankly anyone who knows me in this town would know that there's no way I'd go for it. I'd be voting for having to drive to Great Barrington every time I want a pack of cigarettes. Plus putting Hank's newsstand on Main out of business, basically."

"Or you could just quit smoking," Hadi said, "but in any case, that's all moot, because I'm not bringing that one to a vote."

"You're not?" Tom said.

"No. As I said, a piece of news. I've already given to Anne Marie, and I'll give to you two now, a letter to be read into the minutes of this meeting."

He slid two copies down the polished table, and Allerton read it, his face flushing. It was a letter of resignation. Afraid of making the wrong move, somehow, Allerton kept his head down, face still, and read the letter again.

"What the hell is this?" Waltz said.

Allerton looked up at Anne Marie, still with her pen held just above the paper, waiting for someone to say something that counted. Her face betrayed nothing. Yet she had known before any of them, for days maybe. She knows where the bodies are buried, was the phrase that went through his head, he didn't know why.

She was probably out of a job now herself—no way she'd work for him, that was for damn sure—yet whatever she was feeling, if she was feeling anything at all, was entombed in her. He did not understand people like that. Creepy.

"It's what it says," Hadi said evenly. "I think the time has come, both for me, professionally speaking, and for the town. It's been a grand experiment, and I think for the most part it's worked really well, but now it's time for new challenges."

"Are you staying here?" Allerton said. "I mean, to live?"

"No."

"Where are you going?"

"Back to New York. So my family is happy about that. And I owe them that much, really."

A silence fell on the room, a silence with which Hadi grew quickly and visibly impatient.

"This is effective when?" Waltz said.

"Effective immediately, John. It says right there in the first sentence."

"Oh yeah," Waltz said.

"This isn't how it works," Allerton said sharply. He wasn't at all sure, in the moment, what he was feeling, whether what was happening was good or bad for him, and it was that sense of being outflanked that made him mad. "We have elections. We just had one. It's a commitment. You can't just walk out on it."

"It was an orderly transition when Marty Solomon died," Hadi said, "and it'll be orderly now. I helped this town through a rough patch. You and John are capable of running things just fine without me. I don't imagine you'd disagree with that, Tom?"

"Marty Solomon died," Allerton said. "He didn't just get bored."

"Oh, I haven't lost interest. This area will always have a special place in my heart."

"Is it because you don't feel sufficiently appreciated? We don't kiss your ass or act grateful enough, is that it?"

Anne Marie, he realized, had no intention of taking down a single word. She would write what she would write, and that would be the record.

"You're looking at it backwards, Tom," Hadi said. "Listen, I'm well aware that the sentiment of the town is turning against me a little bit. I think that's inevitable, actually, which is why it's important that people not hang on to power for too long. Now, the election, and the charter of the town, technically empower me not to give a damn about any of that. I'm entitled to continue to govern until the end of my term. But why would I want to do that? I'm not some tyrant. I have no desire to govern without the full consent of the governed."

"How will," Waltz began, and then he seemed to be groping for a word or phrase. "How will we let the people know?"

"Tomorrow I will give it to the *Gazette* and ask them, or ask her I guess, to just run it as is. Reproduce it. No interview or anything like that. I don't want to do anything to make it seem like a bigger deal than it is. Which is, as I've said, in the grand scheme of this town's history not a very big deal."

"So the *Gazette* comes out tomorrow," Allerton said, "so this won't be in there for another week. In the meantime we should just, what?"

"In the meantime I think you should just sit on this news if you can. I know the timing is awkward, but the only way around that would have been to give the letter to the *Gazette* before I gave it to you, and I didn't think that would be right."

He glanced around the table at each of them, including Anne Marie, whose eyes were now on him as well.

"In fact," he said, "I'll bet you a lot of people will be happy about it. I'm happy too. Win-win. Now, if there's no other new business?"

Allerton thought it unrealistic that the news of Hadi's resignation wouldn't get out somehow before it appeared in the newspaper. Gone were the days when anyone learned actual news, even local news, from a weekly paper. He didn't necessarily trust himself to keep a secret like that. But he did keep it, and so did the others. It was less about honoring Hadi's last request than about fear of the news's consequences, and reluctance to bring them on.

For even though he knew it on some not entirely conscious level, he did not fully understand how much of Howland's funding came out of Hadi's own pocket until he sat with the treasurer and the mostly useless Waltz and went through the books.

Hadi had given the town's two school bus drivers a raise, in the form of yearly bonuses. He'd paid all of last year's groundskeeping expenses for the town green, the war memorial, and the Babe Ruth League field. He paid the Animal Control officer's entire salary, despite the fact that the Animal Control officer, as far as Tom could remember, had not been called upon to actually do anything, other than fill out government forms, for a few years. He paid for the flowers in the flower boxes on Main Street every Memorial Day, Fourth of July, and Labor Day. He'd written a personal check to the fireworks company. He'd paid for septic repairs at the high school, a problem Allerton had never even heard about.

As for whatever small personal checks he might have written to tide over local businesses, charities, and even individual homeowners, that was not considered official town business and so there was no record of it anywhere.

He'd done all this, of course, while actually lowering the town's tax rate to levels not seen since before any of them had lived there. Which meant—as Allerton kept trying to impress upon his new co-chief officer of the government—they were going to have to raise those property tax levels again, soon, sharply, and a reassessment of every commercial and residential property in the town limits would have to follow.

"No effing way," Waltz said. "They'll kill us."

"Okay, well, the money has to come from somewhere. What do you suggest we do?"

"Pull a Hadi?" he said, and laughed.

Mark was so angry he didn't even feel he could call his brother on the phone. Instead he sent him an email: *Nice work, jackass,* it said. *Happy now?*

Just pay me what you owe me, Gerry wrote back. *If everybody in this town would just pay each other what they owed, instead of looking for excuses not to, then things would straighten themselves out pretty quick.*

Two weeks after the letter was published, in facsimile form as Hadi had wanted, on the front page of the *Gazette,* the monthly town meeting was scheduled to take place. Allerton sat in his chair in his office and watched the parking lot fill. He tried to think of some pretext for canceling, even now as he could hear the footsteps in the hallways, but that would only have led to more adversarial feeling. These meetings, pointless though they usually were, were a tradition. Anyway, even if he waited until the last citizen had arrived, snuck out to the lot, and drove home, that would only have left Waltz in charge, and God knew what might emerge from a meeting like that.

He entered the auditorium and took his seat at the folding table just in front of the old stage. There weren't enough chairs to seat everyone. The cookies were already gone. Belatedly it occurred to him that there was no longer anyone to take the minutes. Anne Marie had decamped along with her boss. There would be no official record of whatever was discussed.

"Before we open the floor to new motions," Allerton said into the microphone, "as is traditional at these gatherings, let me briefly go over a few basic facts." They were already looking at him angrily. "The former First Selectman was, as per his campaign promise, funding some of the town's essential operations personally. More, probably, than you, or we for that matter, were aware."

"So he's going to stop doing that?" somebody shouted. "Do we know that for sure?"

Allerton closed his eyes, trying to stay patient. "Yes, obviously, he is going to stop doing that. He's left office, he's left town, he will find something else to get interested in, presumably. But Howland ran just fine for a long time before he got here, and it will run just fine after. He was a blip. He did some damage that we will have to undo"—there was a scary, throaty noise of discord in the crowd—"but fundamentally, big-picture-wise, nothing has really changed."

He paused. Hands were raised, but in the interest of procedure, he ignored them.

"In concert with the treasurer and the tax collector, we have made some calculations that might help you to see the nature of the challenge in front of us," he went on. "Were we to continue to fund all of the town's current government operations—"

"He's not asking for any of the money back, is he?" someone said.

"No. He never said any such thing. And I think he would have, if that was his intent. Anyway, if we continued spending at its current levels, and revenue also at its current levels, in one year's time we would have run up a deficit of approximately four hundred and eighty-five thousand dollars."

Consternation in the hall.

"You mean we're in debt four hundred and eighty-five thousand dollars?"

"No, that's not what I said."

"What are you saying?"

"I'm saying that if we want to continue providing certain services, then the money for those services, which previously came from a private source, is going to have to come from somewhere else."

"Like from where?"

"From all of us, together. The way it's always been."

"You can't say the actual word, can you?"

"From me, just as from you. I live in this town too."

"Yeah, but we pay your salary! Hadi didn't even *have* a salary!"

"You'll be paying me the same salary you have all along. Unlike my predecessor, I am not able to work for free. I have a family."

"Oh, excuse me, you have a *family*!"

"Really we're only talking about restoring things to their previous level. We're not actually raising anything."

"Things! Just say the word. You can't even say it."

"There will be some pain, but we'll all share the burden equally."

"Oh my God, Tom, you should be working in Washington. You're a natural. I've never heard such silver-tongued bullshit in my entire life. How can you raise taxes on us? We didn't even elect you!"

"Now, yes you did! You think I want to be in this position right now? I had no choice."

He glanced over in hatred at the town clerk, who sat with his eyes wide. "Jesus," Allerton whispered, not quite softly enough, "are you just going to sit there? Isn't there some kind of procedural something you can invoke? Let's move on!"

The clerk looked at his gavel for a moment as if afraid of it, as if it had been left there menacingly for him like a fish in a newspaper, then he picked it up and hammered away with it until the room was mostly silent. "Open the floor for new motions," he called hoarsely.

In anticipation of this there was already a man standing patiently at the microphone, his hands clasped in front of him, and Allerton saw that it was Gerry Firth. Good, he thought, let that asshole bear the brunt of this for a while; directly or indirectly, he deserved it. Allerton pointed a finger at him to permit him to speak.

"Everybody's pretty upset," Gerry said. Allerton scanned the other faces in the crowd; his understanding, well before tonight, was that people didn't like Gerry particularly, nor his brother. "But I think we should look at this instead as an opportunity. The Hadi regime was kind of a fool's paradise all along, right? I mean it was fun while it lasted, but if we really assumed it was going to last forever, that's on us.

"But it did one constructive thing, even if by accident. It broke this town's government. I think we can all agree that the government of Howland, of Massachusetts, of the United States, has grown much, much too powerful and arrogant, has grown out of control? I see you nodding. I see most people nodding. Okay, so, here is a golden opportunity, in our own backyard, to start over. The town's tax structure is gone. So let's think hard for a minute before we just vote to put it back the way it was. Did we really like the way it was? The system of services—things like a youth center, shuttle bus service, flowers on Main Street—a lot of which was pretty much invented just in order to justify the taxes being there in the first place: that's gone too. There was a kind of image, a projection, of these things for the last five years, but now the projector has been turned off and we see what's really there, which is rubble, basically. And I say good. We have become too dependent on power. Now there's nobody left to depend on. If we fail, we fail, but if we succeed, we do it the only way it's worth doing."

No one else had risen to wait a turn to speak, so Allerton didn't see how he could justify telling Gerry his time was up. While he was thinking this, their eyes met.

"Tom Allerton is a good man," Gerry said, "and I think he appreciates that it's a series of accidents that put him where he is today, and I think he wants to be responsive, to carry out our will rather than try to ignore or overrule it. So let's ask for his pledge today, and that of Mr. Waltz too: No new taxes without a direct referendum to approve those taxes. No new spending without the money on hand. No debt. We will take care of ourselves by not asking anyone else to take care of us. First comes the money, and only then comes the decision about how to spend it. Just the way each of us does it in our own lives. We will get along just fine. We will put our own house in order. We will shovel our own damn snow and drive our own kids to school. It is time for self-reliance. And if we succeed here, we'll send a message to the rest of the Berkshires and beyond."

Gerry sat down. There was not a sound in the hall. He turned and looked behind him, hoping Penny was there—he thought he'd seen her car in the lot—and while he couldn't find her face in the crowd, he could feel she was present.

The idea of a referendum on new taxes was a hoot, Allerton thought. As if any such vote would ever be decided in the affirmative. It was intimidating, though—the idea of a genuine popular will. The negative energy it could unleash. He and Waltz would have the full force of the law behind them if they raised everyone's property taxes overnight, in order to pay for the services everyone expected to receive. But that didn't mean he was going to risk it.

And the risk didn't involve anything as mundane as reelection, either. Reelection was about the last thing on his wish list right now.

The mood in the town was dark; everyone felt under attack. The response was not to come together but rather to protect everything one had against the depredations, real or imagined, of others. People became fiercely, philosophically self-centered. Whatever your problem might be, its origin was within you, and for that reason, Allerton came to understand, your problem was not my problem.

Any sort of collective action was automatically suspect, suspect by definition. It couldn't work. Because if it worked, then we wouldn't be in the mess we were now in, would we? The idea of unselfishness was discredited and shameful.

So the people wanted austerity, and they were going to get it and see how they liked it. Still, there remained a distinction, at least in Allerton's mind, between austerity and anarchy. There were other ways to generate revenue besides raising taxes. The problem with taxes generally was that they were too fair, too evenhanded and democratic: to justify taking money from your constituents, you needed to single people out, you needed to introduce a moral element, an element of punishment. So Allerton went through every permit law on the books—for sidewalk displays, for signage, for use of the bandstand, for yard sales—and doubled the fees. He pulled the zoning-permits list and did the same. Waltz was useless; he would agree passively to anything rather than have to develop an argument to the contrary. There were low-level criminal affairs for which the punishment was a fine; Allerton raised those too, and then he asked Trooper Constable to take a walk with him.

They walked down Main Street to Melville; it was an unseasonably hot June day, and many people flowed around them. On foot, they were faster than the Main Street traffic. Two storefronts on Main—Diabolique and Creative Kidz—had FOR RENT OR LEASE signs in the windows, larger signs than Allerton thought was strictly necessary.

"That's not a good look," he said. "For the town, I mean."

"No, sir," Constable said.

"Right on Route 7 too. Like an advertisement. Listen, I wanted to talk to you about something. A kind of new initiative. There are pretty strict parking regulations in Howland, did you know that?"

"I guess I did."

"Laws of the land. Literally."

Constable nodded.

"But you don't enforce them. I mean, I'm not putting it all on you, I'm saying that, traditionally, they're not that strictly enforced."

"The way it's traditionally worked," Constable said, "is that I'll only come ticket in response to a complaint from a merchant—like if the same car's been parked in front of his window for two days, that sort of thing."

"Yes, right. Well, that's about to change. The fines for parking offenses of all sorts have just gone up. And I'm instructing you to enforce them vigorously. In fact, I am giving you a target in terms of the number of violations you should cite. A monthly target."

"A quota, then," Constable said.

"Not a quota per se. Let's call it a target. Things like your performance review will take those targets into account."

"Why not just install parking meters?" Constable said, reddening.

"With what money?" Allerton said. "Whereas you, we're already paying. Also, everybody has to feed a meter, but only lawbreakers have to pay a fine. It's more just this way."

"I do have other duties," Constable said, trying to keep his tone respectful. "More important duties."

"It's not like I'm asking you to do anything corrupt. In fact I resent the suggestion. I'm asking you to enforce existing laws, which is, I think it's fair to say, your fucking job. If you consider certain duties to be beneath you, or certain laws to be laws you won't enforce because you disagree with them, I'm sure I could find someone a little less activist. But I would have to replace you with that person, since the time is not really right for a town payroll increase at the moment."

They'll hate me, is what Constable was thinking—sullenly, for he knew that he should not care about such a thing from a professional standpoint, yet he did—and over the summer and fall that came to pass. People he'd known for years, casually at least, swore openly at him when they saw him patrolling the street on foot. He knew it was important not to shrug or apologize. He told them tersely that if they didn't like it, they should take more care to park legally. Amazingly, they wouldn't do it. They refused to change their behavior. If anything the financial quota the selectman had set for him was too low, yet Constable always stopped ticketing once he had reached it, an act of passive solidarity with no audience.

Christmas shaped up as less than pleasant because Mark and Gerry weren't really speaking to each other. Neither of them discussed the matter with Candace because they knew they could expect no sympathy there. She heard what little she heard mostly from Haley. As for Karen, she was all but paralyzed by bafflement over why she should have to cook some elaborate holiday dinner for a group of people who now seemed to enjoy each other's company even less than she enjoyed any of theirs.

"It's tradition," Mark said tersely.

"Jesus. Well, it used to be tradition to go to your parents' old place before they sold it, and before that it was tradition for us to have Christmas with my family."

"I know you're not suggesting we go all the way up there," Mark said.

"My point is that a thing's not a tradition just because you declare it a tradition. Sometimes it's just a habit. These things end, for all kinds of reasons. A house is just a house, a table is just a table."

"They should come here. We have the most room by far. And if they resent that, too bad."

"Well," Karen said acidly, "as long as we're all together."

She'd never told her husband what she'd discovered about his sister running some kind of half-assed, off-the-books youth hostel at the Howland Free Library. The days when every single interesting thing she saw or learned was reflexively to be shared with her husband, if those days had ever really existed, were long gone. She didn't mean to keep it from him; she just resisted entering into yet another Firth family drama. And she could not escape feeling that the whole thing, at least as it involved Haley, represented a failure on her part, a failure that would have given Mark, whether he admitted it or not, some petty satisfaction. She thought she could put it right.

That part wasn't going so well. Haley had an animal instinct for every attempt her mother made to Get Closer, or to Talk About Feelings, and eluded her in those moments with a callous finality that left Karen frustrated and afraid. She scoured the internet for danger signs in Haley's behavior but frankly there weren't any. She just seemed to have found affinities of her own. She wasn't outwardly rebellious. Karen knew mothers who had trouble just keeping their kids in the house all night; Haley wasn't like that, but Karen almost wished she were, because locking a bedroom door from the outside or standing beneath an upstairs window seemed relatively straightforward next to figuring out how to compel your child to stop contradicting you. No matter what you said to her, she was determined to imagine some opposing point of view and then defend it as if it were her own. Creative Kidz went out of business, Karen would say, remember how much you used to love that place? and Haley would answer, falsely, that in fact she'd always hated that place, with its expensive designer "IQ games" that were basically practice for the SATs, although she did feel sorry for the low-paid cashiers and stockboys who were now jobless, not that anybody ever gave much thought to them. Karen hadn't even mentioned them, she was talking about something else entirely! She couldn't say anything these days without being taken to task for something she hadn't said instead.

Candace was late, so late that they went through the gift exchange without her. As had become the tradition, the only presents were for Haley, so it didn't take long. Karen, standing at the stove, was just about to say fuck it and serve dinner when her sister-in-law finally arrived at the front door with her parents.

"Happy Boxing Day!" Mark said.

"Very funny," Candace said, and pointed with her thumb at their mother and father, both of whom were still standing expectantly in the foyer with their coats on as if they had never been there before. Karen, even though she had several other things to do, finally went over to help them, since no one else was moving to do it.

"Little trouble getting them out the door," Candace said to her brothers, not all that discreetly.

"No holiday for the ornery," Gerry said.

They sat and ate. There was no grace said, nothing more than a two-word "Merry Christmas" toast from Mark at the head of the table, which still managed to irritate his siblings by virtue of its condescending, patriarchal tone, as if Christmas itself were something that took place under Mark's auspices. Their parents eschewed the toast because both had declined the offer of a glass of wine.

Karen had ordered a ham by mail, bought fully cooked and spiral cut, from a smokehouse in Vermont. Nobody begrudged this, because it was not a family in which anyone had any major culinary skills. There were rolls, and peas, and scalloped potatoes that Karen was relieved had come out reasonably well—she'd had bad luck with that dish before. They ate in a silence punctuated only by occasional wordless sounds of appreciation. Her father-in-law mostly just pushed the food around his plate.

"Sure you won't have some wine, at least, Dad?" she said.

Mark looked at her quizzically. It was rare for Karen to call him Dad, so rare he took there to be more sarcasm than affection in it. The old man said, "What the hell," and poured some of the Chardonnay into his glass. He put the bottle down between his plate and his wife's. She gazed at it while the others went on eating. She reached out for it once tentatively, pulled her hand back. Then she reached out again and took it by the neck and poured it over the ham and potatoes on her plate.

"Mom!" Candace said, pushing her chair back and starting around the table.

"Oh," her mother said.

"I think you may be on to something there, Mom," Gerry said, smiling.

"Here, let me have that. Haley, take Grandma's plate to the kitchen and bring her a clean one, please," Candace said.

Haley heard her but her eyes were on her grandfather's face. He looked furious. At whom? she wondered. He looked as if one touch, one remark, would cause him to explode.

Karen said, "I'll do it," and cleared her mother-in-law's place entirely, happy for the excuse to be out of the room. The old lady sat expressionless, her hands in her lap. Candace went back around the table to her own chair, across from her mother's, and sat, breathing heavily.

Mark, after a long moment so awkward it would have seemed to him impolite not to break it, started cutting off another bite of his ham.

"So no one is going to say anything," Candace said.

"For the love of God," her father said, "will you shut up."

"Dad!" Mark said.

"You amaze me," Candace said. "The two of you." Haley understood from her aunt's gaze that she was referring not to her grandparents but to her uncle and her father. "Right in front of your eyes. But you'll do anything to not see it."

"See it and do what about it?" Gerry said. "Do what about it?"

"Because if I'm the only one who sees it," Candace said, "then it's only my problem."

"It sure as hell isn't your problem," her father said.

"Old people make mistakes," Mark said. "You always get so hysterical. You act like they're the first people in the history of the world who ever got old."

"Shut up now, all of you," their father said.

Gerry rose out of his chair to reach across the table, grab the wine bottle from in front of his mother, and pour himself another glass.

"Every day now, it's something like this," Candace said. "Like this or worse."

"You're humiliating her," Mark said.

"You're their sons," she said. "You have to do something."

"When is Renee coming?" their mother asked.

"God *damn* it!" their father said. Neither the tone nor the volume of his voice caused his wife to react in any way.

"No, Mom," Candace said. "I told you this in the car. Renee is not coming. Renee lives too far away."

She looked briefly at Haley, almost as if she were sorry Haley was there.

"I'm not going to let you stick me with this, you sexist assholes," she said, looking down into her lap. "They're your mother and father. You owe them. You can't just blow that off. It's not right."

"Let's get one thing straight," Haley's grandfather said. "No one at this table owes me a god damn thing."

After the school bus driver stopped showing up for work because he hadn't been paid, Waltz scared up an old, retired buddy who said he was willing to do it as a civic duty, for free; that solution only took them up until Christmas, though, because he spent his winters in Fort Lauderdale. Merchants were still complaining to the board, months later, about Railroad Days, because their extra revenue had barely exceeded the various new permit fees for parking, signage, sidewalk sales, etc. It had led to hard feelings, no matter how delightful the old-timey atmosphere.

Even so, Allerton had calculated that the spike in revenue from fees and fines, while ingenious in its way (the zoning commissioner wasn't even speaking to him anymore), would not get them through the winter. The Town of Howland had its own lawyer, as had been the case since at least the 1970s—a nice old guy in Springfield, at a fancy, white-shoe firm there—and Allerton planned to let him go in order to save the annual $16K retainer, but before doing so he put the lawyer onto a particular problem that had been on his mind for a while, which was how to dissolve or otherwise break the town's land trust.

"There has to be a way," Allerton said. "I mean come on." It was the largest single parcel of land, by far, within the town limits, and the revenue from selling it, on top of the increase in taxes from whatever was built on it, would get them out of the hole in one motion.

The lawyer called back a week later and said there was no way. The trust had been drawn up by some of the most prominent men in Boston, which meant in the world, and the language of it banished ambiguity. "It's actually quite impressive," the lawyer said. "I'm glad I got to look at it. I teach a class at UMass's law school in Springfield and I might—"

"Who does it benefit?" Allerton asked.

"Sorry?"

"Who is this trust for? What keeps it going? Who does it, you know, please?"

The lawyer thought about it. "The public," he said. "The town. That was the idea."

"So the people whom it gratified to create this trust are all long dead. Yet the trust itself just keeps hurtling forward forever, like a piece of space junk or something."

"In a manner of speaking," the lawyer said stiffly.

"Lawyers," Allerton said, and hung up the phone. A few days later he called back and fired him, making no particular effort to correct the impression that it was due to his failure on the land-trust issue. Next on his list—a mental list; he was careful these days not to write anything down if he could avoid it—was the library. That was a touchy one, though the more he thought about it, the less he understood why it should be: people just assumed a small town should have a library, it was a mark of civilization, and Howland had had a free library in some form since before the Civil War. But Tom had no room in his calculations for symbolism. The library itself was a building Howland owned outright. The operating budget seemed modest until you remembered that hardly anyone used the place at all, except for mothers looking for free daycare and a few old Yankees too cheap to pay for their own newspaper. And the librarian was salaried—the fifth-highest salary on the town payroll. Hadi had hired someone with no library science degree (whatever the hell that was anyway), no relevant previous experience, no qualifications whatsoever, and just installed her in the job because it pleased him, which was his rationale for everything. Her name was Firth but there was no way that could be the same family, except maybe distantly. There were Firths all over western Mass.

Having never once set foot in there, Allerton stopped by the library twice in two weeks, and Candace was smart enough to guess why. She couldn't lose another job. She couldn't start over; she didn't have enough faith in the future to start over. With Haley watching from across the main reading room, Candace phoned Gerry the moment the selectman left for the second time.

"You have to talk to your boy," she said. "He's fixing to shut down the library. Probably turn it into a Rite Aid. And throw me out on the street, coincidentally."

"He's not my boy," Gerry said. "We don't even talk. I haven't talked to him in months."

"Well, maybe you should reach out. Is this really what you want? Why don't we all just start building moats and spike pits around our houses and be done with it?"

"First of all, the fact that no one uses the library speaks for itself. I kind of admire what he's doing, if he's actually doing what you say. This isn't *Little House on the Prairie*. There are other places to get books, if you're somebody who still reads books. It's an outdated idea. Just because government always *has* spent money on a particular thing is no argument for its continuing to do so."

"Right," Candace said, "great. Terrific. And what's second of all?"

"Second of all," Gerry said, "is who's 'we'? Technically you don't live here."

Haley overheard so much of that call that there seemed to Candace little point in not filling her in on the rest of it. So she did. Haley was distraught, not that she herself might lose access to the library but out of concern for her aunt, who would have her job, which seemed very much like her home, taken away. Haley, still in her first year of high school, had only a hazy idea what happened to people with no job, which made her fear more atavistic. It upset her enough that she brought it up at the dinner table, even though she knew that the mere invocation of Aunt Candace's name could put her parents in a confrontational mood.

"They're going to just close the library and sell it," Haley said. "I mean, what kind of a place are we living in? How screwed up is that?"

"Language," Mark said.

"Who's 'they'?" Karen said.

"What do you mean? They! Them! The government!"

"We're doing it, is my point," Karen said. "The government, *c'est nous,* or whatever. This is all our own doing."

"Well, then stop doing it!"

"I keep going back, in my head," Mark said, wiping his mouth, "to the fact that everything was going great around here until a small group of agitators, my idiot brother among them, decided that everything has to be a conflict, that there's no such thing as a rich guy who's not evil."

"Oh please," Karen said.

"Oh please what?"

"Can we stay on the subject here?" Haley said, a little catch in her voice that she'd been trying to avoid. "This is important to me!"

Karen's jaw set; she could feel herself hardening, inside and out, against this particular display. "Well," she said at length, "this town is going down the tubes, that's true, but I'm sorry, the Howland library is not going to be my line in the sand. Believe me, if everybody in town knew what I know about the shenanigans going on there, the town budget might not be its biggest problem."

"What?" Haley said.

"What?" Mark said.

"Believe me," Karen said.

After dinner, when Haley had cleared the table and withdrawn to her room, Mark said to Karen, "I wish you wouldn't do that."

"Do what?"

Mark started dropping things into the blender, to make one of his infuriating smoothies. He hadn't eaten much dinner. You could make a dinner that Haley would eat or you could make a dinner that Mark would eat, but, increasingly, not both. "Talk about how the town is going down the tubes," Mark said.

"What? Why not? It is."

"Well, regardless of what you think, it's just not a real positive force for people to hear you talking in that kind of negative way, or even for you to be thinking like that."

"For people to hear me? What are you talking about? I'm in my own home!"

"Regardless," Mark said.

He hit the button on the blender and, in the time it took for him to turn it off again, in the high-pitched, grating roar, Karen believed she figured out what was really going on.

"How's your business doing?" she said.

He looked at her over the top of whatever he was drinking. He made such a fetish out of his own health, for all the good that vanity would do him in the end. "Fine," he said. "Very well."

"All the bad news I keep reading about, that hasn't had any negative effect on you?"

"I don't know what you mean specifically by bad news."

"The crash or the bubble or whatever you want to call it?"

He looked off to one side, rather theatrically, she thought. "It's a fact," he said, "that optimism in a given market has a positive effect on that market. That's not something I made up, stupid though you may think it is. But anyway, my business is doing very well, all that stuff about Wall Street guys trading mortgages to each other doesn't really affect it, so you don't need to concern yourself with that."

She shook her head, as if to clear it. "So optimism affects value," she said. "So pessimism too."

"Correct."

"And that's pretty much all you hear lately, everywhere, when it comes to real estate: pessimism. And that's your business. Real estate."

"More or less, yeah."

"So the value of what you own has gone down. Yet somehow we're doing just fine."

Mark bit his lip. "You want things to go badly?" he said. "You want me to fail? Is that it?"

"I want you to not fucking spin me," she said.

"I wasn't aware," he said, "that asking you to have some faith in me constitutes spinning you."

They heard a noise from upstairs, just a chair moving, but they both stared up at the ceiling.

"I can't help it," Karen said more softly. "I'm sorry. I can't. I'm just trying to brace for the crash this time. It'll be less hard on me if I'm braced for it. That's how I'm thinking."

"You have to cut yourself off from the past," Mark said. "You can't let it frighten you. If you do, you're dead. That's the whole secret."

He said it so passionately, she wanted to believe it, but by the morning she was back to worrying that she was married to a crazy person unaware of his own limitations who would gamble their house right out from under them. She decided, with enough of a touch of perversity to make her feel she wasn't betraying herself, to check out his hypothesis, to take him at his word. She called up Asana, the yoga retreat in Stockbridge, and tried to check herself in for a week. The deposit alone would have been enough to max out one of their credit cards.

But the first available date, for a three-day stay, was in eleven months. Karen felt like crying—not because she wanted so badly to go, but because her idea had been a naïve one, ignorant, assuming the sort of thing an inconsequential outsider like herself would assume. But then the young woman on the other end of the phone, perhaps hearing the distress and embarrassment in Karen's voice, asked if she would be interested in a day pass instead. You wouldn't get the full experience, obviously, not getting to fall asleep in that environment, not waking up in it. But she could take part in all the workshops and meditations, with plenty of time to herself as well, to roam the grounds and meet similarly spiritual people, and commune with herself and others as she chose.

Meet similarly spiritual people, Karen thought: that's the ticket. She didn't hope to commune with them but rather to pass herself off as one of them; that would be funny, she imagined. Just because she was there, they'd believe she was another idle wife from New York or Boston with nothing but time and money to spend, and not just some local, a working mother, a secretary without a rich boss, a wife of an erstwhile contractor who was great with his hands but whose self-image would not stay put. Maybe she would even run into Rachel Hadi there. That would be the best. Unlikely, though. The Hadis were now gone for good, into some realm where they could not be followed.

She said yes to the day pass, and purchased it over the phone. The only disappointing thing about this revised plan was that it would get less of a reaction from Mark. For nights she had rehearsed how she would tell him she was decamping to Asana for a week, and how much that would cost, and how much of that pesky negative energy of hers she hoped to leave behind there; he would struggle to come up with reasons why he couldn't be expected to take care of Haley all by himself because he was so busy, when in fact he wasn't, he seemed to have all the time in the world. But no one would miss her for just one day. He might even be happy for her now, say it sounded like a great idea, which would spoil it for her considerably.

The parking lot was only about half full when she got there. It was freakish weather for January. She wore no coat, just a long sweater with a sash; she had tried to put as little thought as possible that morning into what she would wear, how she would appear. The closer she drew to the place—just as had been happening the closer she drew in time to the day itself—the less the whole excursion felt to her like an act of revenge or an ironic domestic protest. She was going to be asked to meditate, and she was nervous. Meditate on what? She was not the type. Yet the thought of failing at it scared her.

The first scheduled event was yoga; she'd been assured it was a beginner-level class, but it sure didn't look like it. She had only a hazy idea what yoga was: like contortionism without applause. The instructor, skinny with boy-cut hair, was as nice as could be, but Karen hadn't even realized that a change of clothes would be a good idea—it just didn't look that strenuous, not even up close. There was something unavoidably sexual about some of the positions the women got themselves into. They were all women. Other than Asana employees, she didn't see a man that whole day.

She followed the crowd to find lunch—they'd given her instructions at registration, but she'd forgotten: it was just like the first day of school—and she saw nearly everyone go inside the Center and reemerge with a tray. There were picnic tables and Adirondack chairs scattered on the vast lawn overlooking a lake. Inside, the Center was a strange, funkily charming mix of the renovated and the unrenovated, the state-of-the-art and the retro: there was, for instance, still a row of old-fashioned phone booths, the kind with accordion doors, in the lobby just off the kitchen. Karen had left her cell phone at home, as she'd been instructed to do. The booths even had phone books. She peeked to see if they still had rotary dials—maybe they didn't work at all anymore, maybe they were just museum pieces—but they weren't quite as vintage as that.

Lunch was vegetarian—not a shock; she couldn't identify everything, but some of the tray compartments were legitimately tasty. She set the tray down on the grass next to her chair and almost immediately someone came and discreetly carried it away. Karen felt mildly guilty—had she accidentally sent some signal that she didn't even know about, because she was new there? She certainly could have bussed her own tray. She tried to put it out of her mind and stared at the empty lake. It glittered under the sun. There was something calming about it, just as advertised.

She didn't want to lose everything. She didn't want to be broke and in debt again, and even if she couldn't really love her husband anymore, nor did she want to hate him—or not hate him so much as live in fear of him, of his lack of guile, his confidence, his inability to judge himself. She felt threatened, defensive, even in what was supposed to be the sanctuary of her own house.

So was this meditating? All the conditions were right for it, the setting was peaceful, and yet left to their own devices her thoughts naturally flowed in the direction of doubt and fear and self-preservation. That's what was in her. Her spirit had been polluted, or corrupted, or maybe neither, maybe this was just who she was. Terrified of losing a life she couldn't defend and didn't really enjoy all that much anyway.

At two she reported to the pavilion, to learn how to meditate properly. She found the proximity of other people inhibiting. Anyway, who were they? She couldn't keep from turning to stare at them. Rich people who led lives full of manufactured stress. Women who worked harder than they needed to, or women who didn't work at all. Their hyper-refined problems expanded to fill the shape of expensive solutions. Like this place. She was not one of them. She tried, tried, tried to empty her thoughts like the white-haired facilitator said, but her mind was not empty, it was a vacuum: all kinds of random shit naturally rushed to fill it. She really just wanted to be back in her chair in front of that lake again, even though she'd felt bad there too.

"Stick with it," the facilitator said to her as she left, taking Karen's hand in both of hers. "Nobody gets there the first time. Come back often. I hope to see you again."

Come back often! It was all just a sales pitch, in the end, and yet when Karen was back on the lawn—colder now, as the afternoon shadows stretched across it—she felt herself starting to cry. Maybe I'm not such a good person, she thought. Maybe that's the root of it. But you can't change who you are. And anyway, any one of these tranquil bitches would respond to threats the same way I do. When someone comes into your home, basically, and tries to claim what's yours, your instincts take over. All you had, all you were, was worse than useless if there was no one to bequeath it to. Nobody was going to take that away. There was family, and then there was blood.

She went back inside the Center, past the dormant cafeteria, and closed herself into one of the phone booths. In the book she looked up the number for Howland's Town Hall. She asked the secretary there to connect her to Selectman Allerton's office; "don't worry, it's not a complaint," she said. At length Allerton picked up the line and said a cautious hello. "I'm a concerned citizen," Karen said. "I know you've been looking into the library situation. I'm calling with a tip, which is that the next time you go to the library, don't go when it's quote-unquote open. Go when it's supposedly closed. Like early in the morning. I think you'll be surprised by what you'll find going on there. It'll give you cover to do what you want to do." She hung up, breathing rapidly, but then within a minute she was calmer than she'd felt all day. She got home in time to make everybody dinner.

Barrett believed that he was on his way to being a better man. He'd made a lot of mistakes. And he continued to fuck up, not a lot, but never for the last time, either. It was like one of those signs they hung in factories—he'd never worked in a factory, never even seen the inside of one, but he'd seen these signs on TV or in movies or cartoons—that said such-and-such days without an accident. Then some guy wasn't paying attention and got a finger cut off or a toe crushed, and the number on the sign got flipped back to zero. That was Barrett's life.

He found a job with a new guy across the line in Hillsdale, and the guy said the work Barrett did on the slate roofing was as good as he'd ever seen; and so the guy hired him twice more, but then randomly they got into a fight about immigration—right on the site, right in front of the client—and Barrett, when he tried to drop it and just go back to work, found he couldn't, and walked off the job. Stupid. People were entitled to their opinions—that was what his wife kept reminding him, loudly sometimes.

Were people really still entitled to their opinions, though, when those opinions did actual damage? What if somebody had his hand in your pocket, trying to get your wallet, your keys, your ID, every-thing, and some asshole's "opinion" was that everybody's pockets should be bigger and looser and easier to access? You were just making it easier for the takers in this world, the people who had it in for you and wanted what you had. If you wanted to hand your own shit over without a fight, then fine, whatever, except that that emboldened the takers further, after they'd burned through your money, to come for mine. So it wasn't really about politeness or tolerance, otherwise known as political correctness. It was about right and wrong.

Just the presence of that idea in his life—right and wrong—was improving him, sharpening him. But he was prone to slips: it was like a balance beam, he could only stay up for so long, then he'd lose his balance and have to climb back up again. Thus he did a night in the Stockbridge jail for getting into a fight in the parking lot of some bar he'd never even been to before. Things like that. He was learning. He had such a passionate nature; it was not an easy thing to regulate in every situation.

One night—two nights—he'd apparently got so passionate his wife felt she couldn't stay in the house. He never laid a hand on her, but she didn't feel safe. She came back in the morning. He'd asked her contritely where she'd been and she'd said "the library," which was obviously such sarcastic bullshit that if he was ever going to hit her he would have done it right then, but he didn't.

You'd think the people with their hands in your pocket would be the needy, the have-nots, the disadvantaged, but no: it was always the powerful. It was always those with more than you—and their instruments, which they called "law" or "government"—who were bent on walking away with what was yours.

He didn't go to the Ship that often anymore, partly because he didn't want to get buttonholed by Gerry Firth again. He didn't like that guy. The more he felt they had in common, politically speaking, the less Barrett liked him, which was weird but true. Maybe it went all the way back to Barrett's never getting the high sign he'd expected after tagging Hadi's house. It was like Gerry was egging him on, and then afterwards wanted nothing to do with him anymore. Expendable. Well, maybe that was the truth about him. And if it was, then maybe there was something liberating about that.

He drove into town one morning in February because he was out of cigarettes. Stevie, who was catching only occasional replacement shifts at the hospital, was still in bed. The guy who ran the newsstand had been there forever; he seemed kind of nicotine-stained himself. Barrett looked at the headlines in the *Gazette* and the *Globe* while the old Yankee rang him up.

"Glad I can still buy these here," Barrett said, gesturing with the pack.

"How's that?" the Yankee said. Though they'd never technically met, Barrett, like everyone else in town, knew his name was Hank.

"I mean because they were gonna outlaw you," Barrett said. "You heard about that, right?"

Hank's face hardened, as if he were tired of the conversation already. "Still a free country," he said.

"For now." Barrett wanted to pull out a cigarette and light up, but he knew that wasn't allowed, absurd as such a law was in a place that sold cigarettes. "So how long you been at this location? Long as I can remember. I used to come here when I was in high school."

The old guy seemed like a kindred spirit; but now he was looking out his steamed-up window, and faintly grinning. "Maybe instead of gabbing," he said, "you might want to get out there."

Barrett looked through the glass pane in the door and saw what the old man was talking about: that motherfucking trooper, dressed up like he was Nanook of the North in giant boots and a hat with earflaps, was standing in front of Barrett's car with his foot on the fender, writing in his little ticket book. Barrett ran outside, the bell attached to the shop door jangling behind him.

"I'm leaving, okay, I'm leaving right now," he said, opening his driver's-side door.

"Okay," Constable said.

"Okay. So why are you still writing?"

Constable didn't answer; he finished the ticket, tore it out, and stuck it under Barrett's wiper blade.

"What the fuck?" Barrett said. "What's your problem?"

"No problem. You're parked illegally. You have thirty days to pay the fine or contest it. If you do neither, the fine will double."

"But you saw I was leaving!"

"Not relevant," Constable said, "and anyway, you haven't left yet, have you?"

His boots crunched as he walked over the frozen crust left by the snowplow, onto the sidewalk to continue his rounds. He looked ridiculous, his job was ridiculous, his power was ridiculous. Barrett was a citizen, a taxpayer. He was Constable's boss. How many times had he been fired for mouthing off to his boss the way Constable had just done? He turned on his wipers, to try to send the ticket flying into the snow, but it curled around the blade and stuck there. Finally he switched them off again, lowered his window, and pulled the piece of paper inside. A hundred and ten fucking dollars.

Barrett would never pay it, that was obvious, but he couldn't put the incident behind him either. That smug little Nazi. He thought he was some kind of authority—he thought he was the law—but he was just a henchman, and what kind of "law" involved stationary cars anyway? It was so arbitrary, so petty, and it brought out pettiness in him as well, for instance the hour he spent on the internet trying to find Constable's home address so he could go park his car right outside it. Or on his lawn. He tried to get Stevie interested in the subject, but she just said, "News flash, cops are assholes," and that was it. Nobody wanted to do anything about anything.

Then he had an idea. Two could play at the surveillance game. He had a little handheld video camera, a pretty good one, that he'd bought secondhand a few years ago because he had an idea about a particular kind of sex tape, but then the idea wasn't something Stevie was down with at all. The thing had a USB port, so he could figure out how to download a video onto his computer; how to take the next step and make a website to play that video was something somebody he knew was bound to be able to help him with.

He drove into town and nursed a cup of coffee at the Undermountain until he saw Constable passing by on the sidewalk. He paid, left, caught up with him, and turned the camera on, from a distance of about twenty feet. He didn't make any attempt to hide what he was doing, but Constable still didn't notice him for quite a while—five minutes or more—until he was writing his first ticket.

"What the hell are you doing?" Constable said.

Barrett said nothing, kept shooting.

Constable, red-faced in the cold, placed the ticket under the offending car's wiper blade, maybe a bit more deliberately than usual, and continued his rounds. He came upon a truck parked rather poorly, Barrett had to admit, a good six feet away from the curb. Constable looked at it for a long while, angling his back toward the camera. Finally he took his book out again and began writing.

"What are you ticketing him for?" Barrett called.

Constable ignored him.

"What law is he breaking, Officer?"

Constable signed the ticket and pinned it to the truck's windshield.

"You made Howland safe from that guy!" Barrett said. "Thank you, Officer!"

This was going to be great, Barrett thought. He hadn't considered adding his own commentary to the footage, but once the idea came to him he understood how much this would improve the whole project. You could see from the cop's face that Barrett was already getting to him. Constable walked all the way to the foot of Main Street and waited for the light before crossing over and working his way back up the other side. Even from behind, even with the parka on, you could see he was like a coiled spring. Barrett followed him, trying to think of witty things to say. He would come to town and do this every day. He would make this little penny-ante storm trooper's life miserable. Constable stopped and began writing a ticket for a car that looked legally parked. It sat beneath a sign that read NO PARKING TU-TH 10 AM–6 PM. Barrett looked at his watch. "Hey," he said to Constable. "Hey, what are you doing?"

Constable did not pause or look up.

"It's 9:58," Barrett said.

Constable put his foot on the car's fender and rested his ticket book on his knee as he wrote.

"It's not ten yet!" Barrett said. He started to close the gap between himself and the cop. "Here, look, the time's on my viewfinder," he said, extending the camera, ruining the shot.

"It's ten," Constable said.

"It's not!"

"It is because I say it is," Constable said, "and now you are under arrest for interfering with a police officer in the performance—"

"The fuck I am!" Barrett said. He lifted the camera to his eye again.

"Stop what you're doing right now," Constable said. "That is an order."

"What am I doing?" Barrett yelled. "Tell me, what am I supposedly doing?"

"This is your last warning," Constable said. He no longer seemed agitated; you could see him going through a kind of script or checklist in his mind.

"I will show the world what you're up to," Barrett said. "I will

351

show everyone who you are. You can't operate in secret anymore. You're not above the law. You are a public servant—"

Constable reached out for Barrett's wrist, as he'd been trained to do in order to turn him around and subdue him, but with the heavy coat on he was a little too slow, and Barrett skipped backwards, into the road. A car honked and swerved around him. The camera itself now lay in the street.

There were a few spectators on the sidewalk, outside the shuttered Creative Kidz. Barrett's eyes slowly filled with intent. He had his audience, and they had seen it all. *"Sic semper tyrannis!"* he screamed, thinking maybe the camera was still operating, and with his hands in the air like he was flying he leaped onto Constable just as the trooper was unholstering his sidearm.

5

No one was sorry to see that year end, and then before they knew it another year had ended as well. Howland settled into a kind of dormancy. People grew accustomed to austerity, on every level; they internalized it. Without really collaborating on it, together they reached a cold equilibrium, and for a long while, little changed, except within some families, but that news was kept where it belonged, where no one else might mistake it for their business.

In a spasm of guilt, Haley's father had given her outright the ancient Escort, telling himself that he only would have gotten a couple hundred for it anyway, and that Haley deserved a sixteenth-birthday present of some magnitude. She'd had a rough year. The serious look on her face, on the mornings she was with him, when she got behind the wheel to drive to school, was of way more value in his own life right now, he figured, than a few hundred bucks would have been, or even a thousand.

She pulled into the lot in front of Howland Regional High—the same lot where her dad had taught her to drive, in the summer when it was empty, with nothing but a few light stanchions to worry about hitting—and found a parking spot that wasn't too intimidatingly tight. Her mom did not think she should be driving solo at all. One more little battleground for her parents. Thus the

Escort stayed at Dad's, even during the weeks when Haley herself did not. But she didn't miss it when she didn't have it. When she was with her mother, she rode to school in the passenger seat, and that was okay with her too. They were always obsessed with her routine, with not disrupting her routine, but what they didn't get was that you could have two routines and that was just fine.

Life wasn't all that unrecognizable, really, at least after the initial upset. She'd always had separate relationships with her parents. She'd always dealt with them differently. Now that difference was more structured. The more time went by—the more each of them relaxed into being fully themselves, without the other around to inhibit or goad them—the more Haley wondered how two such antagonistic people ever found each other in the first place. She even asked them that, and they didn't seem to have much of an answer, at least not that they wanted to talk about. What she missed most was the old house, specifically her room, which was the only room she'd ever known. But that was still such a sore subject that she tried not to upset either parent by admitting that was the change in her life that felt most like loss.

Much more so than the change in schools. Something about that switch had proved tonic, enlightening even, although not immediately. The absences she felt most achingly that first September away from Mullins were absences she didn't feel at all by October. Her close friendships there turned out to be too flimsy to survive the test of not seeing each other every day. She still kept in touch with some of them via social media, but that was more like good intentions than actual friendship. That seemed right, though, in a way. These were the years of impermanence, the years when everything that defined you was still in flux, even arbitrary to some degree, and it felt correct to be a little detached from all of it, from her classmates, her family, her hometown: a little above it.

Howland Regional helped in that regard. The classes were bigger—too big for anybody to make any real connection with you, least of all the teachers—and the work was so easy you rarely had to engage with it all that fully. She'd made a few new friends, though some of them backed off a bit when Haley made it clear she wasn't going to drive them everywhere. She bounced up the worn steps and made it just in time for her 8:50 class, which was AP U.S. History.

The teacher, whose name was Mr. McMenamin—Mac to his students when he wasn't in earshot, Mr. Mac when he was—did forty-five minutes on the civil rights movement and then, ominously, wrapped up about five minutes before the bell. He was famous for his ability to end his lessons on some kind of pithy zinger just at the moment the bell rang, almost as if he controlled it himself. Haley liked him; he could really talk, he enjoyed talking, and even when you thought you were tuning him out you'd be surprised later by some random fact you'd retained. The rumor was that he was fired from his previous job in Vermont for having sex with a senior, but the rumor was probably just a by-product of the fact that he was considered good-looking, if only because he was the one non-obese male teacher in the school. Over the course of her junior year he'd grown a beard, which in Haley's opinion did not strengthen his case.

"End-of-year stuff," Mr. Mac announced. "I know it seems far off but it's not. This year, in addition to the final—"

Groans of protest from the students.

"Yes, in addition to it," he said, "there will also be a research paper. Twelve to fifteen pages, due the last day of exam period."

"That is *so* unfair," said a girl near the front of the room.

"Hey," Mr. Mac said, "this is AP. You all are the crème de la crème." He smiled teasingly. "Anyway, this is a new requirement, district-wide, so there's no use complaining to me about it. Not to mention that I happen to think it's a great idea. But look, I had a thought that might possibly make it a little more fun for you."

He glanced at the clock, a clock the students couldn't see without turning around in their seats, and perched on the front edge of his desk. "We've been trying to reinhabit America's past all year," he said. "It's not the ancient world or anything, but still, I know that even something as recent as the civil rights movement is pretty abstract to you. I can see it in your written work. I can see it in your eyes sometimes. But you know, there's a hell of a lot of history right here under our feet, in the Berkshires. Howland was a town before America was even a country. So your assignment is to write a research paper about a piece of local history. Doesn't have to be Howland, can be anywhere in southwestern Mass, within reason. There were Revolutionary War battles fought near here, for goodness sakes. Not that you have to go that far back. There's more recent history here too."

"Police-involved shootings," one boy said, smirking.

"Nope. Meaning no, you may not choose that topic, and no, that isn't funny. Massachusetts, people! The cradle of the American experiment! We've talked about it and talked about it. Now take a look at it. Pick a topic and get it approved by me by the fifteenth. That's two weeks, for those of you who aren't in AP math."

The bell rang. Mr. Mac smiled.

She didn't usually discuss her assignments, or anything about school, with her parents, but in this case she thought they might be of some help. Her dad suggested the mills on the Housatonic, some of which were still standing, though not operating, except as stores or galleries. But they'd done a unit on the mills in class, months ago, back when they were talking about the labor movement, and she felt they'd exhausted the subject then. Her dad didn't seem to take it amiss when she rejected his first idea, but then he didn't offer a second one. If there was one major difference in him, post-divorce, post-bankruptcy, it was that his feelings seemed more easily hurt. All winter the radiator in her bedroom at his place kept waking her up at night, but she never mentioned it to him, because any complaint about the place he was renting—especially if it was justified—made him go quiet.

Haley's mother was more helpful, though not right away; first Haley had to listen to the usual complaints about the school. "Your Mr. Mcwhatshisface makes it sound like this is his idea," she said, "but this all comes straight from the school board. Some new thing called the Patriotic Curriculum Initiative or some such bullshit. The board's stacked with wackos now. They lose their minds if you get caught teaching anything about America that doesn't make it sound like paradise on earth. A couple of years ago, the old history teacher had his kids debate the decision to drop the bomb on Hiroshima, and long story short, that's why your Mr. Mac has that job now."

But then she said something useful. "It seems like a no-brainer to me. Do Caldwell House. It's got a ton of history, it's well documented, and obviously you have a rare access to it. Done. Done and dusted, as my mother used to say."

It wasn't a bad idea—in part (though she wouldn't have said so to her mother) because she'd always felt there was something a little shady about that place. Not its current operation, but the story of it. There was a little reek of the sentimental, the official—same difference—that always made her roll her eyes. Her mom, over the years, had bought into it pretty much completely. She'd gotten a title promotion and a raise, and that was their lifeline, no longer a backup or a contingency but the whole thing. She had to believe in the Caldwell narrative, like it was Tinker Bell. If people started questioning it, the whole structure it gave life to might vanish.

The library and its superior internet connection were gone, so in her room at her mom's she Googled Winston Caldwell and started down that rabbit hole. It was so much worse than she'd imagined that for a while all she could do was find it funny. Caldwell started a coke business—coke was the raw material for the manufacture of steel: she remembered that from earlier in the year, mostly because the idiot boys in class kept snickering over it—with two friends from high school. Within a year he had casually screwed both those friends out of their founding stake. He sold the company to a larger company controlled by Andrew Carnegie and used the money to bribe Pennsylvania government officials into granting him contracts to construct and operate various trolley lines, a business about which he knew nothing. He knew how to save money, though, how to cut corners. He was threatened with arrest after a fatal derailment caused by faulty track materials; fortunately, the trolley was empty at the time, so only two track workers were killed.

Katarina Herzfeld was the daughter of a man who owned a company with which Caldwell wanted to merge. She was sickly and had trouble attracting suitors; Caldwell's asking her father for her hand sealed the deal. His new father-in-law's company, which built railway cars, had union problems. Caldwell promised to make them go away, and that he did. He sent spies to live in company barracks. He fired anyone who declined to sign a loyalty oath. He was on record as recommending, to a meeting of his fellow industrialists, a common pledge not to hire laborers of the "darker races," like Italians or certain of the Irish. And when his best efforts were still unable to prevent a strike against the railway car company in 1902, he called in the Pinkertons, who shot and killed four strikers, claiming self-defense. The strike was broken and Caldwell's reputation rose, for decades, with occasional antitrust actions to fight off, but otherwise no bumps in the road.

Even the story of how he first came to Howland turned out to be bullshit. He bought the land itself without even seeing it, on the recommendation of a fellow member of the Century Club in New York City who was pressed for cash. Caldwell was looking for a place his wife would like well enough to stay there for long periods without him, so that he could lead the kind of after-hours life in the city that he felt a man of his stature was entitled to lead. But when he got her up there, she declared the house and property both too small; she coveted the adjoining land, which belonged to a longtime

Howland resident who owned a carriage business. Caldwell invited the First Selectman out to dinner, and gave him a cash gift for the town to spend as the First Selectman saw fit, and requested that he bring to bear what influence he could over the negotiation (though it was no such thing) for the purchase of the carriage maker's land. The carriage maker was unmoved, and declined. Two months later, his stables burned to the ground. Caldwell House was built on their foundation.

Haley didn't have to do any sort of investigative reporting to learn any of this. It was all right there. She never even had to leave her desk. Most of it was on Wikipedia. It was the history of the town, and yet it wasn't, because people didn't want it to be.

She turned in her paper to Mr. Mac; he handed it back with the comment, "Wow! Nice job!" and a grade of A-minus, on account of her not using as much primary-source material as she might have. She didn't tell him that she'd been through the entire Caldwell House "archive," courtesy of her mother; it consisted mostly of Katarina's journals and was sanitized to the point of uselessness. She showed her work to her mother, and that did not go well. Karen didn't say much, but it was clear that she viewed Haley's conclusions as a personal attack, meant to hurt her by denigrating something on which their survival depended, by which her own sense of integration with the town was defined. "I don't know why you have to be so negative," she said. "I know you're a teenager and all that, but still."

Haley's knowing the truth changed nothing. She got a summer job as a busser at the fancy Todd Van Dyke restaurant where the Benihana used to be. Two hundred bucks per person for dinner and it was packed every night. She never recognized anyone in there. She wanted to talk to them, ask who they were and why they had come there, but the bussers had been told unambiguously on day one that they were never to speak to diners unless asked a question.

The training for the job was insane. Literally her only duty was to take away people's dirty plates—which was more than enough to do, considering there were usually sixteen or more courses to each meal—yet it was considered necessary for her and the other back staff to spend a day tramping around a local organic farm, listening to lectures about soil and where vegetables come from. They took themselves so seriously. You'd think their job was feeding the poor, rather than the rich, who could fend for themselves just fine. To make things even more awkward, Haley learned on this field trip that one of her fellow summer employees was Allegra Durning, her former friend from Mullins. She felt some hostility there, that hybrid of hostility and condescension that reminded her of the school itself. Small towns were hard to grow up in, because inevitably you moved on from certain friendships but then the friends themselves remained right where they were, injured and resentful. Haley was already thinking how liberating it would be to move away from Howland, when she was able, to show up somewhere else where nobody was working off of some old version of you.

Something was changing about her—in her. She had less patience. She felt she saw things more clearly than other people, saw other people more clearly than they saw themselves. She tried to keep these insights private, but it wasn't always easy. One night at the restaurant, the maître d' seated in her area a family of five: father, mother, two girls and a boy, the oldest maybe nine or ten. Over the next hour and a half, Haley cleared away course after course that the children hadn't touched. They didn't complain, or even look especially miserable; they endured in silence, while their parents, who seemed quite happy—rapturous, even—talked to each other, mostly about the food. Haley couldn't decide whether to feel solidarity with these strange children, clearly brought there against their will by their hideous parents whom they would probably grow up to resemble, or to feel like slapping them for refusing to eat a turnip or a carrot, because waste and money clearly meant nothing to them. Course thirteen was a small bowl of new potatoes in a chervil sauce; Haley watched the children stare impassively into their bowls for about five minutes and headed over to the table to clear their places again.

"Whoa, one second," the mother said. "Kids, are you done with those?"

Haley was conscious of keeping her mouth from falling open. None of the kids had so much as tasted anything put in front of them for the past hour. They stared balefully at their mother and said nothing.

"All right," she said to Haley, and resumed talking to her husband. But Haley must have stood there a moment too long before beginning to clear, because the mother—whose hair was black, who wore long earrings that looked like diamonds and a sleeveless dress to show off the sloped muscles in her arms—turned back to her: irritated, for just a second, and then self-deprecating. "I know," she said. "It's an awful waste. I'm sure they'd rather just go to the Taco Bell we passed on the way here, but we're going to raise them to appreciate good things, instead of just succumbing to the ocean of crap. Am I right?"

"Are you?" Haley said.

She had the father's attention now too. The mother gave it another try. "They've always been incredibly picky eaters," she said, smiling. "They always want to know where everything comes from."

"I was just wondering that about you," Haley said.

She was fired. Both her parents were pretty angry at her, in their different ways; her dad gave her a lecture about disrespect and about the fad for hating wealthy people, and her mom pointed out how hard it would be to keep college admissions officers from noticing the anomaly of her early dismissal from what was supposed to be a summer job. It was already August, too late to find anything else. Her mom said she was damned if Haley would be rewarded for her bad behavior by getting to lounge around at home all month and watch TV, so she made Haley come to work with her at Caldwell House, to do some filing and copying and answer the phone. The work was off the books, but Karen said she'd pay Haley something if she did a decent job and managed not to mouth off judgmentally to any strangers.

It was the first time Haley had been inside the place since writing her research paper. Strangely, until she'd learned about the greed and venality of the people who built it, who lived and died in it, she'd never really looked at it as an actual home. It was more of a mock-up, a museum with beds in it. Now she saw traces of the Caldwells everywhere, even the poor dead children. The sterility of the house was their sterility. She felt like a trespasser. But in a good way. She retyped some of her mother's boss's correspondence, and she made sure the little glossy pamphlets, with their utterly bogus tragic history of the Caldwells, were stocked in the wooden boxes in the foyer and at the entrance to the gardens.

"You know," Haley said, holding a stack of pamphlets, "the families of the strikers Caldwell's guards killed were evicted from company housing that same day. Children too."

"That was a hundred years ago," Karen said, "and all of those people are dead now one way or the other, and you know what survives? This house. The beauty of it. Which also manages somehow to put a roof over our heads. So why don't we try to focus on that?"

One afternoon Haley answered the phone—"Caldwell Foundation, how can I help you?"—and a woman on the other end asked if the second-floor bedrooms were reopened to visitors yet.

"They're still undergoing renovation," Haley said, which was what her mother had instructed her to say if this question came up. She said goodbye, and then sat and thought for a while. Her mother was out at the groundskeeping shed, talking to Richie, the head gardener. Haley left the desk and went upstairs to the master bedroom. There didn't seem to be any trace of renovation going on.

The bed, huge and ornate, had a plastic-encased mattress on it, with no sheets or pillows. It didn't look particularly attractive, nor comfortable, but still, there was no reason Haley could see why people shouldn't even be allowed to look at it.

What was a house, anyway, and what wasn't? Her aunt had been fired and then pretty well driven out of the Berkshires (not that she would have stayed) not so much for providing shelter as for providing the wrong kind of shelter, unauthorized shelter. The space she thought was hers, she'd been angrily corrected, was not hers, nor its usefulness hers to determine. And now Haley found herself in this space, which scorned usefulness itself. As a child, she had never once imagined her room as someone else's room before it was hers, but of course it was exactly that: it was a space, and over time you and others passed through it. A house passed from occupant to occupant, and its history, or the memory of its history, was wiped clean each time. She could see an argument for taking the Caldwells' house out of that rotation, so to speak, as a way of immortalizing the crime of its construction. But that's not what was happening here at all. The people of Howland preserved it, guarded it, took pride in it, when they should have gotten together and somberly burned it to the ground.

One Friday afternoon toward the end of August, her mom had a doctor's appointment. Friday, according to the custody schedule, was the day Haley switched houses; Karen asked her to ask her father if he would mind picking her up from work. "You don't have to worry about locking up the house," she said, "I'll get Richie to do that." Haley said okay. At three, her mother kissed her goodbye and said she'd see her Monday morning and drove off. Haley sat in the empty office. Then she went out and sat in the empty dining room, watching, from the cool indoor gloom, the mothers and children on the manicured lawn. She recalled the "progressive dinner," something she hadn't thought about in years: the feeling, in the aftermath, of having struck some sort of blow, but secretly, allegorically, and without consequences. She still saw that Walker kid sometimes in the hallways at Regional, but they didn't have any of the same classes. She went back into the office behind the kitchen and dialed her father's number.

"Daddy," she said, "I'm so sorry to spring this on you last minute, but a friend of mine from the restaurant invited me to the Cape with her family for the weekend. Is it okay with you if I go?"

"Well, sure, honey," her dad said, "I guess. What are they, giving you a ride?"

"Yeah. They're picking me up straight from here. From work."

"It's okay with your mom?"

"Well, yeah, plus it's technically your week or whatever now, so."

"You need me to bring you any stuff?"

"No," she said, though only when she said it did it occur to her that she didn't have anything with her but what she wore. "They want to come back early Monday morning, to avoid the traffic, so I'll just have them drop me off straight here, okay?"

"Okay," he said, sounding a little quiet like he sometimes did now in the face of disappointment. She loved him for that. "I'll see you, what, Monday night then I guess?"

"I guess," she said. "Thanks. Love you."

Around four forty-five, Haley turned out all the office lights and walked quietly upstairs to the Caldwells' master bedroom. Almost an hour later, she heard the front door open. Richie's footsteps resounded as he walked through the first floor and switched off the lamps in the front parlor, the dining room, the ballroom, the foyer. He exited again, and Haley heard the chirps of the alarm-system keypad as he locked up the house behind him for the weekend.

There were still hours of daylight left, which meant she wasn't all alone in total darkness but also necessitated staying away from the windows. Not that there was much chance of her being seen— not once the grounds were closed, anyway; the house was set too far back from the road for its windows to be visible through the trees. Still, she was relieved when night fell. When fatigue overcame her, she slipped off her shoes and climbed onto the Caldwells' bed. The mattress was a good one, though she did miss the presence of at least a sheet. She thought she might have seen, once, where the house linens were kept, but it was too dark now, she would have to look in the morning.

She'd gamed out so little of what she was doing that she hadn't even thought about food. She remembered her mother leaving a yogurt in the office fridge, but when she looked for it Saturday morning, it wasn't there. The solution, she decided, wasn't so complicated; she knew the code for disarming the security system (her mother hadn't shown her, exactly, but Haley had watched her do it enough times), so she just punched in the numbers and left the house to walk into town. It was less than a mile each way to the Price Chopper, open but empty at that hour; she bought some snacks, drinks, protein bars, and the like—nothing that needed to be cooked—and in the parking lot she transferred it all from the plastic Price Chopper bag to her backpack. She felt nervous walking back up the driveway to the house, and she realized that was because she'd forgotten to lock the front door behind her. She felt that kind of ownership of the place, like it was hers and she'd left it exposed. As quickly as that. Inside, she locked the door behind her and reset the alarm.

The house was closed to visitors on the weekend but the grounds were kept open. Haley dragged a heavy wooden chair over to the window, then pulled it back a few feet, and sat watching the strangers on the grass at the foot of the great house, vicariously entertained, like an invalid, while she thoughtfully ate a protein bar. She imagined one of the children looking up at the window and trying to convince his impatient mother that he had seen a ghost.

She tested on herself various theories or explanations of what the hell she was doing. A political protest. Mental illness. The cheap thrill of petty crime. Running away from home. Performance art. All these explanations could be made to fit but didn't convince. The truth was that she had no easily articulated idea of the why of what she was doing. She was doing it in the first place in order to figure that out.

All that time alone, in silence, unstimulated, undistracted, would invite a person to think, and she did spend most of the weekend thinking; yet if you'd asked her on Sunday night, as she asked herself, what she'd thought about, she wouldn't have been able to tell you. Monday morning she made sure every trace of her presence was gone—food wrappers gathered, chair dragged back from the window; there wasn't much other than that, really—and waited nervously for her mother. She heard lawnmowers buzzing outside. She realized she couldn't explain being inside the house—her mother didn't know she knew the code—so she deactivated the alarm, went outside, reset it, and sat on the steps. Ten minutes later Karen's car pulled into the lot. She unlocked the front door and looked alertly around the front hall before her eyes landed back on her daughter, who was wearing the same clothes she'd worn to work on Friday. "Jesus, doesn't he even make you brush your hair?" Karen said.

There were guided tours every other Wednesday, but otherwise those who had purchased a grounds pass were free to walk around and explore as they pleased. It agitated Haley to hear, or even to imagine, people—strangers, the public—walking in and out of the house, up and down the stairs, leaning over the CLOSED FOR RENOVATION signs in the bedroom doorways. At four thirty Haley's father pulled into the parking lot and waited for her—he never came into the house—to take her home. It wasn't so bad at her father's. A little depressing, but that was mostly just because she could feel how much it depressed him. And it felt so temporary. They could never make it theirs. She kissed her mother goodbye, went out to the lot, kissed her father hello, and rode home.

She took a long shower before dinner. Her dad struggled hero-ically with cooking for her; tonight it was a version of something her mom used to make, ziti with sausage and broccoli. He ate only the broccoli.

"So how was the Cape?" he said.

"Amazing," Haley said. "I had no idea how rich these people were. The house was huge. Big enough for three families. And they're only there like four or five times a year. The rest of the time it just sits empty."

She felt, out of nowhere, the sting of tears, but she managed to suppress it.

"Isn't that messed up?" she said.

Her dad smiled faintly. "Yeah, well," he said. "There's a lot of houses like that around here too. Family places. Not your home, but a place you can come home to. And you can have more than one place that feels like home to you, as you well know. Houses are a strange business. It's rarely got to do with need, literal need I mean."

"Not a lot of justice to it," Haley said. "That business."

"I don't know if it's a question of justice, really," Mark said.

She went to bed that night exhausted and fell asleep instantly but then woke in the dead of night, as if she had jet lag or some-thing. She'd been sleeping in that bedroom for almost a year—not right after they sold the old house, there was another short-term rental in between. She hardly remembered that place now at all. All the stuff in this current room was her stuff. In the middle of the night she had to pick out various objects in the darkness and reas-sure herself where she was.

She drove herself to work at the mansion the next morning, and left again that afternoon. It occurred to her, at one point—looking up at Caldwell House from the parking lot, waiting for the Escort to start, trying not to flood it as she'd been taught—that she was very likely the first person to have spent a night under that roof in fifty or sixty years, maybe more. That didn't make her feel proud or subversive. It made her feel outraged. Why was this, the grandest, certainly the largest house in town, built by cold-blooded invaders, supposed to just sit there? Why was that supposed to be beautiful? It belonged to each of them if it belonged to anyone at all. But instead they made a fetish of it, and they told themselves that fetish was their history. Which it was, just not in the way they thought.

That night, after she'd said good night to her dad and closed her bedroom door, she stuffed a duffel bag and a backpack with as many clothes and simple toiletries as she could fit. There was no way to wake up earlier than he did, but in the morning she waited in her room until the noise in the pipes behind her wall told her he was in the shower, and she dragged her bags through the house and onto the back seat of the Escort. She was very calm. She looked through his cabinets for any nonperishable food but there wasn't much: nuts, mostly, and vitamins. "Ready already?" he said when he entered the kitchen. His hair looked thin when it was wet. He looked beaten and sad. She noticed these changes in him this morning just as if she hadn't seen him for years.

"See you tonight," he said, and hugged her.

Haley made it through the day, helping with the menial tasks that kept the empty mansion running, and then at four fifteen her mother turned to her and smiled and said, "You want to knock off early today?"

"No," Haley said.

Karen's smile flattened. "I mean, I have to stay and lock up, but you can call it a day if you want."

"I've decided I'm not going."

"What are you talking about?"

"I'm going to stay here in the house for a while."

Her mom misunderstood, of course. "Is something going on between you and your father? You have to tell me what it is. Of course it's okay with me if you stay at my place, but I'll need to talk to him—"

"No," Haley said, "I don't want to go to your place either."

Karen stared at her. "So where do you want to go?" she said slowly.

"Nowhere. I want to stay right here. Plenty of room."

She felt quite calm but her mother's strangely cautious reaction reflected that she must not have appeared that way. "Here in this house?" Karen asked.

"Yes."

"Why?"

"It's hard to explain. I just—"

"For how long?"

"I'm not sure."

"But you mean like overnight?"

"Yes. I have some stuff in the car."

In the cubicle, they were close enough to lean forward and touch each other's knees, but they didn't.

"What the hell are you talking about?" Karen said.

"This place is so fucked up, Mom," Haley said. "It's the nicest house in town and nobody's allowed to live in it. Nobody owns it but you have to pay to get in. The people who built it were monsters, but everybody still kisses their ass even though they're dead. It's so fucked up that I just can't get over how fucked up it is. It seems like a crime for it to just sit here unoccupied. Some other family lives in our old house now. Why is this any different? They don't get to decide that no one else can sleep here after they're dead. They don't get to decide that! Thinking about it just makes me crazy all of a sudden. So I thought I'd sleep here for a while, just to prove a point. Maybe until school starts in a couple of weeks. Maybe longer. What difference would that make to anybody?"

"So it's a political thing," her mother said disdainfully. "Like a protest?"

"Maybe, yeah."

"To get what? To demand what?"

Haley didn't have a ready answer. Her mother seemed unnerved.

"Well, it's obviously out of the question. It's against the law, for one thing. And for another, it'll get me fired. Maybe that's what you want?"

"No."

They stared at each other. Haley could feel the tension building, not in an abstract way either, and she knew a moment before it happened that her mother would reach out and try to grab her by the wrist, as if she were a child.

"Stand up," Karen said. "Stand up! Stop this right now! Get out of this house!"

"You know you can't make me," Haley said reasonably. "Definitely not like that."

Real panic was starting to show in her mother's eyes. She stood up and left the cubicle. Haley heard the echo of her footsteps in the great room, then she heard her on her cell phone.

"It's me," she said. "No, everything is not okay. Did you put your daughter up to this? Do you even have any idea what's going on? She's lost her mind, that's what. You need to get over here. I mean now. Yes, to Caldwell House, god damn it. I don't give a shit if you're on a site. This is an emergency."

She stopped talking but didn't reenter the room where Haley sat; Haley could hear her pacing around the kitchen. Twenty minutes later the front door opened and she heard the familiar low tones of her parents' angry voices.

She walked out to meet them; she didn't like the idea of the three of them crowding into her mother's cubicle. It seemed like that kind of proximity might lead to something physical. Better to be out here, where there was some space. It both was and wasn't odd to see them together again, uncomfortable and faking unity, in the grand entrance hall of a huge house where they didn't seem to belong. "So, Haley, explain to me what this is about?" her father said. "You don't want to come home?"

She faltered—he looked so hurt, where her mother had just looked so furious—but she was trying to ride on instinct alone for the moment. "I just want to sleep here, in the house," she said, "and it seems wrong to me that I can't."

"Why do you want to stay here? It's creepy. There's probably no wi-fi, have you thought about that?"

"There is, actually," Haley said, a little insulted, though in fact she had thought about that.

"Okay, there is." He tried to smile, and then his expression collapsed. "Haley, honey, I'm sorry," he said. "I'm so sorry that your home is gone. It broke my heart to sell the house, because I wanted that to be your home forever, even after we're gone. But I had no choice. That's my failure. Mine, not your mother's or anybody else's. I know you can't like where we're living right now very much. It isn't fair to you."

"It's not about that," Haley said. She wiped her eyes. "It's not about you, about either of you, I swear."

"Then what's it about?"

"It's about this place. Just the—the fact of it. I'm sorry I can't explain it any better than that. Maybe I have to do it to find out why I want to do it."

He looked around the darkening entrance hall and comically rolled his eyes. "I don't see what there is particularly to love about this place."

"I don't love it," Haley said. "If anything I kind of hate it."

Mark laughed a little. There followed a silence in which the triangle the family formed was undisturbed. "That's it?" Karen said, to Mark.

"That's what?"

"That's all you're going to do?"

"Well," Mark said, "do you want me to physically overpower her?"

"Yes! She's your child!"

"Well, I'm not going to do that," Mark said.

Haley felt a thrill run through her as she saw that an old dynamic was coming to her rescue; he would come up with some rationale for not doing what Karen was asking him to do, just because of the way she was asking him to do it.

"There's something she needs to get out of her system," he said, "so let's just let her do that, okay? She's right, it doesn't hurt anybody. And who's she going to get in trouble with? Don't you run this place?"

"Daddy," Haley said. "I have a bag and a backpack in my car. Would you please carry it in for me?" She was pretty sure that if she went to the parking lot herself, her mother would lock her out of the house.

Mark shook his head in wonder and went out to her car. Haley and her mother stared at each other.

"Have you told anybody what you're doing, besides us?" Karen said.

"No. I swear."

"One night. Do not touch anything. I guess you and I could use a night apart at this point anyway. Maybe I can use it to figure out why you hate me so much."

She left, without locking up as she normally would have; a few minutes later Haley's father dropped her bags in the foyer and he left too. Neither of them had touched her; they seemed afraid to. Haley took her clothes upstairs to her room. She planned to put them in Katarina's dresser, but the drawers were swollen shut.

She experimented with the wi-fi, carrying her laptop from room to room, and discovered that while there were a few dead spots upstairs, like the old servants' quarters, the signal was mostly pretty strong. And while there were no working light fixtures any-where except in the little suite of cubicles behind the kitchen, the electrical outlets worked both upstairs and down, presumably for the convenience of the housecleaning staff. So Haley was able to spend most of her time on the second floor. She felt more comfort-able there, less vulnerable maybe, even though it was a long walk down to the office any time she needed to use the bathroom or wanted running water for any other reason.

Was it wrong that she liked so much space, liked having it to herself? If what she was doing was a protest, maybe she should have invited other people to join her. Even like-minded people whom she didn't know. There was something attractive about that scenario, but still she didn't put it out there, via social media or any other way—didn't communicate at all with anyone except her dad, who texted her to ask if she was okay, if she was warm enough, if she needed anything, and then texted her to say good night, just as he would have done if Haley had been in her bedroom at her mom's. That progressive-dinner crowd—they were really just van-dals, which she didn't mean in a bad way, but they were restless and physical and if she invited them in then this whole thing, whatever it was, would surely turn into something different. Strangers would have been even worse. It was enough, she told herself, that some-one was living here now, instead of no one. It wasn't about num-bers. One living person was as much of a defiance as ten or twenty would have been.

Still, she wanted to talk to someone, and so before it got too late she dialed her Aunt Candace. They hadn't spoken in a while; Can-dace hadn't even heard about Haley's getting fired from her restau-rant job. So she had to tell that whole story first. Hearing an adult laugh at it allowed Haley to see it as a little funny for the first time herself. Candace was living across the state line in Copake now, really not that far away at all, but they hadn't seen each other in a long time.

"So what's going on?" Candace said, and Haley explained where she was calling from.

"Huh," Candace said, and then was silent.

"Say something," Haley said. "Do you think I'm crazy?"

"Of course you're crazy," Candace said, but nicely, teasingly. "What are your mom and dad saying?"

"They think it's because of the divorce. They think it's about them."

"Well, sure, they'd think that. So what is it about?"

"Everybody keeps asking me that. I should have a better answer by now. Do you know anything about the actual Caldwells, who built this place? They were literally evil. But, what, because you have money, you get to tell me where I can go even after you die? You know what I'm doing here? Sleeping. That's it. That's my big protest. I'm sleeping. Everybody can just get over it."

"Easy," Candace said.

"Sorry. Was I yelling? I'm sorry." Haley stared out the window at the moonlit garden.

"Honey," her aunt said, "is there anything you want me to do for you?"

Haley smiled. "Wanna come have the worst sleepover ever?"

"Yeah, tempting, but no. They'd probably shoot me on sight if I came back to Howland anyway. But here's what I will do, I'll call your dad. Mellow him out a little. Tell him that you're not crazy."

"Okay," Haley said.

"And please don't let things get out of control, okay? Call me if you think things are getting out of control."

"What do you mean?"

"I don't know," Candace said.

In the morning her mother arrived for work as usual. Haley saw her from behind the bedroom door, but if Karen so much as glanced upstairs, Haley didn't catch it. She changed her clothes and brushed her hair and went downstairs to sit at her station in the cubicle.

"Are you all right?" Karen said evenly.

"I'm fine. What needs doing?"

Her mother stared at her. "We need to order more brochures," she said. "You want to take care of that for me?"

"Sure," Haley said. And the air between them was pretty friendly after that; but gradually Haley realized that this was because her mother took Haley's coming to work as usual as a sort of passive or face-saving apology, which Karen had tacitly accepted. Sure enough, at the end of the day Karen turned to her and said brightly, with a sigh, "Ready to go?"

"No," Haley said. "I'm not ready to go."

Karen's face fell and then slowly its expression hardened. "What are you up to, do you think?" she said.

"I don't know."

"How do you see this ending, exactly?"

"I don't know."

Her mother nodded, looking down into her lap. "Go upstairs and get your things right now," she said. "Enough is enough. That is an order."

"No," Haley said.

"Van Aswegen pops in unannounced once a week or so, you know. Do you want me to lose my job? What do you think will become of us if that happens?"

Haley, though weakened a bit by this, said nothing.

"Well, you know what? Here's the upside to divorce, I guess. Today is Thursday and it's still your week with your father and so technically this insanity is his problem." She grabbed her purse and walked out. Haley heard the echo of the massive front door clicking shut behind her.

But later, after the grounds were closed, Haley looked out of the servants'-quarters window, from which most of the parking lot was visible, and her mother's car was still there. She couldn't see well enough to be able to tell if anyone was inside it. The next morning, when Haley woke, the car was in the same space. Though that didn't necessarily rule out that her mother had gone home and come back again.

Friday Karen placed a sign on the steps outside the front door saying the entire house was closed for maintenance. Saturday passed uneventfully—it was raining, so the grounds were empty—until about three in the afternoon, when Haley heard the electronic sound of someone deactivating the security system to let themselves in. Haley peeked downstairs from behind the balustrade and saw a middle-aged woman carrying an upright vacuum cleaner. A few minutes later, from the direction of the dining room, she heard it roar, loud when it was on the hardwood, muffled when dragged onto one of the carpets.

She was screwed. She could probably make a run for it herself, but there was no way she could have gotten all her stuff down the staircase and out the front door without being seen. She listened to the vacuum—the slight change in pitch as it went back and forth, the silent interludes when it was necessary to switch outlets—and gradually relaxed into the drone of it, to the point where, when she heard the woman struggling to haul the machine up the grand staircase, her breathing barely sped up at all. The woman appeared in the doorway of the master bedroom and saw Haley sitting yoga-style on the bed.

"Hi," Haley said, and the woman screamed. Maybe she believes in ghosts, Haley thought, as she listened to the footsteps pound back down the stairs and out the door. The vacuum cleaner stood upright outside the bedroom door where it had been dropped.

It wasn't more than twenty minutes before a police car rolled into the parking lot. Haley retreated and sat on the bed, scared now. What am I doing? she thought. She heard a loud knock on the door. "It's open," she tried to yell, but her mouth was too dry. Then, unexpectedly, the sound of the keypad. She heard low voices coming up the stairs and knew what had happened. In a few moments the large silhouette of the town cop filled the bedroom doorway; over his shoulder appeared the face of Haley's mother.

"May I ask what you're doing here?" the cop said, very gently. Around his waist was a belt holding a holstered gun and a number of other tools or accoutrements Haley couldn't identify. She was too frightened to speak. The nameplate over the cop's shirt pocket said Pratt.

"She's been staying here," Karen said rapidly. "She works here, with me, I'm her mother. And I'm in charge of this place, and I said it was okay."

"You're in charge of this place?" Pratt said skeptically, without turning around.

"In the day-to-day sense, yes," Karen said, "so it's okay, I said it was okay."

"Why isn't she at home with you?"

Mother's and daughter's eyes met over the trooper's shoulder, as if they were asking each other for suggestions. "I told you," Karen said, "she works here. She has my permission."

"Well, that's nice, but permission isn't yours to give just because you work here too. Are these your clothes?" he asked Haley. "Did you spend the night here?"

"Yes, of course they're her clothes, who else's would they be?" Karen said. "Listen, you can release her into my custody or whatever it's called, right? Haley, you'll agree to be released into my custody?"

Haley nodded vigorously.

"You know," the trooper said, finally taking a step out of the doorway and into the bedroom, "custody, permission, you seem to have a kind of hazy understanding of these words. Miss, would you stand up and turn around, please?"

"What?" Karen said. "No!" She ran around the large figure of the trooper and stood between him and the bed where Haley sat, hugging her knees and crying.

"Ma'am, there's no need for me to arrest you both, is there?"

"There's no need to arrest anybody! Do not put your hands on her. I'm warning you!"

"You're warning me?" The cop laughed, but his demeanor changed. "Lady, what is your name again?"

"Karen Firth."

"If you interfere with me, and especially if you physically attempt to obstruct me, this is going to turn into a much more serious matter, okay?"

"Mom!" Haley said, to her mother's taut back.

"If you want to touch her, you're going to have to go through me," Karen said.

"Mom!"

"You've heard what happened with the guy who was the trooper here before you, right?" Karen said. Her arms were spread wide apart.

Something in the trooper stiffened. He tried to establish eye contact with Haley around her mother's body.

"Anyway it's not a crime, it's a protest," Karen said, her voice shaking. "A political protest. Free speech."

"A protest," Officer Pratt said skeptically. "Against what?"

They both turned to look at Haley on the bed.

"Miss?" the officer said. "What are your demands?"

"What?"

"Demands. Conditions. I mean, if it's some kind of sit-in or something, then you are refusing to leave the premises until X happens, right? So what's X? Because then I can relay those demands to whomever," he said, turning back to Karen, "and we can negotiate, and that buys you some time."

"I don't have any demands," Haley said.

"You *what*?"

"I never had any demands. That would be stupid. I'm not in a position to demand anything from anybody."

"Okay," Karen said, "we are three reasonable people, we're talking reasonably now, let's give this one more try. Officer, I am asking you as humbly as I know how, I'm begging you, please let us just pack up my daughter's few things and we will leave this place and not come back. I mean, I'll come back, because I have to. But she will never come back."

Pratt gazed above her head and said nothing.

"If you arrest us both, there's a record, and there's publicity, and that won't look great for anyone," Karen said. "It's in our power right now to make this whole thing go away, to make it exactly like none of it ever happened at all."

"How do I know she won't publicize it?" Pratt said. "Or hasn't publicized it already. Why else do it? What's the point of this kind of agitation if you just keep it to yourself?"

In witnessing this encounter between her mother and the cop, this confrontation between authorities that was resolving itself into a collaboration, Haley felt beginning to descend on her the understanding that she'd been hoping for all along.

"She won't," Karen said. "We give you our word. I mean, she hasn't yet, has she? Haley, does anyone else know about this?"

"Just Dad," she said.

"See?" Karen said. "It's not political like that. Just a kid rebelling."

Pratt looked much more irritated than relieved. "If you're lying to me and this is not the end of it," he said, "next time we meet there won't be all this debating going on. Understood?"

Karen nodded meekly.

"I'll go downstairs and I will give you five minutes to collect your things and remove all trace of yourselves from the premises. Also, you have to understand that it is still within the rights of whoever actually owns this place to file a criminal complaint against you, if they ever hear about it, and should that happen, it's beyond my discretion. Understood?"

"Yes," Karen said. "Thank you, Officer. Haley, say thank you to the officer."

"Thank you," Haley whispered.

He left the bedroom. Silently they packed Haley's clothes and together walked down the broad stairs and out the front door. Pratt waited in his cruiser. Outside, Karen entered the code. Pratt followed them until they were back on the main road, then he turned left and Karen turned right.

"My car's still in the lot," Haley said.

"It'll be safe there until we go get it," her mom said. "Where do you want to go right now? I mean you probably want to go home and take a shower or something but are you hungry right now?"

There was a new Denny's on Route 7, so they went there, in part because it seemed unlikely they would run into anyone they knew. Haley ate ravenously, trying to hold back tears, although she didn't know why. Should she have resisted? But what kind of resistance could she have offered? She looked up at her mother, who had put her body on the line. Karen ate a little but then got lost in a long texting exchange. "Your father needs to see you," she said gently.

They drove to his house in silence, for a while anyway, past the greenery preserved by the eternal land trust, another space to be revered, a space governed by the dead. "I'm sorry, Haley," Karen said suddenly. "I'm sorry that you're so unhappy. I mean it. I guess I've been in denial about it because on some level I know it must be my fault. I've tried, I really have, but it's so hard to know what's the right thing to do, even when that's the only thing you're trying to do. But I'll keep trying. Maybe we ought to get you into some kind of therapy or something. We can certainly figure out some way to do that, your father and I."

"Okay," Haley said. She wasn't unhappy, and she had no intention of going through any sort of therapy, but in the moment she just needed to bring that whole line of conversation to a close, to do or say whatever in order to keep her mom from further upset.

They pulled to the curb in front of Mark's apartment, the left half of a condo-style construction that shared a wall with another unit. She could see her father's face in the window. She hugged her mother, pulled on the backpack and grabbed the duffel, and started up the path. It was only about twenty or thirty feet to the front steps, but still it felt exhilaratingly strange, in the moment, that neither of her parents came out to help her, that they were each contained inside and she was in the heavy August heat and open air between them all alone.

Was she a political person? Probably not, she thought; political people were probably more focused than she was, less distracted by what was in their own hearts. Still, she'd been right, she felt, not to make any demands, even when the opportunity was presented to her. She saw how that had made them all afraid of her. And what demand could she have made, really? To ask for any redress from the powerful, however small or just, was a tactical mistake. You gave up the only weapon available to you, which was to deprive them of their power to say no.

THE LØCALS

Jonathan Dee

A READER'S GUIDE

An Interview with Jonathan Dee

Adapted from Signature

Q: *The Locals* ends years before the recent election, but it seems almost spookily prescient in its exploration of the growing rage and disenfranchisement of working-class characters who wind up acting against their own best interests. How many of your characters do you think would have voted for Trump, had the novel extended into 2016?

A: Several of them, and not all for the same reasons. But I don't want to name names, for the same reason I never mention any of the characters' party affiliations in the novel: in the current climate those labels have become more of an obstacle to thought than an aid to it. I will say that Philip Hadi, despite playing a somewhat Trumpish role in the book, would surely be repulsed by Trump himself. So loud, so thin-skinned, so proudly impulsive! Back in the day, I'm sure Hadi went home early from more than one New York charity gala just because Trump was there.

Q: Having written the book, were you surprised by the outcome of the election? Did writing the novel make you think differently about what it means to be an American, and what American voters want in a leader?

A: Yes, even after having written the book I was as gobsmacked as nearly everyone else (Trump included) on election night. But, you know, even if he had lost, it's not like the tremendous hostility, distrust, racism, misogyny, pessimism, and savagery he tapped into, a current that runs through the lives of tens of millions of Americans, would somehow have disappeared. It's that volatile incivility, that retreat into paranoid self-interest, that I wanted to write about in the first place.

Q: One line that is repeated in the novel is "Your problems are not my problems." I read that as implying that this philosophy enabled the rapacious capitalism that built towns like Howland and, by extension, our country. Almost all of your characters, whether rich or poor, liberal or conservative, share this viewpoint (the exceptions being the youngest character, Haley, and her aunt, Candace.) Even the presumably liberal, progressive restaurateur is hoping to buy a farm out from under its owners, who have fallen on hard times. Why does this philosophy work better for some than for others?

A: Capitalism tends toward self-interest, that's true, and away from collective action for the common good (because it's an article of faith that the sum of self-interest produces that common good). But even beyond that, I feel like something particular has crept into American public discourse in the last fifteen to twenty years: the mainstreaming of the idea of the dismantling of the state, social programs in particular, which goes far beyond conservatism and into a kind of epic political regression. The idea embodied by the anti-tax activist Grover Norquist's famous remark about wanting to shrink government until it was small enough to drown in the bathtub. (At one point I wanted to title the novel itself *The Bathtub*, but nobody would have found that funny except me.)

Q: You open the novel in New York City on September 12, 2001. The story begins from the point of view of a first-person narrator who is baffled and irritated by the outpouring of public grief, and is relieved when he sees New Yorkers going back to being uncivil and selfish. We never see him again, and the rest of the book takes place in a rural town and is told in the close third person from the viewpoint of alternating characters. Can you talk about your decision to open the book this way? Was this always your beginning, or did you add it later to set the stage for some of the ideas developed through the novel?

A: This was always the beginning, and it's unusual enough that I had to fight for it a bit, editorially. I felt like I had to begin with at least an invocation of 9/11, if not the day itself, because that day instigated a long political reaction that we didn't recognize as a reaction for quite some time. By the same token, you don't want the opening scene of your novel to consist of a bunch of characters sitting on their couches watching TV and crying. So I hit upon the idea of this nameless sort of underground man, an invisible ur–New Yorker who has a bizarre encounter with an out-of-town stranger who then turns out to be the novel's actual main character. So the reader's introduction to Mark Firth is the opposite of intimate—a weirdly jaded first impression, off the mark in some ways but pretty sharp in others.

Q: Another process question: your cast of characters is vast, including nearly the entire population of Howland. How did you keep track of all of them over the course of the book? Did you plot each one separately or did you write it straight through?

A: I wrote each long chapter straight through, then revised it fully before going on to the next chapter. I did, at one point early in the process, sit down and write a sort of mini-biography of each individual character, so if at any point later on I felt as though I was losing the thread, I could refer back to those. There's a lot of material in those biographies that had to get chucked overboard, so to speak, for the sake of maintaining the forward momentum of the whole. But that's almost always the case. It's a bad sign if the book ends up containing everything you once thought it was going to contain.

Q: Through the book, you transition from one character's point of view to another's within chapters and even within paragraphs, almost as though they are passing a baton—we will be in one character's head as she picks up the phone to make a call, then switch to another character's perspective when she answers. The implication, it seems to me, is that we are all more interconnected than we think, so your problem *is* in fact my problem. Can you talk a bit about the transitions between characters? It seems a particularly tricky technique to pull off, almost like shooting long scenes in a movie where the camera switches from following one actor to another without cutting in between.

A: Each chapter has one little formal quirk that distinguishes it from the others (even if only to me), and in Chapter 2 it's this: no space breaks. So all the point-of-view transitions have to be accomplished in some other, subtler way. That kind of technical challenge is fun for me (I did something similar in the first chapter of *The Privileges*), but still, formal quirks of any kind are hard to justify unless they're there to reflect or enhance something about or within the story itself. So yes, the implication there is that our lives are all interconnected—especially lives in a small town like Howland—but there's a flip side to that, a kind of emotional claustrophobia. People in that kind of setting— your family, your neighbors—tend to be a little bit more up in your business than you might wish they were.

Q: The only character whose point of view we don't see is Hadi, the Michael Bloomberg–like billionaire who moves to town and starts throwing around money and surveillance devices. Why did you omit his perspective? Was it necessary for the reader to see Hadi as as much of an enigma as the citizens of Howland do? How is he different as a character from the also very wealthy people you wrote about in your Pulitzer Prize–nominated novel *The Privileges*?

A: Who is Hadi? What does he want? Can we believe what he says? These are the questions that consume the citizens of Howland; keeping the narration outside Hadi's own head is a way of furthering that mystery, but also of not playing favorites among the characters, because if I let you know what Hadi's thinking, then the other characters are suddenly either right or wrong, and your relationship to them changes. . . . But you've also hit upon something here that brings up a political similarity between Hadi and Trump—or between Hadi and Obama, for that matter: the less an electorate knows about a prospective leader, the more wholeheartedly it will project onto that leader either its hopes or its terrors. Sometimes it's simpler, more affirmative, to keep ourselves in the dark.

Questions and Topics for Discussion

1. In Chapter 0, we get the point of view of an unnamed narrator on September 11, 2001. Why do you think Jonathan Dee decided to use this narrator to introduce *The Locals*? What do we learn from this character? How did this first impression of Mark Firth inform your view of his character throughout the rest of the novel?

2. How would you characterize the town of Howland? How does the divide between tourists and locals affect the lives of those on both sides? If the town had its own personality, how would you describe it?

3. Each of the Firth siblings—Mark, Gerry, Candace, and Renee—seem to represent a different reaction to the national character of the post-9/11 years. What are the ways in which they process their changing country? Do you identify with one of them more than the others?

4. On his blog, Gerry writes: "The fight back begins on the local level, right here." In your experience, and after reading *The Locals*, do you agree with him? How does his blog allow him

to "fight back"? What are the ways in which social media has changed political activism?

5. What did you think of Philip Hadi's role as First Selectman? When Hadi crosses the line from tourist to local, how did you see his relationship with the town changing? Do you think he ultimately had good intentions for Howland, or were there other motives at work?

6. Through Mark Firth and Philip Hadi, Dee depicts different points of view on two central American beliefs. Mark espouses his faith in the American Dream, saying: "But this is America. . . . You're supposed to better yourself. You're supposed to think big. Right?" Hadi, while serving as First Selectman, declares, "Democracy doesn't really work anymore." How do you reconcile these opinions? What is the relationship between American democracy and the American Dream? How does Howland as a town demonstrate the benefits and limitations of both?

7. How is Karen and Mark's marriage portrayed throughout the novel? What role does their financial situation—from Mark being swindled by a financial advisor to his ambitions in the housing market—play in their relationship?

8. How do you interpret the significance of Caldwell House, and the way it is perceived by the town? How does it relate to the divide between the locals and the summer residents?

9. At the end of the novel, Haley Firth has a realization about her own political activism: "To ask for any redress from the powerful, however small or just, was a tactical mistake. You gave up the only weapon available to you, which was to deprive them of

their power to say no." Why do you think Dee chose to end the book with this idea? Do you agree with Haley?

10. *The Locals* spans several significant years in recent American history, touching on such events as 9/11, the Iraq War, the housing boom, and the recession of 2008. How do you feel the town of Howland reflects the larger issues taking hold of American society? Has your own experience of recent national events been similar to that of Howland, or different?

PHOTO: © JESSICA MARX

JONATHAN DEE is the author of six previous novels, most recently *A Thousand Pardons*. His novel *The Privileges* was a finalist for the 2011 Pulitzer Prize and winner of the 2011 Prix Fitzgerald and the St. Francis College Literary Prize. A former contributing writer for *The New York Times Magazine*, a senior editor of *The Paris Review*, and a National Magazine Award-nominated literary critic for *Harper's*, he has received fellowships from the National Endowment of the Arts and the Guggenheim Foundation. He lives in Syracuse, New York.